Rise of the Magical Three

House of Phoenix Chronicles Book I

Rise of the Magical Three

House of Phoenix Chronicles
Book I

by
Kurt W. Oster

All Genders Press

an imprint of
Perceptions Press
Victoria, BC
Canada

2023

Rise of the Magical Three
House of Phoenix Chronicles Book I

Revised edition published in paperback in 2023
First published in paperback in 2021, Wilhelm P. Ostir

Cover Design: Margot Wilson (Midjourney)
Illustrations: Kurt W. Oster (Canva Pro)

ISBN: 978-1-998924-73-8 (paperback)
ISBN: 978-1-998924-74-5 (Kindle-e-book)

Published in Canada by
All Genders Press
www.allgenderspress.ca

an imprint of
Perceptions Press
www.perceptionspress.ca
Victoria BC, Canada

Contents

Preface

Across the land and sea on the landmass of the United Kingdom, a red-haired, pale skinned woman in red and purple robes looks out over the cliffs at the roaring ocean as a tear rolls down her face. She holds out her hand, trying to summon water from the ocean to her but, as always, nothing happens. Looking around, she pulls her wand from beneath her robes and begins to conjure a spell when she hears screams. Freezing on the spot, she listens and hears screams for a second time, as the winds carry the sounds to her. The witch kneels to put her palms flat on the ground.

"May the magic of earth protect those who need it the most. Alezander, I know you are out there somewhere. Hear me and hear the cries of the light. It is your time, and the earth needs the light. Bring it back to us. Bring the light of the three back to the earth."

The old witch rises to her feet as she hears the screams echo again. This time, she closes her eyes to listen more closely to the wind. Suddenly, when she opens her eyes, gazing into the realm of the Arcane to observe what is transpiring, a white stallion appears. The woman mounts the horse, and they gallop through a portal.

Definitions

Arcane: known or knowable only to a few people, secret, mysterious, obscure, esoteric, magical, a mystical, enigmatic force in the world, heavenly or spiritual, arcane magic entails forces or phenomena that somehow transcend the natural laws that govern the world by directly manipulating unknown energies that bend the fabric of reality to create a desired effect.

Mundane: of this earthly world, relating to, belonging to, or characteristic of the earth, earthly, in relation to the immediate concerns and activities of human beings.

Prologue
How it All Begins

To tell you our story, we have first to tell you about our family. You see, we are the "Magical Three." For us, life has been... well, rather different. At school, we live normal lives. We play sports. We enjoy times with our friends. We even enjoy our classes, except for history with Ms. Destiny. But that is a story for another time.

At home... well, that is where things get weird. You know, the type of weird where you see a snake slithering towards you and then, all of the sudden, it transforms into a zombie.

"Stop! Don't scare them too much. They won't want to hear the story."

"Ok. Now, where were we? Oh, yes, at home..."

We never had a normal childhood. In fact, our childhoods were downright bizarre. We grew up in the house our parents bought when I was born. When we were younger, our home was like a giant funhouse. It has hidden rooms that expand, appear, disappear, and rearrange themselves. You never know what you may find on our kitchen shelves and avoid the pantry unless you fancy rat liver or dragon toe. One of our favorite rooms is the family library. All of us love books, but that is where things can get really weird, especially with the books in our home.

We live with our grandmother, Dawn, Uncle Hawke, and our dog, Autumn.

"No, tell the truth! You always like to tell everyone that Autumn is a dog, rather than a science experiment gone wrong."

"Such a bizarre creature!"

"She is *not* bizarre! She's just different. Pay those two no mind. They're twins and like to argue and to always be right."

Now, where to start our story? There are so many points in time from which to begin and where in time to begin is an important question.

You see, time is an interesting construct, designed to allow one to know where one is. But, in a moment, time can break. It can change. There one minute and gone the next. Those who can control time can create what is called an "echo," an alteration to the never-ending timeline, what you would call a continuous loop. Time is as ancient as the universe and seems to have no beginning or end. So, at this very moment, we are at a point in time where one can say that our story has already happened or is yet to happen. So, in that sense, our story begins where it also ends.

You, the "Mundane," do not experience time in the same way. Your lives are too brief. But when you have borne witness to the passing of generations, to the segregation of the Arcane and Mundane worlds, and the inception of new realms hidden from the common senses, when you have seen these things and more, time starts to cause trouble. Past and future become tangled up in each other. Thus, what has already come to pass, what is, and what will be, reveal themselves to be singular and ever-present. Nothing happens that was not fated from the beginning, and every ending contains within itself all the elements that preceded it.

So, our story does not hold to one particular moment in time: rather, for us, time does not exist in the same way. You could say that it misbehaves. Well, sometimes, it does behave. But, more often than not, it acts up. And, as I have said, time behaves strangely for us. And this is where it gets a bit bizarre because we can re-live any moment in time over and over, sometimes stepping backward and sometimes stepping forward, altering the story.

But to truly understand us, you have to know something about magic. You see, we are called the "Arcane," or the "magically-gifted." Our magic comes from an ancient bloodline, what some call "pure" Arcane blood. You see, our great grandfather is… well, Merlin—yes Merlin, the wizard of King Arthur's court—not something to get very excited about. You don't know him the way we do.

Merlin taught that magic has rules, and the rules are meant to be followed. But that does not happen for us. Our magic transcends all rules. Now, magic that does not follow the rules has its pros and cons but, ultimately, our magic can cause time to become confusing. To understand our magic, we should start at the end. Inevitably, that sheds light on the beginning because endings and beginnings are, after all, one and the same. We should know. Having seen both firsthand, we are uniquely qualified to say so.

But you didn't come here to hear us talk about ourselves, did you? Still, we are curious about which of the stories led you here to us. But, before we begin, please allow us a moment to gather our thoughts and recollections and, more importantly, to choose a starting place from which to begin the story. We must pick a place, a time, or an event—a compelling moment— that will anchor us, even if only for a few brief moments, so that we can get a sense of the story.

Where shall we begin?

❧

A dozen cloaked figures, the last of the Council of the Arcane, flee from a village engulfed in flames, riding on horseback toward a nearby castle. Flanked on both sides by a pair of golden lions, the figures ride in silence, driving their horses as fast as they dare. They know full well the dangers that follow on their heels.

The rider at the head of the column wields a staff of twisted oak vines with a star affixed to its crown—the last beacon of light in a world of growing darkness and evil.

The riders reach the castle just as the drawbridge opens with a loud thud. The lead rider throws back his cowl and dismounts, striding rapidly across the drawbridge. He is an elderly man with gray hair and beard, and despite the speed of his movements, he leans heavily on his twisted oak staff. At the center of the drawbridge, he greets the king and queen. They are old friends and at risk of being struck by the darkness if they are not careful.

The wizard and his wife turn, touch their hands together palm-to-palm. When they pull their hands apart, they cast magical enchantments around the kingdom. The riders watch as the elderly wizard and his wife transform. Made young again by magic, the two look at each other and then mount the back of a giant dragon with silver and white scales who takes to the air.

The wizard and his wife wave goodbye to the king and queen, and the castle and its inhabitants disappear on the spot. The magical enchantments around the castle will protect it, making it invisible, time standing completely still for the future to come. Across the plain, beneath the soaring dragon, gallop the riders on their horses.

The riders pick up speed as the darkness emerges from the ground, grabbing at the horses and reaching for the riders. One dark shadow latches onto the back of one of the Arcane riders. Suddenly, one of the lions jumps onto the back of the horse, bites the shadow, and tackles it to the ground. Looking back, the Arcane riders notice that the lion has ripped the head of the dark shadow clean off. From above, the dragon carrying the wizard and his wife bellows fire down upon the darkness as the shadows disappear, screaming as the dragon descends. The riders stop at the edge of a cliff overlooking the ocean as the dragon lands, and the wizard and his wife dismount from the great beast.

As the eight riders dismount and hold up their staves, the wizard and his wife begin drawing pentagrams, while the two lions roar. The combined magical efforts of these individuals begin to create a new magical land.

Other wizards and witches, from all over the world, begin to appear, forming a protective barrier that allows safe passage for other magical creatures. When the last of them has entered the gateway, it disappears.

Within hours, the magical beings of the new land appoint the twelve individuals to be the high Arcane Council that will rule over the new kingdom with the wizard and his wife as their king and queen, the protectors of the land. The king and his wife declare the day of their crowning to be a holiday, celebrating the salvation of magic. Both know that the Arcane can no longer live among the Mundane if they wish to be safe.

While everyone is celebrating only a few know what actually occurred that day. It is a history that the wizard king takes great care to hide from all, fearing that the truth will give the Mundane the ability to rise against him and the newly formed Council.

Merlin's objective is to protect the future lineage of magic from undoing the work he has already done. A history that until now was clouded in mystery, Merlin believes that if the Mundane discovered his intention it would mean the undoing of all magic for the world.

☙

Oh, dear. This always seems to happen. Picking a place in time, while apparently simple, can also cause a great haze to occur as if the story has ended. Although we can manipulate time, for some reason, our visions cloud up and don't always show us what we need to know. To sort out this haze, we sometimes have to intervene. So, let's teleport ourselves 25 years into the future.

The hazy magical image before us appears to rip but, by reaching up and touching the broken edges, we fall through. As we descend from the sky, we pull our wands, point them at the ground, and stop mere inches above it. As we each pull up our wands, we land on our feet and brush ourselves off. Our magic allows us to soar over the land and we love to walk quietly through the images of the past and the future until an unusual piece of magic catches our eye.

♋

The vast land has not changed much in twenty-five years: the trees are more prominent, and the rivers run fuller. Small villages sprawl over the hillside as far as one can see. It is at this very moment that the quiet valley echoes with sudden screams.

In the distance, two children are playing in the River Thena when, all of a sudden, for the second time, screams echo across the valleys, the forests, and the waterways. Shadows move over the children, freezing them in place. In the distance, hooves ring out over the land as Arcane riders approach the spot where the two children lie frozen in time. Standing above them, transforming out of the darkness, laughing at the sight of what has just occurred, is the witch, Morgana, and her apprentice, Lord Aden.

Upon seeing Merlin, his wife (the Witch Queen, the Great Lady Nimuway), and the other Arcane riders, who were members of the Arcane Council, approaching, Morgana, who hates Merlin more than she hates the Mundane, points her finger at him, causing his cloak to catch fire. Before anyone can react, the Arcane riders find themselves engaged in battle with creatures of the dark, including Lord Aden and Morgana.

Snuffing out the fire on his cloak and having fought this witch before, Merlin summons forth his magic and, with one blast, throws Morgana into the trees. Vines rise from the nearby tree roots, entrapping her arms and legs. Lord Aden blasts one of the Arcane Council members with dark magic, killing him instantly.

The Lady Nimuway walks through the darkness, summoning forth water, earth, fire, and wind, hitting

Morgana with each element, one after another. Each blow weakens Morgana, causing more of her dark followers to disappear. As Merlin summons forth his magic to finish the battle, Lord Aden stabs him in the back with his sword. Merlin and Nimuway seize Lord Aden in a magic prison and cast him into the Neverlands of the outer realms. Merlin, weakened by the attack, falls to the ground, releasing his hold on Morgana. Nimuway moves quickly to engage Morgana in a magical duel, fighting to save her husband.

The Lady Nimuway's magical power is not equal to Morgana's, and she falls within seconds. Morgana then turns her attention to Merlin. As Morgana levitates above the ground, members of the Arcane Council, the guards, and legions fly backward, unable to stop her as she grows stronger with each passing minute. Merlin rises to his feet, brushes himself off, and summons forth the last ounce of magic he possesses, spinning his hands together, releasing one plasma bolt after another towards Morgana.

Morgana laughs as the bolts hurtle toward her. With one quick movement of her wand, she turns them into flowers.

"Ah, Merlin. Getting old, are we? Have we forgotten that every spell has a counter?"

Morgana laughs as she points her wand at her throat and begins breathing fire. Merlin and Morgana point their wands toward each other. As Morgana summons the darkness, Merlin, with a wave of his hand, creates a magical spinning helix that surrounds the two of them, causing them both to vanish instantly.

What seems like hours is mere seconds when Merlin finally reappears and collapses into the arms of his son, Titus. In his last minutes, Merlin names his son and his daughter-in-law, Flora, to be the new rulers of the Arcane Kingdom and protectors of all that is magical. In his last moment, Merlin touches his son's forehead, takes in one final breath, and dissolves into the winds. The Arcane Council members know that, with that touch, Merlin has passed a living memory on to his son.

As Titus rises to his feet, he scoops up his father's crown and declares himself the new ruler of the Arcane kingdom.

For the next 100 years, the country prospers under the rule of Titus and Flora.

Over the years, many inquire about the vision that Titus received from Merlin. However, the great king never speaks of it. Those closest to him state that the image is a secret that destroys Titus slowly, day by day. Still, Titus swears that he will do anything to prevent his father's past from destroying the future of his people. Titus keeps the secret so well protected that even his closest advisors do not know where he has sealed the scroll with the history of the Arcane and all that is magical, including the images his father has shown him.

⌘

Titus and his wife, Flora, are just and fair rulers, which allows for enormous growth of the kingdom under their rule. Titus and Flora have three children. Their firstborn is the High Prince Kelvin. Someday, Kelvin will take on the responsibilities for ruling the Arcane Kingdom. Their second son is Prince Wade, and their daughter is Princess Terra. The children grow in the magical arts and learn the stories of Merlin and Nimuway, of Camelot and Avalon from our grandparents.

While King Titus and his Council pass many rules regulating the use of magic and forbidding contact with the Mundane realm, Kelvin grows restless and yearns for more. After all, he is a prince, the eldest son of Titus and the eldest grandson of Merlin, and he has grown up in the land of magic. His wife, Nadia, on the other hand, is a child of the two realms.

A powerful witch who comes from one of the last remaining magical families who stayed in the realm of the Mundane, Nadia, by the time she was 15 years of age, had found ways to shift the rules of magic to work in her favor. From writing new spells and spending hours in front of the cauldron learning new potions to leveling an entire wing of her Mundane High school by speaking one-word spells, Nadia's magic seems limitless. Kelvin, being a romantic, is instantly attracted to Nadia. They date for over two years before they marry.

Kelvin and Nadia hope to bridge the differences between the Arcane and Mundane realms. Kelvin knows all too well that the Arcane kingdom will be theirs to rule someday. However, it is a responsibility that the young prince does not want. Both Kelvin and Nadia believe that both the Arcane and the Mundane have much to learn from each other and that they can live together in harmony. Firm in this belief, Kelvin and Nadia choose to reside in the realm of the Mundane and raise their children there, although they travel to the realm of the Arcane multiple times throughout the week.

One cold fall evening, Kelvin and Nadia travel with their three young children to the Arcane realm to join King Titus and Queen Flora for the Fall Harvest Dinner. Kelvin plans to speak with Titus and Flora about stepping down and leaving the kingdom to live fulltime among the Mundane. Kelvin intends to leave the throne to his younger brother, Wade.

Although he plans to speak with his parents after dinner, this conversation never occurs. On that cold, rainy night, while walking in the castle grounds on their way to the dining room, Queen Flora and Princess Terra notice the markings of dark magic on the castle walls. What is about to happen explains why Kelvin and Nadia's children do not reside in the castle in the Arcane realm but are growing up in the Mundane realm instead. After touching the markings, Queen Flora runs quickly into the castle with Princess Terra following close behind. They know all too well what the marks mean.

When Terra arrives in the entry hall, she sees Queen Flora fall to the ground. A dark being stands behind her with a wand in hand. As Terra watches her mother's lifeless body hit the ground, she lets out a scream, alerting the castle of danger. Then, she pulls out her wand and begins deflecting the magic of the dark shadows moving around her. Terra encircles herself in a helix of white light. But, as ten dark shadows strike the helix, she drops to one knee from the strength of their blows. King Titus rounds the corner to find his beautiful wife frozen, just like his father found those two children many years earlier. Kelvin and Wade run to their sister's side with wands drawn and begin pushing the shadows back with lightfields. Kelvin spins his wand, tracing helixes of light to protect his father and siblings.

Horns sound as members of the Council appear with wands and staves drawn. Lightning hits the courtyard as Titus and Morgana fight each other in a battle similar to the one between Merlin and Morgana.

As members of the Council fight to keep Morgana's creatures at bay, Titus, with the help of his sons, subdues Morgana, stripping her of her wand, opening a portal under her, and banishing her to the Neverlands.

The portal explodes immediately after Morgana disappears through it, consuming a third of the castle in the process. Members of the Council rush to seal the portal, but it multiplies exponentially, sucking several members into it.

King Titus turns and summons magical incantations to seal the portal.

"Everyone, stay back!" he shouts.

Titus holds the portal within his hands and works hard to momentarily contain its powers before it explodes again.

Kelvin rushes into the castle looking for someone or something. As he turns the corner, he finds a woman nestled in the bedroom, guarding three children. Nadia points her wand over his shoulder as Kelvin turns to see that three shadows have followed him into the room.

Nadia's eyes begin to glow blue, and the dark cloaked creatures fly back, slamming into the wall and falling to the floor unconscious.

Knowing they have very little time to say goodbye, Kelvin and Nadia race with their children toward the front of the castle. Running down the corridors, they see several nightriders advancing toward them. Upon turning another corner, Kelvin and Nadia come upon the High Prince of the Elves, with sword drawn, waiting to protect the family. Kelvin motions for Nadia to take the children. As she passes,

Kelvin places his hand on the elf prince's shoulder, and as he turns to follow his wife, the elf prince strikes down three of the nightriders with one swing of his sword. A fourth shadow rises up, looks at the elf prince, and begins to laugh. The elf prince, wielding an extremely rare form of his people's magic, raises his hand, levitates the laughing creature off its feet as it begins to choke, and its body is flung back and forth. Finally, it explodes.

The High Prince of the Elves raises his hands and casts the spell,

Magia custodiet Ipsos viam. Protegat haec nullum malum eorum transiet, sic educas festucam fieri.

Magic guard the way. Protect this path so no evil shall pass, so mote it be.

In speaking the spell, the elf prince creates a magical barrier of vines, bushes, trees, and rocks to block the walkway.

When the prince and princess reach the grand walkway, Kelvin raises his wand and shoots sparks into the air. Seconds later, two figures approach. Nadia hands her one-year-old daughter to her mother. As Nadia's brother appears at his sister's side, he takes Kelvin and Nadia's three-year-old twin sons by the hand. After kissing her daughter, Nadia kneels and hugs her boys.

"Be brave, my little ones. Be brave. May your magic grow strong so you may protect all that is dear to you."

As several cloaked figures approach, Nadia rises to her feet and opens the portal that will carry her mother, brother, and children to safety.

Chapter 1
Time is Bizarre

"Ugh! Volleyball again, is that all Coach Griff knows?"

"How come your brother's and my sister's class always get to do the fun stuff, and we are stuck with Greasy Griff who only wants to play volleyball every P.E. class?"

"He is better than Ms. Lopez who only wanted to do figurative dance."

"That girl next to me, complaining about our P.E. teacher is one of my best friends, Brooke. Her older sister, Olivia, and my older brother, Oliver… well, they are a thing. Let me tell you a little about who we are."

&

My brother Oliver and his girlfriend Olivia are seniors and voted most likely to "marry after high school and start a family." Oliver is the star quarterback and has played for all four years. Olivia is head cheerleader and anyone who is anyone in the school wants to be their friends.

My brother is loved by every teacher and can get away with pretty much anything. Olivia and Brooke come from old money, passed down from generation to generation. Now, when I say they come from old money, you know what I mean. Those families that amass wealth over many generations? That is them. That ridiculous mansion with the half-mile long driveway, the security gate, and guard house off Oak Drive? That is their place. Theirs is the house that always wins the community home of the year prize for their three pools, five hundred gargoyles, 12 sculptures, and rose garden. Olivia and Brooke's mother is a professor of history and romantic literature, and their father travels all the time for work.

Oliver and Olivia have the type of sappy teen love that makes you want to vomit. They have been best friends since kindergarten, and he finally got up the nerve to ask her out in 7th grade. Ever since, they have been together and inseparable.

Now, the guy standing next to my brother, wearing glasses and the *faux* hawk haircut, who is identical to Oliver but 2 inches taller, that is my other brother, Ethan. Yes, they are twins, identical yet different. Oliver is charming, the ladies' man, athletic, and popular. Ethan, on the other hand, while also athletic and the track star who has taken this school to multiple state championships, is a book worm, driven by his love of science and technology, and he desires to be perfect at everything.

Currently, Ethan is the only senior who does not have a girlfriend. Oliver has made multiple attempts to hook Ethan up with numerous girls, but Ethan politely refuses and notes that he is happy with his books. The two, being identical twins, can only be told apart by their haircuts and height difference. Other than that, it is scary to see how easily they can be confused for each other.

Now, if you were to take those two aside and ask them what they want to do after high school, Oliver would tell you that he wants to go to Junior College and possibly work. Ethan, on the other hand, wants to go to Harvard or Yale, and then get a job as a scientist. My brothers are two years older than me.

Do you see that charming, 6'4" Junior over there next to Claire? That is my other best friend, Zander. Much like Oliver and Olivia, Zander and I have known each other since kindergarten. We do almost everything together. Zander has always been awkward but, between you and me, I think he is rather handsome. Secretly, I do have a crush on him, but he is my best friend, so it is kind of weird.

Anyways, he is one of the tallest boys in our school. He is a blend of athlete, theater sage, and bookworm. His love for theater is amazing to watch. Somehow, he has this magic to him, and it brings his characters to life. He lives with his uncle in a small house at the base of the foothills. Every girl in the school, at some point or another, has been after him in more than one way, and the guys are intimidated by his size.

Between Zander and my two brothers, I do not worry about being bullied or having issues with anyone in the school. It also helps that I am friends with Olivia and Brooke. I have protection and popularity through them.

৵

You seem pretty cool, so let me ask you this? "What do you notice about everyone in the gym?"

"Give up? Yes, it is a typical high school gym, with raging hormones and people ignoring each other or hanging with their respective social groups."

Speaking of respective social groups, do not try to have those conversations with my charming brothers. They have always been cool with their respective group, that is until I come along.

My brothers were so upset at the start of the school year that they complained to Grandma about me having the same P.E. period as them. They told her they would rather die than deal with it and how uncool it was. I guess it is embarrassing having your 16-year-old sister, who skipped a grade and is a Junior, in the same period of P.E. as you.

Then, you have me. I am Rose. I hate P.E. What teen does not? I love the arts and old books and want to be a librarian someday. Currently, I am Vice-President of the Student Council, involved with every social and service club on campus, and an honor roll student.

Now, Oliver would die if he knew I was telling you this, but when Ethan is busy studying or off blowing something up, Oliver will sit with me and have me tutor him in his subjects. But then, at school, I do not exist.

As we have gotten older, the three of us have gotten closer, but we still have our moments. What siblings do not? I have a unique relationship with each of my brothers, but, together, they are impossible to manage. They get in too much trouble and egg each other on.

The three of us live in the strangest home in our community. Our house is solid gray, an old three-story Victorian, that stands at the end of Magical Way. Yes, that is the actual name of the street. Weird, I know.

Our home looks like an old, scary, haunted house and Halloweens are always fun as Grandma turns the front yard into a graveyard. Over the years, many of our classmates have teased that all our house is missing is ghosts. When I was younger, my brothers used to tell me that the house was haunted just to scare me and build on our classmates' jokes.

So, that is our childhood home, which is owned by our parents. We have lived in the same house for our entire lives. My brothers and I live with our mother's mother, our grandmother, with whom the three of us have a love-hate relationship. Our mom's brother, Uncle Hawke, and our dog, Autumn, live with us too.

Ah, yes, Autumn. She is the oldest living member of the family. Because of this, my brothers like to say that she is a science experiment gone wrong. She is 16 years old but acts like a puppy. She runs circles around the other dogs in the neighborhood as if it is nothing.

Our parents are not around and… well, that is a rather unusual story. If you ask Grandma, she says that our parents died and left us the family estate. But, if you ask Uncle Hawke, he says that our parents are off on an adventure. My brothers and I have come to the realization that those two are hiding something. We just can't figure it out. So, yeah, we live a pretty normal life up to a point.

❧

"Rose why don't you tell them about the week leading up to your sixteenth birthday?"

"Great idea, Ethan! But let me tell it. You and Oliver always mess up the details."

The week of my sixteenth birthday starts out like any other week. Boring! Slow and never exciting. Now, those two charming brothers of mine, never paid attention to anything during their senior year, except their grades, social lives, and sports. I, on the other hand, notice everything, particularly that last week before my sixteenth birthday.

That Monday, I was running late getting to school and Uncle Hawke dropped me off in the parking lot. That is when things got weird. Coming from the parking lot and ascending the steps of the school, the wind was whistling exceptionally loudly behind me, much louder than normal. Then, suddenly, calmness. No sound. Nothing. No one moving around. That is when time froze.

Looking around, what happened next showed me how time can be… well, rather bizarre. The two-story brick school, which normally rises up out of the landscape, is suddenly laid to waste, the school leveled, the door completely ripped off the hinges, and the smell of charred wood in the background. Rubble is lying everywhere. I walk over to the grand archway and, when I walk through to look at the school that has been laid to waste, I find that time has returned to normal, and the halls of the school are bustling with students. Curiously, as I step back through the archway, the school returns to rubble, but, this time, the destruction looks different. Before, the archway was the only thing left standing, but now, there is the archway and part of the wall.

Walking back into the school, it has returned to normal: so, I head to class.

❧

You know that teacher you have in school that the sheer thought of walking into their class makes you want to run and hide? Well, that is this class. Give me a class with Coach Griffy any day of the week over this class.

Ms. Destiny was the strangest teacher of them all. Oliver and Ethan had her throughout the years: then, I ended up with her. She has an aura about her that no one likes. She is mean. Many of us have never seen her smile. She hates athletes: the cheerleaders get yelled at daily in her class. There was one day when we walked through the door and she said that because she hates children, she felt like giving each student detention. However, for some strange reason, my brothers and I never get in trouble with her. And we always seem to avoid detention. None of us can explain it. While she is yelling at my peers, she is always sweet to me and calls on me in class. It is rather annoying.

The worse part of all of this is that she always looks over the top of her glasses and snorts at everything. A student asks why they got an F, she snorts. A student asks to use the restroom, she snorts. Everything is a snort to her. Many of us swear she has a pig hidden in the classroom somewhere.

Now, we all make fun of Coach Griffy and call him "greasy" because of the sheer amount of hair gel that the man wears, but Ms. Destiny has a sense of fashion that is… well, eccentric. She looks like something out of the High Renaissance. Ethan always laughs and asks if she just came from a cosplay event or robbed some Renaissance re-enactment tent. You know the socialite girls at school, the ones that carry their coffees, and talk to each other on their cell phones? Yes, those girls: they even jump up and down and giggle at everything. Take all fifteen of them, combine them together, and they still cannot top Ms. Destiny.

Ethan and Oliver swear that if she is not something out of a cosplay, then it has to be the history books. Oliver simply despises the woman and I… well, I dread her class as I swear, she is Arcane. There are little things she does that cannot be explained otherwise. Ethan and Oliver could never explain it, and many of my Mundane classmates never noticed. But anytime Ms. Destiny gives a lecture and needs to turn off the lights, she claps her hands together and the blinds of the room always close. She never once touches them, never moves from where she is standing. There are also many times, when Ethan or Oliver would be up to no good and she is right there, watching over their shoulders. They always know she is there because she clears her throat. That is rather annoying too.

And, of course, dear Grandma always tells the three of us to "leave that woman alone," that she is just "odd." Right, Grandma, the woman is odd! When I told Grandma that I thought Ms. Destiny was an Arcane, Grandma noted that is impossible because outside of the five of us, no other Arcane survives.

☙

"Oh, wait, did I forget to tell you that? My brothers and I are Arcane. Try living a normal life among the Mundane and not use magic. It is easier said than done. And it is next to impossible to have people over, not with the way our house acts. We are just trying to be three normal teens living life, hiding a secret that no one else ever would understand.

Anyway, where was I? Oh yes, that's right, telling you about the horrors of Ms. Destiny's class.

Now, hers is the one class where I slip through the door and try to sneak into one of the seats in the back. The only great thing about this class is that my best friend Zander is in the class to help keep me balanced.

However, on this one particular day Ms. Destiny is out. These are the days when every student wants to run up and down the hallway rejoicing that she is absent. Heck, we will all take a substitute any day of the week in this class. But if there is one way to get an entire class to groan and protest it is to have a substitute tell you that, once again, your teacher has left another lesson about King Arthur and the Knights of the Roundtable. Blah, Blah, Blah! If Ms. Destiny is not already weird enough, this world history teacher only teaches one type of history— King Arthur. Do not get me wrong! I love Arthurian legend like anyone else, but when you have heard it for over 10 years' worth of schooling, you get tired of it.

Not interested in the movie or listening to the groans of my classmates, I put in my earbuds and pull my book from my bag and start reading. Of course, Zander always shakes his head, laughing at me, and leans on his right arm, pretending to be awake but actually falling asleep anytime a movie is put on regarding King Arthur.

Here is the thing. Ms. Destiny's love of Arthurian legend, while interesting, is not always the most accurate. Remember how I said time has a tendency to act bizarrely with my brothers and me? Well, I do not need a poorly made movie to know what happens in the life and times of King Arthur and his court. Let me tell you a little secret about my, and my brother's, magic. We can be in multiple places at once. The only problem with this is that the magic can be unpredictable. So, looking up from my book, I notice that the film is about the pre-historic era of Arthur. Great! More false history. Instead of watching that boring movie, let's go see what actually happened. Oh, by the way, if you have never time jumped, it is rather simple. Just plant your feet firmly on the ground and hold on.

There, that was not so bad, was it? Now, the fog will clear and, oh, I need to warn you, watch out for the dead bodies lying on the ground. Other than that, shall we go explore? Oh, and pay no attention to the screams you hear. Unfortunately, they are the screams of falling Arcane. It is rather normal for this part of the story.

The history of King Arthur always starts at the very moment of his birth, but what no one ever explores is what happened beforehand. Magic comes from the energy of all things. The Council of Arcane Light, the most powerful group of light-bearing Arcane, governed the use of magic. Nothing can happen magically without their blessing. This is where the rules or rather the etiquette of magic use comes from, which is great. But as there is a Council of Arcane Light, there is, of course, a Council of Arcane Darkness, a group of Arcane who did not care who they killed as long as they gained more power.

Now, the Council of Arcane Light was so beloved that when the shadows attacked, many of the Arcane races—elves, dwarfs, fairies, and even multiple vampire clans—came to their assistance. Those are the bodies that I told you to never mind. Here is where the biggest problem comes: if you are Arcane and you are killed by a shadow, you yourself become a shadow. Let's just say it is how the darkness amasses their huge army. Because of this, the history of the Arcane is never talked about and Merlin did not help the situation by hiding that history.

By the way, you might want to step over there. Things are going to start to get interesting.

&

Scream after scream continues to ring out as three cloaked figures run down the corridor towards a large grand door. One of the cloaked individuals turns around long enough to see the shadows continuing to rise out of the ground. Further down the hall, one of the cloaked individuals proceeds ahead of the other two. When they stop and flip off their cloaks, each summons lightfields in order to hold off the darkness. One individual turns, raises their staff, and summons a massive lightfield that pushes the shadows backward. The three quickly work to unify their lightfields by connecting them together at various pillars. Throwing their hands in front of them, the lightfields expand and start to connect to every pillar, locking the darkness into squares of solid light.

Once the lightfields are in place, the three individuals reach the door. "Sir, you may want to hurry. The barriers are holding but how long they will hold against the shadows is the question."

As they pull the door closed, they enter the great hall. Behind them, the darkness is still trying to reach them and as they look around, they see a cloaked figure at the far wall who lowers her hood.

"Quickly! Get these items moved."

The four individuals levitate the items away from the wall.

More cloaked individuals show up, working to help get the items moved. In the distance, two pillars crash, signaling the weakening of the lightfields. A loud pop echoes over the hall as two more cloaked figures arrive. The taller of the two lowers his hood, pulls his wand, and, with a quick wave, slams the doors shut. The group continues to move quickly as the elderly wizard seals the door and summons a lightfield across it.

"You all must hurry; I do not know how long before the field shatters."

Crash! As the doors of the great hall fly off their hinges, the darkness hits the lightfield. The woman leading the group turns and throws the last of the items out of the way. The individuals hold up their wands as the wall opens. With the wall now open, a figure dressed all in white robes with only her long blonde hair and bright red lips visible emerges. When she reaches the edge of the wall, the smaller of the two cloaked figures lowers her hood, revealing a young girl.

The woman leading the group places a saddlebag over the girl's head onto her shoulders, kisses her on the head, hugs her, and pushes her toward the opening. When the girl reaches the woman in white, the lightfield explodes and the darkness engulfs the room. The young girl disappears on the spot, then reappears in front of the elderly wizard.

The young girl opens her hand, and a glowing crystal levitates into the air. The girl starts humming and the dark shadows start screaming and exploding. With each attack and strike against the young girl's lightfield, the crystal grows brighter. When the girl closes her eyes and reopens them, the creatures explode.

The woman in white, pulls her wand, mutters something quietly under her breath, and the young girl flies backwards through the opening in the wall. When the wall slams shut, the hall is overtaken by darkness for the second time. The woman leading the group pulls her wand back and throws her arm forward as the wall blows up, giving the darkness no chance to reach the young girl.

∾

"Interesting, isn't it?"

But before we jump again, here is where it gets really curious. As I have said, time does weird things for me and my siblings. The young girl has a crystal that she levitates in her hand. That is the same crystal that I now wear around my neck. No, I did not kill the girl for it.

Somehow, she lost it and I ended up with it. Here is where the freakiness comes in—that crystal has never done anything until my brothers, and I found this part of the timeline. The first time we discovered this story, I levitated in the air and flew around the room. Apparently, the necklace has no sense of control.

You are probably wondering where the girl and the woman in white went. Well, we did not know until one day when the story revealed more of itself to us.

Hold on, and this time, you won't have to step over dead bodies. I hope you have your jacket with you. Just one quick wave of the hand and… ah yes, I love this part of the story… a beautiful field and, if you look right over there—give it a minute, 3…2…1… There they are. Follow me or you will miss time playing its bizarre tricks.

The young girl and woman appear, standing on a hill. They pull their wands and point them at the night sky. Across the river, a village rises out of the ground. Smoke bellows from the chimneys, people are bustling in the street: but then, the city disappears and reappears, laid to waste, the once standing village now in rubble.

Are you as frustrated as I am? Okay, good. Yes, see how weird time can be?! Time has messed with the story—one minute a bustling city, the next a wasteland.

My brothers and I have not been able to figure it out. What we know is that whoever that young girl is, no reference to her appears in any of the texts we have examined. The shadows that attacked the hall were also different. The story of this very moment in time is unique. We have seen nothing like it since and almost every time we enter it, we learn something more. It is as if time is catching up and moving the story forward.

Remember that story I told you at the beginning about Merlin creating the magical land of Arcane? Well, there is one little detail I did not mention because I did not want to give it away.

As the timeline catches up, one night, I discover something unique about the story. So, I follow it as it plays out. After my brothers, who were 3 years old, and I, a mere 1 year old infant, escaped with our grandmother and uncle, the portal that opened to capture Morgana continues to engulf the castle.

Now, my parents worked quickly, sealing the portal that carried my brothers and me to safety and turned their attention to the larger portal, which was growing rapidly. My parents were about to hit the portal with the full strength of their magic, when five cloaked individuals walked up. The leader pulled a pocket watch, tapped his finger on it, and threw it up in the air.

In that very moment, time froze everything. I went back later with my brothers and the three of us concluded that the pocket watch could possibly be the very same Arcane instrument that is altering various parts of the story and timeline.

My dear charming brothers and I were able to retrieve that watch, and it is currently held in an enchanted box so we can examine how it is that one watch could freeze time and possibly our parents. Wow, look at the time! It appears that class will be ending in a few moments. Shall we go back? Hold on as we jump now.

&

Meanwhile, across time, in the Arcane realm…

"How do I end up working with such stupid people? The Lord Aden is worthless! You give him a direction, and nothing happens. Then, you have Raven. She is not the sharpest tool in the shed! And do not get me going on Sebastian, Liam, and Miss prissy Bethany."

"Who am I? You want to know who I am?"

"Mere Mundane, I am Morgana. Do you think I am going to let pesky Rose tell the whole story?

It is going on 15 years since the magical three were sent to the realm of the Mundane and it took me over five years to dig my way out of the Neverlands. Talk about a nightmare! Do not get me going on the Neverlands. What is anyone supposed to do there? I remember one evening when Lord Aden and Raven were in a disagreement over how to handle the magical three. I was in one of my moods and walked out of the flames in the fireplace.

That evening, Raven, had caught two of the Council guards and brought them to Lord Aden for questioning. I remember questioning the two guards, then blacking out. It wasn't until the next day that I was told by Raven that the two were dead. That made me upset. I am looking for two things and no one seems to know where they are.

By chance, have you… yes you! Do not ignore me! —have you seen two swords? Never mind, you would not know. You are just a Mundane!

Those swords are Gabriel and Excalibur, two of the most powerful swords around. Yes, Excalibur, the one with which the heroic King Arthur fought. These swords are imbued with great Arcane power. I need them in order to restore the timeline. You see, my dears, I want the same thing—to restore the timeline.

Upon leaving, I hear that Raven and Lord Aden sent nightriders out looking for any sign of resistance and if those three magical brats have returned. Perhaps they are still afraid to face me.

Chapter 2
The Beginning of a Journey

I remember it very clearly. It was 9:30 pm when Zander dropped me off at home after a nice night out. When I came home, I found that Grandma was waiting on the porch for me. She hugged me as I came in. I gave her a kiss on the cheek and headed for my bedroom. In the distance, I could hear the TV running as the fire crackled in the fireplace in the main parlor.

My room was dark that evening and I quickly waved my hand over the light switch so that the lights popped on. I threw my gloves on top of my dresser, kicked my shoes off, and went to my side table where I retrieved my journal and wrote.

October 25th, 2016

Dear Diary,

Today, was truly magical & amazing. My best friend, Zander, showed up & surprised me for my birthday. We went out to lunch, and then, we strolled to the movie theatre after we went for dessert at the ice cream parlor next to the theatre. As we left the mall, we stopped at the little corner jewelry store & he bought me a beautiful necklace and matching earrings, in the shape of the Phoenix. He smiled & said the Phoenix reminds him of me. I wish today did not have to come to an end.

Tomorrow promises to be interesting, oh yes, interesting indeed. You see, tomorrow marks the beginning of a new time in my life. A time that... well, I do not know what to say or even where to begin. My family has always been different. You see, tomorrow, I will be the last of my kind—a witch. My grandmother & uncle say that my mother & father sacrificed themselves while using all of their magic to save me & my older twin brothers. My brothers and I have learned through our visions of times past that this may be true.

The three of us know that our grandparent's home was destroyed, although Uncle Hawke continues to spend time looking for any remaining Arcane, who might have survived. I know that my parents disappeared, riding off into the night on the back of a dragon. While I have first-hand knowledge of this, we really do not know what happened.

Grandma does not speak of the Arcane realm, but instead, she only speaks of the great mystery remaining around an Arcane village & school, which stand in the Mundane realm. Diary, my brothers and I do not speak of this, but we saw what happened the night we were brought here. So many questions come to mind. Did Mom and Dad escape? Who were the five hooded figures? Who is the elf? The hooded figure using the pocket watch to stop time utilized a genuinely fascinating feat of magic! The ability to arrest time is not a magical ability many have, and it leaves so many unanswered questions. Oliver, Ethan, and I know time is bizarre. But, to control time is next to impossible and this individual did it! My brothers and I were able to retrieve the watch, and it appears to be ancient as it comes with markings of the elves and dwarves. It is a truly majestic piece of craftsmanship.

Up to this time, Uncle Hawke has found no one of Arcane descent. Still, tomorrow should prove to be exciting! You see, a witch's or wizard's 16th birthday marks the finishing of their basic training, the time when wizards and witches are taught by their family. But anything they choose to learn after that is on their own, a rule that Grandmother said was passed by the Arcane Council that existed for many years. I laugh because a life of essential magic seems boring because, many times, magic proves to be a fantastic but bizarre tool.

Tomorrow marks a new dawn. You see, Dear Diary, I will be able to create spells, potions, & possibly keep up with those two charming, but mischievous, twin brothers of mine.

No one knows this, not even my best friend, but I hear my mother at night. I listen to her calling to me. I hear her voice, her laughter. I can feel her sadness & worry. I also continue to see a young blind elf boy of eminent power: he watches from afar in my dreams and visions, always with a curious look on his face. Anytime that I try to get close, he disappears. He has never spoken but just watches. To me, he appears to be a younger version of the elf from the vision of my parents the night they disappeared.

Grandma says that when she & my uncle went back looking for my parents, they were gone—vanished—& my paternal grandparent's home was in ruins. Parts of it here & parts of it there, torn apart by time itself, they say. I do continue, quietly though, to hold hope, that, someday, my *brothers & I will reunite with our parents. For now, Dear Diary, this stays between us. For now, I entrust in you the secrets that I know.*

Rose

❧

Yawning, I shut the journal and seal the clasp, falling asleep as my book slides to my side on the bed. Every night, I slip in and out of one dream after another and, on this particular night, I find myself walking in the land of Arcane. There are children running in the distance as dragons roam the countryside.

I have had this dream many times. It is the same one of a woman who is crying as she attempts to pull water from the river with her wand. Nothing happens and the woman continues to try, over and over summoning magic to her. It is the same dream every night. The woman is never able to pull the water to her in order to water the flowers.

Throughout, the night I continue to travel, jumping from one dream to the next but always ending at the vision of the woman crying because her magic does not work. Toward dawn, I attempt something I had not tried before. I push forward to approach the lady. Finally, when I am able to approach the woman, she looks up, smiles, and motions for me to come closer. Cautiously, I do as the woman motions when she reaches down and summons a book from the water. She motions for me to take the book, and I graciously accept it. I turn it over several times in my hands examining the binding and the hand-stitched cover.

Then, just like that, I come out of my dream, being woken by Autumn, standing on the bed, licking my face, and barking.

"Silly dog! Down."

Now, of course, she licks my face again before she jumps down. I sit up in the bed, stretching, when I notice that the book from my dream is sitting on the bed. Before I can pick it up, I find a rainbow in my room, and hummingbirds buzzing around.

Getting up, I put on my robe and pull the blanket over the book.

"Oliver, didn't you see the sign? It says, "Do not disturb."

"Which sign? Oh, you mean that one?

"You burned it?"

"No. Ethan did."

"Seriously?"

"Yes, he used fire wisps."

As I follow Oliver downstairs, I see the funniest sight.

There is my brother, Ethan, covered from head to toe in flour.

"Who won?"

"Ha ha! Very funny! I am not as skilled in the kitchen as you and Grandma."

Ethan brushes himself off and sits down with Oliver and me. Then, Grandma joins us.

"Good morning, children, and Happy Birthday, Rose. My kitchen…! Boys? What did you do?"

"Sorry, Grandma! We are not as skilled as you in the kitchen. We had a mishap with the summoning spell."

Now, being a teenager is hard enough: but mix in your normal, run-of-the-mill summoning spell, and you have a mess in the kitchen like there's no tomorrow.

"Apparently! But it is okay."

Grandma is always skilled in cleaning up their messes and, with one wave of her hand, the kitchen sparkles and everyone is clean again.

&

Over the next two hours, the four of us sit, chat, and enjoy our breakfast. My brothers never get it and roll their eyes when I stand up, snap my fingers, and my clothes change on the spot.

"Show off!"

I smile at Oliver and kiss him and Ethan on the tops of their heads.

"Now, if you will excuse me. I would like to read the new book that Zander got me."

No sooner do I sit down to start reading, when those two charming brothers of mine come strolling in.

"Ask her."

Now, just to annoy Ethan, I tell them, "No!" and go back to reading my book.

"Rose, you don't even know what we are going to ask."

"You see, Ethan? I told you she would say "no." She already knows what we are going to ask before we can even ask it. How many times do we have to go through this?"

&

Now, let's have some fun. Besides, I told them "No," and I do want to read. Do you know how to make your brother mad? Got any ideas? Just keep telling them "No."

Dear Ethan. I have to admire him for his persistence. At the five-minute mark, he asks if he and Oliver can interest me in heading outside.

Now, I love my brothers, but I want to read my book. So, I tell him a stern "no" and go back to reading.

Ethan, you will find, does not like to back down from a challenge. But, after a while, particularly with me, he will start to give up. Oliver has noted every time this happens, and it is amusing to him, but he knows that neither of us is going to give in.

"Now that I have finished reading the first three chapters, we can go outside. But remember what Grandma said at breakfast."

"Yeah, yeah, we know."

The one thing my brothers never argue about is their wardrobes, which always seem to match. Those two just snap their fingers and are in their fall wardrobe with cloaks that touch the ground in opposite colors to each other. Oliver is in a black cloak with purple trim and Ethan in a purple robe and black trim. Just as we head outside, we hear Grandmother clear her throat.

"Boys, remember I have placed a magical barrier around the property just in case you two decide to do something stupid with your magic or your sister's magic acts up as she is not used to the full extent of it yet."

The three of us begin to walk to the back porch when we notice Grandma coming out behind us with her needlepoint. Before heading down the hill, I ask her, "Grandma, where is Uncle?"

"Rose, he is out getting your birthday present. He got up early before the crack of dawn and left. He should be back around dinner."

The three of us look at each other and know not to ask any more questions. As we descend the hill, you can see the dismay on Oliver's face when Ethan motions for him to look back up the hill.

"Really? One of these days. I am going to hex that dog."

"Oliver, leave her be. She is just sitting and watching."

"Watching turns into her being on top of us next."

"Enough, leave her be. Besides, you are the one who always says that she is protective of us."

Holding my wand in my hand, I spin it around and a geyser of water explodes into the air.

Ethan starts laughing as Oliver waves his wand, calming the water.

"My magic appears to be a lot more powerful than before. This will take some getting used to."

However, before I can try another spell, I notice a small ball of bright light flying around. Quietly, so as not to disturb it, I approach with my hand out as it grows brighter. It lands on my hand, then takes off again, back into the air.

"It appears that the fairies have come to bid you a Happy Birthday, sis."

"I thought that magical creatures did not exist."

"These days, only a few do, here and there, but nothing more than maybe one or two, occasionally."

Walking toward the giant oak tree in the yard is when the weirdest thing occurs. The ground begins to shake under us. I place my palm on the tree, trying to support myself, but also to feel what is occurring. As the three of us look at each other, Autumn stands in front of us and, suddenly, Grandma is next to us with her wand drawn. Emerging out of the ground is a young man about our age, with bright peach skin, and brown, green, and silver hair, pulled back in a ponytail. He brushes the dirt and leaves off of himself and, as he spins his hands, much like my brothers and I do, his torn clothes transform into robes that match the color of his hair.

"My apologies, good sirs and good ladies. I hope my appearance did not frighten anyone. Allow me to introduce myself. I am Leaf, the son of...."

This is where my brothers learn why Autumn is always close by. Before the young man can finish what he is trying to say, Autumn pins him to the ground.

"Would someone be so kind as to get this beast off of me?"

"She will be called off when you explain who you are."

With that, my grandmother raises her wand and points it right at the young man, while my brothers step in front of me.

"My Lady, if you would not mind, please look at the mark on the inside of my arm."

Autumn moves her right paw over the young man's sleeve revealing the mark of a tree within a lion's head.

"Does that marking tell you who I am?"

"Autumn get off him. Now!"

"Thank you, My Lady." The young man says to my grandmother as he rises up off of the ground, as he brushes himself off again, and looks around.

"Next time, I won't be nice, beast. I will show my true form. Now, where was I? Oh, yes, shall we go inside? It is not safe out here."

"Who are you?"

"Ahh, yes. You are the shorter of the identical twins. Then, you must be Oliver. I am Leaf, the son of Leo and Lucy. My parents are high ranking members of the Arcane Council."

"The Arcane Council?" my brothers say looking at each other.

"Oh dear, I take it that you are not aware of the Council?"

"We are but only in legend."

"Rose, Oliver, and Ethan, that is a conversation for later. I am curious about how Leaf got here?"

"Yes. How *did* you get here? Or better yet, where did you come from?"

"That is the funny part. One minute, I am asleep: but then, when I wake up, I am in a field with the Lady of White standing over me with the great Belinda."

Now, my brothers and I all notice that when Leaf mentions the name of the great Belinda, Autumn bows her head, showing respect for this beast. Now, our interaction with Leaf raises many questions for my brothers and I as we have been told a very different story. Yet, here, standing in front of us, is an Arcane telling us something entirely different. We also notice that the longer we stand out here talking, the more nervous Leaf is becoming.

☙

"You speak of the Lady of White. Who is she?"

"Ethan, while I am willing to answer your question, I would rather not have that conversation out here."

"Why are you so nervous?"

"Not to sound rude, but, these days, we do not know who is listening. What I am saying is that we should go inside for safety."

Quietly, we walk up the hill, my brothers and I holding tight to our wands and watching Leaf. Once inside, Grandma spins her wand and the doors lock, the shutters slam shut, and, if you watch closely, you will see that a lightfield arises around the house.

Grandma sits in her armchair in the parlor, her eyes narrowed as she asks Leaf, "Now, do you care to explain this? Are you mad? Why would you risk coming here, revealing the identity of the Arcane kingdom?"

"Lady Dawn, I mean no harm. Let me explain. As I said earlier, I went to sleep and when I woke, I was in a field with the Lady of White and Belinda. They told me it was vital that I find the three of you and bring each of you a gift. The Lady of White raised her hand and opened a portal. Before entering the portal, Belinda and the Lady of White noted that I should start running and should not stop until my legs carried me to the Magical Three."

"You see, My Lady, once I got through the portal, I found that several fairies were helping to guide me to all of you. "

With that, Leaf walks to the middle of the room where he extends his right hand and, magically, three beautifully hand-carved walking staves appear and float towards the three of us.

Of course, Oliver and Ethan were first to grab theirs and examine them. I, on the other hand, am more cautious. Although the three of us grew up with each other's magic and the magic of our grandmother and uncle, we learned to be very cautious of all Arcane items. Some are not as helpful or friendly as one might think. But here is something that many do not understand. Those charming brothers of mine experience magic differently. They have no concerns about grabbing and examining the staves in front of them. I, on the other hand, circle the third staff examining it. The markings of ancient runes are breathtaking, but, to me, that does not mean anything. Here is where I differ from my brothers. Many times, they will do something on impulse: I, on the other hand, not so much. When I finally decide to approach the staff and reach for it, time freezes.

Within seconds, everything is back to normal. I am sitting down on the window bench, examining the staff, taking note of each rune in my head and where I may have seen that rune before. I notice one special rune, run my finger over it, and hold back my emotions.

"Leaf. Thank you. These belong to our family, but I am more curious as to who is the Lady of White?" I ask.

"Yes, who is the Lady of White?"

"Oliver, she is a mythological person, until now no one believed she actually existed."

That is when Grandma sits back in her chair and quietly begins to think.

"Would anyone care to explain what does she mean by 'myth'"?

When Ethan asks this question, our grandmother looks at all of us and proceeds to tell us a story.

"Children, The Lady of White is noted in the ancient Arcane texts as the balance of the Arcane realm. The stories told that Merlin and Nimuway created her to protect the Arcane realm. Other accounts say she was created by the high Arcane Council to be a guardian, a beacon of light and hope for all Arcane.

"The legend tells that she will come to the world of the Mundane and bring all lost Arcane creatures, Arcane beings, and any Mundane human who seeks Arcane teaching back to the Arcane kingdom. In folktales and myth, she is a controversial figure as she is associated with life and death, light and dark, good and evil. But if she appeared to Leaf, then she is no myth."

My brothers and I sit quietly processing what we have just heard, when Leaf breaks the silence in the room.

"My Lady is correct. However, that is only one story of the Lady of White."

At that, a surprised look of concern comes over Ethan's face. The three of us have learned a long time ago, never to question or challenge Grandma and yet, this young Arcane has not only challenged her but has declared that her story is only half right. Here is where Grandma could become really difficult to deal with.

"Ha! A young boy your age, knowing the other legends? Impossible!"

Her laugh and expression, which the three of us knew all too well, can pierce your skin and sting.

"Leaf, since you know the 'other' stories, please enlighten us. This should be amusing."

But before our grandmother can say another word, Leaf walks to the center of the room and spins his hands. The room darkens and the three of us, along with Leaf, disappear on the spot. Although we are used to visions, this is unlike anything we have ever seen. We are surrounded by absolute darkness, a coldness coming over us.

The three of us reach around in the dark, and, as we find each other's hands and hold on, we start glowing, lighting the area around us. The three of us know where each other is, but we cannot see Leaf. We can only hear him speaking spell after spell. Now, in my visions, I can tell you, if we leave standing, we normally arrive standing. In this vision, however, we can tell that we are free falling.

The next thing we know, we land on the ground where the Lady of White stands in front of us. As the vision comes into clarity, we watch as she walks around a room, her hands behind her back, speaking to a young girl, who is observing the darkness moving over the earth through a crystal ball.

Quietly, I look around, noting that we're on the balcony of a castle, high enough in the air to be able to look down. In the distance, Arcane warriors can be seen fighting back the darkness. Dragons fly overhead and mystical creatures are arriving from all around the realm, attacking the darkness.

Before we even have a chance to continue to observe the scene that is playing out, we fall into the darkness again. This time, we land on a hillside, a vision the three of us know all too well now presents itself with greater clarity. The young girl appears in the field. The woman with her appears to be the Lady of White.

They raise their wands and cast magic across the river. Rising out of the ground is a beautiful, small village, a temple, and a school. In a flash, they stand in ruins, much like the other day when I experienced something similar at school. But, unlike my experience, where the school was there, then gone, then there again, the village, in this vision, is there, then gone, but does not return to normal.

This is an example of why we say that time sometimes becomes bizarre. Before the vision is finished, we fall again, this time, landing with loud thuds on the ground. Getting up and brushing ourselves off, we notice that Leaf is in the background, and the Lady of White is speaking to him. Oliver, Ethan, and I look back and forth at each other as we realize that this is a vision of the story we have just heard from Leaf, and we realize that Belinda is a giant dragon that is much larger than anything we have ever seen in any previous vision. The majestic beast towers over Leaf and the Lady of White. Her silver and white scales glisten in the sunlight. She has the most majestic green eyes and when you look into them, they look as if they are piercing your soul.

You can tell that she is an older dragon, by the looks of it, one of the originals. Embedded on her right leg, as if etched into her scales, are the symbols of the four divine creatures, the markings of the chief dragon, lion, the unicorn, and the phoenix.

As always, just as the vision starts to get interesting, it suddenly ends.

৵

We find ourselves standing back in the parlor of our house. This is the first time; Oliver and I have ever experienced Ethan winded from a vision. He leans over catching his breath, resting his hands on his knees.

"Leaf, how did the Lady of White acquire those staves?"

"Oliver, that is what I do not understand. As your grandmother notes, the Lady of White was thought to be a myth until earlier today when she revealed herself to me. For many of us, the realm of the Arcane is all we know. No one will believe it back home when I tell them the portals between the realms still exist and function."

Our grandmother, who is still sitting in her chair, looks very annoyed at the mention of the portals.

"Leaf, what do you mean the portals still exist?"

"Oliver, that is not a discussion that needs to happen?"

"Grandma, yes, it is. If they exist, then the realm we are from exists. Mom and Dad...."

"Oliver, your uncle and I swore to protect the three of you. You are the last..."

"My Lady, do they know...?"

"No, Leaf, they do not."

"Then, they must be told."

Realizing that she can no longer control what we know, Grandmother waves her hand, motioning him to share.

"The night when time stood still, the portals exploded. One minute they were there, the next, they were gone. The Arcane believe that the connection between the Arcane and Mundane realms has been lost forever but, clearly, it is not. They are just hidden from sight."

"Yes, and how powerful is Belinda?"

My brothers always find it surprising, when I manage to come up with the perfect magical text to answer their questions. Taking down an old, tattered-looking book from the bookcase, I read aloud. According to the texts I've read, Belinda is as old as they come, believed to be born around the time when magic was first given to the earth. She is the chief of the four divine creatures: the markings we saw going up her right leg, designate her status. While reading the passage about Belinda, my brothers motion with their heads for me to look over at Autumn who is sitting next to Leaf and hanging on every word.

Now, this is the second time that this has occurred, where we see our dog acting bizarrely at the mention of Belinda's name. I continue to read aloud.

Belinda is the queen dragon, mother of all Arcane creatures, one of four leaders and, as the texts note, one of the most magical Arcane. Her knowledge of magic, and Arcane history dates back centuries. She is the one noted from our original vision, she is the one who aided

Merlin and Nimuway and was there when the Arcane realm was created.

"Rose is correct. Belinda is the great queen of the dragons and has been loyal to your family for years. She has aided them in many battles. She went missing for many years but now has returned to help you three take back your family home."

"Wait! What? Take back our home? It still exists? Our family's real home?"

"Leaf, enough of this. They are not ready."

"Lady Dawn, while I respect your concern, I am under orders from Belinda to show them."

Leaf extends his hand to me and knowing all too well what is about to come, I reach down and take Ethan's hand as Oliver grabs ahold of Ethan's shoulder. The room begins to spin when we hear Leaf speak through the engulfing fog.

"You see, My Lady, you are not the only one with the gift of visions."

We land in a cold wet field, dew still dripping off the blades of grass. The morning fog is starting to part and the air is crisp. The three of us look around trying to figure out where we are when we hear Leaf say, "Walk with me."

With Leaf walking in front of us, Oliver and Ethan stop to gaze about, examining the area. Not wanting to lose Leaf, I pick up my pace in order to keep up with him, while those two take their time looking around. Leaf and I are the first to reach the edge of a cliff. In the distance, a dark haze can be observed. Leaf points out over the valley.

"This is your land, the realm of the Arcane… well, what remains."

"I take it that the dark haze is our home?"

"Yes, Oliver, the darkness is why the land in the distance is ripping apart."

"What do you mean ripping apart?"

"Really, Ethan! Don't you know? The night your parents cast the spell to protect you three, that not only sent you to the Mundane realm, but it also froze time. Freezing time, caused magic to become chaotic and locked down all the portals, causing them to explode. The place where time froze is the site of the castle of the royal family. When time froze, the bustling castle became uninhabitable. For nearly sixteen years, the castle and a good portion of the realm stood as a barren wasteland."

"Leaf, why would our parents be at the castle?"

"Oliver, you seriously do not know?"

"Leaf, please, for us, much about the Arcane realm remains a mystery.

"Well then. Your family is the Noble House of Phoenix, you know, the royal Arcane family as declared by the ancients and the original Arcane Council of this land. You three are supposed to not only be the living heirs but the three who will save all magic."

"Leaf, you mentioned a spell that froze time. That form of Arcane magic is forbidden and not talked about in any of the books we have read."

"Rose, that is what a lot of us thought too. You see, many of the remaining members of the Arcane Council have searched the grounds of the castle for any remaining evidence of your family, but nothing has been found, not even a single magical item. It is believed by many Arcane that your family died in the events of that night. However, my father, mother, and a few others believe that if your parents were able to cast Arcane time magic, then they could have teleported to safety. But the larger question remains of whether Morgana made it out alive. If she did, then she knows of the existence of Arcane time spells and will be seeking a way to acquire them. We fear that she will seek to learn this magic for herself in order to control all time. Another large concern is that she will travel through time looking for the young Princess Mora, the young girl from the first vision."

"Leaf, why would she seek this Mora of whom you speak?"

"Good question, Ethan. Legend has it that Mora is the beginning of all magic. She is the essence of all magic. Morgana wants that magical power for herself. What better way to get it than from the ultimate source? Mora is the noble being through whom all magic came."

While Leaf is talking, the ground under us begins to shake and we return to the parlor.

❧

After we catch our breath, Ethan sits down on one of the chairs. Oliver begins pacing the floor while I hug Leaf.

"Thank you for showing us that and thank you for the gifts you brought."

As I finish hugging him, our grandmother rejoins us in the parlor.

"Well, I see you four are back."

"Why didn't you tell us that it was a time spell that our parents used? Or, better yet, that we are royalty?"

"Oliver, your uncle and I made a vow to protect you three. We felt until the time was right, we did not want you to know that your father's family is the royal family of Arcane. And to answer your question about the spell, we cannot be sure. Your uncle and I mustered and used almost all of our magic the next day to open a portal. We went back looking for your parents. Nothing! The Arcane Council believed it to be a time spell, but the Arcane time spells are held by only one person—the Lady Mora, an ancient, noble, magical being of great power. No one could be sure."

"How do we know then?

"Rose, we do not. Remember the young girl you saw, the one advised by the woman? That young girl is Mora. She is the daughter of Arcane light and magic. She was the only one who knows the spells to alter time, to time travel, and to change the timeline altogether. Something that no one has ever understood or tried to understand, is that Arcane times spells are next to impossible to reproduce."

Now, our grandmother never agrees with anyone but, in this case, she nods to show that she agrees with what Leaf is saying.

"Well, the three of us get this, but, apparently, our parents knew."

"Ethan, that is more rumor than anything. Some more outlandish than the next."

"Outlandish in what ways?"

Our grandmother spins her hands, and an orb appears, and images step out. "The first outlandish theory is that a young elf prince, who was close to the princess, learned the spells and then taught them to your mother and father. In the second theory, there were five elves, who were seen on the spot of the attack and aided your parents in opening the portal. They are believed to have some access to Arcane time magic. The best of these theories (and many swear by this one) is that older versions of yourselves came from the future to open the portal and allow your younger selves to escape.

As you can see, one interesting theory after the next. However, two do not address the fact that time froze. That is the largest puzzlement for everyone."

As we sit listening to these theories and as Oliver and Ethan agree that each is more outlandish than the next, a strange thing occurs. I hear a voice. It is very quiet, but it continues to call my name. Finally, I quietly answer "Yes," under my breath.

"The stories are true," the voice says quietly. "None of them are outlandish. Listen to me. Your brothers and you have found that the stories of time spells are true. Listen to what your heart tells you. The three of you have seen too many visions not to believe. You have seen the portal opening and have seen the five hooded figures. The spell lives in the three of you. You already know it. You just have to dig deep and remember how it works."

Then, like that, the voice is gone, and I quickly rejoin the conversation so that I do not draw attention to my inattentiveness. My brothers and grandmother have learned that my inattentiveness is me stepping in and out of visions. After the conversation ends, the three of us spend time asking Leaf about himself, exploring various aspects of the Arcane realm, and learning everything we possibly can about the Lady of White, Mora, Belinda, and our family.

Now, if hearing the voice in the first place isn't bad enough, I continue to hear it chiming in at various points in the conversation, reassuring me that everything Leaf is telling us is correct. The weirdest part of our conversation with Leaf is that any time the name of Belinda is said by any one of the four of us, Autumn is sitting right there listening.

Suddenly, a loud pop echoes through the room from the entry hall, signaling the return of Uncle Hawke. There, covered from head to toe in dirt and with blood running down his nose from a gash across his face, stands Uncle Hawke.

"Uncle Hawke! What has happened?"

"A snag teleporting, Oliver."

"At least you're okay, Uncle."

"Nothing that magic cannot mend or fix. Anyways, my dear boy, did you get it?"

"Yes, Mom, but it was not easy to find, and the Arcane magic surrounding it was far more powerful than expected."

The three of us have always known our Uncle Hawke to be magically talented. So, we look at each other with concern when he pushes back his cloak revealing that his right leg is sliced and bleeding.

"Never mind that. Rose, Happy Birthday!"

And, with that, my sweet uncle hands me a bouquet of flowers from behind his back. He always uses his magic as if he is a magician on stage, always hiding his hands behind his back and revealing the surprise. To entertain Ethan and Oliver when they were younger, he used to do the pulling-a-rabbit out-of-the-hat trick.

"Uncle, thank you. They are beautiful."

Just as we turn to walk back into the parlor, Oliver and I notice Uncle Hawke's eyes narrow.

"Well, I see that we have a visitor. Who is this? He appears to be Arcane and smells like an Arcane beast who just got back from running through the fields."

As our uncle settles in, we introduce him to Leaf and explain what we have learned and witnessed through our time jumps. Uncle is very interested in hearing who is still around and continues to ask Leaf about many different Arcane individuals by name.

"Well, you three, it appears there are more that survived than your grandmother and I thought." Fifteen minutes go by as we continue to explain what is going on. Then, we hear the kettle in the kitchen whistling, letting us know dinner is ready.

We enjoy a beautifully cooked turkey with all the fixings, and, with a wave of a hand from my grandmother, the table is clean. Everyone starts to depart the kitchen back to the parlor when my grandmother stops me.

"Rose, how do you like the staff?"

"Grandma, it is nice. It was my mother's."

My grandmother looks at me with a puzzled look.

"How did you know that, child? You had a vision, didn't you, when you touched it?"

"No, the energy is that of a woman. Second, it is calming and, third, the high rune marking on the staff indicates that it was my mother's."

"Interesting. Shall we join the men and open presents?"

"Yes, Grandma. You go ahead. I will be there in a moment."

After she leaves, I take a moment to compose myself. My head is racing with the thought that I have my mother's staff. How did the Lady of White get it? Whose is the voice I am hearing? A lot is going on, and I become emotional over the fact that my mother and father are not around. Finally, I pull myself together and head for the parlor.

Upon entering, I discover that Oliver and Leaf are playing a round of wizard cards. Ethan and Autumn are playing with her toy. Uncle is sitting in his overstuffed armchair smoking his pipe, and Grandma is sitting next to the radio listening to tribal folk chants. I start to get settled in when my cell phone starts buzzing. What? Do not think that, because I am magical, I do not have technology around. I look down to find that Zander has sent a huge Happy Birthday text, followed by one from Brooke and Olivia. Everyone is wishing me a Happy 16th! I would have loved to spend it with them, but Grandma was concerned about magical mishaps.

The next hour is spent opening presents. Of course, my brothers give me some new cloaks, noting that it is time for me to dress like a true Arcane witch. I snap my fingers and try on all of them, one after another in less than a minute. I open several other presents, new quills, some gift cards, and then, at the bottom of the pile, one present remains. A package wrapped in brown paper, that is extremely dusty.

This package catches the attention of my brothers, and Grandma and Uncle watch as I tear back the wrapping. Looking at the giant book in my hands, I turn it over, examining it, knowing all too well that it is a spell book. Running my hand over the clasp, I notice that the key lock is the same shape as my crystal necklace that I wear. I retrieve the necklace from under my shirt and find that, indeed, it unlocks the clasp. As I click it open, the room begins to spin as Ethan, Oliver, and I find ourselves standing in what looks to be a castle.

As the three of us begin to look around, we notice an image moving in the mirror. As Oliver approaches to check it out, the room becomes engulfed in darkness. We pull our wands and cast light orbs into the area and running to each other, turn back-to-back so that we can see every part of the room. A figure approaches us in the distance. It looks like a ghost, but upon the figure getting closer, a path appears. We are standing in the middle of the path as this individual approaches. Oliver is the first to respond.

"Mom?"

"My children, it appears that your sister has turned 16 years old. Happy Birthday, dear! What an exciting time! This marks the year that Rose becomes the last of her kind, a fully trained witch. What I am about to tell you is essential. First, as you three have all mastered the basics of magic, there is now no limit to your power or potential in magic. Rules do not exist for the three of you. The blood of two very ancient Arcane bloodlines flow through your veins and give you your magical abilities.

Secondly, and on a more critical note, a dangerous and dark sorceress, known as Morgana le Fey, has returned. She escaped from her prison in the Neverlands and is now building a large army. She seeks to use it to destroy you three and then, take over the Mundane world. Although she may try, she will not succeed without help, and it is for this reason, that I am contacting you. It is essential that you three know that the Council of the Dark Arcane fuels her dark magic. She is one of the most dangerous Arcane and has caused the death of many, including your great grandparents and your grandparents. Each of you alone cannot win against her. You will need each other and to work together. Only then will you succeed. In times of great darkness, remember you will find light, in weakness, you will find strength, and in loneliness, you will find togetherness.

You three must be ready and learn to work together, as no one knows what may come your way. Be prepared and trust no one, as darkness is everywhere, takes many forms, and has amassed many allies. Things are not as they seem, and you will all learn many truths along the way. As you continue to learn more, there will be many truths that will reveal themselves to you. Some will be welcomed and some you may not want to know. Remember, magic comes from all living things. Hold tight to the light within, find that light in others, and no darkness will ever be able to touch you. My children...."

๛

Within seconds, the image of our mother disappears, and we find ourselves back in the parlor. As we come to, the three of us are lying on the floor and Uncle Hawke, Grandma, and Leaf help us up.

"A vision, I take it?"

"Yes, but it did not finish."

"Oliver, that is normal."

I sit in the window seat, as Ethan and Oliver share with Grandma, Uncle Hawke, and Leaf what we observed and were told. I sit reading my new spell book for a little bit, while Ethan watches as Leaf and Oliver continue their game of wizard cards. As I quietly flip the pages of my book, I discover a letter tucked into the binding. I turn to the next page, mark the spot, and close the book, sealing the clasp.

I wish everyone a good night and note that I am tired and off to bed, turning in for the night. I move quickly to get to my room, the book in hand, pull my wand, and seal my bedroom door and windows. I retrieve the crystal, pop the clasp, and pull out the letter. Sitting on my bed, I start to read.

My darling Rose,

This day marks a historic day for you, your sixteenth birthday. To you, my daughter, Happy Birthday, and magical blessings. I write this letter to you, as you can see the future. You and I both are gifted seers. In time, you and your brothers will return to the Arcane kingdom. But, for now, you three are safe among the Mundane. This is the realm of your birth and darkness cannot find you there. It is critical that you and your brothers protect the Mundane realm from darkness. If they succeed in destroying the realm of the Mundane, they will also destroy the Arcane kingdom. One realm cannot exist without the other.

You see, you and your brothers are of the two realms. Please, I beg of you, do not come searching for us. You three are the last hope for magic and the salvation of the Arcane. Your father and I are alive but are on the move, trying to rebuild the portals to save the Arcane. If you and your brothers journey here, it could bring Morgana with a great fury.

Your father and I love you three and want what is best for you. We never wanted to send you away, but we knew we had to, for your safety. The night we sent you away, your paternal grandparents' beloved homeland fell under attack by Morgana and her forces. In an attempt to save what magic we could, we sent you and your brothers into hiding. In time, you will understand why we did this. By sending you away, we secured the fate of the Arcane realm by giving it a chance to survive through you three.

Within this book, there is a chapter I have written especially for you. As you know, you have the ability of telepathy. I know you have heard me speak to you many times before. My daughter, that chapter will teach you how to communicate with me in whichever realm either of us may be.

When your father and I froze the realm, we destroyed the portals between our worlds. In time, you and your brothers will learn how to reopen and re-establish those portals. Many believe that to re-establish those portals, the journey begins with Camelot. Yes, Camelot is part of the necessary key to the quest for the portals.

It is time that you know this truth: you and your brothers are not alone. Outside of your grandmother and your uncle, several other high ranking Arcane fled and continue to protect you. They know who the three of you are but watch from a distance until the right time comes. You will only know them by the mark of the Arcane. If they claim to be Arcane but cannot produce this mark or seal, then they cannot be trusted.

Roslynn, you must trust your heart. You, Oliver, and Ethan are the only hope for our people, for the Arcane. It is vital that you and your brothers' journey to find the two swords of Arcane time. These swords of which I speak are entrusted with some of the greatest Arcane power and can help protect you on your journey. More importantly, the Arcane magic of the swords not only protects those who hold them but represent two of the Arcane artifacts you will need to protect both realms.

While there is still so much to tell you, I have very little time. My child, I love you. Be safe and may the Arcane powers of the universe protect you.

Your mother,
Nadia

Upon finishing the letter, a tear runs down my face and falls on the letter. I wipe my face and start flipping through the book, looking for the chapter my mother has referenced. After finding the chapter, I take a deep breath to calm my mind, and sit back on my bed. I jump, having forgotten about the other book I had been given in my dream. I retrieve it from under the sheets, look at it again, and place it in my side table. I quickly turn my attention back to reading. I read into the early hours of the morning and, before long, my dear brother Ethan is in my room trying to wake me to get ready for school.

Chapter 3
School

Morning, the most horrible time of the day. Then, to top it off, that charming brother of mine is waking me, shooting fire pixies around the room.

"All right. I am getting up. I will be down in 15 minutes and get these pixies out of here."

I am sure my snappy tone always makes both of my brothers happy with me. After getting out of bed and putting on my robe, I notice the spell book laying open. I gather it up, remove the necklace from the clasp and seal the book. I place the necklace back around my neck, hiding it out of sight and place the book in my nightstand. As I shut the drawer, locks magically appear on the outside sealing it from any intruders.

Twenty-minutes later, I am ready for school and head downstairs to find an interesting sight.

Ethan is decked out in his usual school attire—blue jeans, boots, and polo shirt—his hair done and, like clockwork, in front of the mirror fighting to get his contacts in, Uncle Hawke fussing at him, Oliver tapping his foot, looking at his watch, complaining about the time it takes Ethan and I to get ready. Oliver is always in his lettermen jacket, and Ethan and I have a joke between us that if Oliver could sleep in his jacket, he would.

Then a rather unusual surprise, Leaf is decked out in what looks to be a mix of Oliver's and Ethan's clothes. The poor guy looks so uncomfortable. He is fumbling around with his wand trying to stow it in his bag.

Grandmother explains to us how she has called ahead and informed the school that our distant cousin has just moved to town and will be joining us in school.

"Children, remember the Mundane are trying to live their simple lives, no magic, no talk about mystical creatures, and no hexing any items in the school to come to life. Oliver and Ethan, Leaf is your responsibility."

Ugh, every morning the same lecture from her about the Mundane and magic, and blah, blah, blah. This morning the ride to school is uneventful or at least I am not paying attention as I think about the spell book and the letter from my mother when Ethan started snapping his fingers in front of my face.

"Earth to Rose. Look a dragon!"

"Not funny Ethan."

"Why do you always zone out?"

"Why do you always butt into my business?"

Of course, once my brothers are in the school, they dash off to see their friends, and I am left with Leaf. We walk quietly to the office. I introduce him to the front office staff. We get his schedule and come to find out Grandma has put him in every one of my classes. So much for Oliver and Ethan being responsible for him.

Walking from the office, we make a sharp right and I show him where the lockers are.

"Good morning."

Now, Zander is always charming. He will grab your hand, make a bow, and then kiss the top of it.

"Morning, Zander. Let me introduce my cousin, Leaf."

"Cousin?"

"Zander, please, not right now. Ask me about it later?"

And saved by the bell. Of course, Zander knows about the magic and the weirdness of my family but how do you explain to your Mundane best friend about the boy who has appeared out of the ground? Do you remember how the other day during gym I was telling you about Ms. Destiny, and I told you that was a conversation for another day? Unfortunately, that day has arrived.

Picture it: 14th century Europe, the Dark Ages, the time of the High Renaissance, and the weird crazy dresses women of the nobility wore. Now, jump forward to the present, and yeah, that is Ms. Destiny, dressed everyday like she just stepped out of the pages of history.

To make it worse, she teaches History of the World… well, more like Arthurian legend all year. Nothing else. She drones on for hours about Arthur, Guinevere, the Knights of the Round Table. Merlin this and Merlin that. It actually becomes rather annoying after a while just listening to her.

Don't get me wrong. I love the stories of Merlin, but 10 years of hearing them is enough to make any student want to go insane. Yes, that is right. Somehow, I have had her for 10 years. Poor Oliver and Ethan are still trying to figure out what curse or hex was put on the three of us as those two have also had her every year. It has gotten to a point where they ditch her class every day.

Then, of course, every morning, it is… wait for it…

"Good morning, my dear scholars. Are we ready to learn, to explore, to engage our mind in ancient wisdom?"

Every morning, the same opening, with the same student's laughing and the same look over the top of her glasses as she mumbles under her breath. Lord knows what she is saying. Oliver swears she is hexing our classmates when she does that.

As Leaf takes his seat, this is where things get interesting. Looking at Ms. Destiny, he mutters under his breath.

"She looks so familiar. It cannot be."

"You, young man. Yes you, the new boy. Please stand up."

"Yes, ma'am. What can I do for you?"

"You are new. What is your name? Please introduce yourself."

"I am Leaf, ma'am, and you are?"

"Well, Leaf, welcome to my class. I want to be the first to welcome you, unlike some others in this class who want to laugh. Mr. Smith, I am looking at you. What is so funny? Why is there so much laughing?"

"Nothing, ma'am"

"Anyway, Leaf, welcome but please keep your muttering about people to yourself. You may sit."

"Why?"

"Detention, for you. This is my classroom. How dare you defy me? You are not making a good first impression. And to answer your question, child, I am Ms. Emma Destiny."

Now, Zander and I shoot each other looks, then watch as Leaf's eyes narrow as he and Ms. Destiny enter into a stare down. Then suddenly, she breaks her glare and proceeds.

"Today, class, we are going to explore the time of one of my favorite kings, King Arthur, and the times of Merlin."

Ugh! Every time this woman talks, her voice is like nails on a chalkboard and those glasses. She always peers over her glasses. This is the one class that I dread. It is always about King Arthur, Merlin, and the Knights. This whole time, Leaf, Zander, and I keep shooting looks at each other. I am hoping for a fire drill.

"Class let us explore a legend from the time of Merlin, a rather unique time in his journey that is not discussed often."

If Oliver, Ethan, Zander, and I each had a quarter for every time Ms. Destiny said that, we would be millionaires. However, this particular day, something weird happens when she mentions the story, something that only Zander, Leaf, and I notice. As Ms. Destiny talks, she winks at me, which, of course, she never does, and—wait for it, here it comes—she claps like an excited little schoolgirl as the shutters slam shut. Every time, it's like magic.

Great, she is doing slides again, another reason we think she might be Arcane. No technology is allowed in her class. The concept of a television is foreign to her. Grandma continues to stand behind her argument that Ms. Destiny is not Arcane, while Oliver, Ethan, and I think that she is, given all the weird things she does.

"Now, before we dive into today's lesson, let me clear up some misconceptions about Merlin and Arthur."

"Oh yes, Merlin, as many of you know, was a wizard and the royal advisor to King Arthur. But things are not as they seem. With Merlin, they never are. One story, while a noted one, is not discussed because of what it means. The story about the Lady Mora. It is believed that Mora was one of the great founders of magic. With this accomplishment, she posed a significant threat to Merlin, so he had her killed. The legends say she returned from death and became the dark witch Morgana, killing everything and everyone in her path. Ultimately, she sought revenge on Merlin."

Several rules, you will learn when in Ms. Destiny's class. Her glare will pierce through you, particularly when her eyes narrow. She has a mean temper, and she has no sense of humor. Take the two football players up there in the front row, watch what happens when they say something about the lesson.

"Wicked," the two football players laughed.

"Gentlemen, what is amusing? Or would you find the principal's office "wicked"? I do not find your analysis helpful. "Wicked"? What type of English is that? One more peep out of anyone and you will have detention for a month."

And to my great surprise, she starts telling the same story about Merlin, Nimuway, and the Knights of the Round Table that I have heard from Grandma a hundred times. Now remember, Ms. Destiny said not a peep. So, watch her blow her stack.

"Ms. Destiny?"

"Yes, Rose? Someone had better be dying! What is so necessary to interrupt me?"

"Ms. Destiny, who is the dragon and the woman in all white?"

But before Ms. Destiny can answer, the room freezes and begins spinning.

There, in a field, stands the Lady of White and, behind her, the great dragon, Belinda. As I approach, the Lady of White pulls her wand and projects magic at me. As I block, our fields of magic intertwine.

"What are you doing? Are you crazy? We are on the same side. Why do you attack…?"

As the dragon rears up, I am suddenly back in my seat in the classroom and the bell rings.

*

"Roslynn, may I have a word with you, please?"

Zander and I look at each other. I roll my eyes, and he knows what I mean.

"Zander, go ahead and take Leaf with you; I will be right there."

Zander, being who he is, grabs Leaf and drags him from the room, knowing all too well that Ms. Destiny is going to be difficult about something.

"Yes, Ms. Destiny?"

"Ah, Rose, my dear child, I was told you have a love of Arthurian legend. In particular, the legends about the powers of light and dark."

"Light and dark?"

"Oh, Rose, silly me! Did I say light and dark? I meant Merlin and Morgana. Well, anyway, here is my new book that I wrote. I wanted to give you the first copy."

"Thank you, Ms. Destiny. I do enjoy Arthurian legend. Is that all?"

"Yes, for now."

With that I quickly depart stowing the book in my bag and heading for the hallway. I run to my next class, meeting up with Zander and Leaf. My head races about the book, but what is perplexing to me is how Ms. Destiny knew my birth name—Roslynn. My school records do not indicate that name. The last time that name was used was when I was three. Over the next two periods, I continue to find my mind wandering, trying to process everything, and thinking about the different experiences my brothers and I have had over the years with Ms. Destiny. Finally, the bell rings and lunch is upon us.

I always sit with Brooke, Olivia, and their cousin, Claire. Oliver and Ethan will join us occasionally and, of course, Zander is not left at another table. As Zander and Leaf approach the table, Claire who is the weird one in the group—imagine the twin to Ms. Destiny—jumps up to introduce herself.

"Hi, I am Claire. These are my cousins, Olivia and Brooke."

"Nice to meet you. I am Leaf."

"Rose, you didn't tell us you had a cousin."

This is the first time the group of us had ever seen Claire talk so much. Leaf sits there listening and eating his lunch, like it is nothing. Our table is always by the big windows overlooking the courtyard of our school. Suddenly, I see a buzzing ball of bright light flying around.

"Hey, I will be back in a few minutes. I am heading to the girl's room."

Quickly, I walk toward the back of the cafeteria, out the double doors, and then, swing around to the courtyard. Upon reaching the courtyard, I find that my hunch is correct. There it is, the small fluttering ball of light, but then, it is gone. I spend a few seconds looking around, but when I turn to go back in, I notice a letter taped to the door. My name is written across it.

Dearest Lady Roslynn,

When this letter reaches you, there will not be much time. Long ago, your parents sent you to this, the Mundane, realm for safety. This realm is your home and is the birthplace of all magic. The necklace you wear comes from this realm. Your necklace is the key to finding the Arcane. When one who is Arcane is around, the necklace will glow. When you give the necklace the command, "Unlock" it will activate its powers.

Second, you must find the Temple of Divine Grace. There, you must make contact with Father Francisco. He holds vital information you will need in your journey against the darkness. You will know him only if he can produce the marking of the Arcane Divine. His knowledge is vital as it will lead you to one of the eldest living members of the realm with direct knowledge of Merlin. He is also the sworn protector of your family.

In order to come back to this realm, you will need Prince Ignatius' help. He will lead you three to safety and will know where your parents are hiding. I must go, but good luck and Godspeed, child. May the powers of your ancestors and the Arcane protect you. You have the blessings of the fairies. Now, good luck and listen to your heart. Oh, one last thing, Morgana knows where you and your brothers are, and she is coming! Be ready!

~Amaryllis, the Lady of the Willow Glen~

I tuck the letter into my pocket and walk back into the lunchroom.

"Rose, you're back. We were discussing Valley High School's debate team. What is your opinion?"

"Olivia, I do not mean to be rude, but I need to talk to Zander. Will you come with me?"

"I was not done with lunch. What is going on?"

"Zander, please watch Leaf. I am heading home to do some research and need to get into the study there."

"Again, what do I tell your brothers and Leaf?"

"Do not worry. I have that handled. However, if I am not back in time, please stall."

"Go, please, before people begin to wonder where you are."

Zander has always been a great friend and very supportive, but I never do magic in front of him, mostly out of respect. Oh, by the way, what I am about to do, no one is to know about. The only way to leave here without drawing attention is to… well, freeze time. Shh, don't say that out loud. If my uncle or grandmother knew, I would be grounded.

I spin the dials of the old pocket watch as a large ghost like image of the watch appears in the hall. The hands move, then everything stops. Time stands still.

"Well, it worked, but let's see for how long. Mora is not the only one who can alter and play with time."

I rummage through my bag, retrieve my wand, point it at the ground and teleport, appearing in the parlor at home. I come out of the parlor, looking around. Perfect, Grandma is at her ladies' luncheon and Uncle and Autumn are out.

Chapter 4
A New Understanding

After checking the house over twice to make sure no one is at home, I head for the kitchen, find the old, tattered cookbook, tap the spine of the book with my wand, and then, pull the book from the shelf. The wall pushes back and slides open, revealing a staircase. As I descend the stairs, the end of my wand lights as the basement has always been dark. Searching through piles of books, I find it.

"Ah yes, the Book of Magical Beings. Here it is."

I pick up the book and because of its weight it slams down on the podium with a loud thud. I start to flip page by page when I realize that, because of the sheer size of the book, it is going to take forever.

"Time to use a trick."

Placing my hands palm facing down over the book, I close my eyes as the pages start to flip quickly. As I open my eyes, it takes me to the section where I need to go.

Here it is, Amaryllis, the Lady of the Willow Glen. Only one way to find out who she is and what she is about.

Stepping into the vision, I find myself in a long hallway reaching for the sky. Walking down the hallway, I look around, observing the various pictures on the wall. They all appear to be of the fairy royalty. At the end of the hall is a grand room where the Lady of White emerges, walking towards a fairy.

"My Lady, you made it."

"I see you are well, Amaryllis."

"Indeed. What news do you bring?"

"Merlin!"

"My dear Lady, there is not a day when that man does not come up. What has he done now?"

"Are you aware of his plan to create a separate Arcane realm?"

"Unfortunately, the wind bag came to visit me and told me all about it the other day."

"Are you going?"

"My dear Lady, yes. I feel it is my duty to help protect the ways of magic. You are the last one I have to remind, but if Merlin breaks the balance of magic, then the magic of earth will die, killing all fairies. So, yes, I am going to protect the realm and all magic."

"Amaryllis, as you know, all things weave magically together. Please do everything you can to keep the magical creatures safe. Your mother would have done the same."

"My Lady, you have nothing to fear."

"You are staying in the realm of Mundane?"

"For now, yes. Someone has to protect them."

"What of the prophecy?"

"Only time will tell."

"Indeed!"

"Amaryllis, when you get there, if you find her—you know of whom I speak—send her home. You are her oldest friend. She will listen to you."

"My Lady, do you believe she will be there?"

"I can only pray. You know she will go after him. She will go where she has to, to protect all magic."

As the Lady of White finishes speaking, the room begins to spin. The pictures on the walls come to life and, within seconds, the room returns to normal, only one candle lit. In the distance, looking from the balcony, I spot Amaryllis.

As I approach, I notice that we are up in a tree, looking down over a valley. Within seconds, the candles throughout the room explode with light as multiple fairies begin to appear, all shouting.

"My Queen!"

"Queen Amaryllis!"

"Our Queen!"

"My children, what is it that brings all of you racing to me, shouting?"

"Our Queen, forgive us. Word has come through the land that Kelvin and Nadia have been spotted."

"Kelvin and Nadia saved a village from the darkness. It is said that Nadia summoned Arcane defense to her and leveled the darkness. Sources from all over the realm saw Nadia while she was passing through the village that was attacked by the shadows. Nadia summoned forth light, dueling with the shadows before using the light to restore the balance of magic to the village. The villagers claim they have never seen magic like that before."

"Our Queen, how is this possible?"

"My children, anything is possible, particularly for Kelvin and Nadia. If what you hear is true and they have been spotted, then Morgana will be looking for them or worse. Oh dear!"

Now, I have seen many forms of magic, but what she does next is amazing. The queen floats above the ground toward a giant pool of water in the room. Waving her hand over it, a large bubble appears, I notice that she is watching Oliver and Ethan.

The other fairies are chattering amongst themselves when a male fairy with a beautiful band on his head approaches.

"Mother?"

"My son, what word do you bring?"

"The word is true. Kelvin and Nadia have been spotted. Divinity and the Council are looking for them."

"Phineas, stay here and monitor the situation, I must get word to those in the Mundane realm. I must ask you to help me secure safe passage. I must do something of great importance."

The great queen starts to float in the air, and, within seconds, I am transported back to the basement.

As the room comes into focus, I find myself sitting on the floor looking around. I get up, brush myself off, and feel excited to know that my brothers' and my hunch is correct, that our parents are still alive. What we now know is that we have friends among the fairies.

Both the vision and the letter from earlier confirm this. When I stand up, I notice that the picture of the dragon, Belinda, appears to be alive, the eyes watching me as I move. Upon reaching the stairs, I turn to examine the room and find that the picture of Belinda is back to normal. I return upstairs and looking around, listen. Still, no one is home and I stow the book back on the shelf, sealing the basement from sight.

Walking by the kitchen island towards the hallway, I grab an apple from the basket on the counter. I notice that another picture of a dragon, at the end of the hallway, has also come to life, the eyes moving as smoke bellows from the snout. As I gaze at it, a black dragon emerges from the picture, its head sticking out and as it inhales, his nostrils glow orange. I pull my wand and when the dragon screams and pulls back, disappearing into the picture, our dog appears from the family room looking at the picture and growling.

"Weird! Crazy dog! That dragon could have eaten you."

I head down the hallway toward the parlor when a cloaked figure appears floating in the air. The spirit raises their arm and points out the window. I quickly move to the window and looking out, note a large group of dark shadows rising up around the house. Not wanting to fight them alone, I pull my wand and summon a protection shield around me.

"Autumn, come here."

She never listens, of course, and takes off running after a shadow that is walking across the family room.

"Stupid dog! Just do not get yourself killed."

Before I can finish my thought, two more dark shadows rise out of the floor. With a quick spin of my wand, I summon the star of power to shield me and teleport on the spot. Grandma is going to be upset to see the star burned into the floor.

I arrive back in the hallway at school, pull the pocket watch from my bag as time unfreezes, and everything returns to normal.

"Well, I calculated that just right."

Peering through the cafeteria doors time is back to normal. I go back in and rejoin my group of friends and brothers. About 15 minutes later, towards the end of lunch period, as we are laughing and talking, a loud clang is heard from the kitchen. Everyone starts laughing, knowing all too well that Ms. Brenden, the school cook, has dropped one of the pans. But this time, the whole room jumps as five more clangs sound, each getting louder. Before anyone can say anything, Ms. Brenden runs backwards out the door, panting and holding a frying pan in her hands.

Students start to get up, others grab their cell phone to record what is causing our school cook to act so weirdly, when a bellow of smoke comes out of the door to the kitchen. Two of the kitchen assistants run out of the door screaming.

"Clear the area! Take cover! Run! Save yourselves! *Dra... Dra... Dragon!*"

Oliver and Ethan are the first to their feet, looking back at me. We nod at each other, knowing all too well that we can no longer hide our identities. Oliver raises his hands as his eyes start glowing, casting a lightshield. Suddenly, a large black dragon bursts through the wall snarling and bellowing fire.

Screams echo through the room. Zander takes cover, pulling Olivia down to the floor as Leaf grabs Brooke and Claire.

I blow out the wall by yelling,

Praemium.

Explode.

"Zander, get them out of here. Now! My brothers, Leaf, and I have this."

Zander nods and quickly gets Olivia, Claire, and Brooke out through the hole in the wall. The dragon continues its rampage and turns to attack us when a loud pop occurs and standing on the table is Autumn.

She turns and looking back at us, says "Run."

"Wait! She talks? I knew it."

"Ethan, not the time."

The four of us run to the door as the black dragon begins backing up at the sight of Autumn.

"Like earlier."

"What earlier? Rose, did you mess with time?"

"Oliver, just a little bit."

"Where did you see this beast?"

"At home, first in the picture of Belinda, then, Dragon A at the end of the hall."

"Roslynn Nadia Phoenix! Are you joking?"

"No, Oliver."

"Guys, stop arguing and look."

Oliver and I turn our attention back to Autumn, as Ethan stands, looking on in amazement. The room is filling with smoke coming from Autumn's nose and she is growing in size. Suddenly, there is a spark of light and there stands Dragon A from the picture.

"It appears that Dragon A is short for Autumn, and she is a dragon."

"I told you she was weird."

"Enough, Oliver, we need to get out of here."

"The hallway…"

We enter the hallway and start running for the double doors to the outside when multiple dark shadows begin rising out of the ground. The shadows grab other students and transform them into dark shadows.

"Okay. So, definitely do not let them touch us. What do we do?"

"Ethan, we have learned that they cannot handle the power of light."

"Then, light it is."

I hold up my hands as I close my eyes and reopen them. Oliver tells me later that my eyes were glowing silver. Helixes of light appear, and the shadows start exploding. Spinning my hands together, the helixes begin circling the room as light explodes everywhere, dropping the darkness.

"Nice job, Rose."

"Thank you, Ethan."

"What was that? No one in the Arcane realm can do magic like that. Even with that sort of power, I would not get excited. There are always more."

"Look!"

The light continues to spin in the space as the wind picks up, pushing the dark shadows back as flames explode out of the ground and a woman appears at the end of the hallway.

Her hair is jet black, her skin ghost white. She wears a black cloak and sports a scar that runs over her right eye. She hisses and screams at the top of her lungs as dark shadows rise up out of the ground. The four of us dive out of the way as rubble goes flying from where Autumn and the black dragon burst through the wall.

The four of us quickly get to our feet as the dark shadows start to charge us. Orbs of light start to appear, causing the darkness to explode. A flame circle encases the four of us as the dark shadows fly backwards from where they are standing.

Orb after orb flies down the hall, trapping the dark shadows and exploding. Ethan and Oliver throw their right arms up in front of themselves as shields appear, reflecting any blasts from the dark shadows. Leaf tugs on my shirt and nods his head to the left. I look back and there, floating above the ground, is none other than Ms. Destiny.

I tap Oliver and Ethan on their shoulders as they look back to see her with electric currents running through her hair and her eyes glowing blue.

"I told you she was Arcane. What is she wearing? She must have an entire wardrobe of those dresses. This time in blue and purple."

"Rose, I do not care, fall back towards her. Now."

"You're in charge, Oliver."

Moving quickly, but as a group, we push our way toward Ms. Destiny. One creature rises up inches from us. It rises off the ground, choking, and then, explodes. Ms. Destiny is pointing her wand where the creature stood.

"Quickly, get behind me. Raven's magic cannot touch you if you are with me."

The four of us move to the sides of Ms. Destiny and watch as the dark creatures continue to rise up out of the ground. The dark witch at the end of the hall starts laughing, then licking her lips, and points her finger at us.

"My pretty creatures, kill them. Bring me their heads."

"Raven, that is not going to happen, not while I am here."

"Destiny, you have no power here, particularly not against me. Ha! Take them, my creatures. Make Mama proud."

The creatures reach into the ground and magically start pulling spears from it. They begin marching five across, shoulder to shoulder, when Ms. Destiny casts a lightshield halfway down the hall, causing the creatures to explode as they march into it. As the creatures continue to march into the field and explode, Raven summons flames around her and begins throwing orbs of fire at the lightfield, causing it to shatter. With one spin of her cloak, the balls of fire take off toward us as Ethan catches one and consumes its powers. Leaf and Rose redirect multiple fireballs as Oliver points his wand at the drinking fountain. The pipes rattle as water explodes from the fountain and begins spinning around the space, extinguishing the flames. The water floods the hallway causing the darkness to back up.

"They hate the power of light, but the power of the elements scares them even more than light. Using the elements will help keep them back."

"We've got it, Rose. Now!"

With that I summon the water around me, pull my hands down and hit the creatures and Raven with multiple blasts of water. As the water hits the darkness, it screams and explodes. Holding them back, I notice Ethan's eyes going gray as lightning appears in them. He reaches up and strikes the column with lightning, supercharging it with his magic.

The power of the lightning and the water causes Raven to drop to one knee trying to shield herself as she flies backwards into the wall.

Raven gets up, brushes herself off, laughs, and points her finger as more creatures of the dark rise up.

"Do they ever stop?"

"Ethan, unfortunately, no. She can keep spawning them. Light, or killing her, is the only way to stop them."

The creatures jump back as the two dragons crash into the hall, fighting and snapping at each other. When Autumn notices us there, she blows a ring of fire around herself and the dark dragon, creating a shield of protection. Suddenly, a loud roar rings out as the dark dragon stumbles backwards and disappears with Raven and the dark creatures. The flames subside, and Autumn collapses.

෨

The three of us race through the remaining flames to get to Autumn. As we approach, we notice that she is bleeding, her eyes are starting to close, and her breath is becoming shallow. The great dragon lowers her head down onto my shoulder.

"Ethan and Oliver, I think she is dying."

"Can we help her?"

"The bite is deep."

"Oliver, we have to try."

I look up as a flash of light illuminates the entire room. There, standing next to Autumn is the Lady of White. Before anyone can say anything, she touches her finger to Autumn's neck and her breathing is restored to normal and all her cuts are healed. When Autumn rises to her feet, she bows to Ms. Destiny, Leaf, and the three of us. A pop announces the arrival of Uncle Hawke and Grandma.

෨

"Oh my! What a mess. What happened here?"

"My Lady, it was Kai, the Shade Dragon, and Raven."

"Autumn, if they are here, then the children are not safe. Ms. Destiny, thank you for protecting them."

"Children, come with us quickly, before they return. You too, Ms. Destiny. Hawke, open a portal back to the home. Quickly!"

"Grandmother, those things were attacking the house."

"We know, your uncle was the first to discover that. The house has been shielded and protected."

As Uncle opens the portal, Grandma and Ms. Destiny raise their hands and speak an interesting spell.

Fiat marcam est et non magia potential videatur hic revertetur ad normalis ludum. Et sic ea est.

Let no mark of magic power be seen here, return the school to normal. So shall it be.

The three of us and Leaf look around as the rubble is gone and the school stands restored. Autumn snorts and walks through the portal, followed by Uncle, then Oliver, Leaf, and Ethan. I wait for Grandma and Ms. Destiny as they go through the portal. Once in the parlor, uncle holds up his hand, captures the portal, and seals it. All of us, look around and breathe a sigh of relief.

"Oliver and Ethan, seal the windows and doors. Hawke, retrieve the emergency bags of supplies. Autumn, take to the air and check the grounds below for any enemies. It is only a matter of time before they realize we are back at the house and breach the field."

After everyone returns to the parlor. We all look around at each other for answers.

"Grandma, please explain what's going on?"

"Yeah. What Oliver said, Grandma."

"Raven has discovered that you three are in the realm of the Mundane. She is the second hand of Morgana as is Kai, the Shade Dragon. Well, Lord Aden's dragon, actually. But that's not the point. The point is that Raven knows where you three are now."

"How do you know this?"

"Wow, Rose and Ethan, do you always ask the same question at the same time?

"Anyway, all the weird things that have happened to you over the years, including me always being your teacher, is because I am a dear friend of your family's and sworn protector of you three. I am, in fact, your godmother and your mother's best friend. I swore to keep you safe in her absence. Hence, why I have always been around.

I may have had to hex a few school administrators and erase a few memories, but I am here to make sure you're safe."

"Wait! Hex some people, and erase some minds? Wicked!"

"Ethan, no, not wicked. She says she hexed people. Seriously?"

"Rose, you worry too much. No one got hurt."

"Would anyone care to explain how Ms. Destiny got here?"

"Ethan, the night your parents sent your uncle and I through the portal with you, they had already sent word to Destiny who had been residing in this realm."

"I do not care about all that."

"Oliver, what's wrong?"

"Rose, this is all too weird. First, Leaf appears, then our dog transforms into a dragon of monumental size, our teacher is our godmother, and some chick named after a bird with a bad attitude wants us dead. What's next?"

"That is actually a good question. Why not ask your sister?"

"Rose, what is Ms. Destiny talking about?"

You will find if there is one thing that I hate in all of this: that is, always being called on by Ms. Destiny to answer questions. I took a deep breath and smiled not wanting to answer.

"What are you wanting me to reference?"

"If you have to ask, then you are not truly as gifted as they say."

Now I remember why I hate Ms. Destiny. Her statements sting and she always smirks when she makes them.

"If you are referring to the swords, that is not up to me."

"What is this about swords?"

"Oliver, she is referencing the Twin Blades of Time. Legend tells of two swords, one forged at the village by Gus the Elf, a blacksmith and exceptional magical being. The other you know as Excalibur, created by Merlin but protected by the Lady of the Lake. They are said to hold exceptional magical powers that could stop Morgana forever: however, no one knows where either sword is located, and they can only be found by you two. The legend notes that the swords imprinted on each of you. The sword Gabriel imprinted on Oliver and Excalibur on Ethan."

"Why us?"

"Because, Ethan, it is said that the swords pick the wielder."

At that and as Ethan mumbles under his breath about the swords, Uncle Hawke enters the room carrying leather bags.

"Okay, so these swords we are supposed to get, where do we even begin to look for them?"

"Ethan, that is simple your books are said to hold a map that will take you to them."

"Are you serious, Grandma?"

"Yes."

"Ethan, let's go grab our books."

Within seconds, the two disappear from the room and then reappear along with pedestals on which to place their books. A knock sounds throughout the house and, of course, Uncle Hawke is the first one on his feet, responding to see who it is.

Uncle Hawke approaches the door, wand in hand, and peers through the peep hole. He quickly unlocks the door and opens it. I peak around the corner to see that it is Zander with a rather confused look on his face.

I hug him. "Zander, come in. What is it?"

"Here. This letter is for all of you?"

Uncle takes the letter and examines it.

"What's wrong?"

"Rose, it appears to be from Raven."

"What does she have to do with anything?"

"More than meets the eye, Oliver. I am sure of that.

What I did next, provided more answers than I think any of us were ready for.

"Zander, may I?"

I place my hands on either side of his face and gaze into his eyes, entering into the vision of what had happened.

The room begins to spin, and I land in the middle of the street. There are Olivia, Claire, and Brooke, walking with Zander. When they round the corner, they are ambushed, and the three girls are captured by the shadows trying to get to Zander. But the shadows quickly back up when a dragon of magnificent proportions appears. Belinda and the Lady of White arrive.

As Belinda lands, the shadows are quick to disappear into the ground, taking the three girls with them. The dragon places herself between Zander and Raven. Within seconds the dark witch and the white witch are intertwined in an Arcane duel. When Kai, the Shade Dragon, attacks, Belinda throws Zander to the ground, protecting him. The great dragon stands up, whistles, and Zander suddenly finds himself at the front door of Rose's house.

"Ethan, she does not look happy?"

"What is it, Rose?"

"Oliver, Raven took Claire, Olivia, and Brooke."

"What?"

"You heard me. Raven has our friends!"

"Okay Rose. Don't yell. What does she want with them?"

"This is Morgana we are talking about. Nothing she does makes sense."

"Leaf, you are correct."

"Knowing Morgana, taking them is intended to draw you three out and force you to the portals to the Arcane realm, thus unleashing her wrath on the Mundane realm."

"Just as the Council of Light predicted, Emma."

"Yes, Hawke, the battle for the realms begins."

"What do we do?"

"We fight, you two."

"Fight? Rose, are you serious?"

"Look, our parents fought to protect us because of the magical gifts they saw in us that no one else has seen before. If we are the three that are meant to stop Morgana and the shadows, then, by all means, let us do it. We have to protect all magic and all people."

Before anyone can say a word, I stand up, snap my fingers, and my clothes transform on the spot. I don my traveling cloak and have my bag in hand.

"Then, it looks like we are coming with you."

With that, Oliver, Ethan, and Leaf follow my lead, snapping their fingers and also donning their traveling cloaks and bags.

"I'm coming too."

"You are a simple Mundane, Zander, you won't last two minutes. Morgana will pick you off first. This should be amusing to watch."

"Seriously, Ms. Destiny? He is going. I am not leaving him here for that witch to capture. Besides, he is the fastest runner on our school's track team next to Ethan."

I walk up to Zander and snap my fingers again, and he is decked out in traveling attire with a sword on his side and a shield across his back.

"What about you three?"

"I will be going with your group," says Ms. Destiny.

"What about you, Grandma, and Uncle Hawke?"

"We will be joining you later. We are going to take the maps and seek out Camelot. This will allow us safe passage. You will all be fine with Ms. Destiny."

"Destiny, please keep them safe."

"Ms. Drake, you have nothing to worry about. They will be safe. Blah, blah, blah."

As we head out the door, Oliver goes to the SUV to load it. Uncle Hawke follows carrying supplies. Once the vehicle is loaded, we hug Grandma and Uncle and get into the vehicle. As Oliver pulls out the gate at the end of our driveway, vines rise out of the ground creating a magical field that seals and protects the house as it disappears out of sight behind us.

The words of our grandmother hang over the three of us as we know what we have to do.

"Good luck! Find the swords as quickly as you can. The survival of the kingdom and the magic of the realms relies on the three of you.

Chapter 5
New Friends

On our journey, we stop and rest at various points, following the map's directions. When we stop to rest, I step into another vision.

Across the land and sea, on the landmass of the United Kingdom, a red-haired, pale-skinned woman in red and purple robes looks out over the cliffs at the roaring ocean as a tear rolls down her face. She holds out her hand, trying to summon water from the ocean to her but, as always, nothing happens. Looking around, she pulls her wand from beneath her robes and begins to conjure a spell when she hears screams. Freezing on the spot, she listens for the screams for a second time, as the winds carry them to her. The witch kneels and puts her palms flat on the ground.

"May the magic of the earth protect those who need it the most. Alexander, I know you are out there somewhere, hear me and hear the cries of the light. It is your time, and the earth needs the light. Bring it back to us. Bring the light of the three back to the earth."

The old witch rises to her feet as she hears the screams echo again. This time, she closes her eyes and listens more closely to the wind. Suddenly she opens her eyes, gazing into the realm of the magical to observe what is transpiring. A white stallion appears. The woman mounts and they gallop through a portal.

Until this point, my visions have only allowed me to see past events, never what is happening in this exact moment. Witnessing what is happening in the Arcane realm was not something I have been able to do until this vision. Now, all of a sudden, my powers have developed, and I am seeing what is occurring in the present time.

There is a cold night breeze blowing through the halls of an ancient dark castle that stands on the hillside. Within its walls, a young, dark wizard sits reading his book, *Demonology Over All Living Things*, while, on the far side of the room, his best friend and his brother practice dueling. The young man's father sits by the fire, gazing into it as screams echo around the castle. Suddenly, with a great crash and a pop, Raven walks into the room hissing through her teeth, then screaming,

"Children, leave us! I wish to speak with Lord Aden."

"Witch, you would be wise not to hiss at my sons and, better yet, explain to me why my dragon is injured."

Lord Aden is furious with Raven. He points his wand at her, raising her off the ground, the witch choking and gasping for air. The room suddenly bursts into flames, and Raven hits the ground as Lord Aden is thrown backward. From the flames of the giant fireplace two black panthers emerge, followed by their mistress, Morgana le Fey.

"Must I do everything around here? I gave you two a simple task and clearly you cannot do it right."

So angry with both of them, Morgana screams, throwing a flask of liquid into the flames.

"My mistress, please forgive me..."

"Raven, I ripped a hole in the realms, I depleted my power so you could travel to the Mundane realm and bring the children of Nadia and Kelvin to me. Instead, you come back empty-handed, and Lord Aden's dragon is injured. What happened? The timeline can only be altered so many times before individuals will start to take notice and start to question what is going on."

She stamped her foot and, the flames exploded from the fireplace, dancing behind her as if mocking Raven and Lord Aden.

"My Lady, I was outnumbered. That witch, Destiny, was there. Leaf was there and…"

Before Raven can finish, Morgana's temper explodes again.

"I do not care. Clearly, I have to do everything myself."

"My Lady. I have captured three of their friends. They will come for them and, when they do, Aden and I will be ready."

"Raven, for your part, pray that they do. For if you fail again, your fate will be worse than theirs."

Morgana walks to the fireplace and throws another vial into the flames. The flames come to life and begin to spread throughout the room, transforming into knights in black armor.

"My elite Nightriders, my precious creatures. General, I want them captured and brought to me or dead. They will be returning to this realm and when they do, they will fall."

Morgana snaps her fingers, walks back into the fire, and disappears. Her two panthers follow behind her and the flames die down, leaving only smoldering wood behind. As soon as Morgana departs, Lord Aden rises to his feet and walks out of the hall. The Nightriders follow behind him down the long path to another group of riders on horses. Leaning over, he whispers something into the ear of the lead rider of the group who takes off down the path, the others following.

From the castle window, the young girl who was dueling earlier now watches what is occurring below. She is hidden out of sight of anyone below, not wanting to be seen. When the coast seems clear, she summons forth two fairies with her wand.

"Go forth and tell them that the Nightriders have come."

When the fairies disappear, the young girl walks down the long, dark hallway. Torches light as she passes them. Reaching an old oak door, she knocks, which echoes down the hallway. The door quickly flies open, and she finds herself pulled into the room and the door slams shut behind her.

"Bethany, what are you doing?"

"Better yet, Sebastian, let me ask you the same question. What are you doing?"

Annoyed by her questions, Sebastian slams shut the drawer of the dresser and begins throwing items into his bag. He turns and points his wand as the books from the other side of the room fly into his bag.

"To answer your question, Bethany, I'm leaving this place in search of my mother, I am tired of my father's ways. Every night, for the past two weeks, Morgana has appeared, barking orders left and right. Besides, my dreams are getting worse. He would never understand them, but he would use them to his advantage. No, I need the one person who I can trust—my mother."

"Sebastian, I understand, and I will go with you. The Council of the Arcane is not going to take well to a dark wizard."

"I am not dark, Bethany, I just pose that way to keep my father happy and to be able to send word back to my mother."

Sebastian points to the stack of books and papers sitting next to Bethany and she brings them over to him. He takes them and places them in his bag.

"Sebastian, I know you are not dark, but you are needed here, you are the link between light and dark. You are more valuable for the light than anything."

"I am no good if I am dead. One-night, Morgana is going to show up, one of us will defy her, and we will be dead, besides my brother suspects me as a traitor. Every time I turn around, he is lurking in the shadows, waiting for me to slip up. Besides, Bethany, the dreams are not making sense."

"Sebastian, how are you going to find your mother?"

"She left me one of the last time stones. She told me to use it if I ever need to find her. Come with me?"

"Sebastian, I'll go with you, but I have to pack my items."

"I already did."

"Figures. And look, you got everything."

"Okay, Sebastian. How do we get out of here? Your father has guards patrolling the grounds. We can't just walk out the door."

"I know he does. Hence, why we will not be traveling by foot. We are going to teleport via the stone."

Walking to the far side of the room, Sebastian taps the wall three times with his wand. As the wall opens, Bethany notices the stone of time and begins sealing the room with her magic. Moving quickly, Sebastian holds the stone in his hand as he motions for Bethany to join him. Just as Bethany reaches Sebastian, the door blows open and Liam and multiple guards rush into the room. With a flash of light, smoke fills the room. Bethany had set off smoke bombs, blinding anyone in the room.

As Bethany places her hand on Sebastian's shoulder, he taps the stone, and the room begins to spin. Within seconds, the two find themselves teleported to a forest with a thick fog around them. Sebastian stows the stone in his bag and hoists it over his shoulder.

"Sebastian, where do we go from here?"

"I don't know. I don't understand. The stone is supposed to take us directly to my mother. Besides, she could be here, and we don't know. We can't see anything with this fog."

"Maybe the stone sensed danger and brought us here instead. Your brother did blow in the door to your room, Sebastian."

"You're right. The stone could have sensed danger. First, we have to clear this fog, and then, figure out where the hell we are. This is ridiculous!"

Clarus.

Clear.

"Sebastian, '*Clarus*' only works when you do the figure-eight motion with your wand. Watch."

Bethany raises her wand and, in a figure eight motion in front of her declares,

Clarus.

The fog clears and the two look around. In the distance, they notice a cloaked figure approaching. The individual's cloak shows markings of dragons and fairies, markings that Sebastian knows all too well. Recognizing the cloak to be his mother's, Sebastian immediately approaches her.

"Mom? Is that you?"

But before the figure responds, Sebastian sees that the figure's wand is drawn. As sparks fly from it, two elite guards who had teleported with them, fall to the ground dead.

"Sebastian, hush! Are you out of your mind? What are you doing here? And to answer your charming friend's question, yes, the magic in the stone is designed to detour the travelers whenever the stone senses danger. Hence, it dropped you here. It has a fail-safe."

"See, Sebastian. I told you the stone sensed danger."

"Now, what is this I hear about a door being blown in? Are you two okay?"

"It was nothing, just Liam trying to stop us."

"Charming. If your brother is anything like your father, I am sure he has alerted him by now. Sebastian, you and your friend cannot continue to stand here in the open, especially with Nightriders having been spotted. Besides, by now, your father has probably sent the entire legion out looking for you. Quickly, let us get to safety."

With one wave of her wand, the Lady Divinity separated the trees forming a path to a giant rock formation, which split open, revealing a passageway. Upon entering the opening, they found a small village. Many species of creatures from the outlying villages were there having their wounds attended to and settling in for the night.

"What happened? I have never seen it this bad."

"This is what happens when your father sends out Nightriders."

"Mom, that is impossible. Those wounds are not caused by Nightriders. It has to have been the Elite Shadow Guards."

"Sebastian, your father's wrath, and that of Morgana, continues to tear the villages apart. We are just fortunate that we were able to get the people out in time."

While talking, the three ascend a staircase up the side of a mountain into an out-cove cliff where a home stands.

"Yes, Sebastian, you are correct. They are both Nightriders and the Elite Shadow Guards. They were sent out to destroy the villages and steal in the name of Morgana le Fey."

"And he sent them out this evening again, because Morgana was furious."

"Indeed, she was furious, but this was not a normal attack. They were looking for someone or something. Sebastian, I need to know what your father is up too."

"From what Bethany and I understand, Morgana sent Raven to the Mundane realm. Something about some witch named Destiny, a guy by the name of Leaf, and the three."

"Oh dear! She found them. We must send word immediately."

With that, multiple fairies begin flying around the Lady Divinity as she whispers to them and motions for them to go.

"Lady Divinity, the three as in the three divine children of light?"

"Yes, they were not born of the Arcane realm, so their parents thought it best to hide them in the Mundane realm of their birth. When High Prince Kelvin and High Princess Nadia sealed the realm, they did so to protect the three, as well as the future of time and magic."

"The future of time? What does that have to do with anything?"

"Everything, Bethany. You see, the three are so powerful that older forms of themselves jumped through time to alter the magical timeline. In doing so, they have altered much of the history. But, for some reason, Morgana le Fey, has held on to this particular moment in time."

The three continue to talk as Sebastian and Bethany set down their bags and look around the home.

"Mom, how is that possible to alter time? It is forbidden!"

"You are correct, Sebastian. It is forbidden. But not for the three of them or their eras. You see, their magic has no rules, nor does it conform to any set standard of the magical arts."

"Mom, what you speak of is impossible."

"Sebastian, we are all taught that magic is bound by the rules of Merlin, and the Council of Light. You do remember the teachings?"

"Of course, I do, Mom. The knowledge has come in handy but how can they break the rules?"

"That we do not know. They are gifted beyond belief. But we will talk more later. For now, you two will find separate bedrooms at the end of the hallway."

"After you are settled in, come down for dinner."

Once they disappear up the stairs, Divinity walks out to the edge of the stone porch as a fairy flies up. Divinity looks around as the fairy lands on her hand.

"My dear friend, send word that the children have been found and are in danger. They will need help. Inform everyone still loyal that help is needed, do not waste time and make haste."

As Divinity raises her hand, the fairy flies off.

Upon settling into their respective rooms, Bethany and Sebastian descend the stairs into the dining area of the home to find that the Lady Divinity has summoned up a feast of food. The three of them sit down at the table and begin eating, while talking throughout the meal about the current state of things, the aspect of the valley, and what should be done moving forward to stop Morgana.

With a giant yawn, Bethany wishes Sebastian and the Lady Divinity good night and heads to bed. Sebastian rises from the table and looks out from the balcony over the valley, the Lady Divinity watching him.

"Sebastian, something seems to be troubling you. What is it my son?"

"Everything. Dad. This place. Morgana's attacks. Not to mention my dreams."

"Your father and Morgana, we will handle. What about this place troubles you?"

"Nothing here troubles me. It is beautiful. It is just sad that everyone has to hide."

"It is one of the last safe places we have, Sebastian. Now, you mentioned something about dreams. What is going on?"

"It's nothing, Mom. Just bits and pieces. Here and there. What is troubling is that I keep ending up in a Mundane high school, watching a teen being bullied. It is weird. But then, there are other dreams: one of a child, one of a battle, and one with multiple elves. None of them make sense."

"My son, dreams never make sense until they happen in real life."

"You're right, Mom, but they seem so real. I am going to turn in. Good night."

When Sebastian is out of sight and the door shuts behind him, a loud pop sounds over the balcony as three witches appear.

They are odd in appearance. The youngest is dressed in all white with tan coloring and has white hair. The second witch wears clothes that are half white and half black. Her hair on the white side is jet black and white on the dark side. The third witch, the eldest, is dressed in all black, with black hair with gray streaks throughout.

The witches follow Divinity into the dining room where the cupboard flies open, and a crystal ball levitates to the table.

"Our Lady, the magic of our realm has weakened. What must we do?"

"Really, Witches Three? In unison? I can hear just fine."

"Lady Divinity, the magic…!"

"My dear Witches Three, I know."

Lady Divinity sits at the table. When she waves her hand over the crystal ball it levitates into the air above the table.

"Our Lady, what do you see?"

"Our kingdom must act, or it will fall. The ball shows me that the three rulers have begun their journey to our realm. Without help, they will never succeed in getting here. On all Hallows Eve, the magic to create a portal will be at full strength and when they pass through a simple portal, their magic will restore the balance of the kingdom. They are the hope and salvation of the Arcane realm."

"What about the time loop, Lady Divinity?"

"Now, that is where the challenge comes in. Yes, the time loop is going to be tricky. Ladies, it is believed that the entry of the magical three through the portal will restore the balance of time as we know it."

"Lady Divinity, you see this in the crystal ball, but time is not that simple, not since… we dare not say anything."

"Not since what…? My dear Witches Three, what are you not telling me?"

"Our Lady, if what you say is true, that the magical three are coming to the Arcane realm, then we must send help to guide them back."

"Let's change the subject for now. I will revisit the question of what you're not telling me later, my dear Witches Three."

"The Councils must be informed, Lady Divinity."

"My dears, the Council here will be notified. The Council of Light should not be troubled. They will be worried about keeping Morgana at bay and not leaving the Arcane realm. Need I remind you what happens if she gets to the Mundane realm. If she finds out the secrets we have taken to protect and hide the magical three, who knows what Morgana will do.

Quietly, the witches look at each other, nodded, and form a circle around the Lady Divinity and the ball. As they close their eyes, the ball flies into the air, higher, glowing as the room lights, and lightning strikes various parts of the room. Lady Divinity raises her arm to cover her eyes from the brightness of the ball.

"Lady Divinity, if darkness moves against the three, then word should be sent to all corners of the kingdom to those closest to them."

"So, shall it be."

With one last flash, the room returns to normal as the crystal ball and the witches three disappear. Lady Divinity sits back in her chair going deep into meditation.

The next morning Sebastian rises early, going for a walk around the village. Strolling down the path, he approaches the farmers market, where he sees villagers begging for food, clothing, and shelter. Stopping to look around, he pays some money for supplies, then continues to walk around until he sees his mother. The Lady Divinity is attending to an elderly elf, wrapping his wounds and giving him water.

Sebastian approaches and the older man turns his head, raises his arm and motions for Sebastian to come closer.

"Young man, it is you. You are the one…."

Before the older elf could finish, he flinches in pain, holding his side.

"Sir, are you okay? What do you mean by the one?

"You, young man, are the one who will save…"

Coughing, the old elf motions Sebastian to him, takes his hand, placing a necklace in Sebastian's hand as he passes in the arms of the Lady Divinity. She closes his eyes, then kisses the gentlemen elf on the forehead as his body dissolves into dust and is carried off by the wind. Sebastian holds up the Phoenix-shaped necklace and examines it.

"Mother, what did he mean?"

"Sebastian, walk with me."

Standing up, the Lady Divinity brushes herself off and heads down the path toward the river. Sebastian quietly puts the necklace around his neck and rises to his feet following his mother. When she reaches the edge of the river she stops and looks out.

"My son, what do you see?"

With a half-smile, half-laugh, Sebastian looks out at the river.

"Mom, is this a joke? It is a river."

"Sebastian, what do you see?"

"I do not understand what you mean?"

"Exactly, my son. There will come a time when you will be forced to use your magic in ways that you have not yet begun to understand. Magic will allow you to see the past, present, and future. You will be challenged to use it as a way to save the ones you love. You will have the ability to enter dreams and protect the ones you love."

"Okay, I understand that now, but how did the elf know?"

"Sebastian, my son, he had unlocked the magic to see the past, present, and future. He was a seer and, like him, you will have the gift as well. It is a rare form of magic that can help you protect all around you. Anyway, the Council is assembling, we must go and hear what is to be said."

As Sebastian and his mother approach the stone circle, Sebastian sees thrones made of stone sitting empty. Following behind his mother, he notices that, as she waves her hand, one of the chairs disappears when she sits down on what looks to be air. Then suddenly, a chair made out of vines materializes under her. Once seated, she summons a staff and taps the ground four times. Upon the fourth tap, magical beings start appearing everywhere around the circle. Watching what is happening, Sebastian sits down in a stone chair next to his mother. When Bethany appears, she hugs him, and they both sit down to listen.

Sebastian leans over and asks his mother who everyone is when, without realizing what she was doing, Bethany begins answering. Puzzled, Sebastian looks at her, ready to question her when he hears his mother speaking.

"My friends, we wait for Lords Leo and Wade. Once they appear, this Council shall be called to order."

A loud pop echoes over the area as a being made of water appears transfiguring into human form. Upon taking human form, he looks around, then nods to members of the Council, and sits in a chair made of solid water, next to Lady Divinity.

"Lord Wade," the Lady Divinity nods to him.

A roar erupts over the chatter of the other Council members as two majestic lions walk up the walkway and sit next to one another beside Lady Divinity.

"Now that we are all here, it is time for this Council to come to order."

Snarling and baring his teeth, Lord Leo catches sight of Sebastian.

"Before we begin, Lady Divinity, would you care to explain who these two young visitors are who are gracing our Council?"

"Of course. For those of you who do not know, this is my son, Sebastian, and his friend, Lady Bethany, the daughter of Lord Wade and the late Lady Beth."

Sebastian freezes, looks at Bethany, then around at the Council.

"Wait! Lady Bethany? Daughter of Lord Wade? That makes you a cousin to the three and a descendant of Merlin. Why didn't you say anything?"

"My son, she did not tell you because she was bound by this Council to keep it from you. We did that to protect the last great-grandchild of Merlin and to keep his line alive. If your father had used his magic to question you and you had known, we most definitely would have lost another member of this Council."

Commotion broke out with members of the Council all whispering to one another. Knowing the gesture all too well, when the Lady Divinity raises her hands up, the Council members quieten down.

As silence falls over the Council, Lady Divinity explains the vision, she had seen the night before to all of them.

"Our Lady, if what you say is true, we must send a team to help the eras get to the portal and get through."

"I agree."

"So, do I. We must send what forces we have to help bring them through."

"Hold it. My wife and I have been told that the Lady Belinda sent our son Leaf to help them."

"Well then, that settles it. If Lady Belinda, sent Lord Leaf, then that shows we must send more to help."

"Beatrice, calm down. Lord Leo, yes, indeed. I too heard that Belinda and the Lady of White sent Leaf to the Mundane realm."

"Lady Divinity, how do we get anyone there. The magic is weak. We run the risk of doing more damage to time. What about help there?"

"Jillian, just come out and say it. If by "help there," you mean the Lady Mora or the Council of Light, no one has heard from either."

"Jillian, the Lady Divinity is right. Also, the covens cannot be trusted as they support Morgana, and many have turned their backs on the Arcane realm. Besides, all of you assume that Lady Mora and the Council are in the Mundane realm. We do not know if they are."

"Thank you, Lord Wade."

"Besides, if you send all your forces, who will protect the remaining villagers?"

"Lady of White, what a pleasant surprise! What brings you here?"

Members of the Council have their wands drawn and pointed right at the witch, waiting to see what she will do. The Lady of White strolls around the circle, looking at the different members of the Council, then simply snaps her fingers and the wands all turn into flowers.

"Can we help you, Our Lady?"

"Help me, Lord Wade? Don't you mean that you all need help? So, the question becomes, 'How can I help you?'"

"Lady of White, what do you want?"

"Simple, Divinity, to be of assistance."

Members of the Council look at each other, shaking their heads and trying to figure out what the Lady of White is up too.

"Dear me. Do not let me interrupt. You were all saying…?"

"Hum…umm… before we were interrupted… There is a way for us to send a few to the Mundane realm."

"Indeed, my wife is right."

"However, it is risky and there is no guarantee that our magic will get the individuals to them."

"Lord Leo, anything is worth a try. Are you and Lucy referring to the magical circle?"

"Yes, Lady Divinity. If we can muster up enough magic among the members of this Council to send two individuals, they will have to find the eras and come back through the portal with them."

"Leo, we understand what you're saying, but the question is who does this Council wish to send?"

"Oh no, Lady Divinity. Absolutely not. Are you out of your mind? My daughter traveling with a dark wizard? No! That is not happening."

"Lord Wade, they are around the same age as the three and so are more relatable."

"No offense, My Lady. While you, my brother, sister, and I grew up together, my daughter can go but I do not trust your son. How do we know he is not in league with Lord Aden?"

As Lord Wade finished, the Lady of White was dancing around the circle, poking at the Lord Sebastian, and mocking everyone.

"Yes, boy, speak up. Indeed, how do we know you are not working for Lord Aden? The Lord Wade wants to know."

"Lady of White, Watch it, old hag, or I'll…"

"You'll what, Lord Wade? Turn me into a toad? Your magic is weak without your brother. Do you really want to try to use it anymore? Besides, what are you going to do, Lord Wade? Throw water at me? Go sit down! Your magic has no power against me, and besides, you are no challenge. Now, the Lady Nadia, or Rose, that is a challenge."

Lord Wade turns red and pulls his wand on her as other members of the Council rise to their feet, drawing their wands, and staves.

"Lady of White, what do you want?"

"Ha! Lord Wade, are you sure it is wise to raise your wands at me when I come to ask if it is smart to drain what remaining magic is left in the kingdom? You said yourselves that the realm is weak, and the covens in the Mundane realm won't help. So, is it wise?"

"Although, I am sure this age-old rivalry is well founded, can we get back to the matter at hand? If we do not try to send anyone, what chance do we have?"

"Bethany, dear child, I knew I liked you. Clearly, you get your charm from your mother. I shall help you. I will light the way and provide my magic."

"Lady of White, your help is appreciated."

"Appreciated? Appreciated you say? Lady Divinity, I do it to remove the trash from the kingdom."

The witch points her finger at Sebastian.

Before anyone can speak or move, Sebastian holds out his hand raising the Lady of White off the ground.

"Now, to answer your question witch. I am not in league with my father if that is what you imply. I cannot stand for what he has done, and I have turned to my mother. I have always been closer to her than to him. I stayed with him as long as I did so I could know what is going on. I used to send word to my mother about his actions."

Angry, the Lord Sebastian turns as the Lady of White drops to the stone circle.

"You did send word, but then nothing,"

"My apology, Lord Wade, my mistake. I should have sent word and led the Nightriders right to your front door."

"Gentlemen, enough! Lord Wade, sit down. Sebastian, I have taught you better. You sit down too. My friends, I think it would be wise to send these two. They are best friends, they are powerfully gifted with magic, and they are of an age to relate to the eras. Besides, getting them to the three will ensure not only Bethany and Sebastian's safety but that of the three as well."

Muffled groans come from members of the Council as they look at each other and nod knowing what needs to be done next. Members of the Council rise to their feet and they all step into the circle.

"My daughter, take this medallion. It was my father's and those loyal to us in either realm will know it."

"My son, you and Bethany must bring the eras back through the portal on all Hollow's Eve. They must come by portal. It is the only way to restore them to full power. Here, I packed this bag of supplies. Good luck."

After receiving hugs from their respective parents, Sebastian and Bethany look at each other and nod. Behind Lady Divinity, the Lady of White can be seen, levitating into the air, glowing white.

In an unpleasant tone that sends chills down everyone's spines, the Lady of White orders everyone to their places.

"I advise, whatever you are going to do, you had better do it now."

Lightning strikes begin to hit the stone circle, as two white helixes begin spinning around Bethany and Sebastian. Roars break out as members of the Council stand in a circle, palm-to-palm, humming. When the Lady of White snaps her fingers, Bethany and Sebastian are gone.

Chapter 6
Introductions

Seconds after they leave the circle, they arrive at the edge of a forest on a cool afternoon. Sebastian and Bethany notice a town in the distance. Both of them look around taking note of their surroundings.

"Bethany is it me or does the air smell horrible here"?

"Zander, my father says it is something about the Mundane realm," Bethany explains as she begins rummaging through her bag in search of a map, while Sebastian takes off his shirt and puts on a sleeveless tunic. When Bethany notices, she laughs, shaking her head.

"What is so funny?" he asks.

"You, Sebastian," she notes.

"What do you mean, Bethany?"

"Sebastian, are you hoping to impress people with your guns?" Bethany inquires sarcastically.

"What? I take pride in my body," he replies lifting his shirt to show off his abs.

"Enough Sebastian! Put the tunic down and pay attention to the task at hand," she says as she returns her attention to the map.

"What Bethany? Am I not allowed to impress the princess or princes?" Sebastian inquires.

"The princess you are referring to is my younger cousin, and she is betrothed to Lord Alezander. As for my male cousins, they are probably like their father, Kelvin, and will find the most powerful witch around," Bethany says.

"What do you mean, like Kelvin?" he inquires.

"Uncle Kelvin was very traditional and married a princess," Bethany states, still searching the map.

"That is all good, Bethany, but there are no princesses here to marry. And, by the way, High King Alezander disappeared many years ago. They say he went mad when the princess left the kingdom," Sebastian notes.

Shaking her head and trying to ignore him, Bethany points northwest saying, "This way."

With a tap of her wand, four small balls of light raise off the map and light the way. The two walk toward the town as the map and the little balls of light lead them toward the source of a magical signature.

At the end of town, down an old dirt road, sits a campground where Oliver, Ethan, Rose, Autumn, Leaf, Destiny, and Zander have settled in for the night. It is late afternoon, as Rose sits by the fire reading her book while Autumn paces the grounds. Ethan and Oliver unpack a chess board, placing it on an old stump, one corner held up with one of the spell books from Ethan's bag, setting the pieces in their appointed spots.

Destiny tends the fire, while Leaf and Zander sit talking. As the group goes about their activities, they hear Autumn begin to growl and see her backing up towards the fire. Suddenly, flames fly around the fire pit as Autumn encircles the group with fire to protect them. Leaf runs up behind her, transforming into a lion. Rose, Oliver, and Ethan stand with their staves drawn but freeze in shock at the sight of Leaf's transformation.

"Wait! You're a lion?" Ethan asks, pointing at Leaf, then looking at Oliver and Rose in disbelief.

"Yes. My pa was not happy when he learned I could transfigure into a human. Anything else he was fine with, but a human! 'You're kidding me!' he screamed," Leaf remarks.

From a distance, they hear a female's voice.

"Please call the dragon and Lord Leaf off. We mean you no harm," Bethany says as she walks out from behind a tree. She raises her hands and bows to the group. Sebastian remains behind her, his wand drawn, gripping it tight and not knowing what to expect from the group in front of them.

"We mean you no harm. I am Lady Bethany, daughter of Wade and Beth, and great grandchild of Merlin."

When the three siblings hear this, they lower their staves. Leaf bows his head, and Autumn stands down. Destiny pushes past everyone and hugs Bethany.

"My child! You have grown! Look at you," Destiny exclaims walking around Bethany.

"Hello, Lady Destiny. How have you been? I see you have not changed one bit," Bethany remarks, smiling.

"Time for reunions later. Lady Bethany, how did you get here and what news do you bring?" Leaf has transformed back to human form. He points and snarls at Sebastian, then looks at Bethany and inquires "An ally? Or were you followed?"

Lowering his wand, Sebastian cautiously approaches. "I mean you no harm. I am not in league with my father, if that is what you mean. I work for the side of good and I bring news from the High Council."

Leaf snarls again and steps forward, shifting his shoulders as if he is going to transform again.

"Tell them who you are, Sebastian," Bethany says over her shoulder to him.

"Oh yes! I am Sebastian, son of Lady Divinity of Light and Lord Aden," he says. He approaches the group slowly, extending his hand.

"Leaf, stand down, please. He will not harm you," Bethany says.

"That is what Kendra said and look at what happened there," Leaf snarls again.

"Leaf, are you really that hung up about it. Kendra would have died a horrible death if she had been captured, but you wouldn't understand," Sebastian tries to explain.

Leaf snarls at him in response.

"Stand down, Leaf. He won't hurt anyone," Bethany demands of him again, this time more firmly.

"Only time will tell, and I will be the judge of that. You're lucky the High King is not here" Leaf glares at Sebastian.

"The High King would not hurt me and you're as charming as your father," Sebastian chuckled at him.

"What is that supposed to mean?" Leaf asks as he pulls his wand and places it at Sebastian's throat, lifting him off the ground.

"Give me one reason, why I should not silence you permanently." He jams the wand deeper into Sebastian's throat. Sebastian raises his own wand and aims it at Leaf in response.

"Enough! Both of you. Acting like children. You two never did get along. Leaf, stand down. Lord Sebastian, it would be wise not to raise a wand on Leaf. I may not be able to get him under control next time" shouts Lady Destiny.

"Now, shall we sit?" Bethany asks trying to relieve some of the tension between the two.

The group sits down as Leaf lowers his wand and drops Sebastian to the ground. Sebastian, hits the ground with a loud thud as Leaf snickers, walking away. Lord Sebastian gets to his feet and brushes the leaves and dirt off.

"Charming that one!"

Both Leaf and Autumn position themselves between the three and the newly arrived visitors. Oliver is the first to break the long, awkward silence.

"What news do you bring?" he asks, his eyes on Bethany.

"Oliver, the realm's magic weakens. Morgana sends more and more shadow and night riders into the villages every day. Her killings have gotten out of control. The magic that once balanced the kingdom has weakened and the covens in this realm have turned their backs and provide no support to the Arcane. It will only take one more major attack to blow our world apart. The two realms will then collide causing more problems than we know how to fix," Sebastian says, staring into the fire.

"But that is not the only thing," he adds.

"My mother, the Lady Divinity, says that it is imperative that you three pass through the last remaining portal that separates the two realms on All Hollow's Eve in order to restore the balance of the kingdom."

"While your mother's visions are always accurate, Sebastian, we go where Rose, Ethan, and Oliver choose to go," Lady Destiny says.

"But Destiny, the portal…" Bethany starts to say when Destiny interrupts. Both of them are stopped by Rose, who puts her hand up and pauses the conversation.

"Bethany, I read about the portal access in my book," she says.

"Your book?"

"Yes, Bethany. My spell book," Rose replies. Looking as if she is confused about why Bethany is perplexed about her having a spell book.

"How is that possible, dear cousin? All the artifacts of the King and Queen are unreachable and frozen in time," Bethany notes looking concerned.

"You know, Bethany, when I first heard it, I wondered the same thing myself. But, hey, this is the three we are talking about. Anything is possible with their magic," Leaf adds.

"Our uncle brought it to Rose on her birthday," Ethan explains. Bethany shoots Sebastian a perplexed look, seeking answers.

"My cousins, only dark magic users can enter that area," Bethany remarks.

"Hey, do not look at me for answers. If it was dark magic that got him there, then it must be a form I am not familiar with. My father has a magical tracker that goes off every time dark magic is utilized," Sebastian says with a shrug.

"Destiny, should we be concerned? I mean, this is Uncle Hawke we are talking about." Rose asked.

"It is nothing to be concerned about. There are still some forms of white magic that darkness does not know about. I hope it is that," Destiny notes.

"Okay, and if it is not?"

"Then, Oliver, I do not want to even begin to think of the issues that it would cause," Destiny says, looking at him.

"Now, Bethany, what were you saying about the portal?" Ethan asks.

Bethany explains to the group about the Lady Divinity's vision and what has to be done.

"All Hollow's Eve is in a week, but first, we are sworn to a journey in search of some items," Oliver states.

"The swords of time?" Sebastian inquires.

"Yes, but how did you know?" Ethan asks.

"Ethan, it is rather a long story that I will explain later," Sebastian says, smiling at Ethan. At that moment, something comes over Sebastian and, suddenly, he understands what the old man from earlier that day had meant.

Ethan looks displeased with Sebastian's response but turns to speak with his brother.

"Here is the thing, Bethany and Sebastian. We have a dilemma. We need to find where this portal is and also where the swords are located," Oliver explains.

"That is easy, Oliver, In the Mundane realm, there are two remaining portals: one in Boston at an old temple and the other in the French Quarter in New Orleans, Louisiana," Bethany states.

"Well, we are three hours from Boston," Ethan remarks.

Thumbing through the pages of her book, Rose quietly laughs.

"What?" Oliver asks.

"It is never easy," Rose says peering over the top of her book.

"Oh no! I do not like the sound of that! Okay, Rose, spill," Ethan demands.

"Ethan, my favorite brother..." Rose begins to say when Ethan interrupts.

"Oliver! She said it! Whenever she starts a sentence with our name followed by 'my favorite brother,' it is never good," Ethan says.

"Rose, share, please," Oliver motions to her.

"As I was saying, Boston is out of the question right now as one of the swords according to legend is hiding in England. So, going to Boston would be pointless," Rose explains.

"And where is the other one?"

"Oliver, that has yet to be revealed and likely won't be until you two find the first sword," Rose replies.

"Great! We could be traveling all over, looking for this sword," Ethan notes.

"Once one sword is found, Ethan, then the location of the other will be revealed," Rose continues to read from the legend.

"Rose, it is never that easy but, what the heck, does the book say anything about which one is easier to find?" Ethan inquires.

"Ethan, the one mentioned would be easier, as the magic protecting the second is magic that you do not want to deal with," Sebastian remarks darkly.

"That bad?" Oliver asks.

"No. He is trying to scare you," Bethany says, giving Sebastian an awkward look and smacking him on the arm. "He likes to joke a lot. Please excuse him."

"Destiny or Bethany, what about the covens? Are you sure they won't be of any help?" Leaf asks.

"The covens have abandoned their duties here. It is believed only a truly powerful magical being can get the covens back on our side," Destiny states.

"What caused them to abandon the ways of our people?" Ethan inquires.

Walking to the fire pit, Destiny kneels down, pulls a small bag from her pocket, sprinkles the dust from it into her hand, and starts to throw it into the fire. The flames begin to dance when a vision appears.

"Ethan, when Morgana took power, she promised to reunify the Arcane and Mundane realms. The covens were supposed to play a big part in that. Morgana promised them each a part of the Mundane world. In a way, she promised the covens a chance to enslave the Mundane. As you can see, that did not happen. It did not happen because time, as charming as it is, played a wicked trick on Morgana who became resentful and spent all her energy trying to battle time, thus leaving the covens to depend only on themselves. Eventually, fighting broke out between the covens, and they went into hiding. Every now and then, chatter is heard about feuds but nothing that ever drew the attention of the Mundane."

The flames die down and the vision disappears. Silence falls over the camp, when Oliver inquires, "Who is the one who can get them back on our side?"

"Rose!" Leaf replies.

"Well, on that note, I am tired and turning in. Good night everyone," Rose says.

On her way, she kisses both of her brothers on the cheek and Zander on the forehead as she walks to the cabin.

"Would anyone care to explain what that was about?" Bethany asks.

"Rose gets very reserved when any mention is made of how powerful we are," Oliver states.

"I am heading to bed also," Leaf says, yawning.

He unrolls his sleeping bag and falls asleep instantly beside the roaring fire. Bethany, Destiny, and Zander all turn in for the night in the small cabin behind Rose's. Oliver, Ethan, Autumn, and Sebastian are left, sitting quietly, watching the flames intently.

"I will take first watch," Oliver states, motioning for Autumn to come with him.

"Ethan, will you be okay?"

"Yes." Ethan states in a stern tone as he glances quickly at Sebastian. An awkward silence falls over the camp as Sebastian gazes up at the sky, looking at the stars.

"The stars in this realm are very beautiful," he says to Ethan, who rolls his eyes, then rises to add more wood on the firepit. As the flames grow, he is pulled into a vision. Seconds later, he wakes to Sebastian helping him up off the ground and handing him a cup of water.

"My Lord! Are you okay?" he asks.

"I am fine" Ethan says, pulling away. "Thank you for helping me," he reluctantly adds.

"I assume that is how you see visions. May I inquire what did you see?" Sebastian asks.

"It was nothing," Ethan says, rubbing his head.

As they sit back down, Sebastian leans over and kisses Ethan. Within seconds, Sebastian finds a wand in his neck for the second time that day.

"What are you doing?" Ethan asks angrily.

"I am sorry, My Lord. That was wrong of me. It will not happen again," Sebastian replies. He pushes the wand from his neck and walks away.

While Ethan watches Sebastian walk away, he turns his attention to the fire where he spends the rest of the evening meditating on what had occurred, the images he had seen, and the kiss.

~

Rose is the first to rise the next morning. As she welcomes the warmth of the sun upon her face, she notices Ethan meditating by the fire pit. She approaches him when a field of magic throws her backward onto the ground. She shakes her head, glancing around, and then gets up and proceeds forward again. The field is gone now, and she is able to approach Ethan.

Sensing Ethan's inner turmoil, Rose places her hand on Ethan's back and before she knows it, she sees the events from the night before. As she stands there, she feels Ethan's confusion, his frustration, his anger, his guilt, and the many questions racing through his mind. As Oliver approaches, Rose quickly lets go of Ethan's shoulder and heads to the fire ring. Three sparks fly from her wand as she quickly hides it from sight. The campgrounds now begin to bustle as other campers and families start to wake. Rose stars cooking breakfast as Oliver hands her wood and supplies. They work quietly.

"Can he be trusted?" Oliver asks, breaking the silence.

"What?"

"Rose, can we trust Sebastian?" Oliver questions again.

Rose pauses. "I believe so, but only time will tell. There are many different versions of the future. In the ones I have seen, he is an ally. But there is something about him that I cannot put my finger on, something that, at this moment, does not make sense."

A quietness falls between the two again as they continue to prepare breakfast. They notice that anyone who walks by Ethan, is thrown backward in the same way Rose had been moments earlier. Oliver sits down with a look of puzzlement on his face. He glances questioningly at Rose for answers. She simply shrugs her shoulders.

"Does someone want to explain what that is about?" Oliver asks nodding toward Ethan as the others gather around the fire.

"It appears, Oliver, that your brother has found a way to create a shield while in meditation. Anyone who hits the field for the first time is flung away. Once he feels their energy, it seems the field is lowered," Bethany remarks.

She sits down on the log, rubbing the backside of the arm she landed on when thrown backwards. While they all sit and begin to eat breakfast, Ethan floats off the ground, then opens his eyes, takes a breath, lowers back down, and standing up, puts on his shirt, and walks towards the fire to join the others.

"Are you okay?" Rose asks.

"Fine. Just needed some time to clear my thoughts," he replies.

"Excuse me for a minute everyone," Rose says, rising to her feet and returning with her book.

"What's wrong, Rose?" Zander asks.

"Zander, I'm still trying to figure out where we are to go for these swords that are supposedly going to help our kingdom." Rose thumbs through the book.

"Camelot," Sebastian says as he buttons his shirt.

All three of the siblings notice the marking of the black dragon tattoo across his right shoulder and onto his chest, signifying a high-ranking user of dark magic.

"Really?" Ethan remarks, glaring at him.

The two lock eyes for a moment and then turn away. Rose and Oliver notice the tension between the two.

"Sebastian, you would know this how?" Oliver asks.

"Last night, I went for a walk and found a temple belonging to an incredibly old coven. The priest was kind enough to sit with me and go over one of their ancient texts. His knowledge of the Mundane is exceptional. Although the coven left the temple, he continues to protect the knowledge within its walls."

"The sword of time is hidden where the journey of Merlin begins," Sebastian states, reading a page ripped out of the book.

"Where Merlin's journey begins," Bethany, thinking out loud, says "would be either Camelot or Avalon. They are the two places where his journey could have begun."

"Rose knows the answer," Destiny says, emerging from thin air with her book in tow.

"Your book! The one you wrote That's it! You left clues for Oliver, Ethan and I!" Rose says. Destiny nods and laughs, handing it to her. Rose holds her hand over the book and closes her eyes. The pages begin to flip rapidly. Once they stop, Rose opens her eyes and speaks: "I know where they are!"

Bethany studies Rose. "Did you read that whole thing?"

"Yes." Rose blushes and continues, "One is in Camelot and the other sword is in Avalon. Avalon is the half-way point between the Arcane and Mundane realms, hence what better place to keep the swords? Genius!" Rose says, closing the book and placing it in her traveling bag.

"Excuse me, Lady Rose," Leaf says, handing her a scroll. "This is for you."

Rose examines the seal as Oliver and Ethan move in close behind her. The three examine the scroll, while Leaf dives into his breakfast. Breaking the seal, Rose begins reading silently. When she is finished, she hands it to Oliver.

"Leaf, where did this scroll come from?" Rose inquires.

"Yes, indeed," Ethan says, looking puzzled.

"The Lady Belinda gave it to me before I left. She said once the journey had begun to give it to you three. She stated I would know when the right time to do so would be. Besides, it was glowing in my bag when I went to pull my shirt out. So, here it is," he adds quickly while eating some bacon.

"What does it say, Rose?" asks Bethany.

"It looks as if we have a second journey," says Rose, sitting down.

Oliver hands the scroll to Bethany who reads it over, then nods.

"This should be interesting! Prince Alezander has not been seen for years," states Bethany.

"Why is finding him so important?" Ethan inquires.

Bethany, Sebastian, Leaf, and Destiny all exchange knowing looks but remain silent.

"Is someone going to explain?" Ethan asks.

"High Prince Alezander is an old friend of your family. It is believed he went mad when you three went into hiding," Bethany remarks, sipping her tea.

"Why did he go mad?" Oliver inquires.

Without missing a beat, Bethany takes another sip of her tea and speaks.

"He is Rose's betrothed and a very ancient wizard. His magic is unlike any power ever seen. He does things that make the rest of our magic look lame and weak."

Oliver and Ethan start to laugh as Rose shoots scornful looks toward both of them.

"So," Bethany continues, "two separate journeys. How do we do this?" Bethany inquires of her cousins.

"Ethan, Sebastian, Destiny, and I will travel to Camelot and Avalon to retrieve the swords," offers Oliver.

"That leaves Bethany, Leaf, Autumn, Zander, and Rose to find this elfish king referred to in the scroll," Ethan says smiling.

Rose gazes sadly at her brothers and then speaks.

"Oliver and Ethan, my brothers, good luck. Be safe. We will meet at the portal to the realms on Halloween."

Rising to her feet, she hugs them both.

"Before you leave, please accept my medallion. It is the crest of our family and will hopefully aid you with safe passage among any of the covens here in the Mundane realm or with any one you may encounter in Camelot," Bethany hands the medallion to Oliver.

"Thank you, Bethany."

"Good luck," adds Ethan.

As the two groups separate, they know their journeys have begun. With one tap of her staff, Rose and her friends disappear from the camp, leaving Oliver, Ethan, Destiny, and Sebastian to find the passage to Camelot.

Chapter 7
The Search for the High King Elf

Half of an ancient archway, several bits and pieces of a stone wall is all that remains of an old temple, the ruins towering over the land, the wind moaning through the walls. In the distance, a woman approaches, her long, red hair blowing in the breeze. Stopping, she looks around and passes through the archway as part of the ancient ruins rematerialize. Placing her hand on the back pew, she raises her other hand as light flies around her, restoring the old temple. As the final stone moves into place, the witch walks down the middle aisle, stops half-way, and points at the front of the temple where the alter appears.

Moving further down the aisle, the witch stops again, this time clapping as tapestry lowers from the ceiling. Listening, she hears the faint sounds of chants. Listening more closely, she can hear the notes of ancient songs sung by ancient priestesses, the words filling her as she feels them coming to life as if her ancient ancestors were there guiding her through the temple.

Continuing to listen, she raises her hands as if waltzing, moving down the center aisle, rising off the ground as if walking on air. The closer to the alter she gets, the louder the singing becomes. The witch flicks her finger, pointing at the different candles in the structure as each light, popping on one after another.

Lowering herself down on the steps ascending to the alter, she looks around and, raising her hand, runs it along the wooden tabletop. Reaching the back side of the alter, she turns looking into the old temple. As she raises her hands above her head, a crystal ball appears. Lowering the ball to eye level, she looks around the room one more time. Then, touching her index finger to the orb's surface, she disappears. The ball falls, hits the ground, and rolls down the central aisle, hitting the sole of a shoe. Reaching down, the priest picks it up, uses his sleeve to brush it off, and raises the crystal to look at it.

He turns quickly, saying, "It appears we will have guests arriving."

&

A bolt of lightning strikes the ground and from it emerge Rose, Bethany, Leaf, Autumn, and Zander.

"How original, a village," Bethany remarks, looking around.

"It appears to be empty," notes Leaf.

"Now the question is, where are we?" Bethany asks as Rose opens the scroll and begins reading.

"It appears, we are still in the United States, somewhere in Maine," Rose says, examining the scroll further.

"Which way, Rose?" Zander inquires.

"This way." Rose points to the road.

As the five walk down the road and through the town, they realize that they are on the border between the Arcane and Mundane realms.

"It appears as if the village was burnt to the ground," Rose says, squatting down and running her hand along the charred ground. Image after image race around her as she witnesses the destruction of the village firsthand. Darkness and light flash around her.

Time comes to a sudden a halt, as Rose looks around. Dark shadows march on the village and multiple wizards and witches lay ruin to the town as Rose walks toward the temple. The wizards spin their wands over their heads and project flames from their wands as the temple explodes and with a flash, the vision changes and everything around is laid to ruins. Walking down the road, the smell of charred wood is heavy in the air. Rose picks up a half-burnt teddy bear, pulls her wand, spins it in the air and reappears with the group, holding the teddy bear in her hand.

"What happened?" Bethany inquires walking out of the fog.

"Dark shadows and wizards marched on the village. They destroyed everything in their path," Rose says handing the teddy bear to Leaf. I see the temple has been laid to waste."

"Yes." Bethany explains, "Right after you disappeared, the temple crumbled."

"Who is that?" Zander inquires, pointing up the road toward a red-haired witch floating above the ground. As the witch enters through the archway, the temple returns to normal.

"Listen," Leaf says as the group hears the ancient chants emerging from the temple. Upon reaching the stone archway, Rose pulls the door open, but the wind pushes her, Leaf, Bethany, Zander, and Autumn backward. Grabbing hands, the group pushes back against the wind. When the witch looks down the aisle, she sees the five pushing against the wind. Then, when she reaches up and touches the crystal orb, time returns to normal.

⟡

"What just happened?" Zander asks, looking around and rubbing his head.

"It appears that, somehow, the four of you got pulled into the vision," Rose remarks as she stands up from where she has been kneeling. Smiling, she begins walking toward the temple when Autumn transforms and takes to the air.

"Where is she going?" Zander asks, looking at Rose.

"She probably senses something. She'll be back," Leaf responds as he motions for the group to proceed toward the temple.

As the group walks down the road toward the ancient building Rose asks Leaf, "Is this what Morgana's rampage, looks like?"

"Yes, but this is mild compared to what we have seen," Leaf responds, looking at Rose and putting a hand on her shoulder to comfort her.

"What's worse is that this village appears to be colliding with the Mundane realm. Since the upset of the magical balance, we have seen this continuously," Bethany adds.

"This village appears to be the home of a former coven. It seems the colliding of the realms always appears where magic is strongest. This means we had better move fast. We have to stop this," Rose responds, looking at the others. Leaf and Bethany look at each other, then shrug their shoulders.

Upon reaching the giant temple, and before anyone can knock, the doors fly open. The four friends look at one another.

"Well, the scroll said to find the old temple, but this is different than the vision," Rose exclaims.

Then, as the four enter the temple, the doors slam shut behind them. Leaf and Zander turn to grab the handles, giving them a pull, but nothing happens. Several individuals sitting in the pews praying, look up. "Shhh!"

"Aren't they pleasant? It appears as if we should proceed forward. Stay close and keep a tight hold on your weapons," Rose states looking down the giant aisle before her.

"It is identical to the vision, only without the floating lady with the orb," Bethany remarks.

Sensing they are being watched by the people in the pews, the four slowly move up the aisle. Pulling tightly on the arrow strung in her bow, Bethany nods towards the alter when Rose, sensing a presence, taps her staff three times on the stone floor. As the four look around, an older gray- and white-haired woman with long, tan, and white robes appears.

"Children, this is a temple, and many are in prayer? May I help you?" she asks, looking at the four.

"Ma'am, we are sorry. We have come a long way and seek sanctuary for the night," Rose explains.

"Sanctuary you say. You mean food, water, and shelter?" the woman inquires.

"Yes, if you wish to call it that," Rose states, lowering her staff.

"That staff," the old woman says as her eyes widen, then narrow.

"My staff? What about it?" Rose asks, holding it up.

"I have seen it before," the old woman states.

"This old thing belonged to a family member." Rose watches the woman carefully.

The old woman comes out from behind the alter, gliding across the floor and touching down in front of them. Extending her arm, she rolls up her sleeve to reveal the crest of the royals.

"I am Mother Francisco, protector of this temple and the last remaining priestess of this village and of the Oak Coven," she states.

Motioning for her friends to stand down, Bethany tightens her grip on her bow and arrow as she takes a seat in the front pew next to Zander and Leaf.

"Priestess Francisco, I am the one they call Roslynn, the daughter of Kelvin and Nadia. This is my cousin, Bethany, daughter of Wade, and my friends, Leaf and Zander," she said bowing her head.

"My lady, you mustn't bow. I should be bowing to you," the priestess replies.

"I bow to you, Priestess, out of respect," Rose responds, standing up and pulling the scroll from under her robe. "My Priestess, this scroll tells of a priest of this temple who holds valuable information about an Elf wizard King who I am to seek out for assistance in my journey."

Quietly, under his breath, Leaf mutters, "I do not like this. The scroll said priest, not priestess."

Bethany turns to look at him and tightens her grip on her bow and arrow.

"Come to the altar, all of you. Hurry!" Priestess Francisco says as she steps back up behind the altar. She puts on her glasses, summoning for a book.

Noticing that the priestesses' hands are shaking, Rose inquires, "Are you okay?"

The old lady looks at her, smiles and returns to what she is doing.

"Who is this King of whom you speak, child?" she asks, opening the book.

"I seek the High Prince, or rather King, Alezander Casper Ambrose Ignatius," Rose replies.

"Interesting. Interesting, indeed," the priestess says, slamming the book shut and sitting down in her chair.

Leaf and Bethany move closer to Rose and Bethany asks, "What is interesting?"

"There was a witch her earlier, with black hair, black lips, black robes, and skin as pale as it comes, looking for the same individual," she replies.

"Raven," Bethany and Leaf say, looking at each other.

"Child, you may be the Queen, but I swore an oath to protect the secrets given to me by the royals," the priestess says. "I am sorry, Lady Rose. I cannot help you, and besides, the King went mad, and has not been seen in years," the Priestess notes, waving her hands to shoo them away.

As the priestess lowers her head, Rose and the others notice multiple dark shadows moving about the room.

"Is it that you won't help me, or are you afraid to help us?" Rose inquires with an inquisitive look.

"Leave this place before I have to get ugly," the priestess snaps, standing up with her hands in front of her, continuing to shoo them away.

Leaf quietly waves his hand back and forth twice at his side, revealing the darkness surrounding them.

As Rose holds tight to her staff, the orb on the end lights, creating a shield of protection around the four.

Looking back over her shoulder, the priestess states, "Door's seal, windows slam, and candles light."

By now, the people in the pews have risen to their feet and are walking toward the main aisle.

"You say that you seek King Alezander, Lady Rose," she asks in a hushed tone.

"Yes. Why?" Rose responds.

"Shh! They are listening," she smiles and points toward the back of the temple as laughter rings out. Rose, Leaf, Zander, and Bethany turn around just in time to see dark creatures moving across the floor as the individuals from the pews produce weapons.

Suddenly, Rose finds a hand wrapped around her neck as the priestess's lifeless body drops to the floor and the dark creature opens its mouth. Black slime comes out followed by snakes that wrap around the figure and transform it into Raven.

Laughing, Raven throws Rose backward down the aisle. Pointing her finger at the ground, Raven projects the other three out of the altar area. Zander flies into the wall, smacking his head and knocking him unconscious. Leaf scrambles to his feet, moving close to Zander to protect him as Rose draws her wand and Bethany begins lobbing arrows at their attackers.

"Your weapons have no effect on me, child. Get them, my beautiful creatures. You will soon join the priestess in death," Raven says as the dark creatures move in to attack.

The dark witch steps over the lifeless body of the priestess laughing.

The three look at each other nodding, knowing what they have to do in order to protect themselves and each other. Lobbing arrow after arrow at the dark creatures, Bethany sets one magical arrow after another. Each arrow, striking the dark creatures, causes different forms of spells to occur. To protect the still unconscious Zander, Leaf summons a lightshield around the two of them to hold off the darkness.

As more and more dark creatures appear in the temple, the room grows darker until nothing—pitch black. Suddenly, a small white light appears to flicker, then an explosion of light overtakes the temple, throwing the darkness into the walls and furniture as Rose stands in the middle of the temple light spinning around her as Bethany falls back to the altar area. Reaching down she checks the pulse of the priestess.

"She is alive, but barely," Bethany says looking at Rose.

The light cast by Rose engulfs the temple, as dark creatures continue to emerge, consuming the back half of the structure, bringing total darkness to the space. Knowing the darkness will continue to try to overtake the space, Rose summons a light orb to her. When the darkness is inches from her, she drops the orb. As it hits the floor, an explosion occurs.

Lightning hits the floor and the fog that has filled the space begins spinning, forming a tornado, dust flying around the space pulling the darkness into the heart of the storm.

Screams echo throughout the hall as the darkness begins to retreat toward the doors that blow open, Autumn begins raining fire down upon the darkness as a man is seen riding on the back of the grand dragon.

"Thank you, Autumn. I leave for 10 minutes, and darkness takes control of my wife, the priestess of this temple. They are getting desperate," Father Francisco says throwing light from his staff at Raven and the darkness.

"Well, he must be the real priest," Leaf says, shooting lightning from his wand at the dark shadows moving against them.

"Silly child, get down and move," Autumn bellows as she lands in the center aisle knocking down rows of pews and blowing fire from her mouth at the dark creatures and members of the dark legions rising out of the ground.

Raven begins laughing as she rises to her feet, spitting blood on the ground. "You think your magic can…"

But before the witch can finish, she falls to the ground screaming.

"What is this….? It has been many years since this…"

Raven cannot finish as she huddles on the ground, holding her head. Another scream echoes over the temple as Raven shakes, the darkness disappearing as the dark witch loses any control over her body, her limbs jerking violently.

"What is going on?" Leaf asks, looking at Bethany and Rose.

"This will be my favorite part," Autumn remarks as the other three try to figure out what she is talking about.

Suddenly, Raven flies into the air and starts flying around the room, being thrown violently from one end of the giant hall to the other. Autumn laughs, as Rose, Bethany and Leaf stand in shock and amazement watching the witch crash into the walls over and over and then into the ceiling. With a thud, Raven falls to the floor and begins crawling toward the great doorway as she summons dark creatures to her.

As the creatures rise from the ground, a wizard looks at Bethany, points his finger at her, and yells, "Charge! Take the traitor."

Liam reaches down to assist Raven to stand up, when she screams and, again, loses control of her body. Distracted by what is occurring, Liam tries to assist Raven, pointing his wand at her casting one spell after another. At the same time, the darkness begins to charge at Rose, Bethany, and Leaf.

"Bethany, help me. Take my hand and repeat after me," Rose calls, holding out her hand. The cousins take each other's hand and cast a spell of protection,

Magia lux, lux Bonum, Defendat, et dirige in via.
Creare Agri in Praesidium.

Light of Magic, Light of Good, protect us and guide the
way. Create a field of protection.

Said in unison, a shield of solid light rises from the ground creating a box around the darkness.

When Raven gets back on her feet, the group notices that Zander is standing in the aisle, his eyes glowing silver and his ears pointed. He had dawned ancient robes. A wind picks up in the temple as Zander raises his hand and the creatures of darkness explode. Looking rather displeased, Raven raises her wand, but flies backwards into the pillar.

"Have you learned nothing in fighting me, witch," Zander inquires.

"Zandi, do you really think you can stop me?" Raven asks as Zander flinches at her comment.

On either side of the temple, dark creatures begin to appear and move down the pews to the center aisle. Father Francisco and the group fall further back toward where Zander is standing.

"What are your orders, My Lady," Leaf asks Rose.

Then, they hear, "Stay back! Protect each other and stay safe. I will handle this."

Zander jumps into the air, landing half-way down the aisle.

"You might need this, Sir," Father Francisco shouts, throwing a pouch to Zander.

As he opens the pouch, Zander retrieves his sword, shield, bow and arrow, his staff, and a small box. Not wasting any time, Zander stows his sword on his belt, places his shield on his back, and taps his staff twice against the stone floor, causing an earthquake to rattle the building, the dark creatures exploding. Turning his staff, three times—one, two, three—and Raven and Liam fly into the ceiling, then to opposite sides of the temple, slamming full strength into the walls.

Getting to her feet, Raven spits blood from her mouth screaming, "I will kill you this time and make my mistress proud of me, you piece of garbage."

Summoning her magic, she hurls orbs of darkness one after another at Zander. The orbs stop midway down the aisle of the temple and explode. Holding out his right hand, Zander stops the next volley of orbs, then closes his hand, causing the orbs to fly back and strike Raven.

"Now, if you're done…" Zander begins.

Raven screams, "Done? I will not be done until you are dead!"

Zander taps the box, which is sitting on the floor, with his foot.

"My turn."

The box lid flies open, and two spinning golden orbs raise into the air above the box. Zander's eyes begin to glow blue as the orbs spin higher into the air. A cyclone begins in the temple as the dark creatures begin turning human again, and Raven is lifted off her feet.

"Liam, get him," Raven yells.

Zander points his finger as the two orbs disappear and reappear, throwing Liam and Raven through the giant oak temple doors.

When they both get to their feet, they charge back through the temple doors, place their hands palm to palm, hold out their wands, and hurl dark lightning and plasma spheres at Zander, throwing him into the alter. Believing he is out of the way, Raven turns her attention to Rose.

Rising to his feet, Zander exclaims,

Cincinno.

Lock.

Raven and Liam fly backward again, this time, their spells backfiring as everyone notices that the necklace Rose wears under her shirt is glowing silver like Zander's eyes. Zander releases the orbs from their spot for a second time. This time, they fly at full speed toward Raven and Liam, while he reaches up, touches his temple, and Raven drops to the ground and begins screaming again. One orb hits Liam at full speed, throwing him off his feet. The other flies around the temple striking various dark creatures, capturing them within the orb. Then, the orbs separate and create a field of magic around Liam, while the darkness around him starts screaming as the orbs grow brighter. Trying to avoid them Liam blasts the orbs back and drops to his knees, weakened from the strength of the magic cast by the orbs.

Catching his breath, Liam rises to his feet, points his wand at the ground as smoke appears and, within seconds, he and Raven are gone.

A roar rings through the temple as Leaf transforms into his true form and, with one roar, cleanses the temple of the darkness. The people who have been transformed from darkness to light bow and clap as the priestess, who is now leaning on her husband, goes to speak with the people. The four and Autumn look around and, for the first time notice the beauty of the temple.

"Do you care to explain, what was all that screaming about with Raven?" Rose asks looking at Zander.

"Raven is the sister of King Alezander and, therefore, they are connected telepathically," Father Francisco states looking at Zander.

"What?" Bethany, Leaf, and Rose ask in unison, their facial expressions showing shock and disbelief.

"He is correct, to a point. Raven is my sister through one mother, but not the other. I will explain later but not now. Also, I am sorry for my deception. I had to keep my distance until you were ready," Zander says, hugging Rose.

"It is okay, I will probably never understand your power, but I am glad my best friend turned out to be the great King of the Elves," Rose says, smiling and reaching up to kiss Zander on the cheek.

Sitting down on the front pew, Rose begins rummaging through her expansive bag, seeking her spell book.

Looking around, she notices several dark creatures lurking in the shadows. Suddenly, they charge down the aisle. Rose gets to her feet, her spell book in hand. The book floats into the air and strikes the darkness head on, causing them to explode.

"What was that?" Leaf asks, shaking his head.

"A form of magic I had only read about," Rose states, laughing.

"What? Wait! You just fought dark creatures using a form of magic you have only read about?" Leaf asks with a look of disbelief.

"Oh, that spell is *Ad undecumum dicendum quod posse fugere efficient,*" Zander replies, realizing that the others do not understand what he is talking about.

"So, in other words, Rose holds the power to make objects fly without the use of a magical conductor such as a wand," Leaf notes.

"Zander and Rose, what Leaf is getting at, is only a witch or wizard can cause orbs to fly. Making other objects, such as a book, fly as a form of a weapon, is unfamiliar to us," Bethany explains.

And, with that, all four look at each other and begin laughing.

Chapter 8
Secrets

"Leaf, Autumn, Bethany, can you give Lady Rose and me some time to talk in private?" Zander inquires. The three nod while Zander reaches down and kisses the top of Rose's hand.

"You three, come with me. I shall help you restock your supplies, food, and water," Father Francisco suggests as the three follow him.

With a quick wave of his hand, a door appears out of thin air. The four walk through and, within seconds, the door disappears. Zander sits down in the front pew, unbuttons his right sleeve, and rolls it up, revealing a tattoo from his wrist all the way up to his elbow.

"That marking is in my book," Rose says, sitting down across from Zander on the front steps to the altar area.

"As it should. It is the only way you would know me," Zander replies. "We do not have much time before the others come back," Zander states.

"Your necklace, may I see it?" he asks looking at Rose and moving from the pew to sit next to her in order to examine it further. Pulling the necklace from under her tunic, Rose notices that it is still glowing white.

Taking it off, Rose places it in Zander's hand as he turns it over several times examining it.

"I take it that 'Cincinno' is the term that locks the necklace," Rose inquires.

"Indeed, it is. Give me a minute. 'Unlock'" Zander commands while he grabs Rose's hand, and they travel through time. They land in a room with a crib and watch as the door opens.

"Alezander, you should not be here. Your people, your kingdom…" Destiny states covering the child.

"Lady Destiny, my people will be fine, I have given my cousin, brother, and sister orders to take our people to the north valley. Besides, I need to see for myself," a younger-looking Alezander states.

With that, he moves his hand over the sleeping baby. A necklace around the baby's neck lights and he moves the sheet back to gaze upon it. As the necklace reveals itself under the dress of the young baby. Rose's necklace also lights, glowing bright white.

"When do they leave for the other realm?" he inquires.

"Tonight," Destiny replies.

"Then, I am going too," Zander responds.

"But you cannot leave. You are needed here. I will be there to protect them," Destiny states.

"I cannot leave her behind. I have to protect them. Old friends of my father live in the Mundane realm. I will live with them and watch from afar until the time is right," Alezander states leaning down to kiss the baby on the forehead.

While this was occurring, Rose reaches up and touches her head as she can feel the kiss and understands who the child is. As the room fades, they jump into another image.

"Secure the palace! Morgana's troops move to seize this place. Get the children to safety now!" a voice Rose recognizes orders. As she looks around, she sees her father and other cloaked figures summoning a portal.

"Get them through now, Nadia. They must leave now, My Queen," Alezander says.

"Keep them safe. We will all be reunited someday but, for now, keep them safe no matter what," Nadia says handing a scroll to Alezander and pushing him through the portal as the entire palace freezes. The High Prince and Princess make it away on the back of a dragon as Morgana, her guards, and all the inhabitants of the palace freeze in place.

Again, the space around them fades and, this time, Rose finds herself with Alezander back in the temple with Bethany, Leaf, and Autumn waiting for them. Rose looks down and the scroll, which had been handed to Alezander in the vision, now rests in her hand. Alezander nods and Rose understands what he means. As she sits down on the step, breaks the seal, and opens the scroll, a secondary, smaller note falls out into Rose's lap.

Lord Alezander,

Where do we begin? While the High Prince and I do not approve of your leaving this realm, we do appreciate the fact that you are going to protect our children and, for that, we are eternally grateful and indebted to you. May your strength and insight guide you, Oliver, Ethan, and Rose along your journey. Please keep them safe. Show them the way of our people and let them know that we love them. Many trials await them when they get older. Be there for them. Guide them and, above all, Alezander, remember who you are.

Your dearest friends,
Nadia & Kelvin

After reading the letter, Rose retrieves the second scroll, opens it, and discovers it is addressed to her and her brothers.

My children,

The time has come to learn of a truth. If you are reading this scroll, then a great truth has occurred. Our dear family friend has joined you on your journey. Let me start by saying this, King Alezander is Rose's betrothed. It has been arranged and they represent the balance of the Mundane and Arcane realms. Because of his age and wisdom, please respect and listen to him. His understanding and knowledge of the ancient ways is what you three will need on your journey to stop Morgana.

Alezander, is the eldest son of King Caspar Ignatius, the late King of the Elves and a dear friend of your father's and mine. This means Alezander, himself, is the New King of the Elves. Against the orders of your father and myself, Alezander left what remained of the Elfish Kingdom in the care of his cousin, sister, and younger brother. He did this to protect the three of you and keep you safe.

While he is over 300 years old in human terms, he is only 25 years old in elfish time. He is the eldest living member of the Arcane realm to date. As such, his age means he has seen the passing of many seasons and he remembers your great grandfather, Merlin. Before Merlin's death, Alezander was able to train with him and understands the magical power of Merlin. It is your father's and my hope that you three will pay close attention to his teachings and learn everything you can about Merlin's way of magic.

Understanding Merlin's magic may be the key to helping our people and saving the Arcane and Mundane realms. At this time, I know you three will not understand the connection you have to the realm of Arcane, but you are now children of both the Mundane and Arcane realms. May the powers of magic protect you.

Your Mother

When Rose has taken in the final words of the scroll, she nods, closes the scroll, holds it tight and, within seconds, it reseals and disappears. Rose looks at Bethany, Leaf, Autumn, and Alezander, stating, "I believe it is time we join my brothers, Sebastian, and Destiny."

"Our Friends…" Father Francisco and his wife Priestess Francisco bows.

"Yes," Rose replies.

"Once you leave our temple, it will remain in limbo between the realms. If any of you need a place to stay or to acquire gear, we are here," he says handing each of them a bag.

"Thank you, Father, for your hospitality," Rose replies, shaking his hand.

As the group steps down from the altar and heads for the doors of the temple, Francisco inquires, "My Lady, the timeline of magic has been altered, shattered, torn apart, and rebuilt. Will you do everything in your power to restore it?"

"Yes indeed. I will, Father, and thank you," Rose replies, smiling at him. "Oh, and Father, I have a task for you. Please find any Arcane in this realm and in the covens. Protect them and convince them to join the fight on the side of good. My brothers and I will be back, and their assistance will be greatly needed."

Father Francisco and Priestess Francisco smiled, put their hands together, and bowed their heads in respect. Standing in the opening of the temple, the four touch their hands together as Autumn blows fire around them and, within seconds, the room begins to spin and, in a voice she has never heard, Alezander speaks.

Ut nos Camelot.
Take us to Camelot.

A dense fog swirls around the four as Autumn begins flapping her wings, trying to reveal where they are. As the fog lifts, the five find themselves standing on the edge of a cliff, a castle stands on the opposite cliff as water separates them. A guard on top of the tower yells down to them, "Who goes there?"

Bethany pulls an arrow from her quiver and shoots it into the air. Exploding in mid-air, the arrow reveals the crest of the House of Phoenix.

"Watch yourselves! The draw bridge is being lowered," yells the guard.

Once the bridge lowers, the five journey across into the grounds of the castle where a small village stands with people bustling about everywhere. A series of knights come up to greet them. One gentleman recognizable to Rose dismounts. Rose bows as the other four follow her lead.

"Rise, Lady Rose, great-granddaughter of Merlin. I should be bowing to you," the gentlemen remarks.

"Your majesty, King Arthur, your reputation proceeds you," Rose states as she follows the king.

"Rose," Destiny says, hugging her and kissing her on the cheek.

"Alezander," she says, looking at him.

"My brothers, where are they?" Rose inquires as Destiny and King Arthur look at each other.

"Why don't I like that look?" Alezander questions.

"Not here," Destiny states.

"To the throne room," Arthur insists.

"I have a bad feeling that something is wrong," Alezander leans over whispering to Rose who is staying close to Bethany and Leaf.

When the group reaches the doorway to ascend the staircase, Rose notices that Destiny is acting strangely. Destiny seems more nervous than normal, not acting at all like herself. Her hands are very shaky, and she keeps looking around as if she is expecting someone. Before anyone can say anything, Destiny is tacked to the wall with arrows from Bethany's bow and Alezander has the King on his knees with a sword at his throat.

"Where is King Arthur? So help me, I will take your head off, demon," he demands as the imposter starts laughing and spitting black venomous magic in Alezander's face. With one quick spin, Alezander takes the head of the imposter clear off its body as the imposter of Destiny transforms into Morgana.

With one blast, Morgana flies through the wall and screams can be heard throughout the kingdom as dark creatures appear.

"Secure my chambers!" a woman screams as she runs down the pathway toward the five, holding a candlestick in one hand.

"My Lady Rose, I am Queen Guinevere my husband is…"

"Locked in the dungeon with the others. I know," Rose responds.

"And you will never get to them," Morgana screams, her hands resting on her knees while she catches her breath and stands up, laughing.

"Lady Guinevere, go with Rose, Bethany, Leaf, and Autumn. Take them to the dungeons and help them free the prisoners," Alexander commands flipping his cloak off his back onto the ground.

"What are you doing?" Rose inquires.

"Handling Morgana. Now, go!" Zander summons his staff and taps it against the ground as Morgana flies backward.

"Now is that any way to treat me, Zanni?" Morgana asks, raising to her feet laughing.

"I hate that name, and you have no right to call me Zanni," he shouts as he blasts her with light rays. Simultaneously, he also kicks a box in front of him, releasing two orbs, which fly around Morgana shooting lightning. One bolt after another strikes her.

"But Zanni is that any way…?" Morgana begins as she throws Zander backward and tries to hit him with magic. But it backfires on her.

"You won't succeed." Zander glares at her.

"But I already have," Morgana argues as she throws more dark magic at him. Zander holds his hands out in front of himself, blocking the magic, but the blasts are so strong that Zander's knees buckle, and his right knee hits the ground as he is pushed backward in the dirt. As he deflects the magic, he rises again to his feet. His eyes turn silver as the magic ricochets back at Morgana. He reaches down to the ground and pulling his hand up causes the dirt to fly into the air. Volley after volley of rocks continue to hurl towards her. Suddenly, Morgana flies into the air, tossed around like a rag doll.

"You see, witch, the last time you fought me, I felt bad for you and lowered my defenses. But, this time, it is not going to be as easy," he declares, spinning his staff and slamming it against the ground causing the dirt to fly up again. This time, rocks smash into Morgana as she continues to be thrown around.

Looking around, Zander snaps his fingers and Morgana falls at full speed, hitting the ground hard. Angry, she starts to rise to her feet when Zander spins his staff, taps it on the ground and blows Morgana off her feet. Then, one of the gold orbs crashes into her at full speed.

Inside the castle, as Rose, Bethany, and Leaf reach the gates of the dungeon, they find Raven there waiting and laughing. Not amused, Rose points her wand at the ground as the stones under Raven flip her backwards into the wall.

Screams echo from all over the dungeon as many of the villagers have been captured and are being tortured by the dark guard. Working quickly, Leaf, Bethany, and Rose begin blowing the locks off of the cell doors, freeing all the prisoners.

"Guards, get these people to safety immediately," Bethany orders.

"I am going to need help here," Rose yells as she blows the cell door off the hinges, not even bothering with the lock.

Rose runs into the dungeon cell spinning magic around her as she shatters the chains that suspend Ethan from the ceiling. He falls to the ground gasping for air.

"Leaf, I need some help," Rose repeats as she hoists Ethan up under his arm.

"We have to get him to safety," Leaf remarks as he takes Ethan's other side to support him.

Rose looks around and notices that some of the cells were still locked.

"How many more cells are there? You know what? Never mind. I am done with this!" Rose shouts as she closes her eyes.

Re-opening them, her eyes glow blue, and she waves her hand as all the locks blow up and the cell doors fly open.

Sebastian is the first to reach the hallway, running to help Leaf and Rose carry Ethan.

"Rose," Oliver says giving her a quick hug as he pulls the swords from a ledge in the guards' chambers. A muffled groan can be heard as Oliver quickly pushes pass the people running from the dungeon.

"Guards, we need help over here. The King is weak," Oliver calls, going back to help Bethany balance Arthur as best they can.

When Oliver and Bethany emerge from the cell, supporting the King, Oliver is stopped by a vine wrapped around his throat.

"Oh, now this is it! Not my brother!" Rose shouts, blasting the vines.

As her eyes turn white, Raven drops to the ground screaming. Rose points her wand at her and Raven freezes, her spirit starting to leave her body. As the vines break, Oliver falls to the ground, choking and gazing up at his sister.

"Rose, snap out of it!" Oliver calls as he gets up and starts shaking her. "Get Ethan out of here and clear the dungeon." Oliver steps backwards, watching his sister's power intensify.

Raven's spirit begins returning to her body as Liam runs quickly toward them, spinning his wand and casting a shield around Raven, trying to restore her to life. Annoyed, Rose walks toward Liam as he flies backwards, and his wand explodes.

"You declared war on the Arcane. You declare war on the Mundane. Then, you have the nerve to attack my brothers?" Rose declares in a deep tone as she tilts her head to the right, looking at Liam.

Scrambling to his feet, Liam throws dark lightning at the group, trying to hold Rose back as she moves her right arm in front of her, extinguishing the lightning instantly. Blast after blast of lightning strikes multiple lightshields but to no avail.

The spirit leaving Raven's body returns fully, and she is helped to her feet by Liam. Rose, now angrier than ever, raises her hand in front of her as a ball of fire appears. Liam grabs Raven's hand and attempts to teleport.

"How is this possible that we can't teleport?" he asks, looking angry.

"You can't teleport because I willed you not too. Are you afraid of fighting me?" Rose inquires as she sends the fireball hurling toward them at full speed. Raven is barely in time to cast a shield as the fireball explodes, taking out the dark creatures and remaining dark guards.

Knowing they are not going to be able to stop Rose, Raven and Liam point their wands at the wall and blow the rocks out into the alleyway leading to the village market. Liam pushes Raven outside as he casts another shield, trying to hold off Rose.

Ascending down the long corridor, Rose picks up speed, moving toward them. Raven and Liam summon the rocks around them and begin projecting them at Rose. They ricochet off her shield and Liam and Raven are thrown into one of the market stalls. At the same time, Raven and Liam hit the stall, Morgana flies head-first into the stone wall.

Alezander appears, his right hand raised, as he walks up to Rose, his staff on his shoulder.

"Hey, it's me. Calm down! Bring the eyes back to normal. They can't hurt us."

Rose and Zander smile at each other and touch their palms together. When they pull them apart, a portal opens. The wind howls around them as Morgana is drawn into the portal with Liam and Raven. From inside the portal, Morgana begins summoning dark creatures but when the five have fully manifested, they fall to the ground and die as Ethan stands behind Zander and Rose, his eyes glowing blue. When the last dark creature falls, Oliver catches Ethan as he collapses.

"I'll take it from here," Zander says, winking at Rose as he spins his hands in a circular motion and the portal seals. With the portal closed, Rose and Alezander run to assist Oliver with Ethan.

"Get the first aid kit out of my bag," Rose says to Oliver.

"The cuts are too deep," Bethany remarks, looking at the marks all over Ethan's body as she begins moving her wand in a sewing motion, trying to heal his wounds.

"What should we do?" Oliver asks.

"Allow me," says Sebastian as he points his wand at the cuts, and they begin to heal.

Ethan gasps for air, sits up looking around, and asks, "Why?"

"Funny! What do you think friends are for?" Sebastian asks putting his wand away and helping Ethan up. Leaf reaches into Ethan's bag and pulls out a tunic and hands it to him.

"Thank you." Ethan says, looking at everyone and blushing as he looks at Sebastian.

"I told you that he is good," Rose remarks, glancing at Oliver.

"You're right," Oliver replies.

Smiling, he walks up to shake Sebastian's hand. Rose sighs and sits down on a crate taking a deep breath. Alezander comes over and sits next to her.

"I guess your mom was right and wrong," he remarks looking at her and her brothers.

"Right about what?" Rose inquires.

"That you, Rose, are one of the most powerful witches around, but we do need to hone your skills. However, I have been around a long time and, Ethan and Rose, what is that trick you just did to take the spiritual force of a living being?" Alezander inquires.

The three siblings looked at each other and shrug in response.

"So, I take it there is a story as to how our friend Zander is King Alezander," Oliver says smiling.

"That is a story for another time. But, right now, Rose, the scrolls please," Alezander says as Rose hands the scrolls to her brother.

Ethan puts on his tunic and walks over to read the first of the scrolls over Oliver's shoulder.

"The swords?" Rose inquires while they are reading.

"Yes, right here. It took forever to get the one that Oliver has," Ethan remarks pulling his sword and showing it to Rose and Alezander.

"Excalibur," Alezander notes in amazement seeing the sword.

"And?" Rose inquires, crossing her arms and tapping her foot looking at Oliver.

Oliver pulls the sword of their father, Kelvin, and shows it to Rose.

"The sword Gabriel," Alezander says looking at it, running a finger down the blade, watching the reflection of the midafternoon sun on it.

"What did you call it?" Oliver asks.

"Gabriel, it is your father's sword, forged at the hands of the elves. Both swords are indestructible and extremely magical," Alezander explains. "Where was it hidden?"

"Do not ask," Oliver states looking at him.

"That bad?" Rose inquires.

"Father's sword was stolen by what is called a 'portal jumper.' Some individuals risk their lives to steal in this realm and sell in the other realm and vice versa. Supposedly, the guy who bought Dad's sword had gotten it from some guy who stole it from the castle. The guy we got it from could not figure out how the portals work," Oliver remarks.

"What was worse is that he wanted an arm and leg for it, literally not figuratively. Rather weird gentlemen actually," Ethan adds.

"How did you get it back then?" Rose asks.

"Sebastian," Oliver states.

"He pulled a sword out of his bag, claimed it to be Excalibur, and the shop owner was very interested in trading. He nearly traded half of his shop for it," Ethan smiles, patting the handle of Excalibur.

"It appears that the one Sebastian had was a replica. When we were in the forest, we ran into the guards from the castle. They brought us here to meet Arthur and, yes, Arthur took us to the lake to meet with the Lady of the Lake. From there, she presented us with the true Excalibur. Arthur said the sword has never let him down and has served him well. Now, it will serve us," Ethan declares.

As the group talks together, Guinevere and Arthur approach.

"Um hum, Our Lords and Ladies, we do not mean to interrupt, but we want to thank you for your help today. Morgana has always been a problem, and it is nice having the Arcane back to help us fight her. Make yourselves comfortable and welcome to Camelot."

"Thank you, Your Majesties. Are you both okay? And are your people, okay?" Rose inquires.

"We are fine. Thank you for asking. Arthur and I are just getting ready to check on our people if you will excuse us, we will be off," Guinevere notes as she and Arthur walk away.

"Destiny? Please show the others where we are staying here in Camelot. We will join you all in a few minutes. Ethan and I wish to speak with Rose and Alezander," Oliver says, placing the scrolls back in Rose's hand.

As the group leaves, Ethan sits down next to Rose, and Alezander kisses her on the top of her hand. Oliver smiles and winks at Rose, showing his approval of Alezander as her betrothed.

"Tomorrow night is our biggest journey yet," Oliver states looking at the other three.

"All Hollow's eve," Rose concurs.

"We must rest. I have a feeling this is going to get interesting," Ethan remarks.

"You may be correct, Ethan. I am concerned," Rose states looking at the other three.

"About?" Alezander inquires, trying not to sound worried.

"Morgana and her troops attacking the portal. If she is here in Camelot, she can already pass between the realms," Rose notes with a worried tone.

"Yes and No! Remember, Camelot is stuck between realms, she cannot get to the Mundane realm without the portal being restored. Besides, she is weak, she was not herself during the battle. Her magic is fading," Alezander states.

"Well, I will say this, most of the kingdom is frozen in magical incantation. Her reach is limited, hence why she has to attack the in-between of the realms," Sebastian states, walking up eating a turkey leg. "I am sorry. I do not mean to interrupt, but Destiny is uneasy after what happened earlier."

"Please tell her that we will be there in a minute," Rose says looking at him sternly.

"He is right. We might want to get inside before Destiny sends the entire kingdom to find us," Ethan remarks, causing the others to laugh.

When the laughter dies down, they walk toward the castle's dining hall.

Entering the hall, the five discover a grand feast.

"Is this what it is like here with the food?" Rose inquires.

"Every meal! I swear Oliver and I have gained fifteen pounds each," Ethan laughs.

Throughout dinner, while everyone was chatting and laughing and enjoying each other's company, Rose sits quietly eating and observing Sebastian, who she notices is watching Ethan's every movement.

"My friends, the palace is yours to explore if you so choose," Arthur invites.

"Our friends, we shall see you all in the morning. Sleep well," Guinevere says as she and Arthur wish everyone a good night.

"Well, I am doing what they are doing and turning in. Please do not leave the grounds of the palace. After what Morgana did today, your parents would kill me if something happened to any of you," Destiny states, looking meaningfully at the group.

When the rest of the group finishes, each goes off to their separate sleeping quarters. An hour later, Rose quietly leaves her room, goes down the hall, and knocks on Sebastian's door.

"Lord Sebastian, may I speak with you?" Rose asks.

"Yes, Princess… My Lady… I mean… Rose, what can I do for you?" he asks tripping over his words and inviting her in and sitting down at the foot of his bed while summoning a chair for her.

"It is fine. Just call me Rose. It is easier. I notice that you… how do I put this? I notice that you have a liking for my brother," she says, glancing at him.

Quiet falls over them as Rose looks directly into Sebastian's eyes. A moment later, she nods.

"Well then, good night."

"Wait! Wouldn't you like an answer?" he inquires.

"No, I'm good. Thank you," she replies, walking out the door.

"Weird," he shrugs as he closes the door.

Rose retreats to her room and begins writing in her journal as she does every night. Soon, she falls asleep on her book and quill. As she sleeps, she dreams and astral projects in and out of visions. When she wakes, she notices a cloaked figure in her room.

Drawing her wand, she slams the cloaked figure against the wall. She gets off the bed, and approaches the figure, pulling back their hood revealing a young man. As she lowers her wand, the young man falls to the floor with a thud.

"Can I help you?" Rose askes.

He smiles, stands, walks up to her, touches her forehead, and pulls her into a vision. The room spins, then comes into focus. Rose looks around. She is standing in an ancient library, old books and scrolls all around her.

"Fascinating place," Rose says aloud to herself, walking around looking at the different books.

Rose begins to reach for a book, when the young man reappears, standing at the end of the shelf and hands a book to her.

"The Prophecies of Merlin," Rose reads aloud.

The young man snatches the book from her, runs to the table, and slams the book down. As he moves his hands over the pages, they begin to flip. Rose's eyes narrow as she has never seen anyone else do this. Cautiously, she approaches the young man but stops in her tracks as the young man is now aging before her eyes, growing older with each flipping page.

"Who are you?" Rose asks looking puzzled.

"Shh," the man says, staring at her.

"No, I will not shh," Rose responds.

Reaching the opposite side of the table, Rose holds tight to her wand as she waves her hand over the book, causing it to slam shut.

The gentlemen standing in front of her is now young again.

"I am Rose. I want to know who you are and why you brought me here?" she demands.

The young man gives her a curious look and raises his hands above his head as a glowing orb appears. He lowers the orb eye level.

"You must look," he says softly.

"What am I looking at?" Rose asks.

"Look, look! No not with your eyes but with your magic. Now, look," he commands.

Cautiously, Rose tightens her grip on her wand, ready to strike if the young man makes one wrong move. Gazing into the orb, she notices Merlin and Titus walking across the courtyard of a castle.

"Rose, it is a trap! Do not look any further," she hears a quiet voice say to her.

Pulling back from the orb, she looks at the young man, and points her wand right in his face as she causes the orb to explode.

"I think I know what is going on here," she tells the young man, who looks very angry.

"I know who you are," she states, a puzzled look on her face as she circles the young man, her wand still pointing at him.

"How is this possible?" she asks, watching his every move. "Release me from this vision."

"That I cannot do. Only you can do it," the young man replies.

"Merlin, I am not asking again. I am demanding that you release me," she says, glaring at him.

"You are not in any position to make any sort of demands right now. Are you?" Merlin laughs as he raises his hands, causing the room to spin.

Rose raises her hands as her eyes turn silver. The room comes to an abrupt halt as Merlin flies across it.

"Are you sure I am Merlin?" the young man demands, pulling a dagger.

Rose blasts the dagger out of his hand and holds her wand at his throat.

"You fail to realize, Merlin, that I recognize your eyes. Your hair is pulled back in the ponytail that Merlin is always seen with in the pictures. Also, you are a silent wizard and can summon items to you without speaking. Lastly, the tattoo of the weird-looking dragon on your arm gave you away," she remarks, raising his sleeve revealing the rest of his dragon tattoo.

Knowing of her magic, he senses her gazing into his soul. He knows that if he does not block her, she will discover what he is up to. So, he closes his eyes, breathes out, and when he reopens his eyes, she has returned to her room in the castle and is lying on the floor. She gets up, walks to the mirror, and peers into it.

"Weird," she remarks, looking at herself. Walking back toward her bed, she notices that the book of prophecies from her vision is lying on the floor.

"What are you up too, Merlin?" she asks out loud and begins examining the book. Turning the first few pages, she finds some paper sticking out from between the pages. She flips to that page, pulls out the paper and examines it.

"Nothing," she notes.

Then, turning the paper over, "No, wait! Those markings were not there before. They are nothing I have ever seen before. But now they're gone," Rose puzzles.

Chapter 9
The Ways of Magic

Over the next few hours Rose reads through the book, seeking answers. Every so often, she examines the piece of paper to see if anything has changed. About to give up, she notices a passage that catches her interest. As she begins to read, the room spins into a vision.

❧

"My Lord and Lady, the boys will need protection," Alezander states.

"We know this, Alezander, but, for now, they will remain where they are," Kelvin explains.

"Kelvin, I understand that but what of the unborn child," Alezander inquires.

"If the legends are true, she will be more powerful than Morgana or any witch or wizard," Nadia smiles, closing her book.

"We shall do what we can to protect her."

"What about the prophecy? What about the time stones?" Alezander asks, sitting down in one of the giant armchairs.

"Sadly, the stones are lost, and we do not speak of the prophecy," Nadia sighs, sitting down across from Alezander.

"But if it is all true, the time stones and your daughter's power could be used to stop Morgana," Zander says, looking hopefully at Nadia and Kelvin.

"Alezander, my old friend." Kelvin places his hand on Alezander's shoulder.

"Whoever finds those stones cannot contain their powers. Those stones will destroy the bearer," Nadia remarks, watching Zander.

"Yes, they are some of the most powerful, ancient runes of magic there are. Also, there is no way to understand their magic," Kelvin says as he leaves the great hall.

Alezander strides across the room to look out of the grand, oversized window of the hall.

"My Lady…" he begins.

"Alezander, no. You have heard Kelvin. Leave them where they are," Nadia bows and walks toward the door.

"Nadia, I have seen her," he declares as she turns to look at him. "She finds them, she merges them, and she uses them. They lead her too… well, the one thing that no one wants coming out," he says when Nadia interrupts.

"I know she does," Nadia states lowering her head, taking a deep breath, then sitting down again, and letting out a huge sigh.

"Then, if you know, why do you fight it?" Alezander said looking at her.

"Alezander, you are one of the wisest and most trusted advisors Kelvin and I have," Nadia said looking at him.

"The strength of those stones could destroy everything, and Morgana knows it. That is why the three stones shall remain separate and hidden for all time. Not to mention the other item," Nadia replies.

"Alezander, do not go looking for them. They will destroy you. Besides, to find them would require you to use magic that you, yourself, have stated you would never use."

Alezander walks toward the door. He turns and nods, looking toward the spot where Rose is standing, observing the vision. He motions for her to follow as if he knows she is there.

Rose follows him and, upon reaching the door, she sees Alezander heading up the stairs. Following him up the stairs, she observes him stopping and looking back every so often as if he is watching her. Upon reaching the room to which he has retreated, she peers through the door.

"I know you are here, young Princess. I can feel you. But I do not know how this is possible. Listen, before you leave, there are three stones. You must find them. Your mother and father are afraid of the stones. I have traveled through time, and I have seen the witch you will become. You have a form of magic that no one understands. The stones will react differently with you. They understand your will. Each stone by itself is weak. Together, they become one of the ultimate weapons of magic. You possess the knowledge of each stone. One is closer to you than you know," he says as his voice fades.

~

The room begins to fade, then comes back into focus as Rose finds herself sitting back on her bed.

She grabs the clock, 2:15 AM. She gets up, puts on her robe, and reaches under her shirt to pull out her necklace. Examining it, she remarks to herself, "I wonder if this could be the stone? He did say it was closer than I know."

Rose looks at the stone dangling in front of her, then walks toward the door. Upon entering the hall, she starts down the quiet and cold halls of Camelot. The only thing occurring at that time of night is the ghost of Ballard who floats up and down the hallway, yelling at the suits of armor, stopping occasionally to challenge the various suits of armor to a duel.

She walks up to the old oak door on the other side of the castle and knocks. Alezander answers, shirtless, only wearing pants.

"May I come in?" Rose asks. Alezander moves out of the way, yawning, allowing her access. Looking around, Rose takes a seat.

Alezander yawns again, "What's up? What brings you knocking this early?"

"A vision," Rose replies.

"A vision of what?"

"You," she replies, looking directly at him.

Sitting on the edge of his bed, Alezander asks, "What was it about?"

"It was interesting. What I want to know is why are you keeping things from me?" she demands.

"What are you talking about?" he asks, leaning forward with his forearms on the footboard.

"The three times stones?" she gazes at him square in the face.

"Oh, what do you want to know?" he responds.

"Everything. Where are they, Alezander?" she inquires.

"Hidden. And do not go looking for them," Alezander gets up and strolls over to the window.

"Why not?"

"Rose, there are things in place that cannot be explained," he replies.

"Zander, if they are the weapons of magic, we need them. Why shouldn't we get them?"

"Because they are gone. We have only the swords left. The stones were lost in time much like other items," he explains, turning to look at her.

"I do not understand," she insists as Zander grabs her hands and looks into her eyes. The room begins to spin, and they land in the vision from which Rose just came. Rose listens to the vision again until Zander freezes it at the part where he says, "I have traveled through time, and I have seen the witch you will become."

"Oh wow! Lost in time. You found them and tried to bring them to our time. When you say they are 'lost in time,' that is true. They are lost," Rose says.

Zander snaps his fingers, and they land back in his room.

"Rose, promise me that you won't go looking for them. Time travel is dangerous. To mess with time can have effects that can destroy everything we know," he explains.

"But you also noted, in that vision, that I need to find them. I do not understand why you would say something you do not mean," she exclaims.

"If you found them, how would you contain the power of the stones once they are combined? There is only one individual who can, but they are not of this time. In fact, they are not even born yet," he states.

"Zander, I know this, but there is the serenity spell in my book. I would not need to touch the stones. Instead, I can cast the spell."

"I was young when I said what I did," he explains.

"Wait! How did you know I was there?"

"There are many things at this time that you still have to learn, Rose. What I know would surprise you. Further, do not seek the stones. You are not ready," Zander notes.

"And you make that decision?" she demands.

"I can if need be. I am older, wiser, and my magic is far more honed than yours," he states calmly.

"Then, shut up and come with me," she insists, reaching up and kissing him.

As they pull apart, he remarks, "You cannot leave now. Your brothers need you. Besides, you would not even know where to begin looking. It is dangerous to pursue them," he insists.

"Fine, I will help them get through the portal. Then, I am off to retrieve the other two," Rose replies.

"Two? There are three. All three are lost," Zander remarks.

Reaching into her shirt, Rose pulls out her necklace and asks, "Then, this is not one of them?"

Zander shakes his head.

"By the magic of my people, I wipe this silly vision out of your head until you are ready," he chants under his breath.

"Good evening. What brought me here to your room?" Rose asks.

"You were coming to say good night," Zander replies, smiling.

"Oh, this early?" she asks, looking at him.

"Don't you remember? You said you couldn't sleep. That is why you came down to my room," he says, walking her to the door. After shutting the door, he hears a voice.

"You cannot keep it from her forever. She will figure it out."

"That is fine. She has to figure it out," he replies, looking around and talking to the air as he notices the mirror on the other side of the room is glowing. Approaching the mirror, he grabs his tunic, puts it on, and then, he extends his hand, reaching into the mirror, and steps into it as his room darkens.

That next morning, the siblings awake early and find one another in the grand entryway of the castle overlooking the village. The three wander the giant hall, looking around. Oliver stops to examine an oil painting of Arthur and Merlin when he discovers that they are not alone. The three reach for their wands as the Lady of White appears from behind a suit of armor.

"Children, why do you wish to harm an old beggar woman?" she inquires of them.

"What do you want?" Oliver asks, lowering his wand.

"Ah, yes, indeed. The mission tonight for the portal," she replies, dancing around.

"How did you know?" Ethan inquires.

"She is a seer," Bethany and Sebastian state at the same time, wands in hand as they walk up.

"Witch, your powers against them will not work," Zander states, appearing next to Ethan and Rose.

"Ah, the young heartfelt prince trying to protect his loved one," she remarks.

"Give up! You won't be able to protect everyone. You failed with the other one and will surely fail again. Anyway, heed my warnings," she sneers.

"Silence!" roars Oliver.

"Disgusting! You roar like a lion. Clearly, you have been around that cat for too long. I will not be silent! I swore to your parents to protect you," she snaps.

"Protect us?" Rose replies, laughing.

Furious, Oliver's eyes glow red. He spins his wand, and sparks shoot out as the guards of the castle come running. Before anyone can respond, Oliver and the Lady of White become entwined in a magical duel. Ethan joins in as his eyes turn white. He raises his hand, and the spirit of the Lady of White starts to leave her body.

"Roslyn, she is here to help. Stop this madness!" a voice commands in her head.

Rose looks down and back up as her eyes go solid gray, and she levitates into the air. With one quick movement of her hand, her brothers and the Lady of White fly backward.

"Enough is enough," Rose says, lowering back down to the ground. Rose walks toward the Lady of White and holds out her hand.

"If you say you are here to help, then show me what you came to warn us about," Rose commands.

With that, Rose pulls her brothers and Zander with her into the vision.

"The portal is under attack from the other side. You must not go through. If you do, you will die," Sebastian shouts as Kai, the Shade Dragon, begins climbing through.

"Run to the edge of the forest! The magical barrier of Avalon is there. It will protect you, go," Bethany calls as Kai snaps and swallows her whole.

"Stop!" Rose shouts, holding up her hand. The image freezes. Rose walks around the scene, studying it.

"This image is incomplete and damaged. Therefore, I do not believe it," she finally says, waving her hand to dismiss the vision.

With that, the image spins and the four find themselves on their backs in the great hall with the Lady of White choking on the other side of the hall.

"What did you do? How can this be? What magic is this?" she demands.

"A magic far more powerful than you think," Rose states brushing herself off as she stands up.

"To date, no wizard or witch has ever been able to do that. Stopping a vision like that is impossible!" The Lady of White declares as her cloaked head tilts to the left.

"What is that?" Rose inquires, peering at the same spot in air that the Lady of White is also staring at.

"Odd," the Lady of White notes, walking around the letter that appears to be floating in midair, sticking out of a crack.

On the front of the envelope are the names "Oliver, Ethan and Rose." Grabbing the letter, Rose begins to read.

My dearest Oliver, Ethan, & Rose,

You have created a rift in time. You have used magic in an extraordinarily powerful way and in doing so, you destroyed all reality and created an echo in time.

Only three powerful users of magic can achieve such a feat. Given that, it is time to share a prophecy with the three of you.

The prophecies foretold of three who would bring balance back to the magic of all worlds. Be careful not to overextend your magic. There will still be much to learn over time. A rift in time is a sign of true power and could restore the balance. Good luck and go forth, my children.

~Your mother~

Rose turns the letter over, scrutinizes it again, then hands it to Ethan. Oliver and Zander read the contents of the letter over Ethan's shoulder.

"A rift in time?" Ethan inquires.

"Huh, you may have created a rift in time, but you will need to be cautious when entering through the portal. I bring warnings of Morgana's intent to attack the portal. Heed them, or not," the Lady of White whispers as she snaps her fingers and disappears.

"I am beginning to hate her," Oliver says.

"As did your parents," Destiny remarks, seizing the letter out of Ethan's hand and examining it.

"Ha! A time rift. That is original. That is magic that many of us have not mastered or tried to master. It is next to impossible," she says, handing the letter back to them.

"What is it exactly?" Ethan inquires.

"A rift in time or an echo of time occurs when the very fabric of time alters in some sense. It echoes the past, present, and future all at once. It will restore the altered fabric of time in that minute," Zander explains.

"I think we should head for breakfast, don't you?" Rose inquires.

The brothers look at each other, nod, and walk toward the dining room for breakfast, where they each sit quietly eating until they are interrupted by King Arthur.

"Uh hum, My Lords and Lady, may I have a word privately with you three?" Arthur inquires and the three siblings follow Arthur.

"I am the oldest friend of your family and as such, I was entrusted with this…. chest," he says, carefully watching them.

"I do not know what the contents of it are, but I was told to keep it safe. It is now yours," Arthur notes, placing his hand on the lid.

"Thank you, King Arthur," Oliver replies, extending his hand. Ethan and Rose follow, shaking Arthur's hand. The two boys pick up the chest and carry it back to the hall. Zander immediately gets up from his seat and moves towards them as he recognizes the chest. Suddenly, he is hurled backwards.

"Odd," Bethany remarks. Moving slowly towards the chest but she too is thrown backwards.

"Well, it appears to have a magical field protecting it," Zander says, rubbing his elbow.

Rose and Oliver look at each other, point their wands at the chest, and command it to open. The chest flies open, and a letter appears on the top with the words,

Oliver, Ethan, & Rose.

Oliver snatches up the letter and reads it with Ethan and Rose looking on.

Oliver, Ethan, & Rose,

Do you think we would let you walk through the main portal and draw attention or an attack from Morgana? Absolutely NOT! Instead, what you have before you is an instrument of great magical power. A powerful relic of an ancient time, it is a safe passage portal. Upon your return, the kingdom will be in danger.

This chest you have been given is "Hope," a safe passage to the Valley of Time and when traveling you cannot be detected by Morgana. Furthermore, this also allows the portals' magic to be restored but will keep them locked so Morgana cannot unleash her fury on the Mundane Realm.

Upon your arrival in the Valley of Time, you must find the High Council of Magic, led by old friends Lady Divinity and Lord Leo. They will help you to secure passage to the palace where you can hopefully re-establish reign over the kingdom and restore all magical balance.

Only you three can restore the symbolic balance of magic and freedom to our people. Morgana wants a perfect nation of perfect witches and wizards, in her words, of 'True Magical Arcane Blood.' Magic cannot be of just all magical ancestry; more and more individuals are born with magical gifts that have no magical lineage. Our family, unlike Morgana, has ruled to include everyone.

The chest will open at the stroke of midnight; all wishing to travel with you must be in the vicinity of the chest. Be aware, if "Hope" senses danger she will not work. Upon your return, please stay strong, help our people, guide the Council, and remember your father and I are always with you. Good luck and be safe.

~Your Mother~

When they finish reading, they hand the letter to Zander who reads it over, Bethany and Sebastian looking over his shoulder.

Finally, Zander closes the letter and speaks.

"If this is 'Hope,' then you have one of the most powerful magical portals. The Valley of Time is where everyone has taken refuge, I assume?"

"Yes. It is home. When the palace and all of the inhabitants froze, the kingdom fell into darkness. The Valley is the only place of light besides the Valley Sheldon," Bethany replies. "The valley has become the way of life, the way of magic, the way of existence. Morgana and her troops control the kingdom. There, our people have to listen to her, obey her rules and orders, or she kills," Bethany continues.

"The Valley is hidden and hated by my father. He wants it gone. It is the last sign of resistance against Morgana," Sebastian explains.

"The Valley, is it magical?" Rose inquires.

"Indeed. Both of the valleys in the Arcane Realm are," Bethany replies.

"The first, the Valley of Time, is the crossroads where time meets the Arcane and Mundane realms. In the Valley Sheldon, time does not exist there. Everything stands still," Sebastian states.

"Also, one of the elder libraries exists within the valley. The other elder library is in the Valley Sheldon, which is the elves' stronghold. It also holds many hidden secrets of the kingdom," Zander explains.

"What is Valley Sheldon?" Oliver inquires.

"Another magical place. It does not exist in the Arcane or Mundane realms. It is the home of the elves and holds many secrets, some of which we still do not know," Sebastian remarks.

"Children, I do not mean to interrupt, but it is ten now. What do you want to do today?" Destiny asks.

"We shall stay here close to the chest. We can find things to do throughout the day," Ethan and Oliver respond, using their unison twin voice.

"My friends, when we arrive home, I must leave for Valley Sheldon. My brother, Marcus, was left in charge and I need to make sure my people are okay," Zander states. "But I am not far away. This horn, the horn of Sheldon, can call me back whenever needed," he continues, handing the horn to Oliver.

"Can I go with you?" Rose inquires.

"No. You will be needed among your people, as I will be needed among mine," Zander declares, kissing Rose on the cheek.

"If I am your future wife then the elves and humans are both my people," Rose replies, kissing him on the cheek.

Zander looks at her, smiles, and hugs her.

"Bethany?" Zander calls.

"Yes."

"Is the elder library still equipped in the Valley of Time?" he inquires.

"It is. What do you seek? The door is sealed." she responds.

"Rose, when you arrive in the Valley, go to Lady Divinity, Sebastian's mother, and inform her that you seek the elder scrolls of time. Go to the library, place this missing piece of wood in the door, and the doors will open. Once inside, begin learning all that you can of time rifts and whatever else you can about altered magical time if you want to help our people," he instructs.

"I understand," Rose replies, wrapping the piece of wood in purple cloth and stowing it in her bag.

That day, the hours rolled by slowly with Oliver and Zander playing chess, Ethan continuing to rummage through his bag trying to organize things, and Rose sitting, reading, and learning about their realm.

A loud pop rings out in the hall as Hawke and Dawn arrive. Rose is the first on her feet to hug them.

"You all made it," Dawn says smiling at them.

"Yes, and I see we have the Lord Alezander in our presence," Hawke notes.

"Hello, Lord Hawke and Lady Dawn," Zander greets them without looking up from the chess board.

Quietly, the rest of the room goes about their business as Dawn speaks with Destiny. Hawke walks around the room, studying everything until he notices the chest.

"What is this?" he inquires.

"Our way home, Sir," Bethany explains, looking up from her conversation with Leaf.

As Hawke walks around the room, Rose sits back pretending to read her book, observing his motions and behaviors from over the top of her book. Dawn and Destiny rejoin the group five minutes later and settle in. Throughout the day, Hawke, Dawn, and Destiny watch over the hall, each taking turns patrolling the space.

At the stroke of five, the castle staff comes to notify the group that dinner is ready, and Dawn walks to the middle of the room, spins her hands, and the dinner appears on a large table in the middle of the room.

While the group is eating, they are laughing and having a good time until a loud crash comes from the hallway. Hawke, Zander, and Oliver are the first on their feet when two guards fly into the room and a cloaked figure walks through the door, wand drawn, and pointed directly at them.

"Where is it?" the figure demands when Hawke and Alezander both disappear from their spots and reappear one on either side of the figure.

"Stand down," Alezander demands, while Hawke reaches for the figure's wand. The figure steps back, raises their hands, and immediately disappears. Seconds later, the figure reappears, this time, on the other side of the room, staring at the chest.

"I wouldn't, if I were you," Rose says, wand in hand as time freezes around her. Rose sits on the lid of the chest as the figure backs up. The figure raises their hand as they notice that it is literally freezing, ice appearing.

"Now, tell me who you are, and I will drop the enchantment and you can go on your way," Rose says, holding her wand in front of her, smiling.

The figure lets out a laugh that would send chills down anyone's spine and snaps their fingers as time unfreezes.

Oliver and Ethan appear next to Rose.

"Wait! Where did they go?" the two inquired in unison.

"Gone. Whoever they were, they can control time," Rose notes, casting a protection lightshield around the chest.

The group looks around the room to make sure it is secure.

"King Arthur, are the guards okay?" Alezander inquires.

"For now, they are in the infirmary being cared for," Arthur responds.

"Alezander, whoever they were, they sure know the way of magic. They slipped past the guards, froze several on the spot, distorted spaces, and knew what they were looking for," Destiny remarks as she approaches.

"Ideas?" Arthur asks Alezander.

"Several. But one more far-fetched then the next," Alezander says, looking around the space. "Arthur, thank you again for your hospitality, but I am going to seal the room to make sure it is secure for traveling."

Alezander places his hand on the King's shoulder.

"Good luck, my friend, and do come to visit," King Arthur remarks as he turns and walks toward the doors. Once he exits and the doors close behind him, Alezander closes his eyes, opens them as they begin to glow green, and, with a wave of his hand, causes walls of light to explode around the room, encasing the group.

"Uh hum," Leaf clears his throat. "My Lords and Ladies, it is 11:50 pm. Shall we prepare for the portal to open?"

"Yes," the three siblings reply as one. The group cleans up and everyone moves around the chest with their gear in hand. At the stroke of midnight, the chest lid flies open, and a whirlwind of sand, smoke, and fog fills the room. Within seconds no one can see. Rose and Ethan are the first to land, feet first, on what appears to be some sort of ancient stone circle.

The fog is too thick to see through. So, Rose spins her wand above her head. As the fog disappears and, as more members of their party arrive, lights emerge around them.

The valley begins to light up as more and more people appear. Oliver is the last through the portal, carrying "Hope" on his shoulder. When the portal closes, lightning strikes the circle in various spots around them, and a roar explodes over the valley. Leaf stands at the edge of the circle in his lion form, roaring to summon the Council.

"We made it," Ethan says, looking around in amazement.

"You made it and welcome," Lord Leo says, approaching the party. "Father," Leaf bows as he transfers back into human form.

"Human! You took the form of a human? Bah. I would have been okay with a rabbit, heck even a turtle, but a human!?" Leo snaps at Leaf.

"Sorry, Father." Leaf snaps his fingers and transforms back into a lion.

Looking displeased with his son, Leo turns his attention to the others.

"Welcome. Your arrival has been expected for some time. I am Lord Leo."

"My son," Lady Divinity runs forward, arms stretched out to hug Sebastian. "I see that you succeeded. I am proud of you," she says as she gazes at him.

"My friends, Lords and Ladies, welcome home," Divinity proclaims bowing toward them.

"Thank you, Divinity," Lady Dawn replies, bowing back.

"Children, these two are your parents' oldest friends, Lady Divinity and Lord Leo," Destiny advises as Dawn and Divinity lead the group out of the circle and down the steps toward the village.

"Lady Divinity, Lord Leo, I do not mean to trouble you, but may I borrow one of your horses? I wish to go to the Valley Sheldon to check on my people," Zander requests, walking quickly to keep up with the group.

"Oh, dear. Zander, I am sorry and afraid to inform you, the darkness has destroyed the elf village of the Valley Sheldon," Lady Divinity replies, a tear running down her face.

"Your brother fought alongside the armies of elves, animals, and dwarves but, unfortunately, they fell. Morgana was much too strong for the forces of the Elfen Army. She knew their every move. I am truly sorry." Divinity places a hand on Zander's shoulder. Zander pulls away to keep from showing any emotion. Rose moves to place a hand on his shoulder in order to comfort him, but he pulls away from her and departs from the group.

"Give him time," Divinity advises Rose.

"Here we are. Sleeping quarters for all of you," Lord Leo announces.

"The boys will be on the left and the girls on the right," Divinity says. "We are sorry that they are not better, but these are the best accommodations that we have."

"It is fine and thank you, Lady Divinity," Rose replies, watching her brothers.

The group settles in for the night in their respective quarters, cottages carved into the side of the valley mountain. Rose re-emerges from her quarters carrying a blanket and walks toward the river where Zander is skipping stones.

"I brought you a blanket to keep you warm," Rose remarks, setting it on top of a large stone.

"Thank you but I'm not cold. I grew up in the Arcane realm. So, I am used to the weather. But thank you anyway," Zander says, continuing to skip stones across the water.

Suddenly, one of the stones bounces back onto the riverbank.

"What?" he and Rose exclaim as a female form emerges from the water.

"Can it be? Oh yes. It most certainly is! Is it true, Lady Nadia, that you have returned?" the female asks as Rose points at herself questioningly.

Then the female laughs and nods, "Yes, you. Aren't you Nadia? If not, then, you must be an enemy spy of Morgana's. Help! Intruder! Someone stop her!" the figure cries, summoning magic to her, ready to attack.

"Lady of the Lake, this is Ros…," Lady Divinity begins to say.

The Lady lowers her magic and blurts, "Princess Roslynn! Can it be? My Lady, welcome," she proclaims.

"Princess?" Rose asks, staring at Lady Divinity, Zander, and the Lady of the Lake.

"She doesn't know? How does she not know?" the Lady of the Lake demands.

"My Lady, she is not used to being called that," Zander explains.

"Lady Rose, we did not realize you were not used to being called Princess. We will talk about it more later…" Lady Divinity begins when the Lady of the Lake interrupts.

"Child, come here. Let me see you. You have Merlin's eyes, Nimuway's nose, and your mother's beauty. Oh yes, indeed, you are Roslynn. I was there when you were baptized. I am here because I heard crying," she announces, looking cautiously at Zander.

"My Lady, it is nothing," he remarks, looking very unhappy.

"Is that the Lady of the Lake?" Ethan asks, walking down the path with Oliver in tow.

"Oh my! Here comes the strapping, young, twin princes," she exclaims.

Rose glances at her brothers as they shrug and smile.

"Ahh, now, this is perfect. The three children of Kelvin and Nadia are here. I have news for all of you," she remarks.

"Morgana's forces move throughout the kingdom, rounding up all she can. She is demanding answers. Her roundups have caused several rifts in time, but one was very odd. It was a surge of energy, then it stopped. No one seems to be able to pinpoint the rift. Several of my sources are looking into it. Also, word comes through the trees that there are three girls by the names of Olivia, Claire, and Brooke, who are being held at the castle of Aden. Lastly, your parents have heard of your arrival," she states, smiling.

"But how ….?" Rose begins to ask.

"My Lady, the way of magic is powerful," she explains, winking.

"Now, before I leave, here is a map of the castle and the valley. Oh, and Rose, darling, can I suggest keeping those two dashing brothers of yours away from Avalon. The nymphs will go wild for them," she laughs, waving and disappearing into the water.

As she disappears, her arm extends from the water, proffering a letter.

"Let me guess. For us?" Oliver remarks, pulling his wand and summoning the letter across the water.

"Yup," Ethan replies as they look at the letter, which is addressed to the Lady Rose and Lords Oliver and Ethan.

Oliver, Ethan, & Rose,

We see your journey has begun. Your father and I love you. Be safe and strong. You will find that many things in the kingdom occur because of the ways of magic. I want the three of you to know that you are here because of the ways of magic. Now to business. Rose, please retrieve your spell book and turn to the chapter about family journeys. Until now, the chapter has been blank. I want the three of you to hold hands, stand around the book, and repeat the spell.

Tempus transmittere per viam magia

Let your journey begin. Good luck,

~Your Mother~

The three look at each other, join hands, stand around the book, and speak the spell:

Tempus transmittere per viam magia.

Tempus transmittere per viam magia.

Tempus transmittere per viam magia.

Forward through time by way of magic.

As they finish the spell, they find themselves in the spinning vortex of time travel. Holding tight, they know not where they will arrive.

Chapter 10
Many Truths

When the three arrive at their location, they recognize it from other visions as the palace that was frozen in time. However, this time is from before it became a barren wasteland. The palace is bustling with activity. The siblings separate, looking around when Ethan overhears a conversation.

"My Lord, we must hurry! The coronation of the King and Queen is about to begin," the man remarks as he chases after Merlin.

"Oliver, Rose, look! It's Merlin," Ethan says, pointing straight ahead.

"Has anyone seen Nimuway?" Merlin snaps, running about the grounds. Merlin darts up the old spiral staircase, calling for Nimuway. The three follow to see what is occurring.

"Rose, is there any way to slow him down?" Oliver asks as they chase after Merlin.

"This is crazy! Merlin is running around like a fool."

Ethan stops and crosses his arms as he leans against the banister of the balcony.

"Let me know when he's done," Ethan laughs.

"You're ridiculous! You know that?" Rose grabs Ethan by the ear and drags him down the hall.

"Nimuway, you must hurry! We will be late," Merlin calls, knocking on the door.

"I am here, Merlin, my love," she says, emerging in a purple and white gown with a long fabric train.

"You look beautiful," Merlin exclaims, kissing her as a baby can be heard crying.

"Oh my!" Nimuway runs back into the room and picks up the crying baby from his crib.

"If life could only be simple for him, but today will mark the beginning of a new era for us," she remarks, regarding her husband.

"We can finally live and raise our son without people fearing his magical ability," Merlin says, smiling at his wife as they walk down the long hallway.

Ethan extends his hand and, in the fashion of his sister, freezes the image.

"Hey, that is my job, Ethan," Rose says, laughing.

"Ha ha! Funny, Rose. Anyway, they left the Mundane realm because people feared them?" he inquires, his eyebrow raised.

"I see nothing has changed. We still have to hide our magic today," Oliver remarks.

"Are you okay, Rose?" Ethan asks, nudging his sister.

"Yes. Just thinking," she replies.

"Shall we continue?" Oliver inquires, looking back and forth between Ethan and Rose.

Rose nods and waves her hand, unfreezing the vision. Nimuway hands the baby to Merlin.

"Go ahead, dear, I forgot my bag. I will be right there."

As Merlin leaves, Nimuway looks around, walks toward the mirror, and taps it with her finger, causing a ripple. She pulls a bag from her drawer as an arm extends from the mirror. The three siblings notice that no one appears in the mirror, not even a reflection of Nimuway.

"What type of magic is that?" Oliver asks.

"I have never read anything about it," Rose remarks, freezing the vision and walking up to the mirror to examine it.

"What do you think?" she inquires of her brothers.

"The only thing I can come up with is… time?" Ethan suggests.

"You might be right, Ethan. Rose, do we know anything about Nimuway controlling time?" Oliver inquires.

"Nothing," Rose states, unfreezing the vision.

Upon the bag reaching the mysterious hand, it is pulled into the mirror and disappears. Nimuway taps the mirror again, and it returns to normal.

Nimuway turns and walks toward the door as the three siblings follow their great grandmother down the hall to a grand courtyard. They separate to look around when they notice many villagers filing into the courtyard. Rose stops and starts laughing as she watches Ethan step around people while Oliver walks right through them. She thinks to herself how awkward this would be if it was real life. Rose stops and notices a young boy holding the hand of a familiar figure. Morgana. *But how?* Rose thinks to herself, noticing a baby in the carrier on Morgana's side.

"She has children! She has children!" Rose screams as Ethan and Oliver come running.

"Is that Mor….?" Oliver begins.

Rose shouts, "Yes!"

"The texts never said anything about this," Rose looks puzzled. Before they can continue, a loud bang is heard from the gazebo. A much younger-looking Divinity walks across the gazebo with the Witches Three. Lord Leo also appears.

"My friends, the time has come to announce our great leaders, Merlin and his wife Nimuway, our King and Queen of the Land," say the Witches Three, holding a crown in the air over Merlin's head.

"Our leaders sought refuge for all of us and helped to create this Arcane realm, where we can live without judgment, fear, or persecution. Here we can start families, practice our craft, and live together in great harmony. So shall it be. We, the Witches Three, hereby crown you, Merlin, King, and you, Nimuway, Queen, of our realm. May the harvest moon bless us and yield a great harvest," intone the Witches Three.

When the Witches Three finish speaking, another loud bang rings out as dark knights and gruesome-looking dark creatures emerge from the ground. The palace guards race to the site only to be thrown backward as Morgana spins her hands, laughing. With an ear-piercing shriek, more dark creatures arrive. Merlin moves against her and finds himself in battle.

"That crown should and will be mine," Morgana screams.

"You have no power here, Sorceress. This is not your kingdom," Merlin cries.

"If you won't give me the crown then maybe your child will upon his 18th year," Morgana states, laughing as she throws Merlin out of the way and going after the baby prince. Members of the Council appear quickly, summoning ropes and vines from their wands, wrapping them around Morgana to hold her back. The witch closes her eyes and, when she opens them, they are glowing red. She wraps her arms tightly in the ropes and pulls on them, slamming the members of the Council together. Then, she throws them out of the way. Standing only feet from the Prince, Nimuway, with one quick movement, steps between Morgana and the baby prince. Spinning her hands, Nimuway casts a hex against Morgana.

Protegere parce, precor, et congelo,

Protegere parce, precor, et congelo,

Protegere parce, precor, et congelo.

Protect by your mercy, I pray, and freeze.

The hex freezes Morgana instantly. Merlin, with the help of members of the Council, opens a portal and sends Morgana's frozen body through. When the last part of her body clears the edge of the portal, members of the Council seal it, while the youngest witch of the Witches Three and other members of the Council tend to the crying children of Morgana.

Merlin picks up his crown and speaks to the audience.

"Any act of witchcraft that is used to harm the crown or my people will be seen as an act of war and will be dealt with as such."

The audience breaks into applauds and praises the King for his actions.

"My King, what is to become of the children?" The young witch asks holding the baby tightly.

"Divinity, send them to live with their father. It will be best and, this way, they will not turn to evil," Merlin declares displeased with being bothered with such a question.

"My Lord…." is all they hear as the vision disappears and the room begins to spin again. Rose, Oliver, and Ethan know what this means, and they move quickly toward one another, join hands, and wait for the fog to lift.

When they find themselves standing in another village, they begin to look around. Screams erupt all around them as fire hits the ground. A dark dragon, Bormism, the Sage Dragon, emerges and begins wreaking havoc on the kingdom. Belinda and Drago, along with Merlin, Nimuway, and a young man, appear. The three watch as a great battle between man and beast commences. Bormism, the Sage Dragon, falls, and Merlin immediately declares that all unfriendly beasts will be destroyed.

"Stop," Rose commands as she approaches the young man and waves her hand over him speaking,

Omne sublime per potentias magicas

regelo iuvenem.

By the powers of all high magic,
unfreeze the young man.

The young man falls off his frozen horse and begins throwing light orbs at Rose.

"Calm down. I mean you no harm." As Rose deflects the orbs, the young man shouts, "Morgana…"

"No! I am from the future. I am Rose. These are my brothers, Oliver and Ethan," Rose explains as her brothers hold out their wands in front of them, ready to strike.

"Who are you? Rose asks.

"Clearly, you are a stupid girl. What? In your time, do you not have history books?" the young man inquires, glaring at the three of them. "Clearly, you have no fashion sense either," he remarks, wrinkling his nose at them in disgust.

"I am sorry if our clothes look different, but we could say the same about you! And, to answer your question, yes, we have history books, but I am just confirming you are the one about whom the books speak," Rose replies, smiling.

"Well then, dumb girl, I am Titus, the crown prince of this land," he starts to say, puffing up his chest, when Rose chants,

Rigescunt Indutae.

Refreeze Titus.

"Charming, isn't he? And that is our grandfather?" Oliver remarks, shaking his head.

"Did he get his manners from Merlin?" Ethan inquires, also shaking his head.

"Really, you two!" Rose says, pushing past them and waving her hand as she casts the reversal spell.

Nunc revertetur.

et restituere ordinem statera, et ita fieri.

What was once done now return order and restore balance,
let him remember none of this. So shall it be.

The image unfreezes and Titus is seated again on his horse and the vision continues as if nothing has happened.

"My son, when you are king, you must rule with a firm hand, or monsters like that one will destroy everything we have worked for…."

Rose holds out her hands as Oliver and Ethan grab hold and the three jump through time again. Now, standing back-to-back, they look around, trying to see through the cyclone of dust and fog. Within seconds, they have arrived back at the lake with Rose's book lying on the ground. Divinity is the first to speak.

"Do I dare ask what that was about?" she starts to say.

"We do not speak of them," Rose responds, picking up the book and brushing it off. "We do have a few questions though?"

"Yes?" Divinity says as she sits down on a boulder.

"Was Morgana once good?" Ethan and Rose inquire in unison, exchanging glances with each other and laughing.

"That is difficult to answer. But the simple answer is "yes and no," Zander replies.

In the beginning, Morgana was good and learned magic from the High Arcane Council of Light: but later, she found the ways of the dark arts and thought it would be the answer to everything. When Merlin found out, he destroyed everything of hers.

In anger, she vowed to destroy him and everything near and dear to him. What he did not realize was that the life force of her magic was the Book of Souls. There are two copies: one Merlin destroyed in his attempt to stop her, the other she had protected. You see, the book she saved is believed to be one of the most powerful, the source of her dark magic. Many believe if the book is destroyed, she will be restored to good."

"Creepy," Ethan declares, looking disgusted.

"And what about the children? Are they a threat?" Oliver inquires.

"The children are not a threat. They have not been seen or heard from in years," Divinity replies, looking at Zander for help to answer the question. Just then, one of the members of the Council interrupts.

"My Lady Divinity, Lord Leo is requesting everyone's presence at the Council circle immediately. It is urgent," a witch from the Council explains.

"My Lord Leo, it was horrible! They are in league with the vampires, centaurs, and trolls. Our troops do not stand a chance," a soldier exclaims, blood running down his forehead.

"Vampires, trolls, and centaurs? Tell me, soldier, what happened?" Rose asks as she approaches the soldier, who steps back.

"May I see your hand?" she asks.

"Who is she, and what magic is this?" the soldier demands.

"The one who could save this kingdom. I am the Lady Roslynn. Your hand. May I see it? I am a gifted seer, and it is my way of seeing what has happened," she explains.

Ethan and Oliver know what to do next and grab her shoulders as they disappear on the spot, leaving the soldier standing frozen and looking confused.

❧

"Rose, can you see anything?" Ethan asks.

"No, I have never been in this much darkness before," she replies. "But look."

A small flicker of light appears in the distance, then another, and another. The three run toward the lights to discover a village being attacked, the guards of light trying to defend it.

"*There are too many*!" one guard shouts.

"The screams are unbearable, watch o...." the guard yells, falling as vampires bite and draw their blood. Centaurs and trolls lay waste to the village while Raven walks over the dead bodies laughing. Suddenly, a blonde-haired woman appears, throwing the creatures back and dropping Raven to the ground. The woman spins around, throwing the darkness back. Liam strikes her with his magic, causing her to fall as the young wizard laughs.

"So much for that witch."

Then, he begins to walk away when, suddenly, he finds himself flying across the ground and striking the side of the building. He falls to the ground unconscious. The witch rises to her feet and attacks the darkness, destroying many in her path as she collapses to one knee before disappearing. The three continue watching until their attention is drawn to a voice that they recognize, calling to them.

"Rose, if you can hear me, the soldier's life force is fading."

It is Zanders' voice in the distance. With that, Rose collects her brothers and returns from the vision to find that the soldier has collapsed.

❧

While Rose, Oliver, and Ethan, continue to hold hands, they restore the soldier's life force.

"Get him to the hospital and let him rest," Oliver says.

"Horses. We need horses," Ethan exclaims.

"Why, My Lord?" inquires one member of the Council.

"We wish to see this village," Ethan replies, looking sternly at the Council member.

"But My Lords and Lady, it is too dangerous," another Council member responds.

"We are the children of light and of the King and Queen, which means we are in charge until our parents are found. Therefore, we must help our people," Oliver states sternly.

"If you insist on riding out, I am coming with you," Leo declares.

"So am I," echoes Divinity.

Oliver and Ethan quickly leave the platform circle and head down the stairs. Rose taps her staff against the ground and regal-looking armor appears on her and her brothers.

"Autumn, take to the air," Zander commands.

With Oliver in the lead, the party rides out. Rose and Ethan immediately behind Oliver, followed by the other five. Members of the Royal Light Guard ride out behind them.

Darkness engulfs the land, as if it was the dead of night. Rose raises her staff, clicks her teeth, and the horse takes off at a gallop as orbs of light launch into the air around the group, lighting the way, and creating a protective field of magic around them. In the distance, they can see the village burning and can smell smoke from where they are. Oliver breaks into a gallop, followed closely by the others. Upon approaching the village, they are met by a child.

"Help my parents," he cries as the screaming continues. Oliver and Ethan pull their swords while Rose flies into the air over her horse, lands on the ground, and sends the dark attacker flying with a blast of her magic. Spinning her staff, light encircles her and her siblings. When two dark creatures move to attack, she raises herself to the sky and unleashes rays of light. The darkness shrieks and tries to run as Ethan and Oliver illuminate their sword blades and further brighten the area. Leo runs toward the victims to check on them when a dark griffin rises from the ground and rears up at the great king. Rose continues to stand her ground, light flying around her and striking down the darkness. Suddenly, a silver spike flies past her and hits a vampire in the chest. Zander lowers his arm, striking a troll with his sword. The vampire drops to the ground as the rest of the team dismounts from their horses, Rose runs to Leo.

"Are they okay?" she inquires.

"No. They are dead, drained of their life force," Leo replies.

Walking up, Divinity considers the victims thoughtfully.

"This is weird. Vampires have been extinct for the past 50 years. Besides, this is unlike vampires. Why take the life force and not turn the person?" she remarks, puzzlement in her voice.

"I wondered the same thing about the people of the village," Zander says, reaching down and closing the eyes of one of the slain villagers. Rose gets up and, in one quick movement, captures an attacking vampire in midair. Gazing at him, she smiles, bows, and turns light on him, causing him to explode on the spot.

"You know, silver spikes are easier," Zander remarks, walking past her towards Sebastian, laughing.

"You do it your way. I'll do it mine," she responds.

"The village is completely destroyed," Sebastian says.

"Guys, I need some help," Bethany calls.

As Oliver, Ethan, and Zander run toward her they notice, that Bethany is holding a baby as more children begin appearing from under the houses. Rose and Sebastian approach, looking around cautiously.

"What? I do not understand," one of the guards says.

"It is not in the nature of centaurs to kill a child. Indeed, it is forbidden!" remarks Divinity. "Now, these children are all without families."

As the children continue to emerge from under the houses, Rose notices a woman lying on the ground. When she kneels beside the woman and turns her over, Zander pushes past everyone.

"Luna," Zander says.

"Alezander, is that you," Luna whispers, raising her hand.

"Luna, what happened? How?" Zander asks as he starts to mend her wounds. Luna turns her head as the group sees dark creatures emerge. Before anyone can respond, Luna raises her hand, and in one last act of protection, destroys the darkness. But her life force is weakened.

"Rose, you must stop her," Luna says faintly.

"How?" Rose asks, looking at the fallen witch.

"Her book. But there is also a second being. Find the one they call M…" Luna says as she fades and disappears. Everything but Luna's necklace of white gems disappears with her. Picking up the necklace and upon touching it, Rose knows exactly who she has to find. Putting the gems in her bag, she rises to her feet, and whistles for her horse.

"Who was she?" Ethan asks.

"A very old spirit who many believed could not die," Zander replies, holding in his hand some of the dirt from where Luna had laid. Getting to his feet, Zander and Rose start loading children onto the back of her horse. After a brief moment of watching them, Oliver, Ethan, and Sebastian followed their lead. The guards also follow.

"Children, I am the one they call Lady Rose. These are my brothers Lord Oliver and Lord Ethan, and our friends, Leo, Divinity, Sebastian, Bethany, and Zander. We are here to help and will take you to a safe place."

Rose stays close to the horses while the others quickly search the village. When members of the group emerge, they begin to walk with the horses and the surviving children. In the distance, they notice riders approaching. Rose pulls her wand from her bag and aims it directly at the riders. With one movement of her wand, a portal opens in the distance and as the riders ride into it, the portal disappears. Several of the riders slip past and start throwing dark magic towards the village when a young elfish girl with blonde hair appears. She turns toward them, smiles, and then, turning back raises her hands as light explodes everywhere. In one quick flash of light, she disappears, and the dark riders lay dead on the ground. Several guards ride out, following Leo, who examines the dark riders.

After examining the dead, Leo hurries to return to the group.

"Dead. All of them. No breath. Nothing. The spirit was completely released out of them. Whoever she was, she is powerful and hit them so hard with magic that their heads exploded."

At that, members of the Council start chatting quietly amongst themselves.

"Who is she?" Sebastian and Oliver inquire at the same time.

"I wondered the same thing," responds Divinity.

"An elf and very powerful?" Rose remarks, looking at Zander for answers.

"You look to me for answers. But I am as confused as you. I have never seen her before. She may be a lone remaining elf," Zander says, looking back at Rose and the rest of the group.

Cautiously, the group approaches the area. Zander reaches down to look at the fallen dark guards.

"Whoever she was, Leo is right. She knew the freedom spell," Zander notes.

"What is a freedom spell?" asks Ethan.

"A spell that releases the spirit of the fallen darken creature. She freed them from this life of enslavement," Zander explains, moving one of the dead bodies with his boot before motioning for the group that it is time to move on.

Once the area is safe, Rose, grabs the reins of her horse and sets off for the valley. The others follow, knowing that the young queen has spoken and not to question her.

Zander walks along at Rose's side, holding tight to the reins of his horse. Throughout the journey back to the valley, many of the children cry, not understanding what is going on. Walking quietly in the lead, Rose and Zander both scan the surroundings, feeling as if they are being watched, neither of them able to explain the feeling or saying anything about it to each other. When the group stops to water the horses, Rose hears a voice.

"You are not alone. Everything is about to change. Stay close to Lord Alezander and listen to your heart."

After watering the horses Ethan takes the reins of Bethany's horse as she walks carrying a small baby in her arms. In the distance, horses' hooves are heard. Autumn soars along the ground and as she rises into the air, Rose and others in the group see in the distance that, behind her, ride other members of the Council and guards, led by Destiny and Hawke.

From a distance, Destiny holds up her hand as orbs of light encircle the group. Then, the guards take off galloping ahead of her and racing toward the group.

"We will take it from here, Your Majesties," the guards state as they grab the reins from the party and take the horses and the children into the valley tunnels. No sooner do members of the Council take the remaining horses carrying the children, when screeches are heard echoing through the night sky. The party knows all too well that trouble is coming. Raven appears in front of them, and Kai, the Shade Dragon, lands behind them, Autumn places herself between Kai and the party while the others stand against Raven.

"Hahaha! Did you like my mistress' surprise? I am sure the looks on those children's faces were adorable," Raven sneers.

"By the way, the next village we attack, no one will..."

But before the witch could finish, Rose and Oliver cast charms, blasting Raven backward into a tree. Instantly, the wood turns to quicksand and starts to drag her in. Zander heads toward Raven, sword drawn, and telepathically attacks her as she begins screaming and crying in pain.

Kai, the Shade Dragon, continues his ruthless attack on Autumn but suddenly flies backward as a huge dragon with silver scales appears blowing a fire circle around the party and Autumn. Liam appears, breaks the tree's hold on Raven, and they both disappear with a pop.

Kai takes to the air as multiple dragons surround him, snapping, biting, and bellowing fire on him. Kai dives towards the party as the great silver dragon snorts and a large force field appears around the spot, protecting them all.

The three siblings notice that Autumn, Leo, Sebastian, Bethany, Divinity, and Zander are all bowing to the silver dragon. She walks past the group toward the three siblings, who also bow to her.

"You three are going to be a handful. I can tell. Or are you just insane?" the dragon remarks, gazing down at them.

"Wow! She can talk," Ethan says looking back at her.

"Yes, and so can my child."

"Mother!" Autumn snaps, landing beside her.

"I am the great Belinda, reigning queen dragon and you three are going to be my favorites," the dragon says, smiling.

"High King Oliver, King Ethan, and the Queen Roslynn, the children of Kelvin and Nadia, I shall walk you and your party back to the Valley of Time. I have to ask what you have learned from your adventures since you arrived?" she inquires.

"Not to trust or believe everything you see," Rose replies, looking directly into the eyes of the dragon.

"The unspoken truths of the kingdom these days stated beautifully. It is as if Nadia is here," Belinda replies, tapping the side of the mountain with her tail.

"This is where I depart, but before I leave, Oliver, do you see the bag hanging under my wing?" she asks.

"Yes, Lady Belinda," Oliver responds.

"Grab the bag and keep it close. Zander and Divinity will know how to use it to summon me, if needed. Good luck," she says, smiling and taking to the air as the party disappears into the tunnel of the great mountain leading to the valley.

Emerging from the tunnel, Zander, Oliver, Ethan, and Sebastian take to helping the children as Bethany heads down the path with the baby she is carrying, Rose stops for a moment, noticing the ghost of a hooded figure watching her. She whispers quietly to it so that the others cannot hear, "Who are you?"

The ghost points to the alcove, then disappears and reappears in the alcove. Quietly, Rose walks over and asks, "Again, I am going to ask who you are?"

"A friend from the past, present, and future. You and your loved ones must return to the birthplace of magic in order to save it. Magic is all around, but it slowly dies with each passing day. You and your brothers, along with help from your husband, must restore the magical balance. Many truths of this kingdom and the birthplace of magic shall be revealed. Now go. Be mindful of things around you and help restore peace," the ghost explains as it disappears.

Rose quietly looks around and nods, knowing what has to be done. She walks out of the alcove and heads up the path that leads to the Council circle, joining the rest of the group.

Chapter 11
The Kingdom in Turmoil

Dear Diary,

It has been a week since our arrival, and it is growing colder here. Winter has come. Although there is no snow yet, I am sure there is plenty back home. Oliver, Ethan, and I are in the libraries studying every minute we are allotted, trying to understand everything we can about Morgana. The children saved from the village are being taken care of by individuals throughout the valley, and many of the children are in tune with their magical side, and Divinity is beginning to train them in the ways of magic.

Ethan, Oliver, and I spend our downtime with Alezander working on our magic and spells. Each night, the raids get worse, and my brothers and I are no closer to figuring out how to help our people. Morgana is growing in power and Zander says it is because of her spell book. Grandma is close by, watching, and Destiny and Uncle Hawke keep close eyes on us. We have not seen the Lady Belinda since that night she appeared to provide a helping hand. The horn that she gave us does not work and won't sound.

I grow restless being here, I want to find my parents and help them. I know Mom and Dad are here. I can hear them more and more with every passing day. The ghost that appeared, I still have not told anyone about, and my studies confirmed that the Mundane realm is truly, indeed, where magic was born. Not here in the Arcane realm like many would have us believe.

Oh, how I miss the Mundane realm. But, if that is the birthplace of magic, then we will all be there sooner or later. The question is when and what do we need to do to save it? Then, there is the question of the witch Mora, the woman shown to me through the gems of Luna. No records or knowledge of her exist and no one speaks of her. When I ask Zander, he shares what little he knows. Divinity suggests that there have to be books on her in the library and the Council remains silent.

Our kingdom is in turmoil and I, the young queen, don't know what to do. I look to the stars for guidance, but they remain silent. The elves are gone. The trolls and centaurs run through the villages like they are nothing. The vampires, who somehow have returned, are stealing souls, and growing stronger with each passing day. My kingdom has very few guards. The dwarves are in hiding, leaving for the mountains of the Mundane realm to protect their gold and gems, and fairies are nowhere to be found.

Diary, I can get lost writing to you. I have no one who understands me. I believe that a restoration of the magical balance can help save us all. I have read the works of

Merlin, and I fear my brothers and I do not believe the same about magic as him. He believes that magic should be contained in the Arcane realm and no Mundane should ever interact with us. This, however, cripples the balance of magic and destroys both realms. No, my brothers and I, we believe differently than Merlin.

~Rose~

"Rose, you summoned for me

?" Destiny inquires, walking up the path to where Rose is sitting under the great oak tree at the far end of the valley.

"Destiny, I do not know who to turn to," Rose says.

"What's wrong, my dear child?" Destiny looks concerned.

"I need your help. I seek to know the truth about many things. I need to jump through time and find answers," Rose replies.

"Ah. I knew this day would come. You are ready. Yes, yes, yes! I will help you but first a gift. Hold out your hands in front of you," Destiny says, setting down her bag and pulling a beautiful broom from it.

"My child, if you are going to time travel, then you will need this," she announces.

"Destiny, it is beautiful. Thank you," Rose replies, grabbing hold of it as it rises off the ground.

"You are welcome. The broom can travel through time within seconds," Destiny explains.

"I am allowing you to do this but, Rose, look at me. Promise you won't tamper with time," Destiny remarks with a concerned look.

"I promise. I am just looking for answers," Rose replies.

"That is fine. Look for answers from a distance but do not tamper with time. Tampering with time will cause a chain reaction and destroy the very fabric of time itself," Destiny warns, watching Rose's reaction closely.

The two nod and with a flick of their wands open a portal.

Rose gets on the broom and takes off through the portal. Destiny reaches up, closes the portal, and winks.

"Good luck, child. May you find the answers you need. Nadia, my dear sister, hear me wherever you are. She is on her way. Your baby girl has set in motions the events to come. May the magic of all Arcane protect you, my dearest niece," with that, Destiny disappears on the spot.

✍

Rose blows through a portal in the sky and lands in a small village.

"Ouch! I need to learn how to land better. I am so glad no one was around to see that landing. It would have been embarrassing," Rose remarks to herself.

Stowing her broom, she starts walking down the path and into the village. At midmorning, the village is bustling with people. She walks past the different merchants looking at what is being sold. She stops to smell the fresh pastries at the bakery when the baker offers her a loaf of bread.

"Welcome! You must be new around here. This is the finest bread in all the villages," the baker notes with pride.

"Thank you, good sir," Rose states as she bows and continues to walk through the market until she notices a woman in the distance, who looks like someone she has seen in pictures many times before. Rose recognizes her as a younger version of her mother.

"Well, I will be! The spell worked," she remarks to herself.

Rose follows Nadia from a distance and discovers the home to which she has retreated. It is a beautiful old manor with vines growing up the side of the home. Three kids, walking by, mutter under their breath.

"There is the home of that crazy witch."

Rose notices a man coming up the road. Ducking behind the bushes, she watches as he approaches. Several members of the lightguard are with him. Rose watches as the guards create a protective formation outside the gates of the home and around the young man. The young man walks up the walkway toward the old manor and taps on the door three times with his wand.

"I come calling upon the beautiful Nadia," the young man calls out.

"My sister will be right down," the young girl replies.

"Thank you, Destiny. Please tell mama that I went out with Kelvin," she says, kissing her sister on the forehead and pulling a blanket around the shoulders of the young girl.

"It appears that Destiny has been keeping things from Oliver, Ethan, and I," Rose says quietly to herself as she continues to watch from a distance.

Kelvin and Nadia hug and then walk down the road, disappearing over the hill, the guards in tow. Rose quietly follows, hoping the guards will leave. To her surprise, they do. *Here is my chance* she thinks as she hurries behind them as they stroll through the countryside. As Rose catches up to them, she begins to speak. Nadia turns, wand pulled, and aimed right at Rose's face.

"Who sent you? Was it that horrid Mildred? The last girl who followed us got hexed. Your fate will be worse!" Nadia declares as Rose puts up her hands to show that she is unarmed and not a threat.

"Excuse me, Lord Kelvin. I am Rose. I come from Valley Sheldon. May I ask you a question?" she inquires, stepping back slowly as Nadia tightens her grip on her wand, which is still pointing directly at Rose.

"Nice to meet you, Rose. but I am not familiar with you, and I know everyone in the Valley. But, of course, you may ask a question. What is it that you would like to know?" Kelvin replies observing her closely, while Nadia keeps her distance, her hand firmly on her wand, ready to attack.

"Your family, they have a library in the Valley Sheldon. Is it at the river?" Rose inquires, looking him dead in the eyes.

"She is direct and brazen, isn't she?" Nadia states, lowering her wand and crossing her arms.

"What an interesting question. Well, yes, there is a library, there is a manor, and, yes, it is by the river. But it is hidden. Why do you ask?" he inquires, reaching into his cloak.

"Lord Kelvin, you do not need to pull your wand. I am a friend, not a foe. My inquiring about the library, well… you would never understand," she said.

"Really? Try me! I am much more open than my father. Whatever you have heard about me is not true. Besides, you are a stranger inquiring about my family's home, so I am curious now," he states, watching her closely for answers.

Rose opens her cloak, revealing the royal medallion from around her neck. Kelvin spins his wand in his hand then stows it back inside his cloak. Nadia looks first at Rose, then at Kelvin, seeking answers.

"I am not from the Valley, nor am I from the Arcane realm. I am a child of both realms. I am from the future," Rose states, tripping over her words.

"And you came here? Why?" Nadia inquired of Rose sternly.

"The kingdom is in danger. That library contains some of the oldest texts of magic, I seek it for answers they hold," Rose explains.

Nadia regards Rose curiously.

"Why not go to the library in your own time? Do you think coming back in time will help to save the kingdom? Time travel, no matter how noble the reason, is dangerous. Shame on you! Do your parents know? They should be ashamed for teaching you such forbidden magic," Nadia scolds at Rose.

"I understand that. I would not have come except that we have no choice. The library is hidden, and we do not know where to find it," she explains.

"We?" Kelvin asks, regarding her sharply.

"Me and my twin older brothers, Sir," Rose replies.

"May I inquire of your lineage, since you carry the medallion of Kelvin's family?" Nadia asks.

"To answer that could alter the very fabric of time," Rose remarks.

"But you think that coming here has not already altered the very essences of time?" Nadia inquires, pointing her wand at Rose, again.

"The houses…" Nadia demands.

Letting out a big sigh, Rose finishes "…. of Phoenix, Ignatius, and Drake."

Kelvin looks at Nadia. She lowers her wand. They smile at each other, shake their heads, and continuing to smile realize that it is safe to talk.

"You are one of ours?" Nadia asks, raising her eyebrow.

"Yes," Rose replies quietly.

"Then, if you are of the three houses of Phoenix, Ignatius, and Drake, I must be your mother," Nadia states.

"And I take it that I am your father?" Kelvin asks.

"Err, yes, Sir," Rose replies, shaking her head.

"But that is all I am prepared to say so as not to disrupt the timeline any more than I already have," Rose declares.

"We understand," Kelvin says. "Come with us," taking Nadia's and Rose's hands.

The area starts to spin, and the next thing Rose knows, she is standing in a rather large manor in Valley Sheldon.

"This is only accessible by three individuals in the family. They have to be of great power and knowledge. You must be who you say you are because the magic protecting this home would detour us from it if you were not," Kelvin states.

"In your time, are we not there to help you with this knowledge that you seek?" Nadia inquires.

"That I cannot answer," Rose replies, looking at her sternly.

As they approach the manor, Rose notices an old man at the door.

"My master Kelvin, and the Lady Nadia! To what do I owe this visit? Supper is not ready." exclaims the old man.

"Cedric, I am bringing a member of my family to the library so that she may do some research that will help her save the very fabric of time itself," Kelvin replies.

"She is no one I've ever seen before," Cedric states in his old raspy voice, placing his monocle over his right eye to examine Rose more closely.

Striding up to Rose, he grabs her hand, examining her further, his nose inches from her.

"She has Nadia's eyes, but smells... oh yes, of the bloodline of the House of Phoenix," Cedric remarks. "Please take no offense, Lady Nadia, but, yuck, the young lady also smells of the House of Drake," he notes.

"Cedric, she is from the future, and she needs our help, old friend," Kelvin explains.

"Sir, if your father knew you were here and that you brought an unknown witch to the home, he would flip his lid. Wait! You said from the future? A witch who time travels? Fascinating indeed. This has not been seen in years," the old Butler says.

"Cedric, I know that. The last one, no one speaks of, old friend. Please take her to the library and let her have access to what she needs, including the special collection," Kelvin says, winking at Rose.

"If you wish, Sir, I will do as you request," the old butler agrees.

"Rose, this is where we leave you. We have to return to the valley before people start to worry or the guards send out the legion to look for us. You are in good hands with Cedric," Kelvin says, hugging her.

"Good luck and be strong. You will find what you seek," Nadia also hugs Rose.

Unbeknownst to Rose, Nadia slides a letter into her back pocket.

"Oh, and young lady, time travel, no matter how noble the cause, is dangerous. Tampering can be dangerous," Nadia winks at Rose as she and Kelvin disappear on the spot.

"My Lady, I am Cedric. I have served the house of Phoenix for years and you are?" Cedric inquires.

"Oh! Where are my manners? I am Roslynn Sophia Nadia Phoenix. I will, eventually, be of the house of Ignatius," she states, smiling at him.

"Fascinating. The house of Phoenix and soon the House of Ignatius. It is a pleasure, My Lady. Would you care to follow me?" Cedric asks, glancing at her as they walk up the grand staircase of the home.

"Cedric, how long have you served the House of Phoenix?" Rose inquires.

"300 years now," Cedric replies.

"Merlin was a dear friend and entrusted me with the knowledge of his family. I know many of the secrets of the kingdom. After the destruction of my people, I sought refuge here," Cedric explains, turning to look directly at her.

"I see. Cedric, I come seeking answers. First, who are Morgana's children?" she inquires.

"Ahh. Morgana has three children: two sons, and a daughter. Merlin told me they were sent to live in the Dale of the Forest Glen. He said that the eldest boy is a bit freaky and can do magic that has never been seen before. The children reside with their father," Cedric explains as they walk along the long corridor.

"Names?" Rose asks.

"Who? The children? Unknown," he responds.

"Do you know what happened to the children and the Dale of the Forest Glen?" Rose asks.

"No. Just a rumor here or there but nothing solid," Cedric says, watching her closely.

"Okay. Then, another question. Who is Mora?" she inquires.

"Ahh yes. The Lady Mora, the daughter of the Council of the Light. She is said to be the opposite of Morgana," he replies.

His hand carrying the candlestick shakes.

"Opposites? Are they related?"

"Ah. One in the same. One solid light and the other solid darkness," he says, pointing his old finger toward the door.

"You see, Mora, when using her magic, created a separate version of herself in hopes of creating an even more powerful twin. However, Mora created a twin who bore darkness against her," Cedric states.

Entering the library behind Cedric, Rose looks around the beautiful room, filled with books and scrolls everywhere.

"Cedric, what you speak of is an impossible form of magic," Rose suggests.

"The ability to make one side light, and the other dark has never been explained. Many have spent years studying what happened. The only thing anyone ever concluded is that Mora altered time," Cedric remarks. "Uh hum. May I ask what that is sticking out of your pocket?" Cedric inquires as Rose walks by him, examining the library.

Rose reaches into her back pocket and pulls out the letter. It is her mother's handwriting. She opens the letter and begins to read.

Roslynn,

My dearest daughter, your coming here is a blessing. It is so wonderful to know that Kelvin and I will create such a beautifully gifted child. But that is not why I write. I write because if you are from the future, then you are more than likely in danger. Or have already experienced the danger head on.

I do not know the details of your time but if you live or have any actions with my mother, the Lady Dawn, she is one of the personal handmaidens to Morgana. She does not think that I know but, Rose, Morgana seeks to destroy everything and everyone. There is an ally, though.

Your father, Kelvin, would disagree with me telling you this, but find the one called the Lady of White. She will protect and get you and your brothers to safety. Do not underestimate the power of Dawn. She is powerful, dangerous, and, in time, will destroy you.

There is one other who can help. He is estranged from the kingdom. He is the last of Merlin's students. He is a gifted wizard, and his magic is far greater than any that has been seen. His name is Alezander, and he will help you.

Lastly, you must promise me, please promise me, you will protect my baby sister, your Aunt Destiny. Your powers are strong. If you can time travel, then you are one

of the greats. Trust no one, except those I named. Oh,
and dear Cedric. He is misunderstood but always loyal.

Your Future mother,
The Lady Nadia

Rose sits on a chair and sighs.

"What do I do?" she asks aloud.

"May I?" Cedric inquires, taking the letter and reading it.

"Ahh, dear, dear, dear! What to do indeed!" he sighs.

"Oh, yes," he says, pointing in the air as he shuffles toward the wardrobe. He pulls an old key from his pocket. His feeble hand shaking, he taps it over the lock of the door. It flies open and out steps the Lady of White. Rose stands up, looking at her, and starts to speak.

"Child, you do not have much time. The safest thing to do is to bring your brothers, Bethany, Sebastian, Leaf, Destiny, and Zander here. Well, to this manor, in your time. You are going to have a battle with Dawn. You have to be ready. Cedric is a friend. He is here to help," the Lady of White declares.

"But I still do not have the answers I need," Rose responds.

"All in due time, child. Come here and the answers will come to you," the Lady of White says.

"Quickly! We do not have much time. Cedric, the amulet," she demands.

Cedric pulls an old crystal amulet out of a box and hands it to Rose.

"Once you have everyone with you within the range of the amulet, it will know what to do and how to help. Hold tight to it. In the hands of your grandmother, or Morgana, it could cause havoc," Cedric says calmly, smiling at her.

"Rose, go! You do not have much time," the Lady of White opens a portal.

Hopping on her broom, Rose flies through the portal and lands at the Council circle. Landing, she catches two of the guards off guard.

"My apologies. I did not mean to alarm you," Rose remarks as she touches the amulet and finds it enhances her ability. She can see through items, can hear things in the distance, and can sense emotion.

Running from the circle, descending the staircase, she rushes past Leaf.

"Rose! Wait up! Why the hurry?" Leaf asks.

"Where are my brothers?" she demands.

"With your grandmother," he replies as Rose runs faster down the path, pulling her wand.

"Leaf, summon the guards! The Valley is in danger!" she shouts as she continues to run down the path. Upon Rose reaching the area of the Valley where her brothers are, the amulet lights. As Rose holds it in her hand, the amulet begins shooting lightning at Dawn and Hawke, while, at the same time, it encircles her brothers in a field of magic.

"That amulet. Where did you get it? Give it to me," Dawn screams as she pulls her wand.

Rose hears a voice say, "Hold tight to it. Do not give in!" while Dawn hurls dark lightning at her granddaughter.

"What the…?" Ethan exclaims looking at his grandmother.

"You bitch! Give me the amulet! Hawke get that necklace for mommy dearest," Dawn exclaims, her eyes turning black as she points her wand at Rose.

"By the fate of the virtues, you will not touch her," Destiny yells pointing her wand at the ground. As the ground begins to shake, Dawn is knocked off her feet. Hawke also falls backward as Zander steps in front of Rose to protect her. Bethany and Sebastian emerge along with Divinity. Dawn rises to her feet and levitates off the ground, her eyes now blood red and her hair standing up.

In a voice they don't recognize, Dawn screams, "You will give me that amulet. My mistress wants it, and she will destroy everything to get it."

As Hawke charges, Rose grabs the amulet and yells, "By the powers of the Houses of Phoenix, Drake, and the virtue of my parents, protect us!"

With that, a field of magic surrounds her and her remaining friends as she locks wands with her grandmother.

"Zander, do you know Cedric?" Rose asks peering over her shoulder.

"I do. Charming old chap," Zander rolls his eyes as he locks wands with Hawke.

"By the virtue of all that is good, take us home," Rose declares as lightning strikes the ground, throwing Dawn backward. Within seconds of the lightning hitting the ground, the magic fields holding Rose and her friends disappear.

Seconds later, Rose, Zander, Oliver, Ethan, Bethany, Leaf, Autumn, Sebastian, and Destiny arrive at the manor in the Valley Sheldon.

"Where are we?" Oliver asks scanning the old grounds of the looming estate.

"Phoenix Manor, home of our family in the Valley Sheldon," Rose explains stowing her wand and opening the gate and walking toward the front door.

"I will explain more once we are inside," she says, looking back at everyone. As they reach the doorstep, the door is flung open and an old, hunched, white-haired man comes shuffling out.

"May I help you?" he asks.

"Cedric, it is me, Rose," she says, holding out the necklace.

"The old man touches it as magic encircles him and returns him to a younger version of himself.

"Ahh, yes. Very well. I never thought you were going to come back," Cedric states, looking around at the others.

"I assume the magic of this amulet helps keep you young?" Rose comments. Cedric nods and moving out of the way allows everyone to enter.

"I was afraid you'd gotten lost in time. It has been nearly 25 years, My Lady. But now I understand to which period of time you belong," Cedric remarks, observing her.

"Well, I am here now," Rose replies, hugging him.

"Rose! Let him go," Zander shouts.

"You?" Cedric declares.

"Me!" Zander shouts in response.

"How dare you step foot in this home?"

"What is he talking about?" Oliver asks.

"Cedric and I have a history that goes way back," Zander explains.

"Enough," Destiny barks. "I am exhausted as I am sure the rest of you are. Whatever issue you two have with each other, put it aside. Can we be shown to our rooms, please?"

"Of course. But, first, introductions?" Cedric suggests. "You two, I know," Cedric says, pointing his finger at Zander and then, at Destiny.

"I am Bethany Minerva Phoenix, daughter of Wade," Bethany introduces herself.

"I am Sebastian Nolan Knight, son of Divinity," he replies.

"I am Leaf, son of Lucy and Leo," Leaf states.

"I am Ethan Ambrose Kenrick Phoenix, and this is my twin brother, Oliver Kelvin Cuinn Phoenix. We are the sons of Kelvin and Nadia."

"My Lords and Ladies, welcome. This home is a safe place. No one can touch you as long as you remain inside the fenced yard. If you pass through the gates, this house cannot protect you and may move locations to protect whoever is here," Cedric explains. "Do not give it a reason to leave you behind. Your parents would kill me."

"Now, the bedrooms are upstairs. But wait for the rules. Boys bunk with boys and girls bunk with girls. Master Merlin's rules. That means Bethany and Rose are together. Ms. Destiny my how you have grown! You shall have a room of your own. Oliver and Ethan will share one room, Sebastian and Leaf another. Zander gets his usual room. Now, upstairs everyone. Pick your rooms and I will prepare dinner," Cedric directs. "Zander, may I have a word with you?"

"But…" Zander starts to say but Cedric gives him a look that brooks no argument.

"What?" Zander asks.

"Do they know?" Cedric walks towards the kitchen.

"No, not yet. They are not ready," Zander replies.

"Fine. But I will be watching you," Cedric responds.

"The King and Queen trust me," Zander begins. But before he could finish, he is interrupted by Cedric.

"Your old room is upstairs. You might want the key to claim it," Cedric says throwing the key to Zander as he walks toward the pantry.

Rose meets Cedric in the kitchen and asks if he needs help. After being chased out of the kitchen, she settles at the large dining room table.

"Sis, last time I checked, I am still the eldest. Move over! You do not get the head of the table," Oliver remarks as he shoos her to a side chair.

"If you want to get technical, Oliver, Zander is actually the oldest," Rose replies, smiling.

"Children, take cover! Quickly! Behind the bookshelves and do not say anything," Cedric calls out.

"Cedric? Cedric?" a voice echoes.

Oliver and Rose are behind the bookshelves when Zander appears behind them.

"Quickly! With me and do not ask questions," he says, moving them along a small corridor.

"Where is everyone else?" Oliver asks.

"Safe," Zander replies.

"Cedric, what is that foul smell? Are you cooking? You are cooking!" a woman screams.

"Yes, my mistress," Cedric replies.

"For whom?" she demands, digging one of her nails into his chin. "Boys, tear the house apart and find whatever monster is in my home," she yells, stomping her foot as she opens her magical compact and looks around.

"I bet you it is that nasty piece of garbage brother of mine and his oh-so-cute, dingbat daughter," the woman shrieks, spitting on the ground.

With that, a suit of armor falls to the floor as one of her boys starts blasting it.

"I am getting tired of those things. They will be the first to go, once you are gone," the woman declares, pointing at Cedric.

"Charming," Cedric says, wrinkling his nose at her.

"Cedric, I am tired of asking, you old goat. Why are you cooking? You have not cooked in years. Who is here? Who is it?" she demands.

"I do not know what you mean."

"Cedric, the only reason you are even here is your abilities. You know too many secrets that you would use against me, so I cannot get rid of you. Otherwise, I would have you gone in minutes," the witch declares, pulling her wand and pointing it at Cedric.

"But you see, My Lady, I cook for fun, never knowing when one of you will stop by. And may I remind you, your brothers will not let you get rid of me," Cedric replies, smiling.

"Wade has always been a waste of time, and when that criminal Kelvin is found and done in, then Wade will have no choice but to join me or suffer Kelvin's fate. Besides, Cedric, you have said yourself that you wish things were back to normal," the woman continues, looking around.

"Now, one last time, where are they?" she demands.

"Right here," Rose says, emerging from behind the bookcase and blasting the woman and two young men into the wall.

"I will not be bullied by anyone," Rose declares.

"Who is she? Brown nappy hair, ugly like Nadia, and she appears to be a teenager. You. You're the one that Morgana wants. Grab her," the woman screams.

As Bethany, Sebastian, and Destiny turn the corner in the entryway, the guards standing there drop to the ground dead. Cedric grabs the woman who he called "mistress" and bites her neck. As the blood runs down her neck, the woman shakes and then he throws her out of the way. When she drops to the floor, Cedric wipes the blood from his face. The two young men who came with the woman are on their feet. One attacks Cedric, his sword drawn. But Cedric catches the blade in his hands. The other locks blades with Oliver who catches the edge of the blade with his, just inches in front of Rose's face.

"Cedric, while my mother would not kill you, I will, you nasty monster," the young man shouts.

"You see, Master Daemon, you would have to not only be able to fight but also be able to catch me."

With that, Cedric pops his cane up, grabs the ball handle on the end, and pulls a sword from it, running the young wizard through. Before anyone can respond, Cedric turns, runs the guard through, then engages the other young man, Eric, running him through as well, grabbing his now bleeding victim by the neck, and biting it, draining him of his blood. The remaining guard stabs Oliver in his arm, knowing fresh blood will draw the vampire. The guard cast a charm that shields himself, then spins his cloak as he and the remaining members of the party disappear.

Cedric wipes his face as he walks up to Oliver, hands him a handkerchief, and pleads, "Please, cover that up before we have problems. While I would never attack anyone of Kelvin's and Nadia's line, the sight and smell of blood is tempting. Are you okay, My Lords and Ladies? I am sorry for that display of aggression."

"Your aggression against our enemies is welcome," Ethan remarks.

"Agreed," says everyone else in unison.

"Who was she?" Rose asks.

"Aunt Terra," Bethany responds, looking displeased.

"Aunt Terra?" Oliver asks, gritting his teeth while Destiny mends his wound with magic.

"She is your father's youngest sibling, and those two charming morons, Daemon and Eric, are her sons," Cedric explains, also looking displeased. He waves his hands and the dead bodies on the floor disappear.

"She will not be pleased that they have died, but I swore an oath to both of your fathers to protect you," Cedric explains as a broom appears, and he starts cleaning up the broken glass.

"Great! An aunt who is trying to kill us!" Ethan exclaims.

"Let me guess. Another one of Morgana's followers?" Oliver speculates as Cedric nods in agreement.

"Over the years, Morgana has amassed a large following of people. They feel that if they follow her, they won't end up dead," Sebastian says.

"But that is not the half of it. Merlin is ten times nastier. He makes Morgana look like a saint," Bethany shares.

Rose sits on the step, shaking her head.

"Rose, what is wrong?" Bethany inquires.

"I do not understand why everyone wants to work for her. But then, if what you say is correct, Merlin is not any better," Rose points out.

"Do they know?" Cedric asks.

"No. They have not been told," Destiny replies.

"Told what?" The three ask, looking at each other.

"Morgana's followers are not her followers. They follow a darker power. She is more or less a puppet in all of this," Zander states solemnly, sitting down next to Rose.

"Puppet? Meaning what exactly?" Ethan inquires.

"Meaning that Morgana has a light side and dark side," Rose explains, looking around at everyone.

"Wait! What? How do you know that? That knowledge is protected," Zander declares, staring at her in amazement.

"I kind of time traveled and came here, met Cedric, and found out that there are two sides of Morgana," Rose replies, giving Zander a half-smile.

"You told her?" Zander accused Cedric, jumping to his feet.

"I was ordered to help her," Cedric replies.

"By whom?"

"By my father and mother," Rose explains.

"Wait, you ran into your mother and father?" Destiny inquires.

"That's how you knew about my mother and brother, isn't it, Rose?"

"Yes."

"Well, I am glad," Destiny responds.

"Any magic dealing with time is forbidden, Rose. If you met your parents, no matter how noble your intent in trying to get answers, you endangered all of us. Never do that again," Zander insists, shaking his head.

"Would you like to share what is going on?" Oliver asks, staring at Destiny and Zander.

"Of course. They have a right to know. Ah ha, to the library at once!" Cedric demands pointing his finger in the air.

"I am hungry. Let's eat," Zander declares, moving toward the table.

"Dinner can wait. If you would all follow me, please," Cedric says as Zander rolls his eyes.

Destiny laughs seeing Zander's frustration.

"You know that he never listens," Destiny teases, nudging Zander.

The group follow Cedric up the stairs to the grand library. Upon everyone entering, Cedric pulls out a book from one of the shelves, picks up the orb on the shelf next to it, taps it against the pages of the book, and the orb flies to the center of the room and illuminates. The room darkens as two figures step out of the orb.

Chapter 12
The Prophecy

Dearest Rose, Ethan, & Oliver,

If you are viewing this, then we know you are safe, and the time has come for you to know of many truths. First and foremost, yes, your great grandfather was King, your grandfather was King, and I would have been King if the kingdom had not fallen. In our absence, you three will be the rulers.

Merlin created this kingdom for all magical beings to live without persecution from those who did not understand what magic was or what it was capable of doing! He believed that since the Mundane did not understand us, they would be quick to pass judgment on our abilities. It is now up to the three of you to protect our people and, more importantly, all forms of magic as it is the very fabric of life and balance.

Next, since you are watching this, you are, therefore, with one of our faithful and oldest friends, Cedric. To answer your questions, yes, he is what you would refer to as a demi-vampire, a rather unique vampire. Because of this, Cedric is the only vampire to date, who can drain the magic essences from any magical being or creature. Once bitten, it takes days, even weeks, for the individual affected to fully regain their magical ability to full strength.

We say this to you three: watch who you trust and only trust those close to you. Many magical individuals in disguise, throughout the kingdom, will seek to destroy you. By now, you should be with our family friend and protector, Alezander. Pay attention to his teachings. Although his past is riddled with mystery, he is most loyal and faithful to the crown.

We say this to the three of you: Merlin foresaw your coming and created this land for you. He knew that you would grow up in a time that would not accept our kind. The three of you are the most powerful Arcane alive to date. Alone you are powerful but together there is no limit to your magical abilities. In some ways, when you are together, your magic becomes unstoppable.

If you have not discovered already, here is something new for you. If you hold hands, your magic creates the strongest shield of protection. So, now we say this, we are proud of you, we have faith in you, and you are the rulers of the kingdom. But do remember that although you may be the rulers, in the end, you are still our children, the children of two realms.

Oliver, you will be the High King of Magic. Ethan, you are the Middle King of all magical beings. Rose, you are the Queen of Arcane and in the near future you will become the Queen of the Elves. Hold tight to your gifts and be ready to use them to protect all people whether Mundane or Arcane. We want you to remember, the Mundane may not understand us, but they are not our enemies. Protect them and keep them safe as well. The three of you must work together, protect those who cannot fight, keep the kingdom safe, and let magic guide you.

In time, we will be back together. Until then, it is up to you three to do what you must to protect the ways of magic. Roslynn, your book holds a chapter written in high elfish. It contains a series of spells that you will need to stand against Morgana. Please give it to Cedric or Alezander. They are fluent and will be able to read it for you. Be safe and good luck.

As the message ends the images disappear. Rose reaches into her bag, pulls out her book, and hands it to Alezander. Cedric moves in close behind Alezander to read over his shoulder and to see what the chapter yields. Alezander skims the pages. Then, he nods and tells them what is written there.

"It appears that your parents left a clean-up spell for you three to help us to regain the castle," he explains.

"A cleanup spell? What do you mean?" asks Ethan.

"It is a spell designed to clean up any magic, good or bad," Destiny says.

"You see, the freezing spell is extremely powerful. Therefore, a clean-up spell is needed to fix the rest of it," Bethany continues.

"She is correct, indeed," says Cedric, who continues to examine the group.

"Zander, I understand that they are to go to the castle: however, it is not like they can just walk up to the front door. Not with Morgana's guards everywhere," Destiny looks concerned.

"Guards?" the three siblings inquire.

"Yes, guards. When Morgana returned, she placed her elite forces at the castle, awaiting your return," Bethany explains.

"That is true. But there is another way to get in. Follow me, please," Cedric says as he walks out of the library and down the long hallway.

He opens the door to a room at the end of the hall, which is empty except for one item that is covered. Cedric enters the room and pulls off the sheet, revealing a large mirror.

"A mirror?" Oliver queries.

"Not just any mirror," Destiny replies, circling the mirror, examining it. "Where does this one dump?" she inquires.

"The castle's back guest wing," Cedric replies. "Morgana and her troops avoid the back wing. They are afraid of it," Cedric says, smiling.

"I take it that a certain vampire keeps them away from that wing?" Rose asks.

"Yes, just in case this moment ever came. This is a way to allow safe passage for the three of you," Cedric remarks.

"Okay, what is the plan?" Ethan inquires.

"The castle sits at the heart of the kingdom. To secure it would be to secure the fate of the kingdom," Zander says.

"So, it's a battle?" Oliver asks.

"Yes," Zander replies.

"However, there are too few of us," Destiny comments.

"We can solve that," Zander responds.

"How?" Rose asks.

"In the castle exists the Horn of Enlightenment. It was your father's and when blown, all Arcane beings will come running to the aid of the summoner. It is the magical way to notify those loyal to the crown, that help is needed," Zander explains.

"The idea is to get to the horn, which hangs in the great hall," Cedric says.

"What happens when we get it?" Ethan asks.

"One of you will have to get to the topmost tower and call for aid," Zander replies, smiling.

"I will do it," Ethan volunteers.

"What?" Oliver says, turning toward his twin.

"I am the fastest of the three of us," Ethan replies.

"I am going with him," Sebastian states.

"Oliver, you are the high King and a lot more advanced than me in magic. Rose, while her magic is more powerful, freaky, and just downright weird, not to mention she can level anything, you two stand a better chance in battle then I do," Ethan places a hand on Oliver's shoulder.

"You won't go down. I will not let them touch you, not as long as I am with you," Sebastian declares to Ethan.

"Then it is decided. Ethan will grab the horn and sound it. Remember, once we are through the mirror portal, there is no turning back," Zander says.

"We understand," the three rulers respond in unison.

"Okay Rose, Bethany and I will take the northern section of the castle. Sebastian, Leaf, and Ethan, you get the horn and head for the topmost tower. Cedric, you and Destiny go with Oliver to secure the throne room," Zander instructs.

"Wait. Autumn, you take to the sky and if you need to unleash hell upon those guards, please do so," Rose says, looking at the dragon who bows and jumps through the mirror.

"Ready?" Zander asks.

"In one minute," Destiny says, pulling her staff and tapping the floor three times.

Immediately, the entire group is decked out in armor, the men carrying shields and the women dressed in beautiful dresses.

"Now, Cedric, take us through," Zander commands.

Cedric turns to the mirror, touches it with his index finger, and the surface of the mirror begins to ripple, Zander steps through, followed closely by Rose. Then, the rest follow. Cedric is the last one through. He seals the portal so no one else can get through to the safe house.

"Good luck, everyone. Our duty is to protect the Kings and the Queen. Let's go," Zander directs.

"Good luck," Rose says to the others as she, Zander, and Bethany run out into the back courtyard of the castle.

As they do so, Bethany points her wand and, in one quick waving motion, the fountain explodes flooding the courtyard as water begins blasting all over. Zander pulls his sword, striking down a dark guard as Rose's eyes light, and she levitates into the air white light flying around her as dark creatures fly toward her across the courtyard.

In one quick telepathic message, the others hear Rose yell, "Go! We will handle this."

While the three hold back the darkness in the courtyard, the others run for the corridors where they are met by more dark creatures.

"Ethan, go! This is our battle. Get the horn and summon help. Go!"

Destiny begins summoning orbs around her, launching one after another at the darkness as Oliver pulls his sword, and starts striking down the dark creatures as they fly into the air and explode. Cedric, the mysterious one, walks through dark creatures and as he gets behind them, he turns to grab them and slams them into the ground at full strength, either killing them or knocking them out. Ethan, Sebastian, and Leaf enter the hall in a mad dash.

"There it is," Leaf points as Ethan bolts for the horn.

As Ethan nears the horn, Liam rises out of the ground with Raven at his side. Ethan has the horn in his hand and bolts for the door as Sebastian pulls down, summoning the room into complete darkness. With a quick move of his wand, Liam, Raven, and the creatures of the dark fly out the back doors of the hall.

"Leaf, go with Ethan. I will handle this," Sebastian shouts as his eyes turn gray and he walks out the door, deflecting the dark magic and throwing it back at the creatures.

Sebastian turns and tells Leaf, "Besides, my brother is my responsibility."

Sebastian dodges the rocks that fly by him. In one quick movement of his hand, he speaks a spell.

Voca fructum mortuis.

Call forth the spirits.

Sebastian repeats the spell three times as multiple spirits rise from the ground and attack Liam and Raven. Leaf runs toward the doorways as he transforms into his lion form, roaring and causing the dark creatures to explode. He continues to run after Ethan. When Ethan reaches the top step of the highest tower, he blows into the horn. As the call echoes across the land, Ethan summons light to him to fight off the dark creatures that are emerging from everywhere on the tower around him.

Suddenly, dark creatures begin flying off the tower into the air as small flickering balls of light converge on the tower. While the balls of light fly around, spirits rise through the stone and attack the darkness. In one quick pass, Ethan summons light rays, which blast the darkness off the tower. He sounds the horn again. A roar is heard in the distance as Leo emerges at the edge of the forest. He and his wife roar again as lines of animals appear, then emerge from the forest, run past them, and descend on the castle. As the animals enter the castle, they begin to fight against the darkness. From the waters, mermaids begin singing their songs, killing dark creatures on the spot.

The horn sounds again, and, in the distance, another horn echoes its call. As the horns echo one another, Zander turns and runs for the gate, launching dark creatures backward as flames rise around them, the light causing them to explode. As the horn sounds again, Zander pulls a bellow horn from under his cloak and lets it sound. The horn sounds yet again as lightning hits the courtyard and all of the dark creatures disappear.

Rose and Bethany run from the courtyard where they find Destiny, Cedric, and Oliver engaging in battle. Zander reaches the courtyard gates, opens them, and sounds his horn again. This time, as he does, elfish soldiers run past him, swords and spears out, striking the darkness and dropping the creatures where they stand.

In the distance, Zander can see Morgana standing with Lord Aden, Lord Hawke, and Lady Dawn. Morgana screams and a column of darkness flies from her mouth. When the dark creatures emerge in the field in front of the castle, a large army of solid darkness appears. The remaining elves turn and form ranks as the little lights flying around them take form and start revealing themselves as some of the most beautiful magical beings. Fairies hover above the ground when Queen Amaryllis suddenly emerges from the crowd.

"The castle is under attack. Protect all that are here with the power of light and our magic. All groups form ranks," Queen Amaryllis commands.

The rest of the fairies fly toward the castle, turn, and formed ranks by locking arms, creating a magical field around the castle. At this moment in time, the animals running through the castle come out over the rampart and take to the land in front of the elves and fairies. While the groups form ranks, the spirits summoned by Sebastian emerge all around ready to fight as well.

Once the animals form ranks, Leaf joins them, standing in front alongside his father and mother. The elves stand shoulder to shoulder, those with swords in the front, followed by spear carriers, then archers, and, finally, the magicians in the very back. Morgana screams and the darkness advances, while Raven and Liam fly over the castle wall and land just feet away from Morgana. In the sky, Rose can be seen levitating above the castle, eyes glowing purple as the elements fly around her.

"Get up, you fools! Take the castle!" Morgana screams, stomping her foot.

"My Mistress, she is crazy," Liam notes, helping Raven up as they point at Rose.

"I do not care. Stop them! I want that castle," Morgana hisses.

Back on the other side of the field, the elves and fairies' part as Destiny, Oliver, Bethany, Ethan, Sebastian, and Cedric emerge from the castle. Once the group of elves and fairies return to their normal forms, the elves in the front of the group hold up their blades while the second group of elves in the back summon forth their magic and equip each blade with great power.

"My children, defend the castle. Do not let them pass. Do your duty to magic," the fairy queen extols.

"We cannot let the darkness pass. We have the castle. We must protect it at all cost!" Zander declares, walking over the rampart, his sword resting on his shoulder.

Morgana points at the group standing in her way and screams, "Kill them!"

As the dark guards and creatures begin to advance, witches and wizards begin to appear, joining the fight to hold the darkness at bay. With each passing second, more animals arrive, running to help their friends. In the distance, centaurs appear charging at full speed. But they hit a magic barrier and are thrown off their hooves.

Great fields of magic begin appearing, pushing the dark creatures back as the elves and fairies quickly work together to deploy lightshields. Suddenly, a group of centaurs come charging from the area around the river. When Sebastian raises his wand, the centaurs disappear only to re-emerge a few feet from Morgana, striking her.

"Hold this line and do not let them pass," Zander shouts as he raises his sword and strikes down a dark guard. Moving quickly against the darkness, Zander runs through the darkness field, striking down each of them as he passes. The soldiers following Zander jump back as the ground around them begins to open and break apart. With each step he takes, Zander discovers the land coming apart as Morgana points her wand at the ground, trying to stop him and the elf guards from advancing.

Rose lands and joins the others when Oliver grabs her and pushes her out of the way. Ethan jumps back as Kai, the Shade Dragon, lands only feet from them. The dragon turns, snapping at them, and raises his head, his nostril starting to smoke and turn orange. Then, the dragon is levitated off the ground and launched across the field by Lady Divinity, who emerges from the ground.

Autumn lands, taking out an entire group of dark soldiers and elite guards. Snapping, then bellowing fire, she blocks Kai from getting to the others. Hissing, Kai snaps back at Autumn, then takes off into the air. Autumn launches herself into the air after him.

Kai races, climbing higher and higher to get away from Autumn. Two other large dragons emerge and join the chase after Kai. Flying as fast as he can, Kai dodges multiple dragons, all joining the chase. Over thirty dragons are now in pursuit of Kai. As the group continue the chase, Belinda and Autumn break off and land on the ground.

The two lock their tails and in what looks like a beautiful waltz, begin to dance in a circular motion, summoning light to them and blowing fire everywhere. As the light hits the ground, the darkness vanishes.

When Rose turns from striking down several dark creatures, she notices that Morgana has disappeared. Seconds later, she and Leo are engaged in battle.

Meanwhile, in the midst of the battle, Raven appears, catching Leo off-guard and stabs a dagger into his back. Weakened, Leo falls to the ground. Leaf goes after Raven and the animals run to assist their protector. Zander and Rose demolish dark creatures and elite guards with light helixes while running towards Leo.

Unable to assist Zander and Rose, Oliver finds himself locked in a magical duel with his grandmother while Destiny duels with her brother, Hawke. With two quick blasts, both Oliver and Destiny throw their opponents backward and disarm them completely. Destiny scoops up both her mother's and brother's wands, snapping them in half as the remaining pieces burst into flames.

As Dawn gets to her feet, Oliver spins his wand and freezes her where she stands. Destiny lifts Hawke off his feet and throws him backwards through a portal that she then slams shut.

In the distance, screams are heard as Leaf rips into the flesh of Raven's arm.

"Nasty beast! Get off me," Raven yells.

Trying to retrieve her wand, she falls to the ground, screaming and holding her head.

"Get out, get out, you monster!" Raven screams as Leaf attacks her again, grabbing her leg and tearing more flesh.

Across the battlefield, Zander stands with his fingers on his temple entering Raven's mind, trying to gain telepathic control over her.

Seeing this, Liam retrieves his wand, stabs two wolves, and starts to summon darkshields. Suddenly, three elfish guards emerge from the ground, stabbing him, once in the gut, once in the shoulder, and once more in the back of his right leg. Wounded, Liam drops to the ground, trying to hold off the elfish guards as Aden charges toward him quickly, casting a darkshield around him and Liam and throwing the elfish guards back. Aden reaches down to help Liam up when another elf guard attacks. Though shielded, the blade of the elf catches the end of Aden's staff, and it explodes on impact.

Hurled off his feet, Aden blows flames around him and his injured son. Then both disappear. At the same time, Hawke reappears at Raven's side, throws Leaf backward, grabs Raven, and begins to disappear as two fairies attack him, stopping him from leaving. The fairies summon vines from the ground, wrapping his legs and preventing him from moving. The vines encircle him as he falls face first on the ground. The fairies raise their hands, then lower them, causing the vines to slam him repeatedly into the ground.

Leaf, now even more furious, roars as the ground shakes, throwing Hawke and Raven off their feet. When Leaf charges Raven, Morgana appears, trying to fight him off with fireballs. When she turns to run from him, he advances, and she finds herself face to face with Cedric. Wasting no time, Cedric grabs her by the throat, slamming her into the ground, then raises her into the air as he sinks his teeth into her neck.

Working together to protect Cedric, Ethan and Oliver spin their wands and hold their hands out in front of themselves, causing lightshields to appear to push back the darkness, preventing it from getting to either Morgana or Cedric.

Screaming and kicking, Morgana tries everything she can to get away from Cedric, even as her arms start to weaken from being drained.

Seeing their leader needing assistance Aden and Hawke run to Morgana's aid, stopping only long enough to cast magic against their enemies. Suddenly, the Lady of White appears and blocks them with a magical barrier.

While drinking from Morgana, everyone notices that Cedric's hair is turning red, and he is growing younger. When he finishes, he drops the shriveled and weakened Morgana to the ground. As she hits the ground, the darkness disappears.

"Enough of this," Oliver declares, pointing his wand straight at Morgana as she begins to transform into stone.

"I agree, but you cannot have all the fun," Ethan remarks as he moves his arms in a circular motion in front of his body, causing vines to emerge from the ground and wrap around Morgana.

In another attempted strike, the dark creatures rise up against Oliver and Ethan. But members of the Council appear around them, wands out, and casting one gigantic lightshields around them.

During this time, Rose remains close to Leo, mending his wounds and trying to preserve his life force while Zander protects both of them.

"No, No! Leo, no!" Rose cries as he takes his last breath.

Aden reappears and attempts to advance against Oliver and Ethan. But, just then, all of the dark creatures explode. A giant orb of white light flies around them. Startled, Oliver and Ethan look first at each other and then at Rose, who is standing with her palm out as the orb flies back to her and floats in the air above her hand.

Walking toward the spot where Morgana is frozen, Rose holds up her other hand causing another orb to appear. The second orb flies around her in the shape of a helix. Multiple dark creatures attack her but explode as they hit the field of light protecting her.

"I am done with this!" Rose declares and the orbs fly into the air when she snaps her fingers.

The orbs grow bright as Rose holds up her hands, summoning an energy orb to her. With one wave of her hand, she releases it, and it begins to fly around the field. Glancing around, she slams her hands together causing an energy shockwave that levels all remaining dark creatures.

Turning, Rose glides above the ground to where Leo's lifeless body lays. Raising her hands, the orbs fly back to her. As she throws her hands down, the orbs launch into the earth under Leo. Sebastian and Leaf run up and take over guarding Morgana, while Oliver and Ethan run toward Rose. The three hold hands and speak in unison.

Expergiscere.

Awaken.

As they close their eyes, and then open them, two columns of light project out of the earth. One heals Leo's wounds and restores his lifeforce. The other encases the frozen Morgana.

The three raise their hands as Leo begins breathing again, and the light column around Morgana freezes the vines and seals her in stone. When the three lower their hands, Rose waves one hand over Leo. The orbs reappear and she launches them at the column holding Morgana. They spin around the column sealing it in a lightshield.

Taking a deep breath, the three regard each other and nod when Dawn, Aden, and Hawke charge the light column protecting Morgana. Dawn hurls lightning at the column, but it bounces back and strikes her. Aden and Hawke appear on either side, grab her, and disappear.

Chapter 13
Dreams

A fire pit roars as smoke rises into the night air. A forest surrounds the pit as pops are heard and cloaked individuals begin to appear.

"We were summoned but no one is here," one of the figures remarks.

"Yes, you were all summoned," Father Francisco responds, walking out of the woods.

At the sight of Father Francisco, the individuals bow.

"Covens, you do not bow to me. It is only for the House of Phoenix that you should bow. As I am not one of them, there is no need," Father Francisco notes, looking at the covens.

"Father Francisco, we bow out of respect," Grace explains.

"Thank you, Spring Coven."

"Father, why are we here?" Grace inquires, glancing at one of the other covens.

"As soon as everyone arrives, I will explain."

Just as Father Francisco finishes speaking, several other covens appear. Tension begins to rise as members of the covens pull their wands and point them at the other covens.

"No. I will have order! No fighting! The enemy is out there, not here," Father Francisco insists. Noticing that the covens are not listening to him, he pulls his own wand, points it at the flames of the fire pit, and causes an explosion to occur, resulting in all of the covens backing up and regarding him cautiously. Slowly, they lower their wands.

"My friends, thank you for joining me. As you are aware the Arcane realm is weakening. I do not lie when I say that Morgana is behind this. Her attacks in the realm of the Arcane, continue to weaken the very essence and life force of magic as we know it. We must come together to stop this tragedy from happening," he states, regarding the covens closely.

"This is all well and good but not one person can stop Morgana," various coven members mutter.

Father Francisco reaches down into the box by his feet and pulls out an orb. The covens back up at the sight of the orb. Father Francisco waves his hand over it, revealing marks embedded in its surface.

"She is alive? The Lady Mora lives?" Grace asks.

"She is, yes, and, as I speak, the magical three have returned to the Arcane realm to find her and stop Morgana. If Morgana comes here, they will need all of your help," Father Francisco replies.

The various covens look around the area, then at each other. The Coven of Earth is the first to speak.

"If the magical three exist, then we shall provide both our blades and magic to aid them. Someday, the young princess will be the queen of our people," Darren notes.

"She would be your queen, great elf, if the King Zander still lived," one of the members of Winter coven remarks, laughing.

"Oh, but he does live! The princess is with him right now. He was in hiding until the time was right to reveal himself. I should know. I was there. Together, they saved the temple and my wife," Father Francisco states.

The members of the various covens break into conversation amongst themselves.

"Then, if what you say is true, as I previously stated, we the Earth Coven of elves pledge our swords and magic to aid in the battle against darkness," Darren vows.

Quickly, the other covens also pledge to fight against the darkness.

"Accordingly, this night marks the time when we take back magical teaching for good. This flame represents the internal flame of magic and stands as the beacon to call the magical three home to this realm. It must be protected at all cost," Father Francisco declares as the covens spread out and begin casting enchantments around the area to protect it.

At that same moment, in the Arcane Realm, Oliver, Ethan, Sebastian, and members of the Council check the area looking for any fallen comrades from the battle that has just ensued.

Zander strides towards the army of elves, holding out his hand to shake that of the young elf who led the remaining elves against the darkness. The two hug and begin speaking, their heads close together.

"What are you doing here?" Zander inquires.

"I heard the horn and knew that our King had returned," the elf replies.

"It is good to see you, Cousin. It is nice to see that some of my people made it," Zander said, regarding them.

"This is the last of us, Cousin," Lucas responds.

"Lucas, it is wonderful to see you again," Zander says, bowing and then hugging his cousin for the second time.

"What happened? Raven killed your brother and my siblings fled with a large group of our people and what remained of our culture. My brother, Max, led a group out of here and never looked back," Lucas remarks, looking worried.

"Any word where Max took them?" Zander inquires.

"Many believe he used the last of his magic to open a portal and take a group somewhere into the mountains in the Mundane realm," Lucas notes.

"He probably went to the original settlement in the mountain region. Knowing your brother, he went looking for the old chiefs," Zander responds.

"Chiefs?" Lucas inquires.

"The native chiefs. The natives of that land believe in the power of nature. Many believe that when Merlin was trying to take over Europe, he knew of the great First Nations and advised against moving against the new land for fear of their magic," Zander explains.

"As I said, Max has not looked back or been in touch. Now, all we can do is hope. If what you say is true, then his knowledge of their ways would be exceptional," Lucas notes.

Nodding in agreement, Zander regards the army of the elves.

"My friends, thank you. Your help is appreciated," Zander remarks as he and Lucas walk through the ranks examining those who remain.

The army of elves separates when the Fairies approach.

Coming up from behind Zander, Rose walks pass him and bows to Queen Amaryllis. Following her lead, Bethany, Destiny, and Cedric do the same thing.

"No, child you do not bow to me, I bow to you," Queen Amaryllis remarks.

"Queen Amaryllis, thank you for your help. Without the fairies, we would surely have lost many more," Rose replies.

"My Queen, it was not a problem. When we heard the horn, we knew our kings and queen were calling for aid," Queen Amaryllis replies, smiling and bowing her head as she lands to walk with the group.

"Bethany?" Queen Amaryllis calls for her.

"Yes."

"Have you met my son, Phineas?" Queen Amaryllis inquires as her son emerges from the ranks of the army.

Phineas is a tall, blonde-haired, green-eyed fairy, donning the traditional silver armor of the fairies and wearing a beautiful crown upon his head. Bethany and Rose both bow and the prince bows to them in return.

"Queen Rose," Phineas says.

"Yes?"

"My I ask for your cousin to walk with me as I examine the guard," Phineas askes as Bethany and Rose regard one another.?

Finally, Rose nods. Bethany stows her bow and arrow on her back and takes the extended hand of the charming prince.

Rose and Queen Amaryllis stop, while the fairy queen bows, and Lucas kisses the hands of both queens.

"My ladies, may I introduce my cousin, Lord Lucas of Glenn Sheldon?" Zander announces.

"I have heard much about you, Lord Lucas. Your help this evening is much appreciated, and our success could not have been without everyone's help," Queen Amaryllis states.

"I agree," Leo states as he approaches the group.

"How do you feel?" Queen Amaryllis asks, examining him.

"Like I am 15 again and could run a thousand marathons," he replies, winking at Rose.

"My Lords and Ladies, I do not mean to break up this party, but may I suggest we begin moving indoors for safety," Cedric suggests, getting up off a boulder on which he was sitting to keep watch.

"Indeed," Oliver replies, walking up.

As the group reach the rampart to the castle, Queen Amaryllis raises her hand and the fairies turn into little balls of light, floating in the air.

"This is where we leave you but know this our people have lived in harmony for years. Anytime help is needed, we will be there," Queen Amaryllis declares as she turns and regards her people.

"My children, we depart," she says, floating into the air and transforming into a little bright light ball. Upon the fairies taking their leave, the group hears the queen's voice, "Phineas, you may stay as long as you need. You know how to call us if you need us." With that, the light flies over Phineas, his armor disappears, and he has donned the royal robes of the Fairy royal family.

With his wings tucked back, his hair spiky and made up, and, on his belt, a sword to the right and a small dagger to the left, he holds out his hand as the fairies fly around his hand. As he raises his hand, the fairies take off, and he smiles and waves.

Then, Phineas turns, bows, and speaks.

"My Kings and Queen, I give you my sword, the dagger of the Fairy Glen, and my magic to protect you three and all people and creatures."

Bethany hugs him while Ethan and Oliver bow.

Zander, who is now holding Rose's hand, bows his head as Rose replies.

"Prince Phineas, thank you. We graciously accept your help."

With that Rose turns, looks at her brothers, and asks, "Shall we?"

Smiling, the three raise their hands and, as they do, three light rays emerge from their wands and combine. As the light rays merge, the three siblings' eyes begin glowing white. Behind them, Zander, Bethany, Destiny, Sebastian, and Phineas do the same. The castle begins to glow as their combined magic restores it back to normal and time unfreezes.

"Now, that is the heart of the kingdom that I remember," Divinity states as she begins spinning her hands and summoning magic around the castle to create a protective barrier around it. The High Council standing with her help to complete the barrier.

With magic restored, the castle comes back to life. Trees turn from barren to full of life. The waterway begins to move again, and the fish start to jump.

Rose, Ethan, and Oliver hold hands as they cast one final spell of protection. Columns of light emerge from the ground and seal the castle in a lightfield. When the last of the darkness is dispelled from the castle, the staff come out through the gates, clapping. The castle again stands as a beacon of hope.

Rose, Ethan, and Oliver walk down the rampart, followed by their friends and the Council. Autumn and Belinda land in the courtyard and roar as the other dragons land around the castle. Looking back as she reaches the end of the rampart, Rose sees that Zander has not crossed. She turns and weaves her way back through the crowd. Zander and Lucas hug, and Rose understands that Lucas and the grand army of the elves are departing.

"Lord Lucas, please wait," Rose says as she approaches. When she pushes her hands out in front of her, beautiful armor appears on the army. Closely behind her are Oliver and Ethan, standing in the archway watching. Rose walks up, kisses the elf on the cheek, bows, and thanks him.

"You have a long way back to Glenn Sheldon. I cannot ask you to make that journey on foot." Rose raises her hand, and, from the archway, her brothers do the same. A portal opens and the guards walk through. Lucas is the last to go through. He bows and, as he walks through, Zander catches the portal and seals it shut.

Oliver and Ethan are leaning against the archway as Zander and Rose walk hand and hand toward them. When they reach Oliver and Ethan, Zander raises Rose's hand and kisses it. Oliver and Ethan turn and the four proceed through the grand entryway into the courtyard, where they find Bethany and Phineas who have summoned up a fire in the pit and are cooking. Destiny is sitting by the fountain while Cedric is consulting in the back hall with what appears to be the staff. Sebastian emerges from the throne room carrying mugs. Rose looks around and smiles. Zander and Destiny are the first to notice this.

"What is it, Rose?" Destiny inquires.

"Is this what the castle was like when Mom and Dad were here?" she inquires.

"It was, indeed," Destiny confirms.

"But before you three get too comfortable, Cedric is checking every inch of this place for any dark portals, guards, anything. He has advised that you three must stay here until he gives the 'all clear,'" Divinity remarks as she joins the group.

Within the hour, Cedric emerges giving the 'all clear.' The rest of the day is spent with the three siblings wandering around the palace, learning the various aspects of its history. Each has their own tour guide: Rose goes with Zander, Oliver and Bethany with Cedric, and Ethan with Destiny. Throughout the day, more and more members of the High Council arrive.

After dinner, each of them retreats to their bedrooms and settles in. Zander is very specific about going through and showing Rose, Ethan, and Oliver where their bedrooms are, and he searches each room to make sure there is no form of dark magic in any of them.

"Master Zander, do you mind? I have already checked their rooms," Cedric complains, very frustrated as Zander looks under the bed.

"Cedric, I know you did, but we cannot be too safe," Zander reassures him as he gives the 'all clear' for Ethan to enter the room. Over the next few days, things in the kingdom are quiet. Rose spends her days wandering the castle and discovers the vast library. On the second day, Cedric is heard complaining about the number of books that are floating out of the mirror and down the hallway into the library.

"Really! Is she emptying the library at the manor?" Bethany asks, chewing on a turkey leg and watching the books float by.

"Cedric is having a fit! Can someone talk to her?" Leaf inquires.

"Ha! You go in there and try. Oliver has already been chased out of the library. Destiny came out with purple hair, and Cedric was chased out by a dragon," Ethan responds, laughing.

"Why don't you try?" Bethany inquires.

"Cousin, I am not crazy! I love my baby sister, but I dare not come between her and the books," Ethan remarks as he watches more villagers come over the rampart and through the gate.

"Bethany, don't they ever stop showing up?" Ethan inquires.

"Nope. We had better go to join Oliver," she suggests as they walk down the hall.

Throughout the week, when Rose's attention is not focused on the library, her attention was on Ethan. Each night, he is having nightmares and wakes the castle screaming. It is usually late in the night and the cries for help are heard ringing throughout the castle.

Rose and Oliver both emerge from their rooms, wrapping their robes around themselves, and run down the hall to Ethan's room. Oliver opens the door carefully as he and Rose find Ethan asleep on the ceiling.

"I have not seen him this bad in a long time," Oliver states looking at Rose.

"What could be going on?" Rose asks.

"I do not know. He won't tell me. He changes the subject every time I ask if he is okay," Oliver replies.

"We are going to have to get him down from there," Rose says as they hold out their wands and lower Ethan to the ground.

As they get him onto the bed, his room starts shaking as Ethan begins to toss and turn. Oliver and Rose back up. Ethan suddenly stops thrashing and everything returns to normal.

"I know I promised both of you that I would never do this, but I need to know how to help him," Rose says as she sits on the side of Ethan's bed and touches her hand to his forehead.

Just as she does this, Oliver grabs hold of Rose's shoulder, and they find themselves spinning in a whirlwind of sand. As the sand departs, they find themselves back at home and, of all places, at their school.

Oliver looks around and asks, "Why are we here?"

Rose shrugs her shoulders. Then, she and Oliver hear a voice that is all too familiar to them.

"Well, well, well! What do we have here?" a classmate of Ethan's inquires, slamming him face first into his locker.

"Brandon, seriously? What do you want?" Ethan asks.

"You know, fag, the only reason we do not beat the living crap out of you is because your brother and his buddies would be after us," Brandon remarks.

Several of the other boys with Brandon, start to laugh when Ethan pushes past them. Furious, Brandon swings and comes inches from hitting Ethan in the face.

"Later, queer!" Brandon laughs, blowing Ethan an air kiss as he and his buddies high five each other and walk away.

After they leave, Ethan sits on the ground and starts crying.

A fog falls over the vision, as Rose and Oliver arrive back in Ethan's room.

"That was it?" Oliver inquires.

"No! His mind is fighting me," Rose replies.

"Do we go back in?" Oliver asks.

"Yes. There is something in these visions that is causing Ethan to not sleep well, and we have to figure it out."

"Rose, I think we did figure it out. It was Brandon," Oliver declares.

"Possibly. But have you learned nothing, dear brother? We have to see as much as possible before we jump to any conclusions," Rose replies, as she places her hand back on Ethan's forehead.

"Not our school again," Oliver complains as Rose rolls her eyes at him and walks down the hall.

"Don't roll your eyes at me! You know I am not a fan of this place, even in dreams," he notes.

"There is Ethan heading to his locker," Rose remarks as the two watch from a distance.

As Ethan sorts things into his locker, Brandon and his buddies show up and push Ethan into the locker.

"Fag! What? Are you going to cry again?" Brandon mocks.

As the group walks by, they throw a crown at him.

"You see, Queenie, you belong back in the closet," Brandon laughs

Knowing the expression on Oliver's face all too well, Rose stops the vision.

"What?"

"Why didn't he tell me, it was Brandon and his buddies who were bullying him?" Oliver inquires.

"I don't know. Maybe he was scared. He knows you too well. He was probably afraid that you and I would hex the school," Rose suggests, looking directly at Oliver.

"Rose, I swear if I ever see Brandon and his buddies again, so help me…. What is that?" Oliver suddenly stops in mid-sentence and points at a murky part of the dream.

The two watch as Ethan slams his locker shut, picks up the crown off the ground, walks down the hall, and dumps it in the trash. The murky haze follows him.

Quickly, Rose and Oliver follow behind, curious to see what is occurring. As Ethan enters the men's restroom, they follow him.

"So, this is what the men's restroom looks like?" Rose asks, wrinkling her nose.

"Ha ha, Rose. Nothing spectacular!" Oliver says.

"Hush! There is Ethan," Rose whispers tapping Oliver on the chest to shut him up.

"Oliver, I don't get it. He is just splashing water on his face, but I see what you mean. That haze is not what it seems. It looks like it is a silhouette of a figure. What the…?" Rose remarks as she observes the scene more closely.

Not paying attention to what is going on around him, Ethan splashes water on his face when, suddenly, Brandon shoves his face into the water.

Rose and Oliver watch as Ethan elbows Brandon. Brandon spins Ethan around when he tries to take a swing at him. But before Brandon could finish, a wand appears from the haze and casts a spell that slams Brandon and his two buddies into the walls. Then, all three are picked up and thrown through the stall doors.

As they hit the ground, they look as though they have seen a ghost and all three scramble out of the bathroom. From the haze, a hand extends toward Ethan. Then, with a loud pop, the haze disappears.

Oliver and Rose find themselves jumping again in the dream. This time, they arrive on the night when they first met Sebastian and Bethany.

The two watch the evening play out.

"Wait! What? Sebastian kissed him?" Oliver inquires, looking at Rose.

"Why didn't I see it before?" he asks.

"Oliver, I didn't know of it either until I touched Ethan's shoulder and saw what happened," Rose remarks.

"They are destined!" Oliver states, looking perplexed.

"Not necessarily," Rose replies.

"Sebastian is certainly interested in him. Which means Ethan either does not necessarily want to be with him or he's hiding it," she suggests.

"Rose, are we sure about that?" Oliver asks.

"No, Oliver, and it is not our place to assume. We have to let him tell us when he is ready," Rose replies as they jump one last time.

❧

This time, they find themselves standing in the large field in front of the castle.

When things finally come into focus, they are observing a battle between Morgana and Oliver, who are locked in an Arcane duel. Suddenly, Liam attacks Sebastian who has emerged from the castle alongside Ethan.

In one quick move, Liam jams his sword through Sebastian's gut and disappears. Blood begins to pour down Ethan's arms as he holds his fallen friend. Tears roll down his face as Sebastian passes away in his arms. Ethan is struck in the back with darkness and before anyone knows what has occurred, his body falls frozen and lifeless.

Oliver and Rose quickly scramble to freeze the image and observe it. Carefully studying every aspect of the vision, Rose makes a discovery.

"Oliver, you might want to see this."

"I told you they were destined. Why else would Ethan be wearing Sebastian's dragon necklace?" Oliver inquires.

"Do you think Sebastian has seen these dreams?" Rose asks.

Oliver shrugs in response.

"I doubt it, but Ethan has been having these dreams for the past few days."

❧

Seconds later, they find themselves back in Ethan's room in the castle, where Ethan is sleeping soundly.

Quietly, Oliver and Rose leave the room. In the hallway, Oliver breaks the silence.

"Do you think he will know that we were in his dreams?"

"No, Oliver. But I know how to fix all this." Rose replies as she hurries down the hall.

"Fix what? Rose, wait! Where are you going?" Oliver asks, chasing after his sister.

Entering her room, wand in hand, Rose spins it, causing her spell book to appear. The pages begin flipping, then stop when Rose reaches the podium.

"What are you doing, Rose?" Oliver watches his sister reading quickly.

"I am looking for a spell," she replies.

"A spell to do what?"

"Oh yes. Sorry. Mom tells of spells for dreams. One of them is where we can alter the dream by making it become real," she remarks, looking up briefly from the book and moving her finger down the page.

"Wait! Are you crazy? You want to do what? Make the dreams real? Why?" Oliver demands.

"No, I am not crazy. I want to make the dream real to a point. You see, I want to connect Sebastian's mind into the dream and see if that helps. It might improve Ethan's ability to rest and prevent him from waking the entire castle with his screaming in the middle of the night," Rose suggests, a half-smile lighting her face.

"Why do I not like that smile? When you say "connect," how does that work?" Oliver inquires.

"It is rather simple, actually. I am going to take Sebastian into Ethan's dreams," Rose states.

"This crosses the line. You are crazy! Or mad! Or both! You know the two of them do not get along, and you want to throw Sebastian into Ethan's dreams?" Oliver says, crossing his arms.

"I do not believe that, Oliver. I believe Ethan likes him but because of you and me and our responsibility, he is hiding his true feelings," Rose replies as she looks up again from her book and regards him.

"Oliver, be a love. Go wake Sebastian and Zander. I am going to need their help for this next part," Rose remarks. Picking up the book, she walks to the middle of the room, places the book on the floor, and steps back as she circles her hands above the book, causing a tornado to appear.

Items fly around the room as the wind picks up. Dust swirls around Rose and when Zander enters the room, he notices that a figure has appeared.

"I see that you have learned how to communicate with me," Nadia remarks.

"Mom, I need your help," Rose replies.

"Indeed. What is it? Wait, this room… Roslynn, you three have the castle and Zander is here?" Nadia asks in an excited tone.

"Mom, focus! Then, I will answer those questions. Ethan is struggling with nightmares. I want to connect a person to his mind and make the dreams real, but I don't know if it will work. Is it dangerous?" she inquires of the ghost-like form of her mother.

"Rose, do you believe anything is possible?" Nadia asks.

"Yes," Rose replies, looking puzzled.

"Then, so shall it be. Rose, those abilities that you keep locked up and protected, you have to unlock them. Once unlocked, you can control dreams, visions, even time itself. Stop being afraid! Your brothers need you to not be afraid," Nadia says, looking at Rose.

"But I have already unlocked my powers. This does not make sense," Rose argues.

"My child, you unlocked them to a point. But your full potential is still to come." Nadia winks at Rose.

As Oliver and Sebastian enter Rose's room, Nadia's eyes narrow and she glides across the floor, circling Sebastian.

"Well, well, well! The legends are true," she exclaims, poking him.

"What do you mean?" Sebastian asks, rubbing the spot on his arm.

"If you have to ask, then you are not as wise as they claim you to be, Sebastian," Nadia remarks, walking back toward the book.

"Rose, you will need Zander's help. But you can enter into the dream if you stay focused," she notes as she gazes at Rose, spins her hands, and dissolves into the light.

❧

"Do I dare ask what she meant?" Sebastian asks, shaking his head.

"Sebastian, I have to ask you a question." Rose states as she approaches Sebastian and places the necklace from the vision in his hand.

Sebastian reaches for his neck, searching for the necklace, but it is gone.

"Oh course, Rose. What is it?" Sebastian asks, examining the necklace.

"You connected to Ethan, didn't you?"

"I did. But I do not know about him," Sebastian sits down on Rose's bed, and lowers his head.

"Sebastian, we need your help. Ethan needs your help," Rose places her hand on his shoulder and, putting her hand under his chin, lifts his head.

"For him, I will do anything." Sebastian quickly wipes a tear from his face.

"Sebastian, Zander and I will merge powers and project you into Ethan's dreams. Once that occurs, you will only be able to get out when he awakens or you have completed the journey and altered the dream," Rose explains.

"Okay. That's fine. I have been in tougher situations," Sebastian laughs, trying to make light of the situation.

"Sebastian, once you're in, Zander and I will not be able to enter the dreams. Neither will Oliver. It will be just the two of you."

"Of course! I understand," Sebastian replies.

"Oliver, when I help Rose, she and I will be out of commission for several minutes. You will be on your own to protect all of us," Zander says, looking at Oliver.

"Zander, I've got your backs. Nothing will happen," he declares.

"If there are any problems, drop this orb and stand back. It is a summoning orb. It will bring everyone to this spot to help," Zander says, handing the orb to Oliver.

As Oliver stows the orb in the bag on his belt, the group gets up, heads for the door, and enters the hallway. Suddenly, Oliver stops and hugs his sister.

"Be safe! You have a power I do not understand but please know that I will use all of the magic I have to help protect you all," Oliver states.

Rose smiles. "Let's pray that does not occur and Mom knows we are here."

Rose is the first to quietly open the door to Ethan's room. Looking around, she finds Ethan asleep under the bed. She and Oliver quietly levitate him back onto the bed. Rose motions for Sebastian to sit in the chair next to Ethan. Once everyone was in place, she touches Sebastian's forehead, then Ethan. As she does, her eyes turn white, and Zander moves in and places both of his hands upon Rose's face. Her eyes stop glowing once the four are connected.

Oliver moves about the room, sealing it and protecting them. Seconds later, he feels a hand on his shoulder and turning, notices Rose and Zander on the other side of the room, sealing it.

"Are you okay?" Oliver asks, studying her carefully.

"Yes. But if it had not been for Zander, I might have leveled the castle," she remarks.

"What now?" Oliver asks.

"We wait," Zander replies.

Chapter 14
Help Arrives

With the fog spinning around him, Sebastian finds his attire transforming on the spot. Pulling his wand, he spins it over his head as the vision begins to materialize, dropping him in the middle of a hallway. Looking around, Sebastian takes note of where he is when he realizes that he is wearing Mundane clothes.

"Blah! Are you kidding me? Mundane clothes! Yuck! But I do dig the boots and, oh hell, is this Mundane school?" Sebastian inquires out loud as he walks down the hallway looking around.

"Double yuck! Definitely some kind of Mundane school," he says aloud to himself.

"Ethan, where are you?" he asks as students rush by. "Weird. Do they always run around like this?" Sebastian mutters under his breath as he continues down the hallway until he turns a corner and notices trouble.

Brandon and his buddies are shoving Ethan into his locker face first. When the three suddenly fly backwards and land on the ground, Ethan notices Sebastian standing at the far end of the hall, his wand in hand.

As Brandon and his buddies get up, brush themselves off, and charge down the hall toward Sebastian, other students stop to watch, many excited to see someone finally standing up to Brandon. Sebastian takes off his jacket, throws it on the floor, and drops his wand on top of it. In one quick motion, he puts his hands up in a guard position as one of the guys swings at him. Blocking the swing easily, Sebastian punches under the guy's arm in an uppercut that knocks him off his feet. Sebastian spins and catches the other guy in the back of the head with a tornado kick. Then, he kicks Brandon in the rib cage, causing him to spit blood.

While Brandon is doubled over, Sebastian notices that one of the other guys had gotten up and is going after Ethan. Quickly, Sebastian rolls over Brandon's back, catches the other guy's fist, spins him around, and strikes him dead in the face, breaking the guy's nose. As he is doubled over holding his nose, Sebastian hits him in the face with his knee, knocking the guy unconscious.

Brandon and his remaining buddy are not happy. They charge at Ethan when they find themselves frozen in the air. Sebastian's eyes turn black as he reaches for Brandon's buddy and throws him into the wall, knocking him out. Sebastian then walks up to Brandon, turns him around, glares at him, puts one finger on his chest and another on his forehead as Brandon unfreezes and flies full speed, like shot out of a cannon, into the locker. As Brandon slides down the locker, out cold, two more guys run up and grab Sebastian's arms. He slams them into each other, slips the hold, and smashes both of them into the lockers face first.

"Punks!" Sebastian spits.

The two guys get up and put up their fists, ready to fight some more. Sebastian steps in front of Ethan, claps his hands together, then pulls them apart, revealing a glowing orb.

"If I were you, I would run," Sebastian declares, looking furious.

The two guys take off, but Sebastian launches the orb at the back of one of them. As he disappears, the orb takes off into the air and within seconds the other guy is also gone.

Sebastian brushes himself off as the other students in the hall break into cheers and applause. Ethan walks up and hands Sebastian his jacket and wand.

"You might want these. But if you do not want the jacket, I will take it," Ethan says, smiling.

"You're cute! But you can have the jacket," Sebastian replies, laughing. "Ethan, you have to understand, I will never leave you or let anything happen to you."

"I've figured that out," Ethan says, turning away to hide the tear rolling down his cheek. Ethan wipes his face but as he hugs Sebastian, he collapses.

"What is going on?" Ethan asks, holding his head. His eyes begin to glow, and he sinks to his knees.

"Ethan, focus on my voice. I have to get you out of here," Sebastian says, holding Ethan up and quickly moving down the hallway while Ethan is doubled over in pain. Rounding the corner, the two hear clapping and a voice that is all too familiar to Sebastian.

"My mistress will love this. How sweet! They like each other," Raven mocks as she projects fireballs at them.

Raven spins her hands together as the area begins to darken. Sebastian holds up his free hand, casting light to protect them. As Raven causes the area to grow even darker, Sebastian responds by causing the light to grow brighter.

"Ethan, I cannot keep holding you up, stop her, and save our butts. Come on! I need you to snap out of it," Sebastian demands.

"Save yourselves," Raven laughs, throwing dark orbs into the air as they fly at full speed toward Sebastian and Ethan.

Pointing his wand at the ground, Sebastian causes an energy field to appear, slowing the orbs to a snail's pace until they finally stop and explode. Furious, Raven tries to throw two more, but they explode in her hands. Looking over the energy shield, Sebastian sees a flickering ball of light moving toward them. Then, a shadowy figure appears.

"I've got him."

Sebastian bows his head at the sight of the silver and gold band on the figure's head as he takes Ethan from Sebastian and lowers him down to the ground.

"What happened?"

"Some form of mind control, I think." Sebastian answers.

In the distance, a second figure battles with Raven. Suddenly, she flies backward, spitting blood. As she stands up, summons an orb, and throws it, the figure waves their hand, and the orb turns into a giant bubble and then pops.

"How lovely! A bubble? Growing weak are you, Nadia?" Raven hisses, throwing another orb.

Nadia raises her hand, and the orb stops in mid-air. Her eyes turn purple as she raises Raven off the ground, causing her to choke. Magical light flies around Raven entrapping her in a prison cell.

Looking back, Nadia exclaims "I have her, Kelvin. Get Ethan and Sebastian out of here. Now!"

Nodding, Kelvin hoists Ethan to his feet and motions for Sebastian to follow.

"Sebastian?" Kelvin asks.

"Yes, My King… I mean, Sir… I mean…." Sebastian trips over his words.

"Sebastian, your job is to hold off any of the darkness advancing on us. And, Sebastian, please call me Kelvin," the figure says, placing his free hand on Sebastian shoulder.

"Yes, Sir," Sebastian tightens his grip on his wand. "Kelvin, you do know that this is Ethan's dream, right?"

"I do. Later, Nadia will explain what we are doing here," Kelvin remarks as he suddenly stops and backs up as Liam materializes out of the ground.

"Well, well, well! Brother, this is a pleasant surprise. You, the traitorous king, and the prince! Oh, when I kill all three of you not only will it be fun, but I will be greatly rewarded," Liam smiles, rubbing his hands together.

"Besides, when you are all out of the way, maybe I will ask that ugly, nasty-looking princess… oh yeah, what is her name?... oh yes, ugly Rose, for her hand in marriage," he tries to say as he finds his self-flying into the air.

Not knowing what's going on, Sebastian looks at Kelvin. Then, when they look at Ethan, they see that he has his staff in hand, and his eyes are glowing blue.

"Ugly! You think my sister is ugly? I will show you ugly," Ethan shouts as vines explode from the ground and begin wrapping themselves around Liam. Scrambling, Liam begins blasting the vines off as Ethan limps forward, twists his staff to the right, and more vines explode from the ground.

"You know, I have grown tired of you," Ethan says, standing nose to nose with Liam, who is now bound by vines. Ethan stows his staff and retrieves his wand. Stepping back, he points the wand straight at Liam, when a cloud of smoke appears and starts wrapping itself around Liam. Ethan's eyes turn gray as the vines begin to snap. Raven flies overhead, landing just a few feet from Liam, quickly casting magic to break the vines' hold.

Laughing, Raven turns her attention toward the group as Nadia appears, orbs flying around her. Angry, Ethan transforms his wand into a staff, spins it three times, then taps it twice, and points it at Raven. A scream is heard, then a second one, as two phoenixes explode into the air, racing at Liam and Raven. Trying to deflect the oncoming phoenixes, Raven and Liam point their wands straight at the birds. The one on the right opens its mouth, releasing a sonic scream and dropping both of them to their knees, dazed and not realizing what is occurring. The two phoenixes continue to fly around them, screaming and pecking at Liam and Raven.

"Now!" Nadia yells as they are distracted. Sebastian levitates Liam and Raven into the air while, at the same moment, Kelvin opens a portal underneath them. Ethan spins his staff, catching the edge of the portal, causing it to grow as the two phoenixes are the first to disappear through it.

&

Back in Ethan's room, Sebastian disappears from the chair and Ethan starts to fade.

"What the…?" Rose moves towards Ethan, but he completely disappears.

"Wait," she calls, running from the room with Zander and Oliver following.

"Wake the castle and summon the guards!" she yells as she runs down the hallway toward the gate, her clothes transforming with each step. As she reaches the gate, she strikes the lever with magic and runs through, barely giving the rampart time to fully drop. Reaching the end of the rampart, she stops and watches as a portal appears in the sky. Disappearing on the spot, she reappears feet from the portal, which explodes as Raven flies out, followed by Liam and the two screaming phoenixes. Liam attacks the phoenixes with his magic, casting darkness against them as Raven hits the portal with the full strength of her magic, trying to seal it.

Casting a lightshield around herself, Rose runs toward Raven, wand drawn, casting one orb of light after another at her. Screaming loudly, one the phoenixes launches Liam back through the portal, but he reappears a second later, hitting the ground face first.

Rising to his feet, Rose notices blood running from Liam's nose and the side of his lip. As he turns to throw three dark orbs at her, they stop in mid-air and explode as everyone is thrown off their feet.

"How is this possible? Stop them! Stop them now! Raven screams as dark creatures appear and begin attacking the portal.

Several of the dark creatures grab the portal but they are hit with the full power of light as Sebastian and Ethan fly out of the portal, landing just feet from Rose.

At the sight of his twin brother, Oliver teleports and lands feet from Rose, Ethan, and Sebastian, throwing the darkness back as Zander emerges out of the ground. In the distance, from the top of the castle, Bethany and Destiny appear with archers lining up behind them. As the last of the guards join the line, Phineas dives from the tower and takes to the air, soaring down the side of the castle and pulling up right before touching the ground as fairies emerge alongside him. Phineas looks back over his shoulder to see that his mother has arrived with a group of the elite guards forming a protective shield around the castle. Looking out over the land, Bethany raises her fist then drops it as arrows zoom past her into the air hitting the dark creatures and dropping them on the spot.

Moving to attack Rose, Raven pulls her wand down and begins to spin it, summoning lightning. Suddenly, the wand explodes in her hand. Holding her hand in pain, Raven flies into the air and is thrown around like a rag doll as Kelvin and Nadia also emerge from the portal. Nadia holds Raven in the air as Kelvin grabs the portal and throws it under the darkness. Nadia drops Raven through the portal and whistles as the portal explodes and begins pulling everything into it. Growing larger, the winds from the portal pick up as Belinda, Drago, Autumn, and the multiple other dragons following them land.

"Get them out of here!" Nadia commands, nodding to the dragons.

Belinda and Drago grab Oliver and Zander by the back of their shirts and throw them onto their backs. Autumn grabs Rose and throws her up into the air. Then, she grabs Ethan while Drago grabs Sebastian. In one swift movement, the three dragons take to the air and fly toward the castle. The other dragons also take to the air next to Belinda, Drago, and Autumn, flying with them as escorts.

Protesting, Rose dives off the back of Autumn but another dragon, flies in, grabs her cloak and holds on tight to her.

"Are you crazy?" Autumn yells.

"I cannot leave my mother," Rose replies, trying to twist out of her cloak.

"Rose, stop! She will be fine," Belinda remarks, soaring alongside Autumn.

As the dragons land behind the fairy guards, they can see that Kelvin and Nadia are glowing and holding hands as the portal grows in size. As Rose begins to run forward, Belinda moves in front of her.

"Rose, I insist you stay back!"

Peeking over the tail of the dragon, Rose and everyone else can hear telepathically.

"Rose, Ethan, Oliver! Stay where you are! You cannot handle the power of the vortex portal and we cannot lose you. Our people need you. Our paths will cross again. We...."

But before Nadia can finish, she spins on the spot, grabs the re-emerging Raven, and launches her through the portal for a second time.

Kelvin walks up, dragging Liam by his collar, and throws him into the portal after Raven. Together, Nadia and Kelvin start to seal the portal, but it explodes again, throwing them off their feet. Spinning out of control, the portal flies up into the sky.

As the vortex grows, Zander walks away from the group, wand out and blasts the vortex with full power. Knowing what has to be done, the others follow. As the portal begins to seal, Rose notices that Belinda is soaring across the ground as Kai, the Shade Dragon, moves in on Kelvin and Nadia. Fire shoots out from Kai's mouth as the beast flies backward and slams into a lightshield.

In the distance, Rose also notices the arrival of Lord Aden. As he starts to pull down, summoning an energy ball, he suddenly finds himself frozen in place. Running across the field, eyes glowing, and wand out is Rose. Zander breaks his spell on the vortex and takes off after Rose.

As he does, he yells, "Stay locked onto the vortex! Get it sealed! I have her!"

Zander begins to catch up to Rose and yells,

Cincinno.

Lock.

The necklace around Rose's neck begins to glow and creates a field of light around her. With each step she takes, the field grows in brightness and power. Suddenly stopping, Rose stands there looking around, as Zander takes the opportunity to catch up to her.

Only feet from her, he flies backwards as she turns her head to look at him, her eyes glowing white as she throws plasma bolt after plasma bolt at Aden. Breaking his magical attack on the lightshield, Aden turns to take on Rose, when he finds himself face-to-face with Zander.

Unaware of Aden's attempted attack, Nadia looks to her left and, as Rose comes into her line of sight, sees that she is fighting Aden. Furious, Aden summons dark creatures, and Kai, the Shade Dragon, appears snapping at Rose who releases lightning at the dragon, causing him to fly up into the air to dodge the attack. Diving towards her at full speed, Kai's nostrils turn orange as he opens his mouth, but Kelvin suddenly appears behind Rose, grabs her, and disappears on the spot. Because of his speed, Kai crashes into the ground.

Spinning light appears around Nadia, transforming her into a being of solid light.

"Kelvin, keep her back," Nadia calls in a deep voice as Aden and all the dark creatures find themselves in the air. As Aden's guards advance on

Nadia, they all begin exploding as Destiny appears and unleashes orb after orb. As each orb hits the dark creatures, they turn to trees, plants, and animals.

The portal in the sky collapses and begins to close as Oliver, Ethan, and Sebastian appear on one side of Nadia in time to hold back Dawn and Hawke who have just appeared.

"Belinda, Drago, Kelvin, one of you get him out of here," Nadia orders telepathically.

"Here Zander. Take her," Kelvin says, handing Rose to him and running toward Oliver.

"Hi," Zander says, smiling at Rose as the two fight off the darkness.

"Mom, I am not afraid. If you have the ability to close the portal, close it," Oliver calls as he pushes Dawn and Hawke back.

"Not with you in the way, Oliver," Nadia replies.

"Rose and Ethan, can you hear me?" Oliver inquires telepathically.

"We can," they reply in unison.

"You know what you have to do," Oliver says as Kelvin, who had just reached him, flies backward.

The darkness screams as Rose and Ethan hold hands tightly as their eyes glow blue.

"We are the guardians of this land. We are the protectors of our people. Our love for everyone is unconditional. We give everything to you," they chant in unison as an energy field explodes from where they stand, leveling all the dark creatures with an energy wave. As the wave rolls over the land, the darkness explodes. When the wave hits Dawn and Hawke, they are thrown from their feet.

Oliver appears next to Rose and takes her hand as a more powerful wave of energy rolls out over the land, causing quakes.

Telepathically, the three siblings connect to their mom and dad.

"Mom, shut it down," Ethan calls as a tear rolls down his cheek, knowing that she may not come back.

"Mom, we love you and we know you will be back. Do what you need to do," Rose says.

Nadia nods, claps three times, and, on the third clap, throws her hands apart. As the portal begins to seal, Kai, the Shade Dragon, flies in, snapping at her. With a flash of light, the two phoenixes appear, screaming and pushing the dragon back as they land one on each of Nadia's shoulders.

Then, Nadia, the phoenixes, and the portal are gone. Kai's motionless body falls from the sky, then disappears inches from the ground.

Night falls over the land as the moon hits the grass, glistening in the night mist. Kelvin extends his arms to Oliver and hugs him as Ethan and Rose run to their father and join in the hug. Close behind, Sebastian, Zander, Bethany, and Destiny watch as the four hug each other. Guards hold out their wands and light the area, while the fairies fly around the group and form a magical field of protection around them. Four guards approach, bow to the King, and jam Hawke and Dawn down onto their knees. Kelvin motions the guards to take them away.

"Wait," Destiny says, approaching her mother.

Placing her wand on Dawn's neck, "Where are they?" she demands.

"Somewhere you would never go, my darling," Dawn laughs.

"So help me, I will take out your voice box," Destiny declares.

"You do not have the nerve or the guts to do so," Hawke sneers as Kelvin walks up and strikes Hawke in the face with the back of his closed fist. Kelvin grabs Hawke by his hair, pulls his head back, and jams his wand into Hawke's neck.

"Now, answer her question! She may not have the nerve, but I do. I will see to it personally…" Kelvin begins to say when Dawn interrupts.

"Don't you remember how you nearly killed all of us the last time you used your brains," she asks sarcastically.

Before anyone can say a word, from where she is standing, Rose hits her grandmother with an energy blast. Destiny turns and looks at Rose over her shoulder. But just as she approaches, the entire Council appears, wands drawn and ready to attack Dawn or Hawke if the need arises. Rose walks past Destiny, grabs the back of her grandmother's shirt, and drags her across the ground.

"What is she doing?" Lucy asks as members of the Council and guard follow, laughing, many left speechless.

At the edge of the water, Rose summons her staff and taps it on the ground. Dawn flies up over the water and as she is suspended there, Rose whistles and mermaids appear.

"Now, where are they?" she screams. Dawn laughs and suddenly finds herself hanging upside down and falling into the water.

"It looks like Lady Rose is going to drown the old lady," one member of the Council remarks as the scene repeats two more times.

"Now, where are they? This time, I will order the mermaids to attack," Rose states, her eyes starting to glow.

"They are at the castle of Aden, in the dungeon guarded by some of the darkest and nastiest creatures around. I hope you go, and I hope they kill you for my mistress," Dawn replies, still smiling.

Rose turns, snaps her fingers, and the old woman falls into the water. When she comes up for air, the mermaids grab her and drag her under. Rose walks up to Hawke, points her wand at his face, and he drops lifelessly to the ground.

"Wow!" Ethan and Oliver say in unison.

"Remind me never to piss you off," Sebastian remarks looking at Rose with respect.

Walking past him, Rose responds, "Captain, get your elite group ready and bring me my horse."

"Yes, ma'am," the captain replies as he runs towards the castle.

"What was that?" Oliver and Ethan ask in unison as Kelvin stands behind them with his arms crossed.

"My way of dealing with a problem," Rose replies.

"A problem? Rose! You just killed them," Ethan says.

"Actually, No." Destiny smiles and hugs Rose. "But how did you figure it out?"

"One of the ancient texts in the library spoke of Avalon and how any member of darkness if thrown to the mermaids would be taken to Avalon and saved by the light," Rose replies, winking at Destiny.

"Okay, that is all well and good. But what about Hawke?" Ethan asks.

"Silly brother! I erased his mind. When he awakens, he will remember nothing," she says, smiling at her brother.

"Well, I think it is time for everyone to head in for those horses that your sister asked for," Kelvin suggests.

"I will be right there. Give me a few moments, please." Ethan requests.

"Go ahead, Dad. We are staying with Ethan," Oliver and Rose both reply.

"I will see you inside," Zander says, kissing Rose on the cheek.

As the group walks over the rampart, Ethan throws rocks into the water while Rose and Oliver watched everyone head in. She and Oliver notice Sebastian, in the distance, standing guard but not approaching, giving the three privacy in which to talk.

"Well?" Rose asks, looking at Ethan.

"Well, little sister, you have to learn not to butt into other people's business," Ethan replies, sitting down on a boulder.

"Butting into others business…" Rose starts to say when Oliver raises his hand, cutting her off.

"Ethan, if you want to be mad, be mad at me. I was the one who asked her to take us into your dreams. As you slept, your screams shook the castle. When we looked in on you, we found you floating on the ceiling or under your bed. You and I have talked about everything. Why didn't you come to me?" Oliver inquires, looking at Ethan.

"Come to you? Come to you?" Ethan yells.

"How do I come to my brother, Mister Popular, and tell him I am being bullied or that I am in love and have seen the person I love killed, not to mention the fact that the person I am in love with is a dude," he snaps.

"Ethan, I would have helped you out with Brandon and his buddies. You know that!" Oliver exclaims, looking stern.

"Just for once, I wanted to be me and not have to always rely on you. We always do everything together and, for once, I just wanted to be me," Ethan replies, glancing at Oliver.

"We do *not* do everything together," Oliver states as Rose shakes her head, indicating that she disagrees.

"Do you have something to say about this?" he asks.

"Yes, I do! I love both of you to pieces. You two are my amazing older twin brothers, but you two each need to develop your own personality. I know you two will always have each other's back, but you need to give each other space to grow and become unique. Also, Ethan, you do not have to keep it from us about being 'gay.' We are cool with it." Rose gets up and hugs Ethan. Oliver joins in the hug.

"Look, Ethan, I am 10 minutes older, and I have always been the protective big brother. I agree and I will let you have space. Now, there is a guy waiting for you up on that hill. Go speak with him. Rose and I are going to head into the castle now," Oliver explains, pushing his brother in a "get going" motion.

Ethan smiles. "Thank you!"

The three start up the hill when they stop.

"Go ahead. I will catch up," Ethan says.

"Sebastian?" Ethan inquires.

"Yes, Your Majesty," he begins to reply when he suddenly finds his lips and Ethan's touching. Confused, Sebastian quickly pulls back and regards Ethan cautiously.

"I never thanked you for what you did," Ethan says, smiling.

"I would do it anytime to protect you," Sebastian replies, looking directly at Ethan now. Ethan smiles and leans in to kiss him again. This time, neither move away. When they are done, Sebastian smiles and notices the captain of the guards approaching with horses.

"Mm hmm. Gentlemen. I do not mean to interrupt."

"No interruption, Captain," Ethan says as he smiles at Sebastian, and they take the reins of the horses from the captain.

Hopping up on the horses, they click their heels, turn the horses, and ride toward the gates of the castle. As they come closer, they find Oliver on his horse and their father on a beautiful white stallion. Looking around, Ethan sees a shadow fly overhead. Landing behind them, Autumn has now donned a beautiful saddle and Rose is mounted on her back. As Autumn roars and bows, Drago lands with Zander mounted on his back. Soaring overhead, Belinda watches as Leo, Lucy, and Leaf walk beside Kelvin.

"Where is she?" Kelvin asks, pulling his pocket watch from his pocket.

"I am here," Destiny replies, riding up on a pony, Oliver and Ethan try to keep straight faces and not laugh. They hit each other in the arm with amusement at the sight of Destiny riding such a diminutive mount.

"Are you sure, you do not want to stay? If that thing goes down, we do not have time to stop and carry you," Kelvin remarks, smiling at her.

"I understand," she replies, bowing her head.

Kelvin turns his horse, looks at the members of the Council, Bethany, Cedric, and Phineas.

"It is up to all of you to keep the castle protected," he declares.

As the horse rears up, Kelvin holds up his staff, lightning striking it, and takes off at a gallop. Behind him, the Captain of the Guards, Ethan, Oliver, and Sebastian follow along with the rest of the guard. When the last of the riders on the ground have started to move, Zander and Rose click the sides of their respective dragons and take to the air.

Chapter 15
The Fight to Save Friends

The night breeze howls as the horses gallop across the land. Leading the group towards Castle Aden is Sebastian. Upon reaching the top of the hillside overlooking the valley where the castle is situated, everyone is scanning the area to ensure its safety.

"How do we get in?" Ethan inquires, examining the dark, looming building.

"There is a passage near the base of the waterfall that my brother and I used in order to avoid our father seeing us," Sebastian replies.

"Will it be guarded?" Kelvin asks, pulling a spy glass from his cloak pocket and scoping out the land around the castle.

"No guarantees, Your Majesty, but it would be the quickest and easiest way into the lower parts of the castle," Sebastian notes as Zander and Rose land and dismount their dragons.

"Lord Kelvin, it appears nightriders are mounting up in the back," Zander declares, looking concerned.

"Look," Rose says, pointing her finger at a large group of riders that have taken off down the path.

"Here is what we are going to do. I am taking Rose, Zander, the dragons, and the guards to go after the nightriders. Oliver, Ethan, and Sebastian go into the castle and find your friends. Then, get out and get back to the castle. We will meet you there," Kelvin instructs as he clicks his heels into the side of his horse and takes off down the path, the guards in tow.

Rose and Zander jump back on the dragons and follow the King and the guards.

Oliver, Sebastian, and Ethan quietly hide their horses, use a silencing spell so no one will hear them and head down the hill on foot. Upon reaching the edge of the water, Sebastian notices that his father has heightened security around the castle.

"Do not touch the water. It appears to be hexed," he warns as they walk over the bridge and quietly slide along the sidewall towards the waterfall.

When they reach the waterfall, they find that the entryway is blocked off.

"What do we do now?" Ethan asks. Sebastian steps back and points his wand at the rubble.

"Stand back," he says as he waves his wand and blows a hole through the pile of rubble.

Perdere.

Destroy.

"We do not have much time. Everyone in the castle, will have heard that," Sebastian remarks as they move quickly through the large hole.

"Great idea! Let's tell the whole castle we are here," Oliver mumbles under his breath as he pulls his wand and flicks balls of light into the space.

Lux in via.

Light the way.

The long hallway lights as Sebastian motions for them to follow as he quickly leads the way down the spiral stairs that lead to the dungeons. As they reach the bottom step, they come face-to-face with the elite guards.

"Alert Lord Aden of intruders," one of the guards orders.

Glacio.

Freeze.

When the guard turns to leave, he finds that his feet are frozen to the ground, and he begins to freeze on the spot. Sebastian spins his wand again.

Glacio Totum.

Freeze everything.

Many of the guards froze on the spot. Those who are not affected by the spell are stopped in their tracks by a wall of vines. As the guards draw their swords and start to cut the vines, they hear,

Item vitem in pariete.

Wall of vines.

With only a few guards remaining, Oliver and Sebastian drop the guards on the spot with sleeping hazes.

"Nice trick," Ethan says, regarding Oliver and Sebastian.

"Thanks. But we have to move quickly and quietly," Oliver remarks as they reach the main cell holding Olivia, Brooke, Claire, and a young elf boy.

With one quick movement, Ethan blows the lock off the door and the three enter the cell.

"Oliver," Olivia says, hugging him as Claire and Brooke rise to their feet. The young boy draws back, watching what is occurring.

"We can have reunions later. We do not have time for this right now," Ethan stresses as he moves toward the door, peering out cautiously to check the surrounding area.

"Oliver, this is Rusty," Olivia introduces the young elf, who bows his head and walks past everyone toward the door.

Once in the hallway, he picks up his cloak and swings it around his shoulders as armor appears on him along with a large staff.

Claire leans toward Oliver and whispers, "He doesn't talk much."

"Thanks, Claire, I can see that," Oliver states, annoyed.

"What's up with his right eye?" Ethan inquires.

"Oh, he is blind," Olivia responds.

"What…?" Oliver begins to ask.

The young man turns and explains, "I am blind in my right eye and have partial vision in my left. Magic enhances my other senses and also allows me to see when I have my staff."

Ethan and Oliver regard one another, shrug their shoulders, then quickly check the area. Upon finding it to be safe, they motion for the others to follow. The group reaches the bottom of the stairs leading to their way out when they are met by Liam and another group of elite guards with their wands and swords drawn. As the seven stop, the three wizards find themselves engaged in magical duels with the guards and Liam.

"Take cover and do not get blasted," Oliver tells Olivia, Claire, and Brooke as they take refuge behind the door to an open cell.

"I do not have time for this," the young man declares as he taps his staff on the ground. The end lights and his eyes start glowing purple.

Aream Purgare.
Clear the area.

As the last word leaves the young elf's mouth, the elite guard drops to the ground dead.

"Really? That spell is forbidden," Sebastian remarks, pushing past the elf and advancing on Liam.

"Not where I am from," the young man says, appearing to be annoyed.

Liam summons magic around him for protection but gets entangled in a magical duel with Oliver.

Annoyed by the continuing attacks by Liam and the darkness, the young elf points his wand at the hinges of the large oak door.

Exsolvo.
Release.

The door flies from the hinges and is launched right into Liam, dazing him as he hits the ground. Trying to get up and catch his breath, Liam places his palm on the ground, summoning more dark creatures.

"There are way too many of them," Ethan cries as he blocks blasts of dark magic.

"Sebastian, is there another way out?" Oliver inquires.

"Yes and No. This is the fastest unless we go through the main castle, but that will be worse," he replies, striking three guards with dark rays, slamming them into the wall.

"Must I do everything?" the three hear as the young elf walks past them, spins his wand, and points it at the elite guard who freeze and explode.

Terminus Haec.
End this.

Liam manages to get up and position himself behind the guards, away from the action as he watches the young elf fight. In a mere second, the frozen guards come back to life, but then, all drop to their knees, holding their ears, as one of the phoenixes Ethan has summoned from his dreams, screams.

"Quickly, follow me," the seven hear as they turn to see Nadia standing there, light orbs flying around her, and her hand out in a fist.

As she opens her hand, the light orbs fly past her and hit the elite guard, blinding them. Oliver, Ethan, and Sebastian guide the three girls and the young elf back towards Nadia. As they turn, Nadia whistles, and the phoenix flies toward them and takes off down the hall, screaming, as they ascend the staircase. At the top of the steps, Sebastian pushes ahead and takes the lead.

"Let's get them out of here. Follow me," he commands.

The group picks up speed as more and more guards chase them down the long corridor.

"There is the door," Sebastian indicates as Liam and Aden rise up out of the ground, laughing and clapping.

As they realize that they are surrounded.

"Well, well, Nadia. It looks as if you will have to surrender, finally," Aden says pointing his wand at her.

When Aden begins moving his hand, the young elf slams his staff on the ground, touches both palms against the ground, and, as he rises to his feet, Aden's wand explodes, and all of the dark creatures disappear instantly.

Furious, Aden moves his hand and raises the young elf off his feet with magic. The elf waves his hand and counters the attack, falling to the ground as Aden releases him. The elf gets to his feet, raises his arm, points his index finger, and as he snaps the fingers on his other hand, Aden's cloak bursts into flames.

The young elf moves out of the way as Nadia spins on the spot, teleporting the group to where Aden and Liam stand. Sebastian pushes the doors open as the others follow just as Liam pulls his wand and goes after Nadia who opens a portal under him. As he falls through, she reseals it behind him.

"Get them out of here," Nadia yells as she pulls down, puts her hands together, and begins to blast light orbs at everything in the castle. As creatures fall, she backs out of the door, watching as the light destroys the castle, the light so powerful that it is blowing the stones of the castle apart and tearing holes in the wall. Rusty, Oliver, Ethan, and Sebastian come up next to Nadia and, in the same move, also begin launching orbs at the castle. Their combined magic causes several towers to fall inwards, into the courtyard as dark creatures begin exploding into the air trying to escape, but they are struck by lightning.

Rusty summons lightning which strikes various parts of the castle and the darkness. Wall by wall, the castle continues to fall in on itself. Then, Nadia slides her palms against each other and opens a portal under the castle and as the portal opens further, it falls through and disappears. Finally, Oliver and Ethan hit the portal with magic.

Signaculum.

Seal.

"Boys, if the portal gets too big, I want you to step back," Nadia explains.

"We've got this. We are not going to let it take you this time," they reply in unison.

As they work to close the portal, Aden and Liam teleport in behind them, and, before anyone knows what is happening, Rusty seizes Liam and Aden in a magic field. Rusty, lifts the two dark wizards into the air and throws them headfirst into the portal. Pulling his hands together, he seals the portal.

Signaculum.

Seal.

Upon the portal closing a huge light column explodes from the spot. The young elf falls to his knees trying to catch his breath as Nadia watches.

"How interesting…" But before she can finish, she hears,

"Oliver! Dad, Rose, Zander, and the guards," Ethan shouts as Sebastian whistles for the horses.

Oliver and Olivia mount the back of one, Ethan and Claire on the other, and Sebastian and Brooke on the third. As the three horses rear up, the beautiful white stallion appears. As Nadia mounts the back of the horse, she extends her hand and pulls Rusty up on the horse behind her. Nadia points her wand in the air as a small ball of light flies from the tip.

Dirige in Via.

Guide the way.

Taking off down the path, the ball of light leads the way as Nadia and the group follow. The four horses carrying them race across the ground as the light guides them toward a village in the distance. When they reach the village, they see fires in the distance with smoke rising in the air. Ethan points his wand, and a pair of phoenixes take off, flying overhead and soaring over the land as beads of water fly up behind them. The phoenixes pick up speed and, in what looks like a synchronized dance, fly over the water, their feet skimming the lake, as they launch into the air, each pulling a column of water up behind them. The phoenixes take off over the village, singing as the water rains down, extinguishing the flames.

In the distance, Nadia observes that dark creatures are still attacking and Kelvin, Rose, Zander, and the guards are fighting them off.

"Rusty?" Nadia calls.

"Yes, ma'am?" he replies, looking at her.

"What do you see?" she asks.

Rusty raises his head as if scanning the land but, actually, he is listening.

"There are 15 guards descending on Kelvin, Rose and Zander, with another 10 in back emerging," he replies.

"Dear child, by chance do you know the ground quake spell?" she asks as she clicks the sides of her horse to go faster.

Without question, Rusty stows his wand, pulls a small stick from his pocket, flicks his hand down as his staff appears at full size. Now standing on the back of the galloping horse, Rusty jumps, flying into the air and landing on his feet in front of the party on the ground.

"What is he doing?" Ethan asks.

"Something, if done correctly, that is truly amazing. Everyone, hold tight to the horses!" Nadia yells as Rusty spins his staff in his hand, causing vines to explode from the ground, grabbing the darkness and slamming it down.

"Looks like we have help," Kelvin remarks as he throws three elite guards back.

Continuing to spin his staff, Rusty summons more vines from the ground. Then, suddenly, he slams the tip of his staff on the ground. The creatures of the dark explode as the ground shakes with one shockwave after another. As the shockwaves roll over the land, the central fountain in the village explodes as the guards direct the water in every direction to extinguish the flames. The young elf turns and walks towards the group as four horses and riders approach, and the phoenixes perch on a nearby downed fence.

Rose raises her wand, shoots four sparks into the air and when the clouds begin to spin, members of the Council land.

"Tend to the people. They need help," she commands as she runs toward Oliver and Ethan and her mom.

"Roslynn," Nadia calls as she holds out her arms and the two hug.

"My Queen," Zander says as he approaches and bows.

Olivia, Brooke, and Claire dismount from the horses and hug Rose and Zander. As everyone starts to smile, Rose notice that the young elf is lurking behind Nadia's horse.

Rose walked toward him, extending her hand.

"Thank you, young man. I am Rose and you are?" she asks as she waits for the young man to take her hand.

"I am Rusty," he says, feeling for her hand, then shaking it as he reaches around the horse, trying to keep his distance.

"Thank you. Where did you come from?" she inquires.

"I was freed by your family, but I got separated from my parents. Those goons seized me and threw me in the dungeons," he explains as he finally comes into full view of Rose and Zander.

As Zander looks at the young man, his eyes narrow.

"You're an elf," he declares as the young elf reaches up and touches his ears.

"It appears I am, Sir. Yes."

Rusty laughs as he looks around at the guards and members of the Council tending to the sick and injured.

"Lady Nadia, please, give your healers this," Rusty says as he reaches into his bag, rummaging around, and pulling out a vial of blue potion.

"The potion of the three rivers," Zander remarks as his eyes narrow even further.

Nadia smiles as she accepts the potion and walks towards Kelvin and the guards.

"What tribe are you from, young man?" Zander inquires scrutinizing Rusty.

"The Dusk Land River," Rusty said looking directly at him.

"Impossible! There is no such tribe," Zander declares.

Shaking his head, Rusty laughs.

"What is so funny, kid?" Zander demands, crossing his arms, clearly not amused.

"My tribe was created by a great and wise Wizard Elf, one of the best of our race. When he and his wife married, they looked for a new way to redefine the elf nation, and our high king and queen adopted the origins of the tribe markings I wear," Rusty explains, looking directly in Zander's face.

Pulling his sword, Zander holds the blade to the elf's throat.

"You lie! How dare you speak ill truths of my people!" Zander cries.

Reaching up, Rusty finds the tip of the blade, taps it, and the sword explodes. When Zander lowers what remains of the sword, it reconstructs.

Zander backs up, looks at the elf, and asks, "What dark magic is this?"

"Not dark magic, Sir. Just the magic of my people. Since I was born blind, the ancient healers worked with my parents and developed a protection spell. Because I was always getting hurt, my parents developed a spell so that nothing can harm me," he explains as he pulls a chain from under his tunic, revealing the same necklace that Rose wears.

Rose walks up.

Cincinno.

Lock.

A field of white light is created around the elf.

"What the heck!?" Ethan exclaims, looking at Rose.

"Unlock," Zander commands, looking at the elf.

"Explain how you got that necklace," Rose insists as she pulls the same one out from under her tunic. The young elf's eyes get large, and he looks at it as if he has seen a ghost. He reaches out his hand and touches the necklace. The light goes out, then flashed blue and silver.

He smiles. "That necklace, this necklace is the lifeline of the elves. It can only be worn by the guardian of our people. Yours was given to you when you were a baby by the Great Prince Zander, and he got it from his father. He gave it to you, High Queen Rose, because you will become his wife. Many years later, you will entrust it to protect the next guardian."

Standing quietly behind Rusty, holding hands, Nadia and Kelvin listen to the conversation.

"Uh hum. We do not mean to interrupt, but we believe this conversation and anything further that he has to say needs to be discussed at the castle, not out here in an open field," Nadia suggests.

"Indeed," Zander agrees.

"Captain, work with Lady Divinity and help her and the Council to heal these people," Kelvin requests. "Also, Captain, if help is needed, just summon."

"Yes, Sir." The captain motions for the guard to follow him.

"Belinda, Autumn, and Drago, my dears, take to the air and keep the area safe," Nadia directs.

Holding out her hand to Rusty, Nadia, Kelvin, and Rusty disappear on the spot, as the others follow. With a large pop, they all arrive in the courtyard of the castle as Destiny runs toward them, arms extended.

"Sis," Destiny says, a tear running down her face as she and Nadia hug one another.

"I owe you, for keeping my kids safe," Nadia says, smiling.

"The pleasure was mine," Destiny replies.

While the group settles in, Bethany and Phineas join them in the courtyard.

"Now, I believe Zander wishes to have a conversation with young Rusty," Kelvin remarks.

"Rusty, if what you say is true, then you are from the future. May I ask why the High Queen would entrust you with that relic necklace?" Zander inquires, folding his arms and tapping his foot as he looks at Rusty.

"I see nothing has changed with our King when he gets angry," Rusty remarks, smiling and laughing at the sight of Zander's ears turning bright red.

"I do not find you amusing," Zander remarks as Rusty walks past him and approaches Rose.

"Is he always like this?" he asks.

"Rusty, he is steeped in tradition and very protective of the elves," she replies.

Rusty turns, walks back over to look at Zander, and starts to unclip his right arm gauntlet. Nadia and Kelvin sit up straight in their chairs, watching, as Rose moves in closer to examine his arm.

Removing the gauntlet, Rusty reveals the same tattoo that Zander has on his arm. Nadia rises to her feet and walks over to examine the tattoo, while Rose, who is standing next to Zander, observes that he is reaching out to grab ahold of Rusty's arm. Examining the marking, Zander's eyes narrow. Determining that time is up, Rusty pulls his arm back and places the gauntlet back over the mark.

❧

"If you must know, I was born in 2056, 40 years into the future from this year. I am the 14-year-old youngest son and child of High King Zander and High Queen Roslynn. Our kingdom has been in great peace. Grandma and Grandpa have retired, and Uncle Oliver is the King of the Magical. Uncle Ethan is the King of Regions, and my mother is High Queen of the Elves. All three of them are beloved by our people, but, about a week ago, and when my mother sent me here, we were attacked.

Morgana returned. She killed many of the Arcane and Mundane. Mom entrusted this necklace to me. She told me to hold tight to it as it would protect me. She opened a portal, kissed me on the forehead, and pushed me through with my bag. I fell from the sky, landed on my back, and ended up in a field. I woke with a bunch of those jerk guards poking me and some dark woman standing over me.

Before I could even respond, she told them to seize me, and they threw me into the dungeon. That's where I met Olivia, Claire, and Brooke. They were kind and shared what food they had. I spent the first two days in deep meditation trying to reach my mom, my dad, my grandma, or anyone in the kingdom. However, my skills of telepathy are not as honed as my mother's. I was able to connect to one of my older sisters, but the connection was lost while I was communicating with her," Rusty says as a tear rolled down his cheek.

❧

Seeing how upset he is, Rose walks over and hugs Rusty comforting him.

"It is okay. You are here and we will take care of you," Rose reassures him.

"Um hum," Nadia clears her throat.

"While Rusty is here, do not inquire about your fate in the future. It can, and will, alter the timeline. He has already said too much," she notes, looking severely at everyone.

"I agree with Nadia. While my future son is here, no asking questions," Zander states.

Rusty is sitting down and rummaging through his bag. When he stops, his hand dances over a box, which he opens. Watching him, Rose instantly knows what is in the box.

"May I?" she asks as she picks up the orb. Walking to the middle of the courtyard, she raises her hand as a podium with a book on it appears. As she taps the orb against the book, it levitates and a much older-looking Rose steps out of it.

❧

"The courtyard... That means Russell Kelvin Alezander Elder Ignatius, my dear son, you made it safely to the time to which I sent you. I am sorry for my deception and for sending you away. Your father, uncles, aunt, grandparents, and I made grave mistakes and underestimated Morgana. I knew what I had to do to ensure your safety and the safety of the Arcane and the Elves. I ask that, someday, you will forgive me for not allowing you to stay. Your siblings are old enough to fight, however, you, being gifted and possessing the magic that you do, warrant me hiding you, Morgana will not be after you in the time to which I have sent you.

"Actually, Morgana, will not even know of your existence and, thus, it will alter the timeline accordingly. The magic I have used to send you to this time will keep you safe and protect you. I want you to hold tight to the magic you have learned. Things for you have not been easy, and I know you have trained with your father. But, Rusty, you are now on your own to remember what you have been taught. I have equipped your bag with some magical items you will need on your journey, including your staff. Keep those items safe. Remember, do not blow things up, or lose anything, and do, please, behave. Also, I have given you the spell book of High Elder Elfish Magic. Remember that you can still achieve greatness even without your sight.

"As everyone continues to watch, the elder Rose turns to speak with the group. Roslynn, Oliver, Zander, and Ethan, if you four can hear me then you need to listen carefully. We underestimated Morgana and the Dark Council. We thought they were gone, but they are not. We overlooked two critical things: one, Morgana's book, the *Book of Dark Shadows*. This book keeps her living even when she has fallen, but there is a greater power we must worry about, the Council of Darkness. While many of us have destroyed five of its seven members, the two most powerful remaining members, keep resurrecting Morgana. Do not underestimate them, the way many of us have! We have lost too many, some very close to us.

"Remember, the greatest power against Morgana is the power of the combined magic of Oliver, Ethan, and myself. Morgana cannot stand or survive when we are combined. But even that cannot stop her fully unless the book and that horrid Council are destroyed. The three of us weaken her and, every time she comes back, she comes back with vengeances that have never been seen before.

"I say to you three, and Zander, dear, if you hear this, protect Rusty. He knows the ways of our people. He has studied all of the magical forms and at fourteen can do things that no one has ever seen before. He possesses the knowledge of the ancient high magic of the elves. And Zander, my love, he will not need to be babied, just watched. He is able to do for himself.

"I hope the knowledge he possesses will help you alter the timeline accordingly and stop Morgana once and for all. Russell Ignatius, I tell you this, young man, you are to respect everyone there. You are to listen. If my younger self gives you a direct order, then that is an order from me. Do not give lip to anyone. You know to whom I am referring in the group. Alezander Caspar Rubious Elderchild Ignatius and Roslynn Sophia Nadia Phoenix-Ignatius, I ask both you to watch over Rusty and keep him safe. In time, many truths will be revealed. Be safe and may the powers of the elders protect you all."

❧

As the last words are spoken, the image of Rose fades and everyone in the courtyard looks around. Alezander gets up and walks over to Rusty's bag, picks it up and slides out the spell book. His eyes widen, then narrow, as he moves his hand along the cover. Nadia and Kelvin rise to their feet, watching Zander.

"Where was this found?" Alezander asks turning to look at Rusty.

"I am not answering that. You are not ready," Rusty replies, looking back at him.

Before anyone can respond, Alezander has his wand out and casts magic over the book. But the magic backfires and Rusty catches it in a charming orb and then dissolves the orb.

Turning the book over, Alezander examines it. When he moves his hand over the clasp of the book, it flies into the air and opens.

Rusty's ears perk up as he scrambles to his feet.

"You fool!" Rusty yells as he runs, wand in hand, pointing it at the book.

The book begins shooting lightning all over the courtyard. Oliver grabs Rose and pulls her behind one of the chairs as Sebastian and Ethan take cover under one of the nearby tables. Rusty, takes to the air, hits the book with the full power of light magic, and immobilizes it when he pulls his necklace from under his tunic,

"Lock it down," he commands as the book slams shut, and lands on the ground with a loud thud, the clasp sealed.

Rusty hits the ground on his knees and reaches for the table next to him to pull himself up.

"Are you nuts?" Nadia taps the book with her staff as Kelvin emerges from behind Nadia, staff drawn, and a dagger in the other hand.

"No. But that book is trouble. I needed to make sure he could handle the power of that book," Alezander replies, glaring in Rusty's direction.

"Alezander, that is fine. But you know the power of that book. No one knows the defenses against it," Kelvin remarks.

"My King, I understand that. But when have I ever been conventional in anything I do?" Alezander asks, looking at King Kelvin and winking.

Kneeling down, Rusty begins to feel around for the book, brushes it off, and says, "Give me three reasons why I shouldn't hex you right now for doing that?"

"One, any hex you would throw at me would bounce off. Two, I am your father and, three, to hex me would… well, you know," he replies, staring at Rusty.

"Lastly, I needed to make sure you could handle that book. The last time that book was seen, the young elf who opened it could not handle its power," Alezander continues, placing a hand on Rusty's shoulder.

"I know the story. It nearly destroyed the kingdom, the valley, and the realm," Rusty declares, glaring at Zander.

"Why would such a book exist?" Oliver asks, walking over to examine it.

"It exists as it contains some of the most ancient magic. My mother and father, next to myself, are the only ones who can control the book, let alone do any of the spells in it," Rusty explains, looking around at all of them.

"Why you three? What makes that book so unique other than being ancient?" Ethan inquires.

"That, Uncle Ethan, is what we do not know. Dad and Mom have been trying to figure out what they can about the book, but its origins are unknown. Its magic is powerful, but I have learned that some more powerful spells exist," Rusty explains as Zander and Sebastian help him up.

"With that said, I believe it is time for you, young man, to get ready for bed," Rose hands him his bag, hoping to redirect the conversation away from the book.

"Yes, ma'am," Rusty follows her as they quietly walk down the hallway until they finally reach their destination.

"This is where you will be sleeping. Your father is next door, and I am down the hall," Rose says, hugging him.

"Wait! Down the hall?" Rusty inquires looking confused.

"Rusty, I am not married to your father yet," Rose explains.

"Oh, wow! I came further back than expected. That is kinda funny, but also weird. Thank you and good night. I am going to turn in," Rusty says, hugging her.

Rose wraps her arms around him and holds him tight.

"Do you need help unpacking?" she asks.

"No, I've got it," Rusty replies, smiling.

"I may be blind, but I can see around the castle. Besides, I can call Cedric if I end up having too many challenges."

"Well then, good night, my child," Rose says as Rusty turns to enter his room.

"Rusty, wait! I will do everything in my power to get you back to your time," she says, smiling at him.

"Thank you, Mom," Rusty replies as he shuts his door.

"You're welcome," she says as she walks down the hallway to the courtyard.

The courtyard is quiet as everyone has turned in. Then, she notices Alezander on the back balcony, overlooking the forest. As she approaches, she hears her mother's voice.

"Alezander, what is wrong?" Nadia asks.

"It is nothing, My Queen," he replies.

"You are struggling with this," Rose remarks, emerging as Alezander turns his head to look at her over his shoulder.

"Not struggling. Just trying to sort things out," he replies as he turns back and leans on the railing.

"You two realize that you have much more responsibility now than you know," Kelvin remarks as he and Nadia look fondly at both of them.

Rose and Alezander nod as Kelvin and Nadia hug both of them, bidding them good night and heading back into the castle.

Rose and Alezander stand quietly, holding hands, looking up at the stars for what seems like an eternity. Finally, Alezander breaks the silence.

"Rose, I need you to listen to me. I am riding out tonight to the village that Lucas oversees. There are way too many questions, particularly if that book exists. I need the elder library to get those answers," he squeezes her hand and looks her straight in the eyes.

"Then, I am coming with you," Rose replies, smiling up at him.

"No. You are needed here to look after Rusty. Besides, I do not think, with your parents just returning, they would be happy if you took off immediately," he suggests, kissing her.

After they finish kissing, Rose remarks, "If that book has the powers that you speak of and it destroyed its last user, then you seeking answers is vital, particularly about how we should handle such a magical item."

Stepping back, Rose summons her staff, taps it twice on the ground as Alezander begins to glow white. When the light disappears, he looks down at the armor he is wearing. He smiles looking at it, then holds up his right arm, pointing at the medallion on the gauntlet.

"Really?" he asks.

"Hush! It was inspired by the one that Rusty wears. I thought maybe it was time we adopted it," she says, winking at him.

"I don't know what to do with you sometimes," Alezander says as they walk over a bridge leading to a back walkway. Cedric approaches, leading a black horse behind him.

Looking around the riding stables, Rose notices that Autumn has transformed back into a dog and is rolling in the hay as the phoenixes perch in the rafters.

Cedric hands the reins of the saddled horse to Alezander.

"Thank you, Cedric. I see that you have him loaded with supplies, and everything I need," Alezander remarks.

"Yes, Lord Alezander, including your sword and your bow and arrows. Do be safe, Sir," Cedric replies, disappearing on the spot.

Alezander kisses Rose, then jumps up into the saddle. The horse rears up, then comes down, hitting the ground at a gallop as Rose casts a portal at the end of the bridge. Alezander rides over the bridge and through the portal as it disappears.

Looking out over the bridge, Rose turns back toward the castle. Then, hearing a voice, she stops.

"Rusty? Rusty? Where are you?" the voice can be heard over the wind. Walking through the back part of the castle into the courtyard, Rose stops and listens again.

"Rusty? Rusty? Where are you?" Louder this time.

"Geez, don't shout," Rose mutters as she quickly ascends the stairs, looking around cautiously, stopping again to listen. This time, the voice is so loud that she has to cover her ears.

"That is loud! They have to be close," she surmises.

She walks quietly past the bedroom door, listening. When she reaches the old double oak doors at the end of the hallway, Rose glances quickly over her shoulder, then places her ear to the door. Inside, she hears the voice again calling out for R-u-s-t-y. Rose pulls her wand, points it at the lock, and the bolt clicks. But when she reaches for the handle to open the door, a fierce wind blows down the hallway, followed by a loud explosion that blows open the doors to the room. Along the hallway, the suits of armor, standing guard, turn their heads, lower their spears, and begin coming to life.

Turning to look into the room, Rose notices a spinning portal. A flashing light shines from the middle of the portal. Again, she hears the female voice calling out for Rusty. But, this time, Rose can also hear dark creatures snarling. Rose tightens her grip on her wand, draws her necklace out from under her shirt, and runs into the portal.

Nadia, Kelvin, and Oliver are the first to appear just as Rose disappears into the portal.

"Roslynn, *no!* The power of that room. *No!*" Nadia screams running toward the double doors that are flying back into place. With a spin of her wand, Nadia takes the doors right off their hinges.

The doors fly down the hall, crashing onto the floor just feet from where Kelvin is standing. As Rose completely disappears into the portal, Nadia summons forth light and sends it into the room and into the portal after her.

Destiny appears next to Nadia, doing the same thing.

"What is she doing? That room and the portal are dangerous," Destiny says.

As the light consumes the room, the energies explode and throw everyone off their feet. Then, in a flash of light, the Lady of White appears and strikes the portal with the full power of light. As Ethan, Sebastian, Bethany, and Phineas come up the stairs, they notice the darkness starting to fill the hallway.

"Nadia, we must seal the room before it can overtake the castle," Kelvin says, levitating the doors off the ground with his wand as Ethan and Oliver join him.

"No, not until Rose is out," Nadia replies as she starts to glow white and a lightfield appears, holding back the darkness.

"Rose! Rose! Rose! Can you hear us?" Nadia yells.

"Quickly! Go find her!" Destiny commands and the suits of armor run into the portal.

Again, the room explodes from the power of the light. This time, the energy hits the lightfield, causing a light show of different colors and the darkness explodes.

Cincinno.

Lock.

Suddenly, Rusty appears, standing behind everyone, his eyes glowing white, his hair a mess, and he has donned the royal robes of the elves. In his extended right hand is the necklace. He places it on the tip of his staff, and taps the end of the staff three times, causing the necklace to glow purple as it begins flickering.

"Look," Destiny points as a solid being of light appears, then another. Both grow brighter as they get closer. The being of light begins to materialize. Within seconds, a cloaked figure is standing in their midst, completely materialized as Rose materializes next to her. Balancing the cloaked figure, Rose carries her through the archway, hands the figure off to her mother. As she turns, her necklace explodes with light, the suits of armor reappear on their pedestals, the doors fly past them and slam against the archway. The hinges reconnect and lock the doors back into place. As the doors slam shut, the figure lowers their hood, and Rose bows her head to a young woman.

"Unlock," Rose commands as her necklace, Rusty's necklace, and the same necklace around the young woman's neck unlock.

Rusty pushes past everyone and runs to hug the young woman.

"Vivian!" Rusty declares.

The young woman extends her arms toward Rusty and hugs him.

"My brother. My dear little brother, you made it safely," the young woman with distinctive elfish traits cries, holding him at arm's length to look at him.

Her long, brown hair, with silver and green highlights, is pulled back in an elf knot, revealing her pointed ears. Under her riding cloak is a beautiful blue and green dress, hanging down the right side of which is a silver and gold looped belt with the markings of the elves. On her side, she carries a curved elfish blade. She carries a riding bag on her left side and her staff is strapped across her back. The young girl regards her surroundings and then bows her head to all the different individuals standing there.

"How…?" Rusty begins to ask as Vivian regards him with a stern look, one she knows he can sense.

"Mom," they say in unison, laughing.

"Everyone else?" Rusty asks.

"Safe for now, at least until Morgana finds them," Vivian replies.

"Rose, what happened? Those doors were to have remained closed and locked because of the portal in that room," Nadia states.

"I heard the screams and came running," Rose explains.

"But still…" Destiny begins to say when Rose puts up her hand to stop her from finishing.

"Aunt Destiny, I heard Vivian calling out for Rusty. I also learned in my studies that that room holds a very powerful portal, one through which Morgana's forces have tried to breach the castle for years. I knew entering the portal would unleash the darkness, but it would also send a message to the darkness that we can and will fight back," Rose replies.

As the group starts to disperse, Vivian and Rusty go into the study to work.

"Sis, do you think Zander is going to take another one being here well?" Ethan inquires.

"Ethan, he is not taking Rusty being here well. And he is definitely not going to take another one of our children from the future being here as well. For now, I have to keep a close eye on them so that they don't get into mischief in the library. Good night." she responds, turning toward the library.

Chapter 16
The Collapse

The following day, a quietness falls over the castle as only a few are moving about. Cedric is overseeing breakfasts with the palace cooks. Destiny strolls to the dining room, reading a book, and Oliver slips in quietly, looking around. Rose comes in, also observing the space, and greets her aunt and brother. As she sits down, she notices Rusty entering the room.

"Good morning," she says, smiling and hugging him.

"Morning," Rusty replies.

"How did you sleep?" Rose asks.

"Restless. I am not sleeping well," Rusty states as his eyes narrow as they alight on a tapestry. Rose looks up at the tapestry at which he is staring.

"Look, Oliver," Rose says, pointing at the tapestry.

"What?" Oliver asks, looking at the tapestry hanging on the wall. Suddenly, Rose bolts from the dining room and down the hall toward the library with Oliver and Rusty close behind. As she runs down the hall, she passes Bethany, Ethan, Olivia, and Vivian.

"What's going on? What's the hurry?" Ethan asks.

"You will see in a minute," Rose replies as she pushes the doors to the library open and runs in, her wand out as several books fly to podiums in the middle of the floor.

Vivian and Rusty shrug at each other, trying to figure out what's going on. As Rose reaches the podiums, she taps the covers of the books, causing the pages to begin flipping. The library doors slam shut, and the room starts to spin.

"Oliver and Ethan, hold on to Olivia and Bethany. They have never been in one of these visions," Rose commands as she makes her way to the middle podium, puts her hands on the book, and lightning comes out of her eyes.

Oliver grabs Olivia's hand as she begins to freak out as the room spins out of control. Ethan reaches Bethany, and they hold hands tightly. Oliver and Ethan look back and notice that Vivian and Rusty are also holding hands, eyes glowing, as they approach the podium where their mother is standing. As they reach out their hands toward her, everything comes into view.

"What was that?" Olivia asks, her hands on her knees, breathing heavily.

"That is a vision jump," Oliver replies, helping her up.

"Where are we?" Bethany asks, peering around.

"Your Majesty, you cannot…" an elf soldier exclaims, chasing after an elder elf, who is wearing a crown.

Vivian looks around and speaks.

"The Hall of the Elder Elves, but I do not know who any of them are," she exclaims as she walks towards the soldier only to have him walk right through her.

"The Hall of Elder Elves is in the Mundane realm and does not exist," Rusty states, staring at her.

"Oh, li'l bro, you still have much to learn," she responds, staring back at him. "What? This hall is where our family went to hide. Morgana cannot enter there, but none of us know why," she explains.

"Rose, what are we doing here?" Ethan inquires, scanning the room.

"Seeking answers," Rose replies, as she watches the various elves coming in and out until all of their attention falls on a cloaked figure standing in the background.

ȣ

"You look good, my old friend," the cloaked figure says.

"Merlin, what brings you here?" King Caspar looks at him inquiringly.

"Your wife," Merlin replies as he lowers his hood and his eyes narrow.

"Merlin, my wife will not hurt anyone, especially now that she has children."

"My friend, do you trust her?"

"Yes, I do. She has changed. She has given up her dark ways," the king replies as a young elf runs into the room.

"Daddy," the young elf says as King Caspar scoops him up and hugs him.

"My son, Alezander, do you know who this is?" asks the king, smiling as the young Alezander nods but plays shy.

Rose and Ethan raise their hands to freeze the image as Rusty and Vivian glance at each other, exchanging looks of concern. Both know what is going to happen. Rose circles the frozen image. Her eyes narrow as she stops and stands in front of Merlin.

"What are you getting at?" she asks him, looking at the necklace around his neck.

"Mom," Rusty says as he reaches out his hand.

"Yes, Rusty?"

"Every question you have will be answered. It is time to unlock the image and let the truths be revealed," he replies as she looks over her shoulder at him.

"Rusty, no! She will alter the timeline," Vivian cautions.

"They need to know," Rusty says as he raises his hand and unfreezes the vision.

❧

"Well, it is a pleasure to see you again, young man," Merlin says, bowing his head.

"Nice to meet you again, Sir," the young Alezander replies as his father lowers him to the ground.

"I see your kingdom will be in good hands, my old friend." Merlin looks at the king as he watches his child run toward his chair.

"What brings you here, Merlin? What is it you want?"

"You know why I am here." Merlin pulls his wand and throws dark magic at the king.

As King Caspar attempts to shield himself against the blast, young Alezander stands up behind his father, his eyes glowing and holding up a shield of magic and Merlin is blasted backward.

"Alezander, run! Get out of here!" the king shouts as he spins his staff and throws light at Merlin.

"Your magic clouds your judgment, my old friend," Merlin states, rising to his feet as the king throws blast after blast of magic at him.

Merlin laughs as he blocks each blast and causes the king to fall to the floor. Merlin advances on the king, kicks the staff away from him, and points his wand at his fallen opponent.

"I told you not to marry that woman. Your son will be the destruction of all we know."

Merlin pulls his wand back but, suddenly, finds himself levitated off the ground as elf guards run into the room. The king scrambles to his feet.

"My wife! What are you doing?" King Caspar shouts.

"Saving you, my dear, and protecting our children," she replies as she spins Merlin in the air and throws him headfirst through the door. "Guards! Lock it down and keep my children protected. Whatever happens, protect Zander and keep him safe," the wife of the King commands as she moves toward the door, wand in hand, armor appearing on her as she runs.

Merlin rises to his feet and starts to throw darkness at her as she blocks one blast after another. In the back of the hall, the King, his wand in his hand, hides his son behind him.

Merlin blasts a stone archway with magic and blows it apart. Rocks fly everywhere. The queen shields herself, but Merlin catches her off guard when he goes after Zander. The queen throws the rocks backward and blasts Merlin at full strength. As her magic hits him, the guards join in, and so does the King. Now in midair, Merlin summons the necklace from around his neck. Seeing this, the King starts to pull the necklace toward him as members of the elf Council run in to witness what is occurring. Merlin pulls his hands together and blasts the magic away from him, landing on his feet and picking up his necklace. As he begins to laugh, Merlin throws the necklace toward the ground, and darkness rises out of it.

"Seize them!" Merlin claps his hands but, without warning, the dark creatures explode, along with Merlin's wand. The necklace rears up and releases a dark creature that chases after the young Alezander, who locks his feet firmly in place and holds up his hand. The dark creature screams and explodes. Alezander's eyes begin to glow as he raises Merlin off the ground, throws him into the stone wall, and pulls down. The stone wall comes to life and draws Merlin in. When the wall freezes, Merlin remains imprisoned in the wall.

The queen races toward her husband, hugs him, and scoops up Alezander, giving him a big hug.

"He is not safe here," the king declares, walking over to the fountain and pulling water around the three of them.

As they begin to disappear, the stone wall holding Merlin explodes as he re-emerges. As the king, his queen, and their son, Alezander, completely disappear, the room begins to spin and they all land in another large hall.

Before anyone can speak, they notice that, on the far side of the room, the queen and king are moving items away from the wall. As they work quickly, several elves appear, one carrying a small child.

The king grabs the young man by his tunic and shouts, "Look at me! Get my children and wife out of here. Now!"

The young man nods, pulls his wand, and launches the furniture out of the way.

"You won't be able to stop him alone," the queen says, looking at her husband and kissing him.

"I will do what I must to give you time to get to safety," the king declares as he kisses her and sends her on her way.

"My Lady, your daughter," an old elf woman says as she screams and falls to the ground. Merlin stands behind her, smiling.

"How sweet," he says as he strikes down four other members of the Council who are standing in the room. Turning with her daughter in her arms, the queen runs toward the opening in the wall, grabbing the young Alezander on the way as the king and Merlin engage in a magical duel.

"My Queen, I must get you three out of here," the young man says.

"Help is here," they hear as Nimuway runs into the room and blasts Merlin backward.

"Lady Mora, get out of here now!" Nimuway yells as she throws shields all over the room, blocking Merlin from moving.

"Look out!" the king shouts as Merlin regains his feet, his eyes glowing, the guards exploding as they charge toward him. The king swings his staff and taps it as vines rise up to hold Merlin back. The shields and vines holding Merlin begin exploding as he continues to advance toward them. Nimuway removes her necklace, the same one as Rose and Rusty wear, and places it over Alezander's head and around his neck.

Cincinno.

Lock.

"You, young man, take them to the furthermost edge of the elder forest, hand them off to the Lady of White," Nimuway commands as she and the Lady Mora push the young elf carrying the baby and holding the hand of Alezander through the portal. Merlin continues to throw dark magic all over the room, exploding the vines and throwing the king backward as he charges after Nimuway and Mora.

Staring at the spot where the portal previously stood, Merlin shouts, "Nimuway, what have you done?"

Then, he lifts her off her feet by her throat and throws her into the wall. As he pulls his dagger and continues his attack on Nimuway, another cloaked figure appears.

"Who are you? No matter! You will die in time," Merlin declares, throwing dark magic at the cloaked figure, who absorbs the magic and blasts the dagger out of Merlin's hand. The figure reaches into his pocket, pulls a broken piece of glass, and throws it into the air. The charging Merlin instantly disappears and reappears in the broken piece of glass. The glass jumps across the floor as Merlin bounds up and down inside of the glass, trying to break free of his prison. The cloaked figure reaches into his other pocket, pulls a pocket watch, spins the dial, and throws it into the air, freezing time.

"We have five minutes. That is all I can allot," he declares, looking at Mora and Nimuway.

"Are you crazy?" Mora inquires, staring back at the figure.

"No. But you know how time acts. I need the item," the figure notes.

Mora opens the flap on her saddle bag, revealing a sizeable purple cloth and what appears to be a book wrapped up in it.

"Look at me! Promise me. Promise me that you will keep it safe. I swore an oath a long time ago to protect it," Mora says.

"If Merlin gets his hands on that, all bets are off. He will control and enslave all of the Arcane and Mundane forever," Nimuway explains.

"That will never happen. He will never be able to match my power. Besides, we have the watch, which is something he wants, and if we have to keep redoing time until we get it right, then we will," the figure replies, moving to stand directly under the watch.

"Do they make it?" Mora inquires of the figure.

"Only time will tell. You will have to wait to find out," the figure remarks as he reaches up, grabs the watch, and disappears. In that very moment, time returns to normal and the glass shatters as Merlin emerges. Mora points her wand at him, and he rises in the air. Nimuway taps her staff on the ground, causing the items in the room to spin as multiple vortexes open, consuming everything in the room.

Floating into the air and glowing white, Nimuway cast enchantments to protect the place they are standing. The guards, Merlin, Mora, King Caspar, and Nimuway find themselves being pulled into the vortex as it seals. The room now crumbles as the stone of the building turns to sand and blows away while the walls fall in on themselves.

⤳

Rose, Oliver, Ethan, Bethany, Olivia, Rusty, and Vivian run toward the middle of the room and grab each other's hands as everything begins spinning around them. Within mere seconds, they land on their backs back in the library. Destiny, Leaf, Nadia, Kelvin, Sebastian, Brooke, and Claire are waiting for them and assist them to stand up. Cedric appears, carrying a tray with a pitcher and glasses on it.

The group brushes themselves off and Rose walks toward the fireplace as it bursts into flames, her back turned to the group. Nadia quietly moves forward to comfort her daughter.

"Merlin is evil," Rose says, glaring into the fireplace.

Nadia freezes, then looks back at Kelvin, nodding to him.

"Everyone, it is time for you all to know," Nadia places a hand on Rose's shoulder.

"Your father and I decided that when the three of you were old enough, we would tell you," Nadia motions for Kelvin to speak.

"My grandfather was the greatest wizard, but he was swayed by darkness in a time when darkness was not needed," Kelvin begins, walking over to the large window, his hands clasped behind his back.

"When my grandmother, Nimuway, opened the portal and sent everything through, she altered the timeline again. Merlin, Mora, and Nimuway retained all memories of what happened, however, time being time, it played its games. Your great-grandmother had hoped that by switching the roles of Merlin and Mora, they would begin to understand each other's powers. Ha! That never occurred. What was only supposed to last for a few days ended up lasting for much longer than anyone expected," Kelvin explains.

"So, to answer Rose's question. Yes, Merlin is evil. Kelvin believes that this particular moment in time is the one that made him evil, but many others believe that Merlin was dark long before that. He did steal the *Liber Mortuus Caelum* (The Book of the Dead)," Nadia notes as Kelvin turns from the window and nods his head in agreement.

"Rusty and Vivian, while we agreed about not asking to know the future, I do need to know one thing. Does your father know?" Rose asks.

"Yes," Vivian and Rusty answer.

"No. Wait! He knows this how?" Nadia inquires, watching them closely.

"Dad figured it out, and when he did, Mom had to pick up the pieces. It was one of the darkest moments for our father," Vivian says, looking directly into her grandmother's face.

"Then, he knows the truth about how his mother split herself in half to protect him?" Nadia inquires.

Vivian nods.

"What do you mean split herself in half?" Oliver asks.

Kelvin waves his hand, and the fire encircles the room providing a visual representation of the story as he explains.

❧

"My grandmother and her best friend, the Lady Mora, as she is known, devised the scheme to teach Merlin a lesson. Mora knew she could use the magic of the Elder Liber (Book) to split herself. However, when she did, her evil side had more power than she had expected. Mora ended up being banished to the Mundane realm to wander the realm without her memory of magic. Morgana, who emerged as Mora's other half, knew that if Mora lived in the Arcane realm, she would pose a threat…"

Before Kelvin could finish his explanation, two of the guards burst through the doors.

"Our King and Queen, you better come quick," they say.

Kelvin and Nadia quickly move toward the door when horns sound. Startled, everyone looks at each other. Then, Rose, Rusty, and Vivian are the first out the door and down the hall to the rampart.

Rose disappears, then reappears in the field in front of the castle, out past the rampart as she pulls her wand as the guards pull multiple injured elves off the backs of horses. Rose begins spinning her magic around them, while water flies out of the river encircling the castle. Each injured individual begins to glow as the combined power of the light and water spin around them, healing their wounds.

Belinda hovers overhead, then dives down and lands to be met by Vivian.

"A young elf girl," Belinda notes as she examines the girl from head to toe. "You smell strangely."

"Hello, Belinda. You always say that," Vivian replies, smiling, and retrieving a flask from her bag as the dragon lowers an elf from her back onto the ground.

Working quickly, Vivian kneels next to the injured elf and begins to pour the potion over the wounds, and they start to disappear.

"Rusty, grab another flask out of my bag. Hurry! Their life forces are fading," Vivian says as Rusty begins to dig through his sisters' bag.

Oliver and Ethan appear, raising their right hands over the chest of another injured elf and his wounds begin to heal.

As more members of the House of Phoenix and the Council arrive, they begin healing the injured. All of the Arcane who are present are helping out, as more members of the Council and guard appear carrying elves on their backs and in their arms, bringing them in every way possible.

After Rose finishes mending the wounds of the two elves she is tending, she begins to look around.

"Rusty?" Vivian calls as she also looks around.

"I know," he replies as he reaches out to take a young elf boy out of the arms of one of the Council members, placing his hand over the boy's forehead, trying to see what had happened.

"Vivian, it appears to have been an attack, but I am not able to make out all the details. This child was in a carriage," he says as he hands the healed child off to one of the guards.

Nadia and Destiny glide over the land, touching the wounded as they heal and rest.

"If they have been healed, guards, let's get them inside," Kelvin commands as he and the guards lift elves and carry them into the castle.

"Guys, this one is not an elf," Ethan says as the young boy cries and shakes, trying to avoid being treated.

"My parents, my parents," the boy cries.

"Shh. It is okay, buddy. I am just trying to help you," Ethan says, holding his hands up as he makes a stuffed teddy bear appear.

"What happened?" Bethany asks, looking around in disbelief at the number of injured.

"We will know in a moment. Here comes Belinda again," Nadia says, pointing up as the dragon lands and lowers a woman off her back onto the ground.

"Martha," Nadia calls as she glides toward the woman, healing her as Destiny arrives from the other direction doing the same.

They notice the young boy running past them to hug the woman.

"My son! You made it," the woman says, barely able to move.

"My Queen, it is one of the worst attacks I have ever seen," Belinda explains.

"Which village?" Oliver inquires.

"Not a village, my young prince, a caravan," Drago replies, landing and lowering more injured individuals off his back.

"It is unlike the elite guard to attack a caravan," Sebastian remarks as he wipes off his hand with a rag.

"Lord Sebastian, we know it is not like them, but it was definitely the elite guard," Drago states, looking down at him.

"This is not good," Sebastian responds as Drago nods in agreement.

"What is not good?" Ethan inquires as he walks towards Sebastian.

"Not here," Sebastian whispers, glancing at Nadia and then at Ethan, who become aware that it was not safe to discuss this in the open.

While the group continues to heal the injured, a loud pop echoes across the field as Leo, Wade, and Lady Divinity appear with more injured.

"This is the last of them," Lady Divinity says as Leo walks past her and lowers down one of the members of the Arcane Council.

"Kaleb has died," Leo states, bowing.

"So has Marques," Wade says, lowering the fallen wizard to the ground.

Rusty pushes past everyone, sensing that something is amiss. Reaching down, he runs his palm over the body of the fallen wizard until a magic mark appears. Tilting his head to look at the mark, he places his hand on the forehead of the man and closes his eyes.

"Would anyone care to explain what he is doing?" Wade inquires.

"Viewing," Vivian answers. "Before you ask, it is an ancient form of telepathy. He is trying to see what happened in order to have a better understanding of what is going on."

Seconds later, Rusty rises to his feet, whistles and, in the distance, a white horse gallops over the ridge. When Vivian sees the horse, she looks down at the fallen Council member, then takes off running toward the castle. At the same time, Rusty begins running toward the horse and leaping into the air, lands on the back of the horse as it rears up. Rusty clicks the side of the horse, and it starts to run. Now at the top of the castle, Vivian pulls out a viewing glass and looks out. She hears the trees rustling, the winds howling in the distance, and hundreds of birds and animals heading toward the castle.

"Just as it was described before," Vivian remarks, continuing to peer through the viewing glass frantically searching for Rusty.

"Where are you?" she asks.

Finally, breathing a sigh of relief, Vivian catches sight of the white horse in the distance with her brother still riding on it. Watching the horse gallop, she suspects that Rusty is rushing toward the cliff.

Riding hard, Rusty closes his eyes and listens to the wind howling as the trees chatter around him. Upon reaching the edge of the cliff, he extends his hand, feeling for any changes in the air.

"No!" He shouts as he reaches into his side saddle and unwraps a horn marked with the head of a Phoenix. "It will be different this time," he declares as he blows the horn three times.

From the top of the castle, Vivian sounds a similar horn three times. Oliver, Rose, and Ethan looked at each other, trying to figure out what is occurring. Then, they notice their father running across the field, his outfit transforming into armor as Drago soars down next to him. Kelvin grabs onto one of the dragon's large scales and climbs up onto the back of the great beast.

Emerging from the castle gates is Cedric as the suits of armor run over the rampart and form a circle around the castle, crossing their spears. The horn sounds again. This time, Vivian is running over the rampart, tapping her staff on the ground, armor appearing on her family and Council members.

"Mother, what is going on?" Oliver asks.

"This is a day we have feared for a long time," she replies, watching birds flying overhead and landing on the castle. As Oliver, Ethan, and Rose look around, Leo and Leaf are off, running as fast as they can toward the forest, as members of the Council continue to move the injured into the castle as quickly as they can.

"What is going on?" Ethan asks again.

"The merging of the realms has begun. The attack of the elite guards has caused a shift in the magic, and the realms are colliding," Sebastian explains.

"What?" Rose screams as she begins to run toward an opening in the field.

"Rose?" Oliver calls as he runs after her.

In the center of the field, Rose turns and points her staff at the castle. "Not if I have something to say or can do about it," she declares as Vivian and Sebastian join her.

"Oliver, Ethan, everyone! Listen to me! Our magic can protect it. There is a spell, a spell of protection. We must protect the castle and everyone within the walls," she messages them telepathically.

In the distance, Rose can see entire villages appearing on the hills as members of the Council and the dragons begin directing them to the castle.

Inside the castle, Cedric directs people to go to certain areas and he goes to give Olivia, Brooke, and Claire a task.

"Ladies, take these wands, I understand you are Mundane, but the castle will respond to you, tap the walls and all the magical artifacts in this place. It will awaken the castle," Cedric notes as the three grab the wands and rush off in different directions.

As they begin casting protection spells, dragons launch themselves into the air overhead, carrying villagers as Leo and Leaf run past them with all the animals following. Nadia and Council members begin spinning their hands over their heads as they start to create lightfields to protect the castle. On the hill, the horse stands quietly as Rusty sits listening. Then, he clicks the side of his horse, and, in that moment, his hair shortens, and silver highlights appear. His eyes glow, and he raises his staff in the air.

"This is not a battle any of you should fight alone," Rusty declares as he points the staff at the castle and a phoenix explodes from it, screaming as light columns burst out of the ground. Everyone lowers their staves to watch.

The horn sounds three more times from the west, then again from the east, then from the south.

"Oliver, Ethan, Bethany, Sebastian, help get these people into the castle now!" Rose yells. But before any of them can say a word, a cloaked figure appears on the hill, standing next to Rusty and his horse. Lowering their hood, a much older looking Zander is revealed.

"Great job, Rusty. Now go," Zander orders as he taps the backside of the horse, which takes off running down the hill as elves on horseback follow.

Zander turns to see the realms colliding and falling apart in front of him. Spinning his hands, magic flies from them as he seizes the different parts of the kingdoms and tries to hold them together.

"Get everyone into the castle now!" Nadia hollers as she directs everyone into the castle.

As Arcane begin to evacuate the realm and head for the castle, having put some distance between her and the group, Rose runs up the hill toward Zander.

"Hi," she says, reaching his side.

"Hello, beautiful," he replies, looking at her tenderly as a tear rolls down his cheek.

"Zander," she says gently, touching his shoulder.

"Rose, listen to me. I have my duty. You must get to the castle. I am not going to be able to hold this much longer. The castle won't leave without you," he says, motioning for her to go.

"Will I see you again?" she asks as she pulls the necklace from around her neck and places it over his head.

"Rose, you must get to us. Now!" Nadia yells as she holds out her hand, reaching for Rose from behind the lightshield.

"You will. But, right now, I have my duty to protect you, our children, and the Arcane. Go now, Rose. Go!" Zander begs.

Reaching up, Rose kisses him and waves her hand as the necklace locks a field of magic around him. Vivian and Rusty understand what their mother has done, and grabbing their own necklaces, start humming, casting additional protection around their father.

Turning, Rose runs down the hill as Drago flies up behind her. Just as he reaches her, he flips onto his side, grabs her in his claws, and soars up into the air with her. As Rose passes through the lightfield, the castle and everyone around her begins to spin. Rose holds on tight to Drago as she begins to climb up onto his back. Suddenly, she feels a hand on her shoulder, pulling her up.

"Hold tight!" her father says as he points his wand into the eye of the cyclone.

Illustro.

Illuminate.

From the castle, Nadia emerges on one of the towers, casting the same spell into the eye of the cyclone.

Upon Drago coming within several feet of the castle, a group of the guards throw a rope to Kelvin to wrap around the great dragon's neck.

Maintaining his grace in the turbulent wind, Drago roars as more dragons appear, encircling the castle. The dragons begin bellowing fire to strengthen the field around the castle. Looking around, Rose notices that Ethan and Oliver have emerged and joined their mother on the tower. In a sudden flash of light, Rusty and Vivian join their grandmother and uncles on the tower. Rusty's necklace is glowing and a heavy whooshing sound is heard as Belinda emerges, soaring through the cyclone.

"What the…?" Rose begins to inquire when Belinda comes into view.

"It appears she is in her *Candentis* state," Kelvin says.

"She is in what?"

"A special glow that only dragons can achieve. It is a combination of their internal energy combined with the sheer strength of their scales," Kelvin explains.

When Rose sees what Belinda holds in her claws, she reaches into her bag, pulls out a miniature broom, and dives off the back of Drago. The broom expands, and Rose takes flight through the cyclone toward Belinda.

Nadia raises her hand as she helps guide Rose through the winds.

"Flying has never been my favorite thing, but I can guide anyone without a problem," she says telepathically to Rose, who turns, looks at her, and smiles.

Reaching Belinda's side, Rose quickly observes that the necklace has worked and is protecting Zander.

"Oliver and Ethan, can you hear me? Our magic, the light. It is who we are. Let's bring this castle down safely, and I know where," Rose relays a message telepathically to her brothers.

Looking at each other, Oliver and Ethan pull their wands, and move to opposite sides of the tower. Nodding, they speak in unison,

Illustro.

Illuminate.

Holding on to the leg of Belinda, Rose grabs the necklace around Zander's neck and closing her eyes, speaks.

"Time to create a new home for our people. Take us to where our journey began. Take us to the internal flame."

Chapter 17
Time is Unpredictable

Rose, Belinda, and Zander teleport into the castle with a sudden jolt. The castle is jostling about in the cyclone as Belinda helps Rose to remain standing. Rose retrieves her wand and twirls it over her head

Divina virtute magicis lumine.
Divine Power of Magical light.

With a sudden quake, the castle lands safely on the ground as members of the coven dive out of the way in order to not get squashed by the castle. Stowing her wand, Rose notices that Zander is starting to stir. She moves her hands out from her side as a circle of fire emerges around her and Zander.

"This should heal him while I go to check the others," she says.

"Belinda, stay with him, please," she requests as Belinda curls her tail around the fire and hunches down near Zander.

As Rose walks out of the door, she heads toward the main hallway.

"Mom," Rusty and Vivian say as they hug her.

"Excellent job! Both of you," she smiles at them.

"I will tend to Father," Vivian says, heading to the room from which Rose has just come.

Glancing around, Rose notices that the gate is open. Walking toward it, she sees her parents and members of the Council also looking around. When Rose taps her staff on the ground, suddenly, everyone is dressed in beautiful clothing, robes, and a magical shield embraces the castle.

"Rose?" Oliver and Ethan call as she emerges from the castle. Nadia and Kelvin glance quickly at each other and run toward Rose. Her hair has turned brown with white highlights throughout. She looks much older and walks with what the people call "divine grace." She hugs her parents.

Kelvin breaks the silence, "How did you figure it out?"

Rose smiles and responds, "You, Mom, Zander, and Rusty."

Walking past her parents Rose points her wand at her brothers and says,

Reditum, quod nunc est, etiam novum.
Return what is now to new.

The two watch as the magic flies around them and they glow with light. They point at each other, laughing as they see each other grow older but also a lot more powerful.

"I have one last thing to do," Rose notes as she spins her hands and casts magic over the whole castle, causing it to first disappear, then reappear.

"A cloaking spell?" Oliver inquires.

"Indeed! We do not want the Mundane to find us just yet," Rose replies, smiling at him.

Then, the three notice multiple people approaching and extending their hands to welcome everyone.

"Father Francisco," Rose says, hugging him.

"My Lady, you made it safely," Father Francisco replies. "Your majesties," he says, bowing to Kelvin and Nadia.

"Thank you, Father. But what is going on?" Kelvin inquires.

"The covens of the Arcane have waited for your arrival," Father Francisco explains.

"Shall we?" Kelvin holds out his hand, motioning that he and the Father should talk privately.

"Everyone! We shall regroup in the castle and figure out what is the best course of action. All covens are welcome," Nadia declares as she turns toward the castle.

The covens follow Nadia as she leads them into the great hall. With one motion of her hand, the shutters slam shut, and, as she spins her hands, the room darkens, and the fire pit explodes into flames. The candles dim, and the children are pushed to the front of the room by the fire pit as Sebastian, Bethany, Phineas, Rusty, Kelvin, and members of the Council file into the back of the room.

Looking into the flames, Nadia blows into the fire as the room spins, and her voice can be heard echoing throughout.

It is time to speak of many truths. Our story begins long ago when the earth was just created. Several ancient beings, the celestials we believe to have emerged from the elements, met to discuss the fate of their mother and the beloved earth.

One of them, the youngest of the siblings, grew angry and wanted all the power and magic for himself. However, the other six siblings rose against him, banishing him into the darkness of the earth. Many years passed. Then, the first human showed magical abilities and was taught how to channel that magic by these celestials, thus creating the first supernatural being. The celestials lived among humans for years, and when they decided to retire from the earth, they made the collective decision to place a great Council of magic in charge. This Council, as we have all come to know it, is the Council of Light.

They ruled over the magical realm with love, justice, and kindness for thousands of years. But many years later, the grand elder of magic took on a student to learn all aspects of magic. The young man emersed himself in every text. He was eager to learn, but members of the Council feared the young man was consumed by power. So, in that moment, they decided to suspend his training. Unaware of his power, the Council went to rest. But the young man sought out the library and stole one of the most influential magic books, the *Liber Mortuus Caelum*, a dark and sinister text. One that would fuel the young man's power.

This text was so dangerous that the Grand Noble Elder of the Council himself did not dare to use the book. As the young man held the book, examining it in his hands, the darkness attacked. At that moment, the young man sacrificed himself to save everyone. After a fire broke out, the members of the Council emerged to find the young man was dead. They combined their collective powers and restored his life force but at a very high cost.

You see, although the darkness had planned to kill him, it knew that the light of the Council would awaken him and release their plan and awaken the demon side of the young wizard. Thus, the young wizard was now dark. Then, that wizard took his post as advisor to one of England's greatest kings.

The wizard is known to all as Merlin. His views threw the country into one war after another. Many called his years of advising King Arthur the "years of chaos." The Council grew concerned about Merlin's power, and when the Elder of the Council and his wife decided it was time to teach Merlin a lesson, they sent their daughter, Mora, to deal with him. Mora was the purest of all witches and she stood fast against Merlin.

Now, Merlin had Arthur and England convinced that they would all surely die if they listened to Mora. Mora used her magic to reverse Merlin's hold on England and Merlin died suddenly one day. The Council believed that his reign of terror had ended. Several years later, magical teaching was at its strongest. Schools were popping up everywhere, and the Mundane accepted wizards, witches, and the Arcane.

Mora settled down and married the Elf High King, Caspar Ignatius, and they had a son, followed three years later by a beautiful daughter. Then, it happened. One day, Merlin arrived at the castle and tried to destroy their son, Zander. It was in that moment that Mora and Nimuway split time even further. Many believe that time shattered in that moment.

What was seconds for the realms and Council was years for Nimuway until she finally arrived and spoke with the Council of Light. Using the time-turning spheres, the Council altered history, past, present, and future. Many believed Nimuway died the night of the attack at the River Thena, but being as powerful as she was, she shifted the timeline one last time and left the spot. When Nimuway arrived at the Council, she collapsed but, before dying, she foretold of a prophecy that Merlin would never hear, a prophecy that until now many believe did not exist.

The prophecy foretold of three siblings, two brothers, and a sister who would not listen to the rules of magic. Their magic would be so strong that they would create many new rules. The prophecy noted that the three realized that the power of darkness had grown, but they would summon forth great magic to protect their people and their way of life while using their magic to reunite the realms.

It was foretold that when this joyous event occurs, it will forever alter the past and present, as well as change the course of the future yet to come. It will begin to set things right for all. These children will be the ones to restore the balance of earthly magic and reestablish the ways of magical teaching.

಄

Everyone in the room watches the visions made from the flames emerge one after another around them. Across the room, Rose notices Zander quietly entering. While she listens to her mother share the story, she approaches Zander and bows her head. He walks over, kisses her, and places the necklace back around her neck. The two hold hands as they watch the fires die down. Everyone looks around when Olivia breaks the silence.

"Great Queen Nadia, I never got a chance to thank you for rescuing me, my sister, and our cousin. But a question, if you don't mind. How does this work? Magical creatures cannot just walk around in the open, and I am sure dragons cannot fly around," Olivia states, looking around at everyone.

"I agree with Olivia," Divinity says as the people and creatures around the room begin whispering to each other, trying to figure out what to do.

"Our way of life has changed. Yes. Indeed, us just being here will alter the path of magic," Rose replies. "However, magic will protect our people and way of life."

"But where do we live?" one member of the Council inquires.

"Yes, indeed. Where? This castle is packed with everyone remaining from the Arcane realm," another explains.

"My friends. We can build a community here. The land will provide for us. Our magic has helped our ancestors and will help us again," Nadia states.

"What about the ancient city and school?" Wade asks, looking to see if anyone cares to respond.

"I will take a small group and look for it," Kelvin suggests.

"Hun, no one knows where it is," Nadia states.

"Then, we will find it," Oliver replies, looking at Sebastian and Ethan, who nod and step forward.

"Then, so it shall be. I will travel with our boys and their friend to find the ancient city and school," Kelvin says.

"What about me?" Rose asks.

"You have your duties here. Besides, our people need their queen and high princess here to help them," Kelvin says, hugging his daughter.

As the others watch, Sebastian, Oliver, Wade, Ethan, and Kelvin spin their hands together and don the clothing of the Mundane realm.

"How do you guys wear this stuff?" Sebastian inquires, trying to move around in his jeans.

"You will get used to them," Ethan laughs.

Kelvin taps his staff on the ground, and, immediately, all five disappear.

Afterward, Zander motions to Rose. She meets him at the door to the great hall. He pulls the doors open, walks down the long hallway to the rampart, and crosses over it. As he reaches the edge of the rampart, he points his wand at the ground. Dirt, wood, and water fly all around them. Suddenly, with one movement of his hand, there stands a small, quiet village. Zander turns to Rose, and walking past her, places a hand on her shoulder.

"I believe this village should be sufficient for everyone here."

The villagers who have gathered on the bridge look cautiously at one another and start for the village. Many of them move toward the shops of their professions: the baker took the bakery, the blacksmith the smithy, and so forth. The Lady Divinity also walks past, turns, hugs Zander, and thanks him. Rose, Rusty, and Vivian stand looking down the street as Nadia joins them.

"I cannot thank you four enough. Our people, our way of life is safe for now," Nadia smiles at them.

"Indeed, it is," Rose responds as she notices that Zander is further down the street.

Curious to see what is occurring, Rusty and Vivian walk toward him. Rose and Nadia watch and then follow behind as Bethany and Phineas join them. When they all reach the fountain in the middle of the square, Zander smiles and nods his head toward the empty fountain. All of them raise their wands and, in one quick movement, water sprays forth.

"I do not mean to interrupt, but who is that?" Bethany inquires, watching a cloaked figure in the distance.

Zander carefully approaches, extending his hand, when the cloaked figure bows his head, spins his wand, and disappears. He reappears, standing next to Rose, hands her a bag, and disappears again.

"Careful," Nadia remarks as Rose uses the tip of her wand to open the flap of the bag.

"It is empty," Rose says as Vivian comes up, closes the flap, taps the clasp, and reopens the bag, revealing scrolls.

"How did you know to do that?" Nadia inquires.

"Mom has this bag. The five of us kids used to play with it all the time. We would take turns hiding things in it," Vivian explains as Rose retrieves the scrolls.

Turning them over, she examines them carefully.

"What are they?" Bethany inquires as Rose holds up one scroll, revealing the crest of the House of Phoenix.

"Should we open them and find out?" Rose inquires, as Rusty and Vivian appear to be nervous.

"What is wrong, you two?" Zander asks.

"I have seen scrolls like that before," Vivian remarks.

"Let me guess. Something you do not want to tell us about?" Rose inquires, looking closely at Rusty and Vivian.

"No. Just that they are rather confusing," Rusty notes.

"Please, nothing can be that confusing," Rose replies, removing the crest and opening the scroll.

"Oh dear," Nadia says, looking over Rose's shoulder as she reads the scroll.

"You are right. This does not make sense," Rose remarks, handing the scroll to Zander.

"They're blank," he says, holding them up to the light.

"No. wait! They're written in invisible ink. Shall we head to the library?" Zander suggests.

The group fades on the spot and reappears in the library. Zander takes the scroll, moves toward the podium, picks up a large clear crystal, and places it on top of the scroll as a vision appears.

Light spins around the room, then stops, everything frozen in time and coming to a halt. Then, it begins to spin again, time, coming back to life. The cloaked figure materializes as various colors swirl around him. The light gets brighter, then dims, the stories playing across the timelines as if projected on small television screens.

The figure spins their hands together as a fog emerges swirling around them. Then, the group finds itself standing in a burned forest. The smell of charred trees is heavy in the air and ash covers the ground. The remaining trees stand glowing orange, showing that the fire has just recently been extinguished. The ash is still glowing and the heat in the air is unbearable.

The cloaked figure reaches down, picks up a handful of ash, puts their palm out flat in front of them, then blows the ashes into the air as a door materializes.

"Neat trick," Vivian notes as the group nods in agreement. As the figure disappears through a doorway, the group follows only to find themselves standing in a greenhouse.

The greenhouse is quiet, the only sound the clipping of branches. Across the room, the figure places their bag on the table and retrieves an item from the side saddle bag wrapped in purple cloth. Unwrapping the item, the figure examines a leather-bound book.

"How one book can be such a problem," the figure remarks out loud to themselves, holding up the book and examining it.

"Indeed, dear brother. I see that you're back," a witch remarks, emerging from behind the plants in the greenhouse, holding clippers in her hand and wearing some goofy-looking magnifying glasses on her head.

Laughing at the strange device, the figure asks, "What are you wearing?" Lowering their hood, the figure reveals himself to have brown and silver hair pulled back in a ponytail, and his ears show his lineage to be elfish.

"Don't you like it, Brother? It allows me to see the plants up close. I made it myself," the witch declares.

"It looks ridiculous. And it makes your ears stick out. Anyway, look what I have," the figure says, sliding the leather-bound book across the work bench.

"Dare I ask where?" the witch inquires, lowering one of the magnifying glasses in order to examine the cover more closely.

"Yes. But it was not easy to come by. I broke over a thousand rules to get this. I had to skip at least ten timelines and ran into members of the various houses, multiple times. I remember the story of Merlin and Mora and the day they switched roles. Ultimately, I went there. Mora is a charm to deal with," the figure remarks, placing his feet on the workbench.

"Dear brother… Wait! You interacted with Mora? You did not reveal who you are?" the witch inquires, looking frantic.

"No! That is the one rule I won't break," the figure responds.

"Brother, you have always been about the rules. Do you not remember your teachings? The rules are different for us, particularly when it comes to time," the witch remarks.

"Your teachings. If you remember, I grew up away from the family. I grew up going to a different school. I grew up not knowing magic until much later. Do I need to remind you?" the figure inquires, looking annoyed.

"I get it, and you do not need to remind me. Have you notified the others of your return?" the witch asks.

"Nope. I came in, examined the book, and sat down to rest. I would rather not deal with them this evening," the figure replies.

"Are you afraid it is going to be hundreds of questions?" the witch asks.

"Yes, and I do not want to hear our dear eldest sister drone on about the book like she is the leading expert," the figure rolls his eyes and holds his hand to his chest, imitating someone giving a lecture.

"Give her a break. She is like…" the witch remarks as she tilts her head, looking at the spot where the group stands observing.

"Brother, where did you leave the timeline?" the witch inquires, walking up to where Rose is standing and, moving multiple magnifying glasses over her left eye, turns the dial as the lens extends out as if she is focusing on Rose.

"I left it in one piece if that is what you mean," he responds.

"Well, it appears the timeline has found us," the witch says, pointing right at Rose.

The room begins to spin and the group lands back in the burned forest, looking around. The door they used to enter the greenhouse is gone, leaving only the framed archway. Rose walks up to it, her arms folded behind her, examining the archway. The group splits up, walking around the area, trying to figure out the vision. A breeze begins to blow, kicking up the ash, and covering the area. By the time they arrived back at the library, none of them can see because of the ash fog swirling around them.

"What in the world was that?" Bethany asks, looking puzzled, while Rose spun her wand clearing the fog.

"That is what everyone is asking," Vivian notes.

"Even in our time, that scroll is one of the most perplexing and that witch has always been able to see others in the timeline," Rusty explains.

"How is it possible for a vision to come to life? It was a vision, wasn't it?" Bethany asks, looking around.

"It is *not* possible. And that is what is interesting about the whole thing, Bethany," Zander agrees.

"Zander is right. However, the individuals who can do it have to be exceptionally powerful," Nadia says.

"That is what Mother believes, that the witch's interesting helmet and glasses have something to do with it," Vivian explains.

Listening carefully, Rose climbs the ladder to reach one of the top shelves.

"Rose, dear, what are you looking for?" her mother asks, looking up at her from the bottom of the ladder.

"There is a book that came over from the villa. It is about elves," Rose says, her fingers running over the spines of the books.

"What you are looking for won't be found," Vivian states as Rose's hand stops moving over the books, and she looks down at her daughter.

"Do you know who those elves are, then?" Rose asks.

"No, and even from our time, we do not know. You have spent many years searching the library, texts, nothing," Rusty replies, shrugging his shoulders.

"That answers the question then," Rose remarks as she slides down the ladder.

"What does it answer? I am confused," Bethany says.

"Bethany, that is simple. Vivian and Rusty say that even in their time, I do not know who the two individuals are. Then, cousin, it tells me that those two individuals were from the future or a different timeline," Rose remarks, picking up an orb and looking into it. Before the group can do anything, Rose drops the sphere and disappears in a flash of light and smoke.

"Where did she go? I have never seen her do that," Rusty says.

"It is a trick she learned to master, taught to her by the time we were four years old," Vivian explains in a puzzled tone.

Nadia and Zander shrug, glancing at each other, looking for answers.

"It appears she knew long before you were born," Zander suggests, laughing as Vivian and Rusty look confused.

"Bedtime, you two. Good night," Zander says as he hugs them and sends them off. When the door shuts, he taps the handle, and the locks click.

"Ideas, Nadia?"

"Several, but I am not willing to guess. We must wait until she returns," Nadia says, strolling to the center of the room as a giant orb appears, floating up out of the floor. When she waves her hand over it, Kelvin appears.

Chapter 18

Search for the Answers of the Past

Dust spins as Rose lands on the ground, standing. Spinning her wand, she clears the air. As she walks down the dirt path, flames in the distance catch her attention. With a quick spin of her wand, she disappears on the spot and reappears at a campfire.

"No one is here," she remarks, looking around as she hears a whistle coming from her right. She quickly ducks behind the shrubs and one of the giant trees just as the cloaked figure emerges carrying a pile of wood. Setting it down, they raise their hand, and two logs levitate onto the flames. The figure sits down, opens the lid to the pot, and stirs the contents. Hearing rustling in the brushes, the figure turns quickly with their wand drawn. Turning back to the fire and the pot of food cooking, they find Rose sitting across the campfire, staring at them.

"Good evening," she says, smiling.

The figure summons a fireball and throws it at Rose. She instantly disappears and reappears behind the figure.

"What the heck?" The figure says, scrambling to their feet.

"The texts say you are powerful, but, interestingly, your magic is boundless," they say as Rose continues to look at them.

"I mean you no harm. May I sit?" she inquires as the figure nods.

"So, tell me about yourself." she says while removing the lid from the pot and stirring the contents.

"Why do you ask such a bizarre question?" the figure inquires.

"In what way is my question bizarre?" Rose asks.

"'So, tell me about yourself.' That is a pretty odd question to ask of a stranger, don't you think?" the figure states, rocking back on the log on which they are sitting.

"No, I do not think it is. It is not as odd as the device that the young elf girl wore on her head that enables her to see me in a vision," Rose replies, placing the lid back on the pot.

"You should see some of the gadgets she has," the figure remarks, laughing.

"Deflection. I see you are trying to change the topic," Rose states.

"No offense, but you are Queen Rose, and it is rather nerve-wracking to have a conversation with you," the figure says.

"You know who I am, but I do not know you. Here is where it gets interesting. You have a book. I am rather interested in that book," Rose says, continuing to scrutinize the figure.

"That book, you are not allowed to have," the figure replies.

"And why is that? If I may ask. Wait! Let me guess. It would affect the timeline." Rose suggests.

"If you have the book in this moment in time, it will change the timeline and not for the better. Besides, I do not have the book. I left it in the place called The Sanctuary of Lore and Legends two years ago," he explains, scrambling to his feet as Rose rises to hers. Without any warning, Rose spins her hand over the flames of the fire, and they appear at the archway.

"Then, take me to the greenhouse," Rose suggests.

"No. You see, Your Majesty, any such interaction would be dangerous to the timeline," the figure notes as he also spins his hands, summoning a portal, and stepping back into it, disappears. The only thing left is a note that flies through the air and lands on the ground. Rose reaches down, picks it up, and breaks the seal.

Dear Queen Rose,

Many years ago, I was taught by a wise witch how to control time. I, much like you, can bend time to my will and make it do bizarre and unique things.

You asked who I was, and I will tell you this. Our paths will cross again but, until then, know that I am neither living nor dead. I breathe but, then again, I do not. I can see but, then again, I cannot. I am Elfish but, then again, I am not, I am Arcane but, then again, I am also Mundane.

To introduce myself would be not to introduce myself. In time, you will learn what this riddle means. The power of time can be bent to fix a damaged past and to build a bright future. Time itself is confused and does not know what it wants. The question for you is, do you know what you want? The power to understand magic is vital in the success of any journey.

~NOEL~

Halfway across the globe, Kelvin, Wade, Oliver, Ethan, and Sebastian arrive in a large field. Kelvin looks around as Wade reaches down and picks up the dirt, letting it run through his fingers.

"England," Wade says.

"Indeed, brother, it is," Kelvin confirms.

The two brothers stand looking around when Kelvin holds out his hand to Oliver and says, "Go into the bag and search for the compass."

Oliver quickly rummages through the bag and pulls the compass out, and hands it to his dad. Kelvin taps it three times with his wand and, as the dial inside begins to spin, the hand whistles and glows. Oliver and Ethan move closer to watch as Kelvin closes his eyes and speaks.

Magicae de Orbis Terrarum et Universum Illustro quod iter enim nobis.

Magic of the world and universe illuminate the path for us.

As he finishes, the compass stops, pointing northeast. Kelvin taps the compass again as three small balls of light fly through the glass and across the grass, marking the way.

"You two look shocked," Kelvin remarks, looking at his sons and laughing.

"We have heard of magic artifacts but have never seen anything like this," Ethan says, reaching for the compass to examine it.

"I am afraid there is no time to explain everything to you. You will have to learn as we go," Kelvin replies as Wade appears in the distance, looking around the field.

"What is he looking for?" Oliver inquires, throwing the bag over his shoulder.

"Trouble. Being in the open like this can draw attention to us," Kelvin says.

"Where is Sebastian?" Ethan asks, as Sebastian jumps down out of a tree, landing on his feet.

"Sorry. I was trying to get up high enough to see what is going on," he explains, smiling at Ethan.

Going through the bag, Kelvin looks up in time to notice the interaction between the two young men. His eyes narrow as he watches them for a minute, then he goes back to rummaging in the bag.

"I see that your delightfully wonderful sister has mastered the expansion spell as well as your mother," Kelvin remarks as he rummaged further into the bag.

"It was one of the first spells she mastered. It took Ethan and me years, and we still have problems with it. The walls collapse, or things disappear," Oliver notes while watching his father's frustration.

"Oh, this is ridiculous!" Kelvin points his wand into the bag, and a map flies into his hand.

"I see you get as frustrated with the expansion spell as Ethan and I do," Oliver laughs, picking up the bag.

"Oliver?" Kelvin looks around to make sure no one else is listening.

"Yes, Dad?"

"Is your brother…?" Kelvin begins, then quickly looks down at the maps as Ethan and Sebastian walk up.

Oliver gives them an awkward look then asks, "What were you asking?"

"It is nothing, Oliver. Don't worry about it," Kelvin replies as Wade also appears.

"Brother, all I see for miles is open pasture, grass, and animals," Wade says as he watches the tiny balls of light flying toward the northeast.

"They will eventually stop, and when they do, we will be at the ancient city. But, for now, so that Nadia can follow us," Kelvin taps the map and ink races across the map, drawing lines that signal the path of the journey the five are taking. Looking around, Kelvin notices that the sun is starting to set.

"I believe we should make camp near the woods. In the morning, we will head out. Besides, I am sure you boys are hungry," he remarks as he points his wand, and the trees separate, revealing a small hidden grove where they can make camp.

"Wade, would you mind looking for food? Sebastian and Oliver, please setup the camp. Ethan, will you gather wood for a fire, please?"

Kelvin begins walking around the grove, apparently speaking to the trees.

After Kelvin is a reasonable distance away, Oliver turns to Ethan.

"You need to speak with Dad. Well, both of you do. I think he has figured it out, and I do not want to be the one to be questioned about it."

Ethan and Sebastian glance at each other with a curious expression. Then, Ethan smiles, nods, and moves toward where his father is walking. As Ethan bends down to pick up some wood, he hears his father's voice.

"What are you doing?" Kelvin asks.

"Gathering firewood, like you requested," Ethan replies.

"Yes, I know the earth trembles, but we must keep the darkness at bay," Kelvin says.

"Excuse me?" Ethan looks up to see a huge tree talking with his father.

The tree turns, looks directly at Ethan, and swats at him with a branch.

"What the…?" Ethan jumps back, dropping the pile of wood and pulling his wand.

Quickly, Kelvin steps between the tree and his son.

"Wow, you two need to stop and become friends. Ethan, this is Elder Oak. Elder Oak, this is one of my sons," Kelvin says as the tree bows.

Ethan lowers his wand, looks at the Elder Tree and bows his head in return. Ethan stands watching as the tree turns and shuffles away.

"Are you okay?" Kelvin inquires.

"Yes, why wouldn't I be?" Ethan responds.

"Elder Oak has a way of being mean with his swat. Elder Oak became a dear friend when I used to run away from your grandparents and hide here. Are you sure that you're okay?"

"I am fine," Ethan replies as he scoops up a pile of wood and turns away.

"I do not understand him," Kelvin remarks out loud as he walks toward the campfire. "Looks good, gentlemen. Where is your uncle?" Kelvin inquires as he sits down on a log.

"Not back yet," Oliver replies, pulling a chess board from the bag and setting it up.

Ethan builds a fire in the pit as Sebastian goes into his tent, takes off his shirt, and changes into a sleeveless tunic. Sitting back, Kelvin watches Ethan's response to Sebastian. Ethan quickly turns his attention to the fire as Kelvin leans back, shaking his head, and chuckling to himself.

"Seriously, will you just use your wand and get that fire started? Then get over here to play a round of chess with me," Oliver says.

"Oliver, building a campfire is a science. Besides, magic is not the answer to everything," Ethan replies, stacking everything nicely.

Sebastian walks up, points his wand at the fire, and the logs fall into order and the fire lights.

"There," Sebastian says as he sits down.

"It is not always about magic," Ethan complains.

"You sound like Rose. Will you stop complaining and get over here and play wizard's chess?" Oliver taps the board as it expands into nine boards at various levels.

Rolling his eyes, Ethan sits down on the log, as Wade walks up, carrying fish and various herbs. He waives his hand, and items appear on the fire cooking in pots and pans.

"What took you so long?" Kelvin asks.

"Trouble," Wade responds, looking displeased.

"Trouble? What kind of trouble?" Kelvin raises his eyebrows.

"Darkness. Don't worry. They did not follow me. I made sure of that," Wade explains as he sits down by the fire to tend to the food.

Halfway through the chess game, as Sebastian reads quietly and watches them play, Oliver says, "Smells good."

"So, Sebastian, what is your story?" Wade inquires.

"Pardon me?" Sebastian asks.

"What is your story? You know, when I first met you in the Valley, you were traveling with my daughter," Wade explains, looking at Sebastian from across the fire.

Kelvin, who has been studying the map, stops, and peeks up to listen to their conversation.

"Lord Wade, if you are suggesting that I am dating your daughter, you have nothing to worry about. Bethany is a good friend. She fancies Phineas, and I am single," Sebastian explains.

"Ah. So, you do not think she is pretty enough to fancy?" Wade asks.

"It isn't that, Lord Wade."

"Then what is it?" Wade demands, aware, at this point, that the other three are watching and listening.

"Lord Wade, if you must know, I do happen to fancy someone. But it is complicated, and I wish to leave it at that," Sebastian replies as he glances around the campfire and puts his nose back into his book.

"You know, you could whip up one of those love drafts and slip your hand over a person's drink when they are not aware," Wade says as Oliver and Ethan shoot each other looks of concern.

"How is dinner coming, Wade?" Kelvin quickly changes the subject.

"Almost done, but…." Wade starts to say when Kelvin interrupts.

"Wade, whoever he chooses to see is none of our business or concern. There will be no love draughts slipped into anyone's drinks. We have larger concerns and need to eat, then head to bed. We have to be up early. I want to get to the ancient city by early afternoon," Kelvin explains, first looking at Wade, then over at Ethan.

Seeing that look, Oliver motions with his head for Ethan to speak with their father.

"Dad, I notice that we need more wood. Would you care to give me a hand?" Ethan asks as Oliver, who is sitting behind Wade, motions with his head for their father to follow Ethan.

"Firewood? Kelvin, we have enough," Wade points at the pile and hands a plate of food to Oliver.

"What is going on?" Wade asks, looking directly at Oliver.

"Nothing," Oliver looks at Sebastian, then starts eating.

Strolling quietly through the trees to an opening overlooking a cliff, Kelvin finds Ethan sitting on a boulder, looking out at the ocean.

"Beautiful, isn't it? This is why I came to this realm. It is so beautiful here," Kelvin remarks as he sits down next to his son.

"It is. But…" Ethan starts to say when he feels his father's hand on his shoulder.

"I want you to know that I know. I figured it out. I also understand what Sebastian means about it being complicated. You and he could never be together because of the laws of the Council and Merlin. But, Ethan, you have a say in the Council far greater than any other member. Also, that law applies in the Arcane realm only, not here. So, what I am saying is that you can be with him if you want."

Ethan stands to walk away, trying not to let his father see that he is weeping.

"But my duties…" Ethan begins when Kelvin walks up behind him, turns him around, and hugs him fiercely.

"I regret not being there for you, your brother, and your sister. But I am here now. Ethan, you are allowed to do what you want. You understand your duties, but your duty is first and foremost to your heart. Your magic will always be yours. No one can take that from you. But if it will make you feel better, I will work with the Council to overturn the law," Kelvin announces as he looks fondly at his son.

Kelvin felt Ethan tighten his hug and, through his tears, hears him say, "Thank you."

"Now, it's time for us to get our dinner before your uncle gets nosey."

Suddenly, Kelvin becomes aware that Ethan is looking concerned. He turns just in time to catch a blast of dark energy hurtling towards him and Ethan. Kelvin closes his hand, opens it, and light explodes around them.

"You think you can protect them?" the darkness asks, laughing as three cloaked beings point their wands at the two of them.

"Oh, look! It is the great King," a female voice declares as the two other figures throw lightning at him.

Before any of them can respond, all three figures are thrown to the ground as Sebastian steps out from the edge of the woods, his eyes black and his arm straight out with his palm out. The dark figures scream and fly into the air as Sebastian raises his hand. When Sebastian lowers his hand again, all three land on the ground hard, coughing and crying. Next, they find themselves levitating into the air, still choking. Sebastian slams his hands together, causing the three to crash into each other.

Wands drawn, Oliver and Wade approach. Ethan's eyes turn blue as a portal explodes open under the dark figures. The dark figures scramble to grab the sides of the portal but, in the end, they start falling through.

Desperately trying to hold on, they start to pull themselves out when high-pitched screams echo over the land as roots fly toward them. Trying to fight back, one of the dark figures falls into the portal and disappears.

"My children, protect the five magical ones of light," Elder Oak bellows as his children wrap branches around the five protecting them.

In the distance, they hear a loud whistle, and, suddenly, animals appear all around them. The wolves howl as rabbits, beavers, and raccoons run past to bite the hands grasping the edges of the portal, causing the other two figures to fall through. The trees release the five as Sebastian and Ethan spin their hands, grab the edges of the portal, and slam it shut. As the portal seals, the darkness around them dissipates.

Once the portal closes, Elder Oak turns with his sons to walk away when he hears Kelvin clear his throat.

"My friend, thank you. Without you, we could not have stopped this evil."

The tree turns, bows, and then turns again to depart. Ethan pets one of the bunnies while Kelvin and Wade check the area.

"It appears to be clear. Let's get back to camp, eat, and go to bed," Kelvin and Wade suggest.

"Who are they? We are not familiar with them," Oliver questions.

"Imagine Morgana. Now multiply her by three. They are members of the Council of Darkness," Sebastian explains.

As they take the path back to the campsite, they see the Lady of White floating above the ground.

"How horrible! Those things came after you," she remarks as they pass her and sit down around the fire.

"What do you want? Rose and the Lady Divinity are not here to keep you safe, witch," Wade says.

"I'm here to warn you that the darkness is moving. But you have already discovered that," she replies.

"Thanks, but you're a little late," Ethan remarks, looking displeased.

"Is there something else we can help you with, Lady of White?" Kelvin inquires when the lady raises her hand, and the campfire grows brighter.

"I know about your journey. You seek the ancient city and the school. I see the path, but it is clouded in darkness. Is it safe to take such a journey? Should the truths of the past be revealed? You have never listened, Your Majesty, but heed well this warning. Where there is death, there will always be de…"

But, before the Lady of White could finish, Ethan and Oliver rise to their feet, wands drawn and blast her backward.

"You dare attack me?" she asks as she takes to the air.

"She can fly?" Ethan asks as his father also rises to his feet, spins his wand in his hand three times, and throws a light orb at the Lady of White, which she dodges.

Laughing, she mocks Kelvin, "Is that all you have, Your Majesty?"

Suddenly, the orbs explode, and a vortex opens, pulling her in, and slamming shut. The only thing remaining is her necklace, which falls towards the earth. Ethan dives to catch it. When the necklace is only inches from Ethan's hands, Kelvin blasts it away from him. Upon the necklace hitting the ground, it opens, and Ethan starts to be pulled in when Sebastian dives in, grabs Ethan, and pulls him out.

Wade and Kelvin quickly move to seal the vortex and restore the ground. When it is finally closed, Wade and Kelvin look at each other, then at Ethan, who is sitting on the ground with Sebastian hugging him from behind.

"You do not know this, and, therefore, we cannot fault you. But a vortex stone is something you do not want to touch," Sebastian explains as he helps Ethan to his feet.

"A what stone?" Ethan asks, looking around.

"The ancient ones and the members of the highest Councils wear vortex stones, stones designed to consume everything in their path," Kelvin says, looking at Ethan and Oliver.

"Let's eat, then off to bed. I will take the watch for the night," Kelvin says.

They eat quietly and turn in. Oliver and Ethan go to their tents as Sebastian approaches Kelvin.

"Your Majesty, may we speak?" Sebastian asks.

"Of course, and Sebastian, please no formalities. Just call me Kelvin," Kelvin replies, bowing his head.

"Kelvin, I know you and my father have been great enemies, and I know you and your brother watch me closely. But, please, understand that I am on your side," Sebastian says as he looks at Kelvin.

"Sebastian, I know you are on our side. You watch over Ethan more than anyone knows, and I have seen the way he looks at you and you at him," Kelvin says.

"So, you are okay with it, Sir?" Sebastian asks.

"Yes. And I am glad you have his back," Kelvin replies, looking directly in Sebastian's face.

"Very much so, Sir…Kelvin. Sir, may I inquire? I know about the law," Sebastian starts to say when Kelvin raises his hand to stop him.

"The Law, as I told Ethan earlier, only applies in the Arcane realm and does not have any baring or power here. I have explained to him that I will work with the Council to overturn and dissolve that law."

Kelvin pats Sebastian on the back.

"Thank you, Kelvin. You are as kind and amazing as the people say. Do I have your permission to date your son?" Sebastian asks.

"Yes. But, Sebastian, if you break his heart, you will have my anger to deal with," Kelvin says as he walks away.

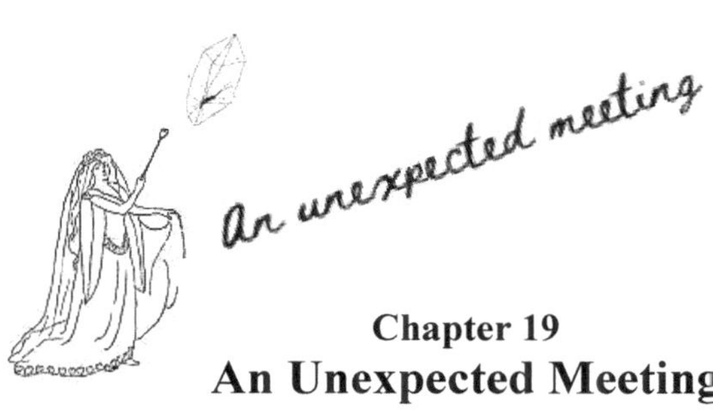

Chapter 19
An Unexpected Meeting

Drifting in and out of sleep that night, Sebastian is suddenly awoken by the smell of breakfast and the sounds of Ethan fussing over the fire pit. Walking out of the tent, putting on his tunic, and looking around. Sebastian notices that it is a cool, crisp morning, the dew still on the blades of grass as the fog is starting to dissipate.

As he approaches the campfire, Sebastian sees Kelvin approaching with Oliver, carrying several bags of fresh fruit just as Wade emerges from his tent. Wade takes over preparing breakfast as the group settles in. Ethan stands up, walks over to the trees, and closes his eyes when he touches the tree, listening as Oliver and Sebastian stand by watching what is occurring, curious to see what Ethan is doing.

Ethan opens his eyes and collapses to his knees. Oliver and Sebastian both run over to him with Kelvin and Wade not far behind.

"Are you okay?" Oliver asks, helping his brother up.

"The earth is trembling. It was last night, and it still is," Ethan replies, looking around dazed.

"I do not understand. What is going on?" Oliver asks, looking with concern at his father and uncle.

"Since the collapse of the portals, the darkness is weak and trying to feed off the energies of all living things. In doing so, they are weakening the earth. Remember that magic comes from everything around you and your heart. The darkness believes that if they feed on the energies of all living things, they will slow us all down. But they have forgotten about the power of the heart and love," Kelvin explains.

Oliver and Sebastian help Ethan up, and the five quickly eat, then pack up the camp. With a quick movement of their wands, everything is packed into their bags, and the group walks out of the woods into the morning breeze of the countryside. Looking around, they notice individuals out tending to the land. When they reach the path and begin walking, Kelvin speaks to Oliver, Ethan, and Sebastian.

"Refrain from the use of magic. The Mundane are around and will not understand it."

Glancing at each other, all three nod their heads in agreement. Just then, a man in a roadster pulls up.

"Good day, mates," the man says.

"Hello," Kelvin replies.

"You gentlemen look lost. Where are you heading? May I be of assistance and provide you with a lift" the man inquires.

"To a place called Catalina," Kelvin says, looking at the man.

"Ah yes, Catalina. Do you need the town or the ancient city?" the man asks.

"You know of the ancient city?" Sebastian inquires.

"Anyone who is anyone does. Of course, you will never reach it on foot. May I be of assistance? I am happy to offer you a ride," the man explains.

Looking around cautiously, the man taps the dash, and the car transforms, expanding to provide enough seats for everyone.

Kelvin motions for them to get in. Once they are all seated, the man takes off driving the car, Kelvin in the front seat next to the man, Wade behind the man, and Oliver behind his father. Wade and Oliver sit quietly in the back, keeping their wands in hand and holding tightly to them.

"Sorry. Where are my manners? I am Erick," the man says, looking directly at Kelvin.

"I am Kelvin. Behind you is my brother, Wade. Behind me is Oliver, one of my sons. Behind him is my other son, Ethan, and my son's boyfriend, Sebastian," Kelvin responds returning the man's stare and waiting for a reaction.

"Nice to meet you, gentlemen. May I inquire, where is Nadia?" Erick asks as Oliver looks over his shoulder at Ethan.

"I never mentioned a Nadia," Kelvin remarks, giving the man driving an alarmed look.

"You didn't have to. You say your name is Kelvin, and there is only one Kelvin who is Arcane. You are married to the divine Lady Nadia, and you are from the Arcane realm," Erick replies as he races down the road.

Kelvin turns to look at Wade and Oliver, who look back at him, trying to figure out what is going on.

"Do not worry. I am not going to hurt you. Divine Ladies Nadia and Destiny, and Lord Hawke are cousins. My father is MJ, the brother of Lady Dawn. My mother was pregnant with me during your and Nadia's wedding," Erick says as he smiles at Kelvin.

"Wait, your father and mother disappeared two days after the wedding," Kelvin says.

"Yup. My parents fled the realm and came here. My parents disagreed with Dawn's way, and my father feared she would become corrupt. He felt it best to protect the power of magic in some way along with the family lineage. So, he and Mom came here," Erick explains as the car slows downed in front of an old English villa.

"Please come in." Erick says as he pulls his wand, points it at the lock, and the gate opens.

"Shall we follow?" Oliver asks.

"Yes," Kelvin replies inquisitively as he follows behind Erick.

"Father, I am home. Where are you?" Erick calls as he walks down the hallway.

"Ah, my lad. You are home," MJ says as he walks across the parlor with a peculiar contraption on his head.

"Oh, Erick, my dear boy! You didn't tell me you were bringing company home," MJ says as he peers past his son, his eyes narrowing.

"Father, our guest...." Erick begins as his father pushes past him, pulling his glasses down to the edge of his nose and staring over the top of them.

He walks around Kelvin studying him carefully.

"Can it be?" MJ inquires, poking at Kelvin as he half-smiles at the older man. Finally, MJ stops and points his finger at Kelvin.

"You?" MJ asks.

"Me!" Kelvin says.

"You are Kelvin Phoenix, the son of Titus, the prince who married my beautiful niece," MJ declares, laughing as Oliver and Ethan glance nervously at each other.

"Indeed, I did, and now, here I stand," Kelvin replies.

"Well, where is she?" MJ asks, looking around, obviously upset.

"At home, with our sister and our niece and nephew," Ethan replies as MJ pushes past Kelvin and examines Ethan.

When he notices Oliver, he says "Ha! Two of them, and they look identical. Yours?" MJ asks, pointing to Oliver, then Ethan, and looking inquisitively at Kelvin.

"Yes, they are. And they are Nadia's as well," Kelvin replies.

"Yes. But where is she? Why didn't she come to visit?" MJ asks as Erick holds up a hand and rushes to his father.

"Father, your great-nephew just told you where she is," Erick says, trying to sound calm, without showing his annoyance.

"Yes, he did. Erick, you brought guests home. Did you offer them tea, you silly boy? Very well. So, what brings you here?" MJ asks, as he holds up a teapot and looks at Kelvin.

"They are here, Father, exploring the countryside and looking around," Erick says, standing behind MJ, giving Kelvin a "just go with it" look.

"Yes, Uncle MJ. That's what we are doing here," Kelvin smiles as he and the others quickly leave the room.

"My apologies," Erick says. "I should've told you he is forgetful. But we never speak of the village since Mother died. Father spends all of his time in his study, doing I don't know what."

"It is okay," Oliver and Ethan say.

"I was hoping he would be able to hold something of a conversation. His knowledge on the subject of the ancient city is fascinating, but he is a no-go today," Erick remarks.

"I can tell you that if you are going to that village, you run the risk of being killed. The Baron is the guardian of the village and one of the most dangerous wizards around," Erick says, looking at them.

"And on that note, that is all I need to hear," Ethan remarks as he walks down the hall, through the front door, and out onto the grass.

Close behind, Sebastian and Oliver are trying to figure out what he is doing. Wade, Erick, and Kelvin follow quickly.

"What in the world?" Erick asks.

Kelvin shrugs his shoulders. Ethan looks around to ensure they are alone and tapping his staff against the ground, says, "Great Earth, my family and I need help. It is time. I summon the powers of the family of magic. Bring them forth."

As Ethan steps back, light beams stream down from the sky as Rose steps out, followed by Nadia, Alezander, Rusty, and Vivian.

Rose smiles, hugs Ethan, and says, "Took you long enough to summon us, dear brother."

"What is the status?" Nadia asks, as she spies the middle-aged man standing on the top step of the villa.

"We have so much to tell you, and we need your help," Oliver replies as Nadia walks past him.

"I am Nadia, daughter of Dawn and Fortis, and you are Erick. Correct?" Nadia states, holding out her arms to hug him.

"I am your cousin, Erick. It is so nice to meet you," he replies, stepping back.

"Kelvin, love, I thought you were going to the village. What has happened?" Nadia inquires.

Erick explains what has occurred.

"So, my loving uncle, MJ, knows the story and the truth. Where is he?" she asks as Erick steps back to reveal MJ coming cut of the villa.

"What is all this noise and ruckus?" He demar_ds, swinging his cane.

Suddenly, he looks down at the grass and notices Rose, Nadia, Rusty, Vivian, and Alezander standing there.

"It cannot be," MJ pronounces as he stumbles down the steps looking directly at Nadia.

Vivian elbows Rusty. They look at each other, then quickly turn toward their dad with concern in their eyes.

"What is wrong, you two? It is like you have seen a ghost," their father says as Rose looks around at them.

Before anyone can move, Vivian pulls her sword and has MJ on the ground, her blade to his throat.

"You will not harm her," Vivian declares as the old man reaches for his wand.

Rose and Oliver quickly disarm him, and Ethan and Sebastian pull their wands on Erick. Kelvin immediately steps between Nadia and the confrontation.

"Silly child! You will all be dead. Merlin will reign supreme over all realms," the old man laughs, as his skin begins to peel back and a dark creature rises from the ground, throwing Vivian backward.

Erick pulls his wand, charging the beast.

"You! Where is he? Where is my fath...?"

As he flies backward, the dark creature reaches for Vivian, but she sweeps his legs out from under him and slashes his arm with the blade of her sword. As the edge makes contact, the dark creature's arm explodes. The creature screams, summoning several dark soldiers who cast dark magic as they advance. The group shields itself frcm attack.

"Vivian, can you handle him?" Zander asks, flipping his cloak off as he pulls his hair back and draws his sword.

"Yes, it would be my pleasure, Father. Keep everyone safe," Vivian says as she flips her cloak off her shoulders.

She draws a second blade and taps the handles together end to end as they magically combine and create a double elfish edge.

Seeing this, the creature of darkness charges, pulling his sword as he strikes Vivian. Becoming overwhelmed, the group falls back toward the house as more dark guards appear, march on them, and cast dark magic against them. While the creatures of darkness continue to appear, Zander spins his staff, striking one of them while he simultaneously blasts three more backward with his wand.

Rusty pulls his sword, striking down one of the dark guards as he pulls a small hand blade and takes another dark creature's arm off. Fighting off the darkness, Nadia and Kelvin throw fireballs at the oncoming dark soldiers. While Ethan and Sebastian point their wands at the fountain, the water begins swirling as it flies across the yard, creating a wall of water.

Ethan holds his wand steady as Sebastian moves to the middle of the wall and hits it with both palms. The wall shoots across the ground, taking the darkness out. Annoyed with the continued volume of dark soldiers advancing on them, Rose's eyes take on a green glow. She slams her hands together as the dark soldiers fly off their feet, exploding in the air.

Rusty fights his way through a group of dark soldiers to reach his sister's side.

"Shall we dance?" he shouts, looking at her.

"Of course," she replies as they take each other's hands and start dancing. The blades of their swords strike the creatures charging them, causing them to explode.

As the darkness continues to advance, the group becomes overwhelmed when, suddenly, time stands still. Everything is frozen in place. Oliver taps one of the dark creatures who is suspended in the air.

Surprised, everyone is trying to figure out what has happened when they notice a young girl standing at the gate, holding a glowing crystal in her outstretched hand. With her head tilted, time starts to unfreeze and when she starts to scream, the creatures begin to explode.

Turning, she raises her right hand as the soldiers fly into the air, and as she moves her left hand across her body, the guards are thrown through the sky. Then, as time finally returns to normal, the one remaining guard charges the young girl but is stopped, blood running from his mouth as he falls face-first on the ground, a dagger sticking out of his back. Across the yard, Zander lowers his arm and walks across the field to pull the dagger from the guard's back.

Backing up, the young girl notices the marking on Zander's arm.

"How is it possible?" she exclaims. "You are Alezander! That cannot be! You look much older now, which means the timeline has been altered."

"You are correct. Time has been altered, Great Princess," Vivian replies, looking at her.

"How do you know my identity? What type of witchcraft is this?" Mora asks, looking at Vivian and holding up the crystal as it begins to glow more brightly.

"We mean you no harm," Vivian says, lowering her blades to the ground and raising her hands.

Quietly, Rose walks over to Zander, who is closely watching what is occurring. Slowly, they all stop and stow their wands and swords, also watching.

"Great Princess Mora, your story is legendary and well-known. My name is Vivian, and I am one of the last of the elves. Your journey did not end when you were cast here, and your family has thrived," Vivian says, bowing her head.

"The Light of the Elves itself called me here to this spot," Mora declares as she looks around.

She spins her hands in front of her chest and transforms into an older woman with brown hair and blonde highlights that comes to her shoulders. An elfish knot headband extends across her forehead, an emerald at its center. Her dress is white with gold and silver inlay. Immediately, the group bows.

"Do you mean this light?" Vivian asks, smiling and pulling her necklace from under her dress and holding it up. Rusty and Rose do the same.

"Can it be? All three of them together! The hope and salvation of magic? The light that can restore the balance?" she asks as a tear rolls down her face, and she touches the stone on Vivian's necklace. As the stone comes into contact with Mora's finger, light bursts forth from the stone and encircles the area.

"Great Princess Mora, I have read your story. I know the prophecy your mother foretold, the one that Merlin never heard. I am Rose, the youngest of the three magically divine, and I am affianced to Alezander," Rose explains as she extends her hand.

Mora grabs Rose's hand and pulls her in for a hug.

"Mora, you may not know me, but long ago, my father fought for you, to protect the village. My father, Fortis Drake, was the head of your guard and Council. My mother is the Lady Dawn," Nadia says as Mora walks over and looks at her curiously.

"You are the one they never found. Your power, your magic, is legendary. You used the greatest power, the love of your family, of your sister, to stop those creatures and Merlin in their tracks. You are the one who weakened him. It was your chaos spell that sent shock waves through the timelines."

"She is also our mother and has protected the Arcane realm for years," Ethan pushes through the group to stand next to Rose.

"The three, the ones who are sent to protect all, whether Arcane or Mundane," Mora says as she bows her head.

"Mmm hmmm. I believe the rest of the introductions can wait. We need to move from outside. The darkness will be here soon, and I would rather us not have to deal with the darkness for the second time today," Alezander exclaims.

"Please, I ask you all to come into my home," Erick invites as the group strolls inside.

Nadia and Kelvin are the last to reach the door.

"You are not alone. I am here," Nadia says as she hugs Erick.

"Thank you, cousin," Erick responds as Kelvin pats him on the back.

The group files into the great room while Mora wanders around, exploring the space.

"She is different than what we heard," Vivian whispers softly under her breath to Rusty.

"Different?" Mora asks, gazing at her.

"Now you've done it," Rusty says.

"We grew up only knowing you as a member of the High Council. Books retrieved from other timelines refer to you as a person, but the images of you portray darkness. Except for Father, no one got to know the real you," Vivian explains.

"So, that is my fate. The timeline alters, and I either sit on the High Council or become dark," Mora states in a disgusted tone.

"In one of the stories, you are wicked and controlled by the book," Rusty says.

"A book? Which book?" Mora inquires as she examines the cuckoo clock.

"The Book of Darkness. The one with the eyes and the mouth sown shut on it," Vivian replies, revealing a picture of it.

"Oh, how charming! I am familiar with it," Mora rolls her eyes, a displeased look on her face.

"How badly are the timelines altered?" she asks.

"That is what we are assessing," Nadia replies, gazing at her.

"This is my fault."

"No. If neither you nor Noble Elder had not altered the timeline, none of us would be here, and darkness would control the earth. As long as the last person or magical being holds that light, we are safe. You believed that, and because of that, we are all here," Vivian states, looking at Mora, who is now examining her closely.

"That saying about the light. Where do you hear that?" Mora inquires, lifting the fabric of Vivian's cloak, examining it.

"We all know it," Rusty and Rose respond in unison.

"My father, Elder Light, would say that. He believed that light is in everything. But he died in the siege on the Council," Mora says, trying to peer into Vivian's eyes.

Vivian quickly closes them as she feels as if the great witch is looking into her soul for answers.

"Curious but yet interesting. You know how to block me," Mora states, stepping back.

"Yes," Vivian replies, looking at her again.

"Then, you have been taught well," Mora states as she takes a seat in the overstuffed chair. "You will have to forgive me. Merlin took everything from me. I lost the village, my parents, my people, and my children. For years, I wandered the Mundane realm trying to regain my memories."

"Mom?" Ethan says with a puzzled look on his face.

"Yes, Ethan. I am also trying to figure it out," Nadia replies, looking first at Oliver, then at Rose and Zander. "Great Princess Mora, what do you mean Merlin took everything?"

"When Merlin attacked my village, my people, you will remember that he killed hundreds: Arcane, Mundane, animals, mystical, elves, fairies. He nearly wiped out the magic of the world. You and your siblings got away with your parents, but many others were not so successful. Merlin told me I would know pain as he took everything. I have wandered the earth looking for the magical, but until the darkness attacked you outside just now, and the light called to me, I could not see the magical. I have lived off the land and done what I could to survive," Mora explains, looking at them sadly.

"You're the mystic that the trees spoke of," Kelvin remarks.

Mora sits back and nods her head, a tear running down her face as Rose kneels next to her, holding her hand. Zander hangs back, quietly listening and watching.

"You said that you could not see magic until we were attacked. I don't understand," Rose says.

Before Mora or Zander can answer, Vivian clears her throat. Rusty looks at her knowing what has to be done. She raises her hand and as Rusty joins her, a silver light orb appears, floating in the air. Nadia and Kelvin exchange looks as Zander moves across the room to look at the orb more closely. He slowly touches it with a finger, then grabs it in his hand, closes his eyes, and light appears around him in a helix. The room darkens as Rose's necklace, which holds the magic and the light of the Nobles, begins to glow. Mora's eyes narrow and then get large when she sees the light coming from Rose's necklace.

Rising to her feet, Mora exclaims, "It cannot be! How is this possible?"

"It is possible because we willed it to be," a voice pronounces as they look around trying to see who has spoken.

"I know that voice," Zander says as he opens his eyes.

"So do I," Mora responds as she starts to glow white, and fog begins to fill the room.

"Rose, what are you doing?" Zander asks.

"It is not me," Rose replies, pulling the necklace out from under her blouse as it glows even brighter than ever before.

Rusty and Vivian also pull their necklaces out from under their shirts, to see that theirs are reacting in the same way as their mom's. Rose turns toward Zander as the room begins to spin and everyone finds themselves floating in the air. Rose is able to grasp Zander's extended hand just as Vivian and Rusty are able to reach Zander and Rose.

"Mom, Dad, Ethan, Oliver?" Rose calls as she reaches out to her parents. The fog is thickening around them when Mora spins light around them and manages to pull all of them together.

"Grab the orb or someone near you and hold on. I am going to try to bring us down," Mora says as light begins to blaze through the fog.

Zander looks over to see Rose's eyes glowing and they see land appearing underneath them.

"Let go," Rose says as everyone lands in a room filled with great stone pillars.

While the group gets their bearings, beings made of various elements step out through the openings between the pillars. A ghost-like figure of a woman peers out from behind one of the beings.

"It's her," Rusty says as he and Vivian bow.

"It cannot be," Zander and Mora say at the same time, turning to look at one another.

"You disbelieve your own eyes?" the ghost asks.

"I saw you die. You died protecting me," Zander replies as the ghost materializes fully before him.

"Alezander didn't you learn anything of my great power," the woman asks as she sits down on one of the chairs as the others follow her lead and sit on other chairs in the room.

"This is the Council of the Elements, the great ones, the ones who brought magic to earth," Rose says as she lowered to one knee, bowing her head to them.

Wade, Erick, Nadia, Kelvin, Sebastian, Ethan, and Oliver did the same.

"Roslynn, you are quite correct. Rise, our friends. No need to bow to us," the woman says.

"You ask how it is that you recognize our voices, Zander. This is your home," the elemental being of water spoke in a calm, quiet voice.

"You see, we never left any of you or the way of magic. We watched from afar and our hearts broke with sorrow. We were hoping and praying that you would all be reunited. When Elder Light and the Council sacrificed their magic to protect you, Mora—and your children and grandchildren after you—we knew the ways of Magic would be protected," the woman explains.

When another voice speaks, Kelvin, Nadia, and Wade look first at each other and then quickly around the room.

"We knew Merlin's plans, and we could not intervene. The three had to be protected and had to live in the Mundane realm. Those who traveled with them to protect them were part of our plan. Roslynn and Zander were destined to be married and unify the kingdoms of magic before they were born. It was written in the stars," Flora remarks as she appears, walking through the room toward them, her arms open to hug Nadia, Wade, and, finally, Kelvin.

"You three question whether you have failed," Flora says as Kelvin looks away.

"You have not," the elements declare in unison.

"But we watched you die. Morgana froze you," Wade says, staring at his mother.

"The Council of Elements can restore life. But the spirits can never leave this place," Rose reads from her spell book.

"Indeed. She is as knowledgeable as the stars, Noble Elder, and Elder Light foretold," elemental fire and wind respond in unison, while gazing down at her.

Then, the silence between the three is broken.

"I do not mean to interrupt, but how did you get here?" Vivian asks the woman in the main chair.

"I have lived between the two worlds for years. I had to do what I could to protect those I love, those this Council loves," the woman explains as she gets up and circles the group.

"It was to protect all of you. Suppose my father and grandfather were here. The Lady of White…" Zander starts to say when the woman raises her hand.

"Yes, Alezander. Your father and grandfather are here. You can speak with them if you wish," the woman says as Zander stares at her incredulously.

"How do you know my thoughts?" Zander asks.

"Child, do you forget about my abilities? What were you going to say about the Lady of White?" the woman inquires.

"Nothing," Zander replies.

"She was there when she was needed," the woman says, turning to look at Zander.

"Needed? She nearly killed me," Ethan raises his voice.

"An imposter! Many try to copy the great Lady of White, but none compares to me. My help is never evil. Although theirs is. You are probably wondering who I am. I am the true Lady of White. I am the one they call the Great Mother. I am the Lady Theresa, daughter of Noble Elder and Lady Elder, and I married the man known as Elder Light. My husband and I are the parents of Mora and the grandparents of Alezander," Lady Theresa explains.

As she walks over and hugs Mora, they both start crying. Zander joins them and Rusty and Vivian follow. The four generations look at one another speechlessly. Flora places a hand on Rose's shoulder and watches silently while no one in the room moves.

"What do we do now?" Rose asks as she reaches up to touch her grandmother's hand. The elementals look questioningly at each other as the spirits standing in the room gaze at each other in confusion.

"What do you mean?" Elemental Earth asks as she glides across the floor. Walking to the fire pit, Rose lights the pit and as she waves her hand over it, the lights dim, and she speaks.

"The Arcane realm is gone. My brothers and I saved our people by bringing them to the Mundane realm. No one knows if the dark wizards and witches still live. However, some form of darkness remains in this realm and knows how badly the timeline is messed up. We still need to find the ancient village and the school. Then, we need to begin looking for and protecting any remaining Arcane who are here, not to mention figuring out what is going on with the timeline itself."

The fire dances in the pit, reflecting her thoughts, and showing the darkness moving over the land.

"When the three of you moved the castle and all the Arcane back to the Mundane realm, you restored the timeline. Now, we are running in actual time. It is destined that all of you would meet. But what you choose to do from here on is up to you. We cannot make that decision for you, but we can support you all in your journey," Theresa says as she looks meaningfully at each of them.

"What about the darkness?" Zander asks, looking at his grandmother.

"They can be handled," she replies, looking back at him.

Oliver and Ethan glance at Rose, and the three can tell what the others are thinking without saying a word. They nod and smile at each other.

"Then, we fight?" Ethan asks.

"Yes! I am not resting until every last dark creature is gone or brought to the light, and the magical can finally live peacefully," Rose replies.

"Is this what the three of you want?" elemental wind and water inquire.

"Yes," the three siblings declare in unison as their parents step up behind them. The rest of the group join them.

The elements rise to their feet. The Lady of White joins them. As the spirits stand with the circle of elders, Flora steps back, also joining the group. The Council members raise their right arms, open their fists, and light begins to circle the room.

"So shall it be. May the powers of this Council, of Light, and of all earthly magic protect our friends who have fought so nobly to protect this Council, the light, and all individuals. Let the magic of this Council protect this group. Our friends, you have taken on a great responsibility. The darkness will fight back even harder than before. Be ready. You have the power to stop them. Listen to each other. Both young and old have something to teach and learn from each other," the Lady of White declares as magic spins around the chambers of the Council and each individual.

Suddenly, they all disappear only to find themselves in a field overlooking the ocean. As they all start to look around, they notice that the cloaks they were wearing have transformed and are much heavier. They are equipped with various metals that add a layer of protection. In the distance, they can see the Lady of White and the Council standing on the hill. They raise their arms, wave goodbye, and disappear.

"What if we need them again?" Oliver asks.

"They are always with us now, particularly with the armor they have provided for us," Kelvin remarks as he smiles and walks past his son looking around.

"What do you suggest?" Rose inquires, walking up to Zander who is watching his mother looking at the water.

Nadia, Wade, and Erick watch and wait for Zander's response.

"I had always been able to hear her voice, and this is how I remember her. When Morgana came, I was in disbelief. I fought against her saying that she was not my mother. I spent many days with Nadia and Kelvin. That is how I became betrothed to you," he says as he kisses Rose on the cheek and walks past her.

"I know there are still many questions we both have for each other, but I assume the Council did not drop us here for just any old reason," Zander remarks, gazing at his mother's back.

Turning with a half-smile, she replies, "No, they dropped us where we needed to go."

The Battle Begins

Chapter 20
The Battle Begins

Mora wanders the hillside studying the ground. She claims that a hidden tunnel would allow for safe passage to the ruined ancient city.

Mora wanders up and down the hill examining every inch, stopping, reaching down, picking up blades of grass, and then throwing them over her shoulder. While she wanders, Nadia and Vivian pour through book after book about the ancient city's history, looking for clues that will help locate the secret passage. Kelvin quietly walks over the hillside, examining the area to see if he might be able to find anything, while Wade and Erick are deep in conversation. Ethan, Oliver, and Sebastian sit quietly watching what is going on.

"Is he okay?" Zander asks Rose, pointing at Rusty, who is up the hill from the group floating above the ground in meditation

"He says he is going to try something, but I don't know what he has in mind," Rose notes, looking puzzled.

The sun shines through the afternoon sky as the group continues with their tasks. As Rose continues to examine the scrolls, Zander keeps an eye on Rusty. Suddenly, Zander takes off to sprint toward Rusty as he begins to fly over the hillside.

"Rose!" Zander yells as she also begins chasing after Zander and Rusty.

Mora stops pacing while Nadia and Vivian look up, all eyes fixed on Rusty, Zander, and Rose. From the opposite direction, Kelvin also sprints after Rusty, trying to catch him. When he reaches the hillside across the way, Rusty stops, and spins in place as his eyes open and an enchanted doorway appears.

Tap, thump, tap, echoes over the field. By then, everyone is standing and watching closely, wands in hands, as Rusty lands on the ground, and walks toward the door.

Tap, thump, tap, this time even louder than the first time. Rusty taps the handle of the door. *Rap, tap, tap.* The door flies open and an older-looking Rose strolls through.

"No regards for the rules! Didn't I say any interactions with the timeline could cause chaos," she complains, crossing her arms and tapping her foot.

"Hi, Mom. We have spent the entire day looking for the passageway to the village. Can you help us, please?" Rusty inquires.

"Children," the older Rose says, shaking her head and walking past Rusty as she circles the younger version of herself.

"Don't be so shocked. We don't have time to pick you… I mean me… I mean… oh you know what I mean… up off the floor. Children! They have a way of always breaking the rules," she remarks, a look of amusement on her face while watching her younger self, who is still frozen.

Whistling orbs of light explode around the older Rose as she raises her hand, and the orbs fly back through the doorway.

"How is it that you can perform the magic of my mother?" Mora inquires.

"A dear friend taught me many things," older Rose says, smiling and winking.

"You called?" a voice asks as several beings emerge out of the doorway and begin to materialize.

The group freezes as Oliver, Zander, Ethan, and Sebastian are confronted with older versions of themselves. The four older and younger versions of themselves look at each other and then laugh.

"Fascinating," they all say in unison.

"Russell! Explain yourself! What is the meaning of breaking the rules of time?" the older Zander demands.

"Sorry. But time has been fixed, which means the Spell of Elfish Purity should work now in this time," Rusty explains, smiling at his father.

"You sly devil! The Spell of Elfish Purity!" the younger Zander exclaims.

"He gets it from us," the older Zander replies, laughing.

"The spell of what?" the younger Ethan asks.

"A spell that allows any witch or wizard of great mystical power to combine two versions of themselves. It is a restoration time spell," Mora explains.

"What?" the younger Sebastian inquires.

"Great-grandmother knew that help might be needed sometime. Mom and Dad, as they got older, took on a lot more responsibility. When they did that, great grandmother Theresa stepped in and taught me everything she knew. Before she passed and ascended for the third and final time to the Council, she told me that someday, a great challenge might occur. I have seen the darkness that lurks in that village. I am not losing anyone, so in meditation, I entered the Light Chambers and looked for the Spell of Elfish

Purity. You see, the six hours we have all been on this hillside was one month for me. Now, all that has to occur is for you five to touch the hands of the older versions of yourself and stand back, *boom, pop, bam,* another part of the timeline will be restored," Rusty explains.

"Okay, and then what?" younger Oliver inquires.

"Well, once you touch hands, the magic will combine, and the two older and younger versions of yourselves will combine, and well… you will be one and have greater knowledge and Arcane mystical power," Rusty explains.

"But the one thing he forgets to mention is that if we do this, then not only will we restore a vital aspect of the timeline, but when Rusty and Vivian return to their own timeline, they will not be able to return until they are born in this time," the older Rose clarifies.

Curiously, watching what is occurring and knowing her brothers too well, Rose knew they would not take this leap of faith. Stepping forward, she nods to the older version of herself and as the two touch palms, light begins to spin around them. Within seconds, Rose transforms. The light flashes and they shield their eyes at the pure brightness. Rose disappears, then reappears, looking older. Then, the group hears a voice.

"All the magic we do, all the magic you do, all the magic around you is to protect you."

"That is the Lady of White is it not?" Ethan inquires, stepping forward as he and his older self touch hands and transform.

Following Ethan's lead, Oliver, Sebastian, and Zander touch palms with their older selves, and the three transform instantly. Each looks older and more distinguished and as the light swirls around, gray highlights appear in the hair of Kelvin, Nadia, Wade, Erick, and Mora.

"Wow, not only do I have my magic, but I have just gained the magical knowledge of my older self," Zander remarks.

"Look," Ethan points at the door, which has disappeared, and, in its place, a tunnel appears in the ground.

"Well, I guess that is the passage we have been looking for," Kelvin notes, walking towards the entry of the tunnel.

Everyone starts gathering up their belongings when, suddenly, they realize that Rose is nowhere to be found.

"Rose?" Zander calls when a flash of light explodes in the air.

"What is going on?" Oliver asks, running up the hill after Zander. At the top, Zander retrieves his wand as the mountain explodes and a substantial, but unknown, dragon flies backward across the ground and getting up, hisses at Zander where he is standing next to Rose.

Stowing his wand, Zander pulls out his elfish edge sword from its cover. As the tip of the blade emerges from the cover, the blade bursts into flames as Zander points the sword at the dragon and fireballs fly at it. Oliver and Ethan appear on the other side of Rose with their swords drawn, and Sebastian carries a spear.

Vivian glides over the land, firing arrows from her bow. Rusty snaps down his arms and two elfish blades appear from the edges of his sleeves. He and Vivian join their parents and uncles in battle just as dark creatures begin emerging from the ground.

Before anyone realizes what is taking place, Rose discovers her newfound power and spins her hands together, causing the creatures of the dark to instantly explode. Picking up her wand, she releases rays of light and light orbs at the dragon, who takes to the air. Soaring high, the dragon rises into the air when three roars are heard as Drago, Belinda, and Autumn charge the creature. Drago and the dark dragon snap at each other; their necks interlocked.

The group watches from the ground as they notice Mora's eyes begin to glow silver, and orbs of light spin around her.

More dragons appear in the sky. When Drago breaks his hold on the dark dragon, it charges Belinda as Autumn flies in, raining fire down upon the dark dragon.

As Autumn holds the dark dragon in a ring of fire, still more dragons appear, joining her. While the fire grows in size and strength, the dark dragon begins to spin. Then, suddenly, bursts into a beautiful dragon with white and silver scales. The newly transformed dragon soars into the air and disappears along with the other dragons, leaving Drago, Belinda, and Autumn. Belinda and Drago are the first to touch down, bowing at the sight of everyone. When Autumn lands, she transforms once more into the family's beloved dog.

"Lady Mora, it is nice to see you, Great Queen," Belinda says, smiling, as Drago lowers his head for Rusty to stroke the scales on the back of his neck.

"Thank you," Rose says as she bows to Belinda.

"For you, Lady Rose, and for our friends, anytime," Belinda says as she extends her neck, looks up into the air, and roars as she takes off.

"Be safe. But before we leave, Autumn…?" As Drago looks down at her, Autumn transforms back into a dragon, "Keep them safe and if you need help, do call," as he rubs his head against hers.

Once Belinda and Drago depart, Rose walks over to a patch of grass on one of the hills, spins her hands, and the ground reopens, revealing a staircase. Mora proceeds cautiously down the stairs as the others follow.

"Ah yes. Here it is. I knew it was here," she remarks.

Then, as the group walks through the underground tunnels, Zander inquires, "Mother is there a reason why we are taking a hidden passage into the village? What are you not telling us?"

Mora stops where she is and waves her hand and the tunnels begin to spin, and as everyone looks around, they see a young girl. Mora's voice begins echoing all around them when the image snaps back and they are all back standing in the tunnel.

&

"I am sorry, I have not done that type of magic in years," Mora admits as she holds her head.

"Hey, I do not mean to interrupt, but this staircase leads into an ancient temple," Rusty says.

Everyone in the group draws their wands and quietly emerge into the temple. As they peer over the balcony, they observe an older man standing with a number of other men, looking around.

"Find it now and bring it to me," the old man demands.

"Baron, Sir, this is the last possible spot. If the staff of Elder Light is not here, then have you considered that it may be lost?" one of the men asks, crouching with his arms up. The Baron turns, points his wand at the alter and it explodes into flames.

"If it is not here, then burn the place down," he commands as the men working for him pull their wands.

But before anyone can say anything, a massive wave of water rips through the temple, extinguishing the flames.

"We are not alone," the Baron remarks, cautiously looking around.

"Oh, Magical One, come out, won't you?" he suggests as Rose emerges from behind a pillar. Kelvin and Wade hold up their arms to stop the others.

"Watch," they say quietly.

"You, girl! What is your name?" The Baron inquires, smiling wickedly as he points his wand at her.

"I am Rose," she says, bowing with her wand and eyes both fixed on him.

"A witch! I see you must be from the realm. No matter, I will handle you like the rest," the Baron declares as he waves his wand. But it explodes in his hand, and he flies backward. Gathering his breath, he points his finger at Rose and screams, "Get her!"

As the others advance on Rose, she spins her hand around her as light explodes from her wand, throwing the attackers back. The attackers hit the wall and disappear as more advanced on her. Rose moves down the main aisle of the temple as attackers disappear one after another until she reaches the spot where the Baron is standing.

"How is this possible?" he asks, staring at her.

"The power of magic runs deep in my veins, and, Baron, you pose a threat to the safety of all creatures and beings," Rose explains as she stares deep into his eyes.

As a result, the Baron drops to the ground, screaming and holding his head.

"Get out! Get out, you monster!"

The Baron continues to shake on the floor, holding his head while Mora and Zander appear next to Rose just as she faints into Zander's arms.

Mora pulls her wand and raises the Baron to his feet, then slamming him into the ceiling. When she lets go, he falls heavily to the floor, dying from the impact. As Zander tends to Rose, the others emerged from behind various pillars, searching the area, and securing the temple. Oliver and Ethan run toward Rose when they notice there is blood on the floor from the Baron.

"Look," Ethan points at the blood as it turns silver. Before anyone can move, Kelvin pokes the silver blood with his wand, and pulling up, the blood springs back into place.

"Vampire blood of the ancient ways," Kelvin remarks as Wade rummages through his bag and pulls out two vials to collect the Baron's fangs.

"Look, brother," Wade says, lifting the lip of the Baron.

"Interesting," Kelvin replies.

Bethany, who is standing behind her father, notices the same thing that her father and uncle are examining.

"Wait. Where did you come from?" Wade inquires as Bethany smiles and winks.

She taps the ground three times with her staff, and, within seconds, a being begins to materialize.

"You rang, Madam Bethany?" Cedric says. "Fascinating," he continues as he moves across the floor and picks up the lifeless body of the Baron.

After examining the Baron carefully, Cedric then sinks his fangs deep into the Baron's neck.

"Hmm. Silver blood tastes like ginger and smells of skunk. Horrible smell, that one," Cedric comments as he throws the Baron's body to the ground and, pulling a handkerchief, wipes off his hands.

"Cedric, what can you determine about his blood?" Kelvin inquires.

"Strappy fellow, gray hair, but carries a wand. What a horrid, nasty beast," Cedric replies as he spits silver blood all over the ground.

Then, looking around, he notices Zander holding Rose. Cedric moves quickly across the space, touches her forehead, and she fully awakens.

"May I?" he asks, extending a hand to help her up.

As Rose rises, she and Cedric glide across the floor together.

"What do you see, My Lady?" Cedric asks as Rose looks around and notices the silver blood. Rose reaches down, looks at the Baron, and touches his forehead. As she pulls her hand back, she shakes her head.

"What is it, Rose?" Ethan inquires.

"His soul was stolen by vampires. When their souls are stolen, their blood turns to silver, and you cannot see into their minds. It is as if…" Rose pauses as she looks at Cedric.

"As if it has been erased," he finishes her sentence.

"Yes. But why?" Rose asks.

"It makes it easier for the dark to control those without souls," Mora explains as she walks around the altar area. Just then, Mora flies back as Raven appears.

"Well, well, well! If it isn't Mother dearest two," Raven sneers, tilting her head and licking her lips.

As Mora gets to her feet, Zander steps in between them to protect Mora.

"Touch her, and I will finish this once and for all, Raven," Zander says.

"Touch her? Oh, I don't intend to touch her. I intend to kill…"

Before Raven can finish, she finds herself locked into a dual with her brother.

"Rose, get them out of here!" Zander shouts as he raises his left hand, and the windows fly open, and Raven is lifted off the floor in a twister of wind.

Multiple dark creatures and a cloaked dark figure appear to assist her. The group works together to fight back the darkness while Vivian and Rusty remain close to Mora. The cloaked dark figure is dueling with Kelvin but when the figure raises his hand, multiple creatures descend on Mora. When one of the creatures is mere inches from Mora, Vivian pulls her sword, cuts both arms off of the beast, and replaces her sword before anyone realizes what is happening.

In that exact moment, Rusty's eyes turn purple, and he multiplies himself, each copy fighting one of the other dark creatures. Annoyed now, the cloaked figure blasts fire at Kelvin. Suddenly, the figure flies backward down the center aisle of the temple, Oliver and Ethan emerging from the side, swords drawn and striking the figure's blade, causing him to fly further down the aisle.

Just as the figure regains his feet, Vivian slides under his legs, grabs the exposed skin on the figure's ankle, causing it to drop back down to the floor, screaming. The gem on Vivian's necklace begins to glow and the figure starts to sink into the ground. Just then, light explodes around the figure as it transforms and an older elf gentleman emerges, bowing his head.

"Thank you," he says as he disappears on the spot.

It becomes increasingly more difficult for everyone in the temple to remain standing as the velocity of the wind picks up. Trying not to get drawn in, the group grabs hold of whatever they can in order to anchor themselves. Cackling laughter echoes around the temple as Raven blasts fireball after fireball at Nadia, Kelvin, and Zander.

Annoyed by this, Zander moves to the middle of the temple with the wind flying around him. When he throws his hands out in front of him, the wind slams into Raven at full velocity, wildly whipping her around the space.

Holding tightly to a pew, Rusty and Vivian pull their wands and shoot a magic rope around the marble statue at the main entryway. Vivian is the first to let go of the bench, flying into the air holding onto the rope as she takes Mora's hand.

"Grandma, let go! I have you," Vivian shouts, and, with that, Mora clings tight to Vivian's hand, letting go of the pew onto which she was holding.

Jerking the wand and snapping the rope, Vivian and Mora propel themselves toward the marble statue and the entryway. Once safe, Vivian motions for the others to follow. Rose is the second one to escape out the door behind Vivian and Mora. As the other party members emerge from the temple, they notice a tall, dark figure approaching and begin drawing their weapons. Rose stands in front of Mora, her ward extended. The figure lowers his hood, revealing someone Rose knows all too well from her dreams and pictures in her books.

"Why couldn't you just mind your own business?" he demands.

"Grandfather?" Kelvin asks as he emerges from the group.

"You were destined to be king. You turned your back on the kingdom I fought to keep away from that woman," he yells, pointing at Mora.

"Your kingdom of lies. Your kingdom where the magical have to fear their safety," Oliver says, stepping up next to Rose as Ethan appears on the other side of her, their wands drawn and their swords at the ready in their other hands.

"Boy, if you know what is best, you will stay out of my way, and maybe I will let you keep the crown for a souvenir for good behavior," Merlin sneers, pointing his finger at Oliver as lightning hurtles toward him.

But with one wave of their wands, the lightning stops, and Ethan, Rose, and Oliver move as one toward Merlin.

"Merlin, take your crown, take your rules, and shove them," Ethan shouts as he grabs one of Rose's hands. Oliver takes her other hand, and a field of magic surrounds Merlin. When the lightfield hits the ground, the three hear a voice speaking to them.

"Hold tight! No matter what happens, you can stop him."

The lightfield begins to encircle Merlin. Furious, he strikes the field with multiple blasts from his wand.

Licuefacio.

Dissolve.

Merlin's wand dissolves into dust as the lightfield begins to close in around him. Even angrier, he points his index finger at the three, and before anyone can react, Rose's eyes turn white, and Merlin's hands are bound to his sides. Without hesitating, the three raise their hands and Arcane begin to appear from all over the world.

As each Arcane arrives, they join their magic with the lightfield containing Merlin's power and immobilizing him. Merlin rears back as he begins to breathe fire into the lightfield, causing it to crack.

"Do not let him break the field," Kelvin calls.

As the lightfield explodes, everyone flies backward. The flames encircle Merlin as his eyes turn black, causing the sun to disappear.

"Fools! Do you think you can contain me?" Merlin inquires as he snaps his fingers, and Raven materializes next to him, and an archway made of fire appears.

Two giant panthers emerge as a sinister cackle rings out over the land, sending chills down the spines of many of those present. This is followed by clapping as Morgana reveals herself.

"Bravo! Bravo! They are all here. This will be easy," Morgana remarks, backing up as dirt begins spinning in the air next to Oliver.

Zander draws his sword as Morgana screams. Black magic flies from her mouth, hurling towards the Arcane. The dark magic is caught by Mora, who spins on the spot and deflects it away from the group. Not pleased, Morgana screams again as Mora catches the darkness, turns it in her hands, and redirects it at Merlin, Raven, and Morgana as light.

Merlin deflects the blast and lobs lightning strike after lightning strike at Mora, hoping to catch her off guard. When he notices that nothing has affected her or the others, he holds up his hand as Morgana and Raven disappear on the spot. He laughs, and as he does, he fades away with magic.

"What in the world?" Ethan inquires, gazing around at the others.

"It is just his way of saying that he is tired of dealing with us," Mora explains.

"We cannot let him get away," Oliver declares.

"We won't, dear brother, but we need to regroup. We have to pull all the forces of magic to be able to stop him, particularly if he has freed Morgana," Rose states, tapping her staff and restoring the sun.

When Mora spins her hands, all of the Arcane disappear.

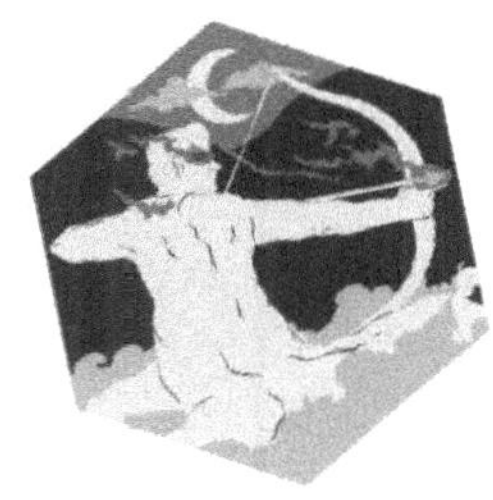

Chapter 21
The Attacks Grow

Appearing at the center of the ancient village, the Arcane begin moving about, regrouping, and disappearing.

"Where are they going?" Ethan asks.

"To get supplies and help," Nadia replies.

"Cedric, go back to the castle and begin activating all magical artifacts. Wade, call the Council. Phineas, call the fairies," Kelvin orders, then stops and watches as Vivian pulls items out of her bag and throws them on the ground.

"I know it is here. But where is it? I hate expanding spells!" she declares as Rusty moves closer to assist her.

"Here, hold this!" she says, putting the bag in his hands as she continues to dig around searching for something.

"What are you looking for?" Rusty inquires, looking annoyed.

"Give me a minute. Ah! Here it is," Vivian says, pulling a box from her bag.

"I believe this is the correct time to give you this," she remarks, handing the box to her father.

Zander takes the box in his hands, looking puzzled. Standing next to Zander, Rose observes as he opens the box, looks down, and a slight smile crosses his face. Mora quietly looks over his shoulder. Her eyes narrow, then light up at the sight of the box.

"How and where did you get this? Better yet, when did you get this?" Zander asks, gazing at the contents of the box.

"Grandma entrusted me with it, and now I re-entrust you with it," Vivian replies.

Stepping from behind Zander, Mora looks first at him and then at the box. Zander reaches in, pulls out a white orb with gold Celtic marks appearing on the surface, and holding it in his hand continues to gaze at it.

"I believe you know what to do with this," Zander says, handing the orb to his mother.

"Oh yes. Indeed, I do!" she replies, taking the orb from Zander. She hugs it as a tear rolls down her cheek. Rusty begins to approach her but

Vivian holds up her arm and shakes her head, indicating that he should let their grandmother be.

Quietly, Mora proceeds down the street to a grand square as everyone follows her. Upon reaching the great square, she holds up the orb and summons light into it. The light flies around everyone as it hits the orb. Magic from the orb starts rebuilding the city. Within seconds, it is restored to its former glory. Mora taps the ground near the fountain with her staff and raises the orb. It flies into the air explodes into light rays over the fountain, creating a column in the air, signaling the return of the great magical kingdom.

Vivian and Rusty raise their hands, holding up the crystals they wear and reflecting more light into the orb. As they do this, a field of great power rises over the city and begins sealing the city from all danger.

"Now, let the darkness attack," Vivian says, looking fondly at her mother and father.

"What about the other village?" Oliver asks.

"It can stay as it is to serve as a second village for the Arcane. Let the people decide where they want to live," Mora replies.

"Merlin has dictated what the Arcane can and cannot do for far too long. Let it be their choice," she remarks as she continues to watch the magic restoring the city.

Zander puts his hand on Rose's shoulder, kisses her cheek, and walks past her.

"The village, our people, our way of life, will fall again if we do not stop the darkness for good this time," Zander says to his mother.

"Indeed. Zander is correct. Merlin will continue to return, and when he does, he will unleash more darkness on earth each time," Nadia agrees.

"Then, we continue to fight as we have done," Ethan and Oliver respond in unison.

"It won't be that easy. Merlin's magic is uncontrollable, but throw the Council of Darkness into the mix, and now that Morgana has been freed from the stone, we will have an interesting fight on our hands," Mora says as she sits down on the stone ledge of the fountain.

"Wait! How did you know about the stone?" Rose asks, looking inquisitively at Mora.

"Because, much like Zander is with Raven, I can feel and hear Morgana's thoughts," Mora explains.

Looking up, Mora notices a small ball of light flying in the distance. As she rises to her feet, Zander and Rose turn to see what has caught her attention. Before anyone knows what is happening, several full-sized fairies appear.

"Our Kings and Queens, we are sorry to trouble you, but darkness, is on the move all over the globe. Merlin has summoned nocturnal gloom to the earth. The magic will surely be weakened," the fairies report in unison.

Then, just as the fairies finish speaking, several rabbits appear, carrying messages from the Arcane.

"Sightings of darkness in Africa, Asia, and Europe," Ethan reads from one of the letters.

"This confirms that they are in North America," Kelvin reports, looking at the letter he holds in his hands.

"So, the darkness is taking over," Rose says, looking at everyone.

"How do we stop this?" Bethany inquires.

"I will go back to the castle. There are some items I need that will help us assess the levels of dark magic," Nadia replies, looking at Phineas and Bethany.

"We will travel with you," they respond and the three disappear on the spot.

Rose raises her wand, points it in the air, and sparks fly. Within seconds, portals open around them as members of the Council, fairies, and animals emerge. In the distance, one remaining portal stands with no activity.

"For whom is that meant?" Oliver says, looking at Rose while more and more of the magical appear.

"The elves," Rose says as she turns her attention back to the group.

"Here is the plan. We split up from here. Ethan, you and Sebastian take a group with you. Head to Africa. Dad, you and Oliver take another group to Asia. Zander and I will take North America. We will each take as many Arcane with us as possible. We have to do everything we can to restore the light," Rose says.

Nodding, they all split into different groups.

"What about the children?" Oliver asks, looking at his niece and nephew.

"We can handle ourselves," Vivian replies, nodding at her brother.

"I am fine with that. Stay close to each other. Let's stop the darkness but don't do anything too dangerous," Zander says giving them a severe look before he disappears.

"Children, stay here. Be careful and help your grandmother," Rose says as she hugs Vivian and Rusty. As she lets go of Rusty, she and the rest also disappear. Mora stands looking out over the area, her hands up, casting light around the village.

"You're staying?" Vivian questions her grandmother.

"Oh child, yes. The darkness will come, and we must be ready. We have no way to stop them if some of us don't remain here," she replies, putting up more lightfields.

"No way to stop them?" Rusty says loudly as Vivian and his grandmother turn toward him.

"There is a way. Yes, there is," Rusty declares as he pulls the spell book from his bag and opens it.

Running his hand over the pages, they flip open, then stop.

"Divine Solaris," he says, running his finger down the page.

"That spell cannot be done without the Lunar gem," Mora remarks, watching as he pulls the necklace out from under his cloak.

"That necklace! How…?" Mora asks, reaching for it, then quickly pulling her hand back.

"Rusty, that is…" Vivian begins with a puzzled look on her face.

"Mom's. Yes, she gave it to me and told me to hold it tight, that it would protect us all. And that is what I plan to do," he responds.

"Rusty, no. Not that spell. It is…." Vivian raises up her hand and touches his face.

"Too powerful?" he says, finishing her sentence. "Vivian, this book was entrusted to me. Dad said I am the only one who can do these spells," Rusty looks directly at Vivian.

"I know, little brother," she says, kissing his cheek.

With that, Rusty rises to his feet, summons his staff, and dons his cloak.

"Look for the light. It will guide the way," Rusty says as he disappears on the spot.

"Grandma, will he be okay?" Vivian asks, looking to Mora for reassurance.

"Yes, child. I believe so," she replies as she gazes past Vivian, pointing to a young girl who has emerged from the portal of elves and is skipping by the fountain.

Vivian turns to see what Mora is looking at.

"Esther? How…?" Vivian asks quietly as she approaches the girl, Mora following behind.

"Hello, I am Vivian, daughter of Zander and Rose. And you are?"

"I am the one they call Lady of Light, but you know me as…"

But before the young girl can finish, she is being hugged tightly by Vivian.

"How did you get here?" Vivian inquires.

"Grandmama Nadia," the girl answers.

Mora watches as the girl summons water from the fountain and spins it into a ball. Before anything more can be said, the three find themselves standing in a room in the castle with Nadia peering into a crystal ball.

"Vivian, Mora, Esther?" Nadia inquires, looking at Esther.

"Grandmama," the girl calls, running toward Nadia and hugging her.

"What is going on?" Nadia asks, looking at Vivian.

"I was hoping you could tell me. One minute, I am with Grandma Mora, next my niece is standing behind us, skipping around the fountain," Vivian replies.

"I sent word, calling for aid from the elves, but it appears it crossed the timelines," Nadia explains as they all notice a light growing brighter in one of the crystal balls.

"You are right, Grandmama. The message called to all of us. Uncle Rusty…?" Esther asks, holding up her hand and looking into the crystal. "It is too powerful," she says finally, glancing back at Vivian.

"Esther, he knows what he is doing," Vivian says returning Esther's gaze.

"He will collapse. He needs help. No! He must not! It is what Bla…. It is what the darkness wants," Esther declares as she turns, whips her cloak around her, and heads down the hallway at a sprint, running toward the courtyard.

Nadia, Mora, and Vivian dash down the hall behind her, watching what is occurring.

"One minute darkness is consuming the earth, then a huge flash of light," Nadia declares as Esther reaches into the water and starts whispering to it.

Gather.

"Who is she? What is the meaning of this? Who is she summoning?" one of the Council members who has remained behind inquires.

Vivian shrugs her shoulders as Esther gets up from the fountain, nods at the Council member, and begins to walk towards the rampart, water streaming behind her.

Esther reaches the end of the rampart and looks down the main walk toward another fountain in the distance. As she raises her hand, the water flies out from behind her and starts to combine with the water in the other fountain. As it does, she reaches into her pocket, retrieving a small bag. Turning the bag upside down, she shakes marbles out into her hand. Esther glances quickly around and raises the hand not holding the marbles and speaks.

"Darkness is rising. Our friends need us. I summon the aid of my people."

As she finishes speaking, she throws the marbles into the water and closes her hand as the light explodes everywhere. The light grows brighter, and Vivian can make out various figures appearing. When the light lifts, an army of elves stands before them and as they reach out with their hands, a portal opens and out steps a series of elves wearing majestic robes and armor. Esther runs past the guards and into the arms of one of the elves.

"Father! Uncle Rusty is calling for aid. Divine Lunar Solaris has been activated," the young girl says, looking first at her father and then at her mother.

"You have done well, Esther. We will take it from here," Ari says as he raises his hand.

Then, he notices Vivian standing in the distance. Before anyone can respond, an older elf, a woman, pushes past them and runs toward Vivian.

"Sister, you made it," Hope cries as Vivian hugs her.

"I did, and help is needed," Vivian replies, gazing at Hope.

"Mom and Dad?" Ari inquires.

"Entwined in the conflict. Rusty went to save them," Vivian says.

"Then, it appears we got here just in time," Ari declares, looking around at Vivian and noticing their grandmothers standing in the distance.

"Ari, we have work to do," a soft-spoken voice says as an elf woman places her hand on the shoulder of the great elf.

"I agree with your wife, brother. There will be time for reunions later," Theo says, drawing his sword.

"Esther, do you know what to do?" Ari inquires, looking at her.

Esther turns, spins her hands as her eyes start to glow blue. In an intense voice, she speaks.

"Guards, my grandparents and family need help. Protect the Mundane, protect the light at all cost."

When she looks up, the guards have disappeared with Theo and Ari. Vivian, Hope, and Amber are left standing with Esther.

"Esther?" Amber says.

"Yes, Mother," Esther responds.

"Go to the globe, monitor the light, and if it begins to weaken, you know what to do," Amber directs, then pauses and continues, "Oh, and dear, do not get into trouble. Understand?"

"Yes, Mother," Esther rolls her eyes as she opens a portal, and Vivian, Hope, and Amber disappear through it. Esther turns, walks past her great grandmothers, and motions for them to follow. As they do, Esther teleports them into the castle and into an old room. As Esther walks around the room, orbs of different shapes and sizes light and start to glow and take to the air.

"The Arcane Nexus? Can it be? I have only read of this place," Nadia says, looking around.

"Yes, it allows me to see what is going on at all times," Esther explains, standing in the center of the room as multiple orbs fly around her with various images showing.

She walks toward one orb, looks into it, and sees members of the Council and covens being overwhelmed by the darkness. She touches the orb and speaks.

"Father, members of the Council are in danger in the streets of New York. Guards are needed."

As members of the Council and covens continue to protect the Mundane, people run, screaming, as darkness continues to rise. When one dark creature descends on a young, crying toddler, Ethan materializes, striking the darkness with the power of light and grabbing the child whose parents lay dead on the ground. Sebastian pulls magic to him, separating the ground and watching the darkness fall in. Members of the Council and covens encircle them as a horn sounds and a group of Mundane runs toward the Council members with darkness on their heels.

Suddenly, the darkness flies backwards. Members of the Council and covens turn to look as elfish magicians appear in the distance, hands out as the darkness is hit with rolling waves of asphalt. Ethan holds the young child and retreats toward the elves. A dark shadow walks through the wall and begins to lob dark energy at members of the Council which Sebastian catches it in his hands as it pushes him backward. Continuing to fight against the darkness, he reflects the dark energy at the creature, which screams and takes to the air.

The dark creature attacks again. This time, Sebastian looks at the beast, his eyes now black, and chants something quietly. The beast freezes, unable to attack. It begins to scream as Sebastian slams his hands together. Pulling them apart, the creature explodes. Sebastian and the remaining members of the Council retreat as Theo appears, carrying his bow, notches an arrow, and lets it go. The arrow flies through the air, exploding as light flies around the darkness. Theo turns and looks at Ethan.

"Well, this is weird, seeing a younger version of you," Theo remarks, continuing to look at Ethan.

"Do I know you?" Ethan inquires.

"Oh, yes. Indeed, you do, and… Oh my!" Theo's eyes narrow, seeing the young child clinging to Ethan.

"I see," Theo says as he raises his bow and shoots an arrow into the air.

"That will be your ride. Take the young child and go. Both of you," Theo says, looking directly at Ethan and Sebastian.

"We have it from here, Your Majesty," the guard says, creating magical fields around the city. Theo walks with Sebastian, Ethan, and the young child to the spinning portal.

"Elf, I did not catch your name," Ethan says as he hands the young child off to Sebastian.

"Go, I will be right behind," Ethan says.

"I am Theo," he replies, looking at Ethan.

"Thank you, Theo. I have a favor to ask. Find my sister, your Queen, and protect her," Ethan requests as he steps into the vortex portal and disappears.

"Believe me, Uncle. We will keep you all safe," Theo declares as he strikes down three dark creatures with a quick blow of his sword.

As the fog lifts, Ethan looks around curiously as he lands in the nexus.

"Oh dear," Esther says as she looks at him and Sebastian.

"A child? What happened?" Nadia asks.

"The kid's parents were killed, and he was about to be attacked when Ethan held them off and saved the child," Sebastian explains.

"Sebastian, stay with the child," Ethan says and Sebastian nods.

Before any further debate can occur, Nadia takes the child from Sebastian as Esther pushes both of them toward an open portal.

"Less talking. Quick! You do not have time. Here, take this and go," Esther declares, handing Ethan a bag as both men jump into the portal.

Looking around and finding Oliver fighting off the darkness.

Ethan opens the bag and pulls out his sword. As Oliver spins, he catches his sword midair, taps it with his wand, and charges the blade. As the darkness strikes, they fly backward. As the two brothers fight off the darkness, members of the Council appear and as the darkness grows in numbers, so do the number of Council members. As more darkness attacks, another group of elves appears, helping to fight back the darkness.

When the darkness advances, the elite guards of elves draw their swords and strike it down, revealing light and restoring the humans who had been turned.

"They have been turning the Mundane into dark creatures. Does Rose know?" Oliver asks, spinning and striking another dark creature as it explodes into light and transforms back to Mundane.

"I have a feeling she might," Ethan notes.

When the last of the darkness disappears, a portal opens. Oliver and Ethan stow their swords and run at full speed, jumping through the portal and landing on the ground in the middle of a battle. Bending backward, Ethan neatly misses dark arrows whizzing past him as Oliver pulls his sword, locking blades with one of the dark guards.

Rose is fighting against Morgana. Zander is fighting against Raven, and their father and Destiny are fighting Aden. Kelvin disarms Aden as Destiny freezes him in place. Then, with a quick movement of her wand, he disappears.

Morgana charges and hurls darkness at Rose but the darkness stops in midair as Ari, Theo, Hope, and Vivian walk up with their wands drawn.

The four siblings work together, throwing light, earth, water, fire, and wind, one element after another, at Morgana. With Morgana distracted, Rose scrambles across the ground and retrieves Morgana's bag.

"No! My creatures, bring me my bag *now*!" Morgana screams, running towards Rose.

Throwing the bag on the ground, Rose holds up a book in her hand as Morgana stares at her. Spinning a dagger in her hand, Rose jams it into the book, which screams, and the dagger flies out of the book, and lands inches away on the ground. The book folds up, screaming, bursts into flames, and disappears.

Knowing that Morgana is at her weakest, everyone strikes Morgana from four different directions with the power of light. When Zander pulls his hands apart, the witch screams, and a portal appears in which he captures

Morgana and seals it. In his hand, he holds an orb with the dark energy of Morgana trapped within it. Zander throws the orb into the air, pulls his wand, and blasts the orb, shattering it into pieces. As Oliver, Rose, and Ethan hugs, Vivian, breaks the silence.

"We are not done yet."

"What do you mean?" Ethan asks.

"One down. One to go. Merlin, if you remember," Ari says, looking at them all.

"Father, you must hurry. Merlin is attacking the field of Divine Solaris created by Uncle Rusty," a voice says, echoing around them.

Before anyone can respond, Vivian opens a portal, and they all teleport. When they land, Zander and Rose realize what is happening.

"No!" Zander shouts, shielding his eyes with his arm, trying to see. "That spell will kill him."

With that, Zander sprints toward Rusty. But, upon reaching the field, he is thrown backward. Merlin and Rusty are so entwined in battle that they fail to notice the others arriving.

"How do we get to him?" Rose asks.

"The magic protecting him and everyone else will be too strong to stop," Zander replies as Oliver and Ethan look at each other.

Just then, Esther walks up.

"Our place is in our time, and this is Uncle Rusty's way of securing that passage for us. He is mighty, like they say," Esther remarks.

"I understand," Zander says as he turns to observe Rose, Oliver, and Ethan. "Magic is what we make of it. It is in everything around us, the trees, the land, the air, the light, and the dark. That is why he came, to teach us that. I understand now. He is not here to stop Merlin but to secure the final battle for us to stop him. Vivian?"

"Yes, Father," she answers, approaching him.

At that moment, Zander hugs her, a tear rolling down his cheek.

"Look at me. Take your siblings. Take the armies and go. The four of us have this. Five taps of the orb on his staff, and all will be restored," Zander hugs her one last time.

Rose quietly hugs Vivian, and says, "I am not afraid of the future seeing who you have become. Go! Go now! Your father, uncles, and I have this."

Rose turns and holds her hand in the air as her staff appears. She slams the tip on the ground, causing Merlin to fly off his feet and land backward. Darkness begins to rise from the ground as the powers of Divine Lunar Solaris grow even brighter. At the fifth tap, the darkness explodes and the five children of Zander and Rose, along with their granddaughter, disappear. Once they are gone, Zander walks over to the staff, pulls it from the ground, spins it, and catches Merlin's magical blast with it.

"You will not win! Rise, my creatures, rise!" Merlin shouts as he touches the tips of his finger to the earth. When nothing happens, he looks around surprised. Then, he does it again.

"How is this possible?" he asks.

"It is possible because the magic does not respond to you anymore, Merlin," Zander declares, looking down at him. Merlin rises to his feet laughing.

"Then, I will have to kill you the old fashion way."

Charging Oliver, Merlin pulls a sword. Their blades clash in the rays of the sun. Merlin pulls out his dagger and throws it at Ethan who blocks the dagger with his sword. As Merlin, Ethan, and Oliver continue entwined in battle, several members of the Council of Darkness appear.

The three remaining members of the Dark Council pull their wands and strike Merlin with their magic. As the blade of Merlin's sword explodes into flames, Rose and Zander hold hands and their eyes turn white.

Nos finem haec.

We end this.

Members of the Dark Council freeze instantly as Sebastian, Bethany, Nadia, Kelvin, and Destiny all appear, opening a portal and blasting the frozen Council members into it and sealing it.

Chapter 22
The Belief Anything is Possible

Although the last Dark Council members are gone, Merlin manages to regain his magical ability. While the battle with Oliver and Ethan continues, two of the frozen Dark Council members reappear and engage in a magical duel with Destiny, Nadia, and Kelvin. Summoning more dark creatures, wave after wave is struck down when the two Dark Council members, in a final attempt, turn their attention to Rose and Zander, who work together to disarm and strike them with the full power of light. Winded, the two dark individuals fall back to Merlin. Angry, the three spin their wands in unison as darkness falls upon the earth.

"How do we deal with this?" Bethany inquires, looking at the others.

"We do this as a team," Rose says as she points her wand at the darkness and light emerges. Darkness continues to fall all around them, the only source of light coming from their wands. Zander waves his hand, and a single spike of light begins to flicker, Then, with each flash, it grows larger.

The light emanates from the staff still stuck in the ground. The Dark Council members raise their hands as darkness flies behind them, swirling, as one individual appears, holding the staff. Then, two more appear beside them, then two more.

Rusty pulls the staff from the ground, spins it in his hands, and with one final tap on the ground, his siblings grab the shoulder of the person in front of them. As Rusty slams the tip of the staff into the ground, the darkness is tossed back.

The three dark wizards emerge with wands drawn, hurling lightning at them. Rusty catches the lightning with his spinning staff, wrapping it around the staff, and reflecting it back at the dark wizards.

Summmone Ignis Nomenis. Summmone Terrae. Summmone Aqua. Summmone Ventus.

Summon fire. Summon earth.
Summon water. Summon wind.

Flames explode around the three dark wizards as the earth and water combine, creating quicksand. The wind picks up speed as it snatches up the dark wizards and slams them together. They fall to the ground, disappearing and leaving Merlin to fight alone. Merlin begins to blast dark magic at Rusty and his siblings, unleashing fire, lightning, and dark energy against them, just as Mora rises out of the ground, touches Merlin's hand, and begins to glow.

"No! What did you do? What did you do?" Merlin screams, backing up as he hits the edge of the cliff, falling backward and exploding into light. Immediately, the darkness disappears, and light returns to the land.

Mora brushes off her hands, smiles, and nods at Rusty, Vivian, Hope, Theo, and Ari.

"The timeline has been restored," she says.

"Yes, indeed. It thanks you," Nadia states, looking at the five siblings, who smile at each other and nod in agreement.

Rusty separates from the other four as he approaches his parents and hugs them.

"This is the last you will see of us," Rusty says.

"We know," Zander replies, hugging him hard.

"We are proud of you, all five of you," Rose declares, hugging him too.

"Before I leave, I still have two things to do," Rusty says.

As he steps away from them, his clothes transform into beautiful robes and his hair is pulled back neatly under his crown. He taps his staff on the ground. Light flies from the orb on the end and encircles the group, then flies up into the air as magic begins restoring everything.

Rusty turns, walks toward his father, and speaks.

"This is for you. A wise leader once told me to keep it safe and protect it until the necessary time came. The person who gave it to me made me swear I would make sure you would get it when my work is done."

With that, Rusty hands his father the spell book, turns over the staff, and joins his siblings. With one tap of a new staff, all five disappear. Magic flies all around and combines with the current light to restore all the remaining damage from the battle. Members of the Council of Light and the covens begin to reappear, using their magic to heal and rebuild as well.

Nadia and Kelvin return to the village to help their people while Rose, Zander, Ethan, Oliver, and Sebastian disappear, only to reappear on the lawns of a sizeable and majestic building in New York.

"It is time for the world to understand," Rose says, climbing the steps of the building. Upon reaching the top step, she pulls her wand, and blast two dark creatures off the ground, slamming them into the wall. Oliver and Ethan summon light, turning the two creatures from dark back into humans. Zander extends a hand and helps the President of the United Nations to her feet.

"Madam President, are you okay?" Zander asks as the woman runs her hands over her face and smiles.

"Yes, I am now. Thank you," she replies, looking curiously at the five of them.

"Madam President, I am Rose. These are my brothers, Ethan and Oliver, and our friends, Sebastian and Zander. We have come to speak with the world leaders."

The President looks inquisitively at Rose, then turns to the other four. She opens the heavy door to the building and holds out her hand, inviting them in.

That day magic is restored to the earth, the timeline is corrected, and the five address the United Nations, sharing who they are and that they are there to help.

As the five prepare to leave, the world ambassadors rise to their feet, breaking into applause. Rose smiles, knowing that she and her brothers have accomplished something that all others fear. They have created an open dialogue that will continue for the weeks and months to come.

࿔

A year since the fall of Merlin and the darkness, and much has changed. On a quiet evening after Rose returns home, she sits down in her study and pulling out her diary, she begins to write.

> *Dear Diary,*
>
> *Where has the time gone? I cannot believe that a year has passed since the fall of Merlin. Lots has happened over the year, and I am still amazed at where we all are.*

After Merlin fell, both Councils and all of the covens worked together to restore the light. Mora returned to the Arcane village and took her place as the head of the School of Arcane Studies upon the request of the Councils. Zander and I moved to the village to be close by and to join her at the school, teaching.

A new group of teachers has been brought on board, and the first-class promises to be interesting. Zander and I married this past fall, and I find that he and I are expecting our first child this August. We laugh and say we will name our first child Ari. Zander and I have not forgotten the impact of those five on us, our family, or the world.

You are probably wondering where Mom and Dad are. Both of them, along with Mora and the High Council, talked and met with the world leaders after Zander, Sebastian, Oliver, Ethan, and I addressed the United Nations. The Council's and senior wizards and witches of the light and the covens helped restore the cities and towns to their former glory.

Although the Mundane know of our existence, they are still perplexed as they cannot see our homes because our magic hides us from them. The Council members gifted each world leader a specialized orb that allows direct communication between the Mundane and Arcane. After careful discussion, Father, Mother, and Uncle Wade dissolved the magical monarchy, and the Arcane voted for their first president—none other than Father. He graciously accepted!

Dad, Mom, and Oliver live in the New Village, transforming the castle into the Arcane headquarters. Cedric still serves the family and travels between each of our homes. The High Council remains intact as the governing body of the Arcane and has added some new members. Mother, Divinity, and Aunt Destiny are the three heads of the Council. With father's and Uncle Wade's help, the Council has overturned many years of impractical laws governing the Arcane.

The elves that were hiding in the mountains have begun moving to the two villages. Many of them have also started living among the Mundane. It poses challenges. But Zander, as the King of the Elves and I, his Queen, work closely to help them transition and the Mundane to understand us. Right before we married, Zander and I traveled to the village in the mountains where we were welcomed with open arms. The elfish culture is breathtaking, and I enjoy everything about it. While the elves have started to live among humans, the high-ranking members of the elves, their Council, healers, and leaders, remain in the mountain village.

After the battle, my dearest brother, Ethan, tried to return the young toddler who he saved that day during the battle but was told that he would have to go into foster care because the child had no family. At that moment, Ethan and Sebastian made a commitment to the young child, married a month later, and then adopted the child.

My beautiful nephew, Matthew, is adorable and will soon have a playmate when Ari is born.

I laugh because Ethan and Sebastian were not expecting the child to be Arcane, but Matthew is showing signs of power. Ethan and Sebastian live in the country just outside of the Magical Village. Sebastian heads up the Arcane guard, a group of wizards, witches, and magical beings whose sole responsibility is to protect our people in the event of attacks. Ethan works at the school and teaches science and potions. You could say he has become one of the best potion experts we have. Divinity is close by and watches young Matthew regularly while helping him explore his magic abilities.

Mom and Dad gave Aunt Destiny the childhood home in which Ethan, Oliver, and I grew up. Aunt Destiny has taken to gardening while keeping a close eye on things as well. To Zander, Ethan, Oliver, Bethany, and my surprise, Aunt Destiny began dating Uncle Wade, and they are becoming serious. Leaf lives in the forest and is always close by, watching with his parents. Leaf works for the Arcane Council as a shapeshifter, keeping an eye on the Mundane. Our magic trick that went wrong, Autumn, lives in the forest behind the school, while her mother, Belinda, stays at the New Village near my mother and father.

Olivia has also moved to the New Village and resides with Oliver. They are engaged to be married this summer. Olivia serves the Council as an advisor on Mundane affairs. The Council asked Bethany to serve as the Arcane ambassador to the United Nations, a position which she graciously accepted. She and Phineas are traveling the world right now, and they are sending postcards, the last sent from Paris. While Bethany loves the traveling life, I am happy here in the village and only venture out when necessary.

Life is treating us well, and things have returned to normal. Magic is a beautiful thing! I am also working at the school these days, but Mother Mora insists that I rest before Ari is born.

I happily accepted the assignment to head the library of Arcane artifacts and texts. While the job allows me to stay in the village, I occasionally travel to find texts and artifacts. Zander travels with me, and we always have fun on our journeys. He teases that I have a way of finding danger. When I am not at school, I have taken to spell writing and have read the entire book of elfish magic that Rusty gave to Zander. There are still so many questions to be answered, but I know those answers will come in time. I often wonder how my devilishly delightful son came upon the book in the first place and hope, someday, to find out.

The cloaked figure from the vision, who was holding Mora's book has never been seen since, and I often wonder if our paths will cross again, or if he has just become an echo in time.

~Rose~

With that, Rose closes her diary and places her quill on top of the book as she seals it. Reaching up, she touches Zander's hand, which is resting on her shoulder. As she looks up at him, they smile at each other, and he bends down to kiss her on the cheek. As she rises from her chair, they hear the horns of the Arcane Guard sounding and Autumn roaring as she takes off into the air. Holding hands, they summon their staffs, tap them three times, and disappear.

Epilogue
Secrets Echoed

Have you heard? A secret exists. Echoes continue to interrupt time as we know it. Do you think the story of the House of Phoenix is over? It is just beginning!!!

The House of Phoenix Chronicles, Volume II, *Secrets Echoed*, is set ten years after the events that changed the very fabric of the Arcane and Mundane communities and set a new era of peace in motion. The incredible journey of Rose, Ethan, and Oliver continues. The Noble House of Phoenix, the most ancient of all Arcane bloodlines, must now forge and navigate new allegiances while living among the Mundane. As the darkness claims control, the three siblings are, once again, thrust into the heat of battle. When multiple disappearances rock the Arcane community, the three siblings put aside their careers, differences, parenthood, the spaces that separate them, and time to join forces, working together again to save their families, friends, and the world as they know it. In this battle of good and evil, the Magical Three learn of the Curpendulums, a most advanced form of magic. Will the Curpendulums provide the answer to their struggles against the darkness? Or will they prove to be the very weapon that the darkness needs to destroy all Arcane bloodlines and enslave the world? Will magic be lost forever? Lines are drawn, sides are taken, and new secrets are revealed, leaving all to wonder if the echoes of a dark past will remain or be forever changed.

Join Rose, Ethan, Oliver, and their friends and families on their next journey in the House of Phoenix Chronicles, Volume II, *Secrets Echoed*, due Summer 2022.

~THE END~

Afterword
Chronicles of Phoenix

Words have the power to transform a person's life in many ways and is one of the most transformative art forms known to man.

~Kurt W. Oster

My writing is very much influenced by my career as a Licensed Therapist. My experience working with Mental Health, Life Coaching, and helping the LGBTQ+ community has very much influenced my story themes, characters, and relationships in the Chronicles of Phoenix.

As readers and writers, in school we are taught many literary themes, and one of the most popular is the *Hero's Journey*. Society has taught us that the majority of the time, the female heroine must be cast as the "damsel in distress" and must be saved by either colorful companions or a man. As a gay man, and as the father of a teenage woman, I felt there are not enough stories with a female heroine in the literary world. The House of Phoenix Chronicles explores the life of a young heroine, her two brothers, and their struggles with love and power that will shape their destinies. I hope this series inspires the next generation with a love for reading, our fellow man, and values that re-define the role and acceptance of all people.

Although I grew up in a family of readers and academic scholars, as a young person, I hated books with a passion. It was not until my high school years that I began to enjoy reading and became engrossed in fantasy fiction. In college, I discovered that I am dyslexic, a common reading disability, and once I had that under control, I thrived in my college education far beyond anything I had expected. As the late Ruth Bader Ginsburg said:

Reading is the key that opens doors to many good things in life. Reading shaped my dreams, and more reading helped make my dreams come true.

Sincerely Yours,

Kurt W. Oster

Character List

The Noble House of Phoenix

Merlin Ambrose Phoenix (Arcane, Sorcerer Warlock)- Advisor of King Arthur's court. King and one of twelve original founders of the Arcane realm. Spouse of Nimuway. Father of Titus Phoenix. Grandfather to Kelvin, Wade, and Terra Phoenix.

Nimuway Gwendolyn Phoenix (Arcane, Mystic, Witch)- Queen and one of twelve original founders of the Arcane realm. Spouse of Merlin. Mother of Titus Phoenix. Grandmother to Kelvin, Wade, and Terra Phoenix.

Titus Marvin Phoenix (Arcane, Wizard)- Head Wizard (until his death) of the Council of the Arcane. Second King of the Arcane realm. Spouse of Flora. Son of Merlin and Nimuway. Father of Kelvin, Wade, and Terra. Grandfather of Oliver, Ethan, and Roslynn Phoenix.

Flora Aine Phoenix (Arcane, Wizard)- Head Witch (until her death) of the Council of the Arcane. Member of Arcane Council of Light. Second Queen of Arcane realm. Spouse of Titus. Mother of Kelvin, Wade, and Terra Phoenix. Grandmother of Oliver, Ethan, and Roslynn Phoenix.

Kelvin Chadd Phoenix (Arcane, Sorcerer)-High Prince of the Arcane realm. Heir to the Throne. Eldest brother of Wade and Terra Phoenix. Spouse of Nadia Drake. Son of Titus and Flora. Grandson of Merlin and Nimuway. Father of Oliver, Ethan, and Roslynn Phoenix. Leader of the Arcane Resistance.

Nadia Freya Phoenix {Maiden Name: Drake} (Arcane, Diviner, Witch Goddess)-High Princess of the Arcane realm. Member of the House of Drake. Sister of Hawke Drake. Daughter of Fortis and Dawn Drake. Spouse of Kelvin. Mother of Oliver, Ethan, and Roslynn Phoenix. Witch Goddess, highest witch of the realm. Child of two realms. Second Leader of the Arcane Resistance.

Oliver Kelvin Cuinn Phoenix (Arcane, ArchSorcerer)- High Prince of the Arcane. ArchSorcerer. Member of the Magical Three. High school senior. Son of Kelvin and Nadia Phoenix. Grandson of Titus and Flora Phoenix and Fortis and Dawn Drake. Boyfriend of Olivia. Great grandson to Merlin and Nimuway Phoenix. Twin brother of Ethan and older brother of Roslynn Phoenix.

Ethan Ambrose Kenrick Phoenix (Arcane, ArchSorcerer)- High Prince of the Arcane. ArchSorcerer. Member of the Magical Three. High school senior. Son of Kelvin and Nadia Phoenix. Grandson of Titus and Flora Phoenix and Fortis and Dawn Drake. Great grandson to Merlin and Nimuway Phoenix. Twin brother of Oliver and older brother of Roslynn Phoenix.

Roslynn (Rose) Sophia Nadia Phoenix (Arcane, ArchSorceress, ArchSeer)- High Princess of the Arcane. Queen Elf. ArchSorceress. Member of the Magical Three. High school junior. Spouse of High Prince Ignatius. Daughter of Kelvin and Nadia Phoenix. Granddaughter of Titus and Flora Phoenix and Fortis and Dawn Drake. Great granddaughter to Merlin and Nimuway Phoenix. Sister of Oliver and Ethan Phoenix. Mother of Ari, Theo, Hope, Vivian, and Russell Ignatius. ArchSeer and Time Cycler. Best friend to Zander, Olivia, and Brooke.

Wade Brennon Phoenix (Arcane, Wizard)- Prince of the Arcane realm. Second heir to the throne behind his brother. Brother of Kelvin and Terra Phoenix. Son of Titus and Flora. Grandson of Merlin and Nimuway. Uncle of Oliver, Ethan, and Roslynn Phoenix. Wizard, Second in Command and Member of the Council of the Arcane.

Terra Discordia Phoenix (Arcane, Witch)- Princess of the Arcane realm. Sister of Kelvin Phoenix and Wade Phoenix. Daughter of Titus and Flora. Granddaughter of Merlin and Nimuway. Aunt of Oliver, Ethan, and Roslynn Phoenix. Member of the Dark Guard.

Daemon Merlin Phoenix (Arcane, Conjurer)- Baron of the Arcane realm. Son of Terra Phoenix. Grandson of Titus and Flora Phoenix. Great grandson to Merlin and Nimuway Phoenix. Member of the Dark Guard. Brother of Eric Phoenix.

Eric Marvin Phoenix (Arcane, Conjurer)- Baron of the Arcane realm. Son of Terra Phoenix. Grandson of Titus and Flora Phoenix. Great grandson to Merlin and Nimuway Phoenix. Member of the Dark Guard. Brother of Daemon Phoenix.

❧

The House of Drake

Fortis Mael Drake (Arcane, Knight, Wizard)- Knight of the Court. Chief of the Guards of Light of the Ancient City. Spouse of Dawn Drake. Father of Nadia and Hawke Drake. Grandfather of Oliver, Ethan, and Roslynn Phoenix.

Dawn Rhiannon Drake (Arcane, Witch)-Spouse of Fortis Drake. Mother of Nadia and Hawke Drake. Grandmother and Guardian of Oliver, Ethan, and Roslynn Phoenix.

Hawke Adie Drake (Arcane, Wizard)- Son of Fortis and Dawn Drake. Uncle of Oliver, Ethan, and Roslynn Phoenix. Brother of Nadia Drake Phoenix.

❧

The House of Knight

Divinity Macha Knight (Arcane, Mystic, Sibyl, Sorceress)-Sorceress. Head of the Arcane Council of Light, one of twelve original founders of the Arcane realm. Head Sibyl. Mother of Sebastian and Liam Knight. Ex-Spouse of Aden Knight. Friend of Kelvin and Nadia Phoenix. Current teacher of Arcane.

Aden Duncan Knight (Arcane, Summoner, Warlock)- Warlock. Summoner of Darkness. Head of the Dark Guard. Father of Sebastian and Liam Knight. Ex-Spouse of Divinity Knight.

Liam Tarlock Knight (Arcane, Summoner, Warlock)- Warlock. Summoner of Darkness. Second Head of the Dark Guard. Son of Aden and Divinity Knight. Younger brother of Sebastian Knight.

Sebastian Nolan Quid Knight (Arcane, Sorcerer, Necromancer)- Sorcerer and Necromancer. General of the Guard. Son of Aden and Divinity Knight. Older brother of Liam Knight.

The House of Ignatius

King Caspar Ignatius (Arcane, Elf, Wizard)- Reigning King of the Elves. Father of Prince Ignatius. Spouse of Mora Elder. Grandfather of Ari, Theo, Hope, Vivian and Russell Ignatius. Friend of Merlin. One of twelve original founders of the Arcane realm

Mora Ignatius {Maiden Name: Elder} (Arcane, Witch Goddess)- Reigning Queen of the Elves. Mother of

Prince Ignatius. Spouse of Caspar Ignatius. Grandmother of Ari, Theo, Hope, Vivian and Russell Ignatius. Witch Goddess and sorceress. Eldest living Elder.

Prince Ignatius (Arcane, Elf, ArchSorcerer)- Reigning King (upon death of father). Student of Merlin. Youngest Member of the Council of Elders. Spouse of Rose Ignatius. Father of Ari, Theo, Hope, Vivian, and Russell. Member of the Elf Royal Family.

Ari Ignatius (Arcane, Elf, Wizard)- Eldest son of Prince Ignatius and Roslynn Phoenix Ignatius. Father of Esther Ignatius. Nephew of Oliver and Ethan Phoenix. Grandson of Kelvin and Nadia Phoenix. Time Traveler. Leader of the Elfish Guard. Member of the Elf Royal Family.

Amber Ignatius (Arcane, Elf, Witch)- Wife of Ari Ignatius. Mother of Esther Ignatius. Elf Seer. Member of the Elf Royal Family.

Theo Ignatius (Arcane, Elf, Wizard)- Second eldest son and child of Prince Ignatius and Roslynn Phoenix Ignatius. Nephew of Oliver and Ethan Phoenix. Grandson of Kelvin and Nadia Phoenix. Time Traveler. Leader of the Elfish Guard. Member of the Elf Royal Family.

Hope Ignatius (Arcane, Elf, Witch)- Third child and eldest daughter of Prince Ignatius and Roslynn Phoenix Ignatius. Niece of Oliver and Ethan Phoenix. Granddaughter of Kelvin and Nadia Phoenix. Time Traveler. Leader of the Elfish Guard. Member of the Elf Royal Family.

Vivian Ignatius (Arcane, Elf, Witch)- Fourth child and second eldest daughter of Prince Ignatius and Roslynn Phoenix Ignatius. Niece of Oliver and Ethan Phoenix. Granddaughter of Kelvin and Nadia Phoenix. Time Traveler. Leader of the Elfish Guard. Member of the Elf Royal Family.

Russell (Rusty) Ignatius (Arcane, Elf, Grand Sorcerer)- Fifth child and third eldest son of Prince Ignatius and Roslynn Phoenix Ignatius. Nephew of Oliver and Ethan Phoenix. Grandson of Kelvin and Nadia Phoenix. Time

Traveler. Leader of the Elfish Guard. Member of the Elf Royal Family. Grand Sorcerer.

Esther Ignatius (Arcane, Elf, Witch)- Elf Witch. Daughter of Ari and Amber Ignatius. Granddaughter of Rose and Prince Ignatius. Seer. Member of the Elf Royal Family. Head of the Magical Nexus.

The House of Noble

Lady of White Noble(Arcane, Elder, Witch)- The Noble Elder Witch. Mysterious. Member of the Arcane Council of Light.

Elder Light Noble (Arcane, Elder, Wizard)- Member of the Arcane Council of Light.Grandfather of Mora Elder.

Lady Elder Noble (Arcane, Elf, Witch)- Member of the Arcane Council of Light. Grandmother of Mora Elder.

Noble Elder (Arcane, Elder, Grand ArchSorcerer)- Member of the Arcane Council of Light. Most powerful living magical being. Father of Elder Light. Grandfather of Lady of White.

Noel (Arcane, Sorcerer)- Mysterious. Time Traveler. Magical power is equal only to Noble Elder, Oliver, Ethan, and Rose Phoenix. Sibling to Willow.

Willow (Arcane, Witch)- Time traveling Leading Arcane Alchemist and Herbalist. Sibling of Noel.

Other Mundane & Arcane

Lady Bethany Minerva (Arcane, Witch)- Best friend of Sebastian. Member of the Arcane Council.

Zander (Mundane)- Best friend of Roslynn Phoenix.

Dragon A (Arcane, Dragon)- The mystery painting hanging in the House of Phoenix estate. Child of the King and Queen Dragon.

Queen Belinda (Arcane, Mother Dragon)- Eldest dragon. Mother of Dragons, Queen of all Arcane beasts. Spouse of Drago.

King Drago (Arcane, Dragon)- Second eldest dragon, Father of Dragons, King of all Arcane beasts. Spouse of Belinda.

Kai, the Shade Dragon- (Arcane, Dragon Warlock)- Dark dragon Warlock. Pet of Aden Knight.

Autumn (Dog, Familial)- Family dog of the Phoenix children.

Cedric (Arcane, Vampire)- Vampire. Butler to the House of Phoenix, Protector of the family estate.

Ms. Emma Destiny (Mundane, Teacher)- Mundane Teacher. Arthurian Historian. Very eccentric.

Raven (Arcane, Summoner, Witch)- Dark Witch. Summoner of Darkness.

Morgana (Arcane, Witch)- Dark Witch. Self-declared Queen of the Arcane.

Leo (Arcane, King, Creature)- The King of Forest. Lion. Spouse of Lucy. One of twelve original founders of the Arcane realm. Member of the Arcane Council.

Lucy (Arcane, Queen, Creature)- The Queen of the Forest. Lion. Spouse of Leo. One of twelve original founders of the Arcane realm. Member of the Arcane Council.

Leaf (Arcane, Wizard)- Friend to the Magical Three. Member of the Arcane Council.

Queen Amaryllis (Arcane, Fairy)- Queen of the Fairies. Mother of Phineas. Friend of the House of Phoenix. One of twelve original founders of the Arcane realm.

Phineas (Arcane, Fairy)- Prince of the Fairies. Son of Queen Amaryllis.

Olivia (Mundane, High School Student)- High school senior. Girlfriend of Oliver Phoenix. Friend of Roslynn and Ethan Phoenix. Older sister of Brooke. Cousin of Claire.

Brooke (Mundane, High School Student)- High school senior. Friend of Roslynn, Oliver, and Ethan Phoenix. Sister of Olivia. Cousin of Claire.

Claire (Mundane, High School Student)- High school freshman. Friend of Roslynn, Oliver, and Ethan Phoenix. Cousin of Olivia and Brooke.

King Arthur Pendragon (Mundane, King)- King of Camelot. Head of the Knights of the Round Table. Spouse of Gwenivere. Friend of Prince Ignatius.

Queen Gwenivere (Mundane, Queen)- Queen of Camelot. Spouse of Arthur Pendragon. Friend of Prince Ignatius.

About the Author

Kurt W. Oster, LICSW, LCSW, MAT, RPT™ is a gay author, clinical social worker, and educator who advocates for the needs of children through his practice as a clinical social worker and as a Registered Play Therapist™.

His writing is devoted to encouraging the transformation of children with attention deficits, autism spectrum disorder, anxiety, OCD, ODD, learning challenges, and coming out issues. He explores these traditionally unspoken topics and brings awareness to neglected groups via his literary works and bibliotherapy that features neurodivergent and LGBTQ characters.

Kurt obtained his Bachelor of Arts (BA) from Rutgers University, a Master's in Social Work (MSW) from the University of Pennsylvania, and Master of Arts in Teaching (MAT) in Elementary Education from the University of Southern California.

Through his writing, Kurt aims to demonstrate that anything can be achieved while making storytelling enjoyable and changing how it is done.

Other Publications from Perceptions Press

Available now from All Genders Press
a division of Perceptions Press
https://allgenderspress.ca/

Secrets Echoed (2022, revised 2023)
House of Phoenix Chronicles Book II
Kurt W. Oster, LICSW, LCSW, MAT, RPT™
Ten years after the events that changed the very fabric of the Arcane and Mundane communities and set a new era of peace in motion, the incredible journey of Rose, Ethan, and Oliver continues. The Noble House of Phoenix, the most ancient of all Arcane bloodlines, must now forge and navigate new allegiances while living among the Mundane.

As the darkness claims control, the three siblings are, once again, thrust into the heat of battle. When multiple disappearances rock the Arcane community, the three siblings put aside their careers, differences, the spaces that separate them, parenthood, and time to join forces, working together again to save their families, friends, and the world as they know it.

In this battle of good and evil, the Magical Three learn of the Curpendulums, a most advanced form of magic. Will the Curpendulums provide the answer to their struggles against the darkness? Or will they prove to be the very weapon that the darkness needs to destroy all Arcane bloodlines and enslave the world? Will magic be lost forever? Lines are drawn, sides are taken, and new secrets are revealed, leaving all to wonder if the echoes of a dark past will remain or be forever changed.
(https://allgenderspress.ca/secrets-echoed/)

The Ignatius 7 (2022, revised 20223)
House of Phoenix Chronicles Book III
Kurt W. Oster LICSW, LCSW, MAT, RPT™

When RJ, a Mundane archeology graduate student, is mysteriously injured during a walk across campus, he makes a discovery that uncovers one of the greatest secrets of the Arcane and Mundane worlds and forever alters how he understands the battle between good and evil.

Learning the truth of Merlin's dark plans and discovering that magic can happen even for those born with no magical power, RJ now holds the key to stopping the destruction of the Mundane across the globe. As time continues to unravel and as missing relics of the past emerge, a bizarre, twisted fate in which the Knights of the Round Table are at the heart of Merlin's plan for total power is revealed.

RJ and his roommate, Dalton, set out to discover their college's history while meeting resistance every step of the way. RJ's journey quickly takes an interesting turn when he receives help from unexpected allies, including the Ignatius 7 and others.

Growing frustrated with the ongoing echoes of time, RJ must formulate a new approach to handling time's bizarre game by channeling the power of technology, mind, magic, and love to bring an end to the battle, save both the Arcane and Mundane, all the while listening to his heart, falling in love, balancing the complex life of a college student, and dealing with his estranged family.

(https://allgenderspress.ca/the-ignatius-7/)

Mystical Way of Time (2023)
Kurt W. Oster, LICSW, LCSW, MAT, RPT™
(A children's book)

In a moment of boredom, young Lord Time stops, thinks for a moment, then gets out his paintbrushes and starts creating.
 What emerges is a beautiful village, with many people, all different but living and working together in harmony.
Take a magical journey with Lord Time and his sister, Citrine, as they stroll along the Mystical Way.

Here everyone is welcome, all are accepted, and each person celebrates the ways in which each one is unique.

When a new library opens, Lord Time and Citrine help create a memorable moment of acceptance for the new librarian in town.

(https://allgenderspress.ca/mystical-way-of-time/)

Bibi The Happy Trans Girl (2023)
Karla May-Strange

Bibi is a vibrant young transgender 7 year old who love everyone, especially herself. Perfectly Trans.
(https://allgenderspress.ca/bibi/)

Eli The Happy Trans Boy Takes Testosterone (2023)
Karla May-Strange

Eli is a tween, a transgender boy tween. He is just starting out on his journey to become a young adult.
(https://allgenderspress.ca/eli-the-happy-trans-boy/)

Norm As I Am! (2023)
Cy Nelson

Late spring brings larvae to the garden. Some are pink and some are blue. However, Norm does not conform to these expectations. Follow the journey to find Norm's rare and beautiful authentic self.

Available in French **Norm Comme Je Suis!**
Available in Spanish **Norm Como Soy!**
Available in Chinese **Norm Jiu Shi Wo!**
(https://allgenderspress.ca/norm-as-i-am/)

PUBLICATION EXPECTED IN 2021
The Gospel of a Witch
Diana Bishop

The 200 angels who procreated with human women and fathered the Nephilim were cast out of Heaven. Their Nephilim children were ordered by God to be destroyed because of their destructive and corruptive behavior on Earth, but not before they fathered children of their own. These children of Nephilim came to be the witches, vampires, and werewolves of lore. It was generally believed by these supernatural beings that God disapproved of them, although they were three-fourths human and were left untouched by the purge. Lena's parents were such Nephilim offspring. They suffered under the same assumption until they met Jesus when he was physically among humankind. They became a part of his discipleship and Lena was born in his presence. They, and, in turn, Lena, were charged by Jesus with the mission of spreading the message among the Nephilim decedents that they were loved by God and were welcome in Heaven upon their death, contingent on the life they had lived. *The Gospel of a Witch* is a part of Lena's story as she endeavors to complete her mission. (https://allgenderspress.ca/the-gospel-of-a-witch/)

Coming in 2024/25 from
All Genders Press
https://allgenderspress.ca/

PUBLICATION EXPECTED IN 2024
Things are Not What They Seem
House of Phoenix Chronicles Book IV
Kurt W. Oster, LICSW, LCSW, MAT, RPT™

Shifting, altering, and replaying over and over, one timeline after another is acting up. When fifteen timelines act up all at once, a new, rebellious Noble Elder must calm the chaos and re-establish the balance of time, magic, and everyday life. Noble Elder grows into their new role despite moments of wanting to throw up their hands and walk away. Traveling through time and meeting hiccup after hiccup along the way, Noble Elder collaborates with six, headstrong Ignatius siblings, learning to navigate complex and, at times, downright awkward relationships with them.

Working together and, sometimes, against each other, the Ignatius 7 quickly learn that things are not what they seem when they discover a truth that rocks the very core of what they know about magic. Noble Elder, tired of the growing attacks of darkness, seeks the help of Arcane and Mundane alike in a battle between light and dark.

When magic stops working because of time disruptions, RJ, Amelia, Minnie, and Dalton return to help and must learn to navigate complex friendship with the Ignatius 7. Will their epic journey to find the Curpendulums, restore time, and bring normalcy to the earth succeed? Will time break the spirit of Noble Elder, and stop time altogether? Or will Noble Elder discover new ways to handle the challenges of life, magic, and darkness? (https://allgenderspress.ca/things-are-not-what-they-seem/)

PUBLICATION EXPECTED IN 2025
The Curpendulums
House of Phoenix Chronicles Book V
Kurt W. Oster, LICSW, LCSW, MAT, RPT™
(https://allgenderspress.ca/the-curpendulums/)

The **House of Phoenix Chronicles** *is planned as a series of books filled with wizards, witches, fairies, elves, dwarfs, centaurs, mermaids, and dragons in the fight of their lives to protect their ways of life, their families, and the earth. The Phoenix siblings, Roslynn and her older identical twin brothers, Oliver and Ethan, embark on a remarkable journey of friendship, romance, hatred, and mystery as truths are revealed, challenges faced, and battles with ancient darkness fought. Bending magic to their will, Roslynn, Ethan and Oliver, step in and out of time, breaking the rules at every stage of their remarkable journey. Along their way, they meet friends from the past, present, and future, and discover an ancient secret that could forever change the fabric of history, including our understanding of Medieval times and the Knights of the Round Table: a curse sent by darkness to unravel time as it is known. One minute, magic was at its height, the center of life and the community. In the next, cities and villages lay in ruins, a mere echo of a time that was. Can the three siblings channel their family's magic, one of the most powerful magical bloodlines ever to live, for good? Or will their efforts backfire, leading to the destruction of all magical beings? Will they be able to break the curse that affects their family? Can they save their bloodline and the ways of magic? Will they help bring magic back to earth, or will they become the continuation of the curse?*

PUBLICATIONS EXPECTED IN 2025
The Two Princes
Masters of the Curpendulum Book I
Kurt W. Oster, LICSW, LCSW, MAT, RPT™(
https://allgenderspress.ca/the-two-princes/)

PUBLICATIONS EXPECTED IN 2024
Holidays at the Mystical Way of Time
Kurt W. Oster, LCSW, RPT™
(A children's book)
Following his moment of boredom when he created a beautiful, magical village (see Mystical Way of Time), Lord Time and his sister, Citrine, continue to welcome villagers from diverse places to the Mystical Way. As a result, the village is bustling and ever-changing. But one shop remains empty. Suddenly, a unique-looking tree appears, and, like magic, snow begins to fall. Curious villagers turn to Lord Time and Citrine to sort out what is happening.
While exploring the situation, Lord Time and Citrine meet a new neighbor who has just moved to the Mystical Way. The villagers soon discover that their new neighbor is rather "odd," leading some of them to become concerned.
Lord Time, with the help of Citrine and Biblia, the librarian, find creative ways to promote acceptance and welcome their new neighbor while, at the same time, dealing with the ever-changing nature of time in the village. https://allgenderspress.ca/holidays-at-the-mystical-way/)

PUBLICATION EXPECTED IN 2024
Dancing Dylan is a Happy Non-binary Child
Karla May-Strange
(A children's book)
Dancing Dylan is a self confident, non-binary teenager. They/Them, Dylan, is enjoying the freedom of being genderqueer and learning how to experience life with an open heart.
(https://allgenderspress.ca/dancing-dylan/)

Publications from Other Divisions of Perceptions Press:

Perceptions Press www.perceptionspress.ca
Stephanie Castle Publications www.stephaniecastle.ca
TransGender Publishing www.transgenderpublishing.ca
Castle Carrington Publishing www.castlecarringtonpublishing.ca